Evelyn Oliver

The Egyptian Guide

From Jihad to Joy

Published by Regina Press
A Division of Regina Foundation of Oregon

REGINA Foundation of Oregon
12042 SE Sunnyside Rd
Suite 486
Clackamas, OR 97015

This is a work of fiction. Names, characters, businesses, places, events and incidents are either the products of the author's imagination or used in a fictitious manner. Any resemblance to actual persons, living or dead, or actual events is purely coincidental.

Copyright 2018 by REGINA Foundation of Oregon
All rights reserved

ISBN-13: 978-0-9966479-4-6

Preface

I first met the author of *The Egyptian Guide* at a conference a couple of years ago, where we chatted about writing. Evelyn had, I learned, been particularly struck by the similarity between the themes in my novels, especially *I Am Margaret* and *Someday*, and Evelyn's own work-in-progress. In a spirit of solidarity with a kindred Catholic author, I agreed to read Evelyn's book when it was finished, and (when I had almost forgotten about the whole thing!) I had a nice surprise when it finally pinged into my inbox.

It turned out to be worth the wait. Evelyn has produced a novel that is reflective, meditative, lyrical, and bursting with the most beautiful metaphors about faith. Yes, it deals with those same pressing issues of our times that drive me to write – aggressive secularism, religious oppression, radical Islam – but in a way very different from my own writing, though most effective.

The Egyptian Guide takes the reader along on Clara's journey of faith and self-discovery, providing a whistle-stop tour of the joys and wonders of the Catholic faith along the way, challenging us to reflect on a whole range of issues, right through from the material, to the spiritual. And indeed, to reflect on the connection between the material and the spiritual, especially with regard to the sanctity of human life. It is a book that will speak to you personally. I was particularly delighted by the appearance of St. Margaret Clitherow, the Pearl of York, whom I consider to be a Patroness of, and inspiration for, my own work. But each reader will find his or her own points of reflection.

The journey is not all contemplation: there's action, and there's certainly sacrifice. As well as being an enchanting meditation on the beauties of Catholicism, *The Egyptian Guide* delivers a powerful, and timely, warning about those twin threats: Aggressive Secularism and Radical Islam, both of which are trying so hard to crush the Church.

Hence it is not only 'old' saints that we meet in *The Egyptian Guide*. The 'new,' fictional saints Evelyn Oliver gives us are so vivid and wonderful that after finishing the book I occasionally found myself on the point of asking for their prayers – only to recollect that they are, well, fictional! Of course, at the moment, similar new martyrs are surely arriving in heaven on a regular basis. We may never know some of them until we (Lord willing) arrive there ourselves; others, we may know on earth in due course, once the wheels of canonisation have finished their careful revolutions. And so parts of this book feel like a compelling glimpse of things to come, a warning of the strife that could be approaching, but still it is a tale of hope, and glory.

Ultimately, one of the greatest challenges Clara faces in *The Egyptian Guide*, probably the greatest challenge, is exactly that faced by my own heroines, Margo in *I Am Margaret* and Ruth in *Someday*: 'Would I die for my faith?' This is a question that has been of vital importance for Christians ever since the earliest days of the Church, though at different times and in different places it has had more or less relevance to Christians' everyday lives. Alas, we are again living in a time when, though we may well hope never to have to give proof of our answer, it is no longer unthinkable that we might. And that is the single most challenging message in *The Egyptian Guide* – that Clara could be any one of us, some day very soon.

Corinna Turner

"They have deceived my people, saying: Peace, and there is no peace."

Ezekiel 13:10

Dedication

In memory of Mark
Who last slept in *The Moon;*
Upon whose youthful smile
The sun shall never set.

28 March 2018

PROLOGUE

The Nile is covered with them. Seen from the aircraft, they look like baskets.

Barges, though, that's what they are. As we prepare for landing, I discern troops through my porthole – probably a hundred on each vessel. Not only infantry, but vehicles, are ferried across the water.

After alighting on the West Bank, the hovercrafts return empty to fetch another load of soldiers. This to and fro has been going on all day, apparently.

It looks quite spectacular, seen from above. A pity that the new bridge isn't complete. But armies are converging on Casablanca and can't delay.

According to the report, most of Cairo is still a vast swamp.

Daily, an evil crop of bones surfaces from the stinky mud. They soon disintegrate in the damp air, or are eaten by animals. Giza is slightly more salubrious, hence our descent onto it at this very minute.

To think that we took off from Kiev less than an hour ago. Officials and more troops are lined up on the tarmac. Like a gigantic drone, AN Force One performs a smooth vertical landing and we disembark.

I haven't been back here for a quarter of a century.

What will it feel like?

I have long forgotten what sentiments are. Over twenty years of war – spent helping children in dire straits – haven't left me time or energy to listen to my inner self. I don't even know if, having just turned fifty-one, I am an old woman.

And yet, on hearing the official anthem of the Anastasis being played by the military, I feel something quiver inside my chest.

The worst is behind us, that music proclaims. Peace is spreading, after decades of horrors, which thick history books will find it hard to summarize.

The Regent is now giving his speech, but I'm distracted. The question asked onboard by that Education Official stirred something in my mind. When did the war begin?

When?

When you are in it up to your neck, you don't have the luxury of reflecting on war. You don't care when it started, because you're desperate to see it end. Now that things are settling down, experts mean to tell us how it all happened. I wish them well.

Obviously, the catalyst was the Flood. When S.I. – that is, "Scimitars of Islam," as they were called – blew up the Aswan Dam, causing nine million innocents to drown within three days, along the Nile Valley, they knew they were triggering a chain reaction.

They forged evidence to incriminate the Copts. The utter devastation fuelled the need for a scapegoat. Despite the fact that most Christians in Egypt had died with the Muslims, churches were burned all across the country – or whatever remained of it.

Music is playing again.

The Regent is now decorating wounded soldiers.

According to the programme, in a few minutes we will walk to the Pyramids, or rather, to where they used to stand.

Fatimah is waving at me. To think she was about my age when we first met. She doesn't look seventy-four. Without her, I wouldn't be here.

As I was saying, religious violence rapidly spread across Africa and other continents, even in countries where Muslims were not the majority of the population.

S.I. had managed to unite hundreds of budding radical groups, from England to the Philippines, and from Nigeria to Sweden. At their signal – and the Flood was quite a signal – mini insurrections occurred, targeting Christian buildings and communities.

Merciless hackers hijacked vital networks such as health services, banks and even the army. National governments declared martial law. Democracies were destabilised. But it wouldn't have ended up in a global conflict, in my opinion, had powerful secularists not taken advantage of the chaos.

First, they allowed radical Islam to "retaliate" against Christians. Mainstream media denounced "Islamophobia" while failing to expose the jihadists' lies holding the Copts responsible for the Flood.

Then, they feigned to wonder at the anarchy they'd allowed to prosper, and affirmed that the only solution was to crack down on all religion, whether Muslim, Christian or other.

It eventually prompted a three way war: Jihadists aggressing Christians; Christians engaging in legitimate defence; and secularists trying to crush both. They would have won. Until...

No one saw it coming: the conversion of Russia – well over a century after it was announced in Portugal! China did not follow Russia (as yet), but soon adopted a policy of benevolent neutrality towards Catholicism, which was enough to bring further millions of convert Chinese to the Church.

But I am late.

Fatimah just sent a member of staff to escort me to the car park.

I must follow the delegation.

The memorial service at the (crumbled) Pyramids lasted only twenty minutes. Everybody's gone now, while I lag behind. The main ceremony will take place tomorrow afternoon, on Flood Day.

I told my colleagues that I would meet them in an hour at the residence.

I need to be alone, for a change.

The missing *nose* of the Giza Sphinx has nothing to do with S.I., we were just told. If there is *one* single destruction of which they are innocent, that is it. Napoleon blew it up (not proven) long before S.I. existed; then he spread war all across Europe (proven).

As to the Sphinx itself, S.I. destroyed it, of course, with much publicity at the time.

It occurred soon after the Flood, once they'd seized power. The Pyramids followed the Sphinx, as well as any temple still standing. In fact, little is left from the wonders which, for centuries, fascinated tourists, artists and scientists all along the Nile Valley.

The debate of the day in Cairo is whether the Sphinx should be rebuilt with its nose or without! One would think that, after over twenty years of oppression,

Egypt would have more urgent issues to consider.

In fairness, the situation is well in hand.

The Interim Government has solved the water shortage; food is available again; the wounded and orphans are properly cared for; even the Internet is now accessible (when there is electricity).

I admit that the Sphinx is a symbol.

It represents Egypt's glorious past.

Rebuilding it would cost comparatively little and would enthuse the population with hope, connecting the survivors with their personal and national history. Hope is in the air, in and outside Egypt – and icons will fan it into flame.

I advised *against* the nose, however.

Our scars tell who we are.

We can't ignore them, even if they remind us of sufferings unspeakable.

Like everybody, I lost almost everything. Now standing alone on Cairo's West Bank, I look in the mud at the scattered blocks, remains of what used to be the Giza Sphinx.

I once stood there, long ago, before the war; before the Flood.

A twenty-four-year-old young woman, I *danced* between its colossal paws, challenging the monster to jump on me, since the man I loved disregarded me. I wish I'd known then, that the statue was called "Abū al-Haul – The Father-of-Dread".

I was vain, possibly sinful, although not as bad as, say, Don Giovanni. (When was Mozart last played on this planet, I wonder?) Like in the opera, though, the statue moved and answered.

The beast of stone leapt upon my beloved.

Then upon my soul.

No wonder it's gone from its pedestal. Over the past twenty-five years, that monster has run wild all over the world, shredding peace, destroying peoples, desecrating hearts. Hatred gone viral.

Why rebuild the Sphinx at all, actually?

I told my Personal Assistant that I preferred to walk.

A privilege of Anastasis officials, my security drone is hovering ahead of me, like a pet. It doesn't bark, but it will beep and fire laser beams if it detects hostiles, whether landmines, crocodiles or runaway S.I.'s.

Will it warn me if dangerous memories pop up?

There is mud everywhere, with items emerging from it, which I try not to look at (I couldn't help notice a jaw near that teddy bear, though).

I wonder: was it fair of me to elude the question of the man on the plane?

How could he know about *Operation Omen*? Even *I* had forgotten the name. He suggested that historians would identify it as the true beginning of the war.

I am tired, and the mud smells awful on either side of the track. But what a pleasant sensation to press my soles against Egyptian soil again after so many years.

In but five minutes, I will be at the residence.

Perhaps I can skip the formal dinner and just go to bed. The government requisitioned all the former hotels in Giza (those still standing). Thousands of tourists used to visit here every day, before the war.

Little did they know what was coming.

Or did they? Did we?

What is *pre*-war?

You can only define it in retrospect. Until war is declared, by definition, you can't be sure it will break out. If you have any sense, you hope it won't. If you are stupid, you take peace for granted.

I was stupid.

Most of us were. We paid the highest price for our irresponsibility. Of course, war was never formally declared, until late in the conflict. Had it not started much earlier than the Flood, though?

Was it not raging while most of us were having fun? Simply, we said the victims were *too small* to count as human. We denied them personhood. We treated them like wheat grains or vermin.

Those are objectively *not* human. This is why nobody calls a harvest or a cleansing a *war*. When disposed of according to our interests, we don't call wheat grains *prisoners*, or dead rats *casualties*.

A *war* is against other *persons*, isn't it? Deny your enemy personhood, and both enemy and war disappear, magically.

You are still killing people, but you don't realise, because it is called *entertainment* (Colosseum, Roman Empire), *management* (Germany, Third Reich) or *healthcare* (pre-Flood Global Order).

In reality, then, peace had ended long before the Flood.

If my expert asks me again tomorrow, I will suggest that the war started in Soviet Russia with the Semashko Decree, on 18 November 1920. But some might imagine an even earlier genesis, in the Garden of Eden.

My drone beeps!

But this is a *safe* beep, merely announcing that we have arrived at our destination.

Indeed, the residence is right over there, behind those few surviving palm trees.

So, where was I?

Yes, to think that Russia converted...

Orthodox churches did not come back *to Rome* though, since Rome was no more – but to the Successor of Peter, strategically exiled in Ivory Coast.

What had started as a sporadic resistance inspired by the Church on several continents soon muscled up with Russian backing. Based in Kiev, it became the *Anastasis* – or the *AN* – a confederation of sovereign states, which replaced the collapsed UN.

On reaching the building, something in the Anastasis flag teases at my memory. I don't know what in particular: not the five red stars circling around the Face; not the closed eyelids; not the beard either.

Sometimes, things become so familiar that one doesn't pay attention anymore. I have seen this emblem everywhere for years, on every official document and vehicle, and again on the badges of the sentries by the entrance door.

Dear boys – I could be their mother. My children...

I have a snack in my suite rather than downstairs with all the brass.

I feel weary and introspective.

My room is in the same wing as the chapel. But God and I aren't on speaking terms. Nothing personal; I simply think that, over the past two decades, we both have been very busy.

After my conversion twenty-seven years ago, I would see His hand everywhere. If it rained, I gave Him thanks; if it bloomed, I gave Him thanks. It was childish of me and surely annoying for my friends.

I felt like a dry sponge suddenly immersed in water or in wine. I absorbed Bible verses, I sucked catechism definitions and imbibed all that I could find or read about Catholicism. To me prayer was never a duty, but a recreation. I meant to tell every soul about Christ, and hammered my joy and my optimism on all, regardless of their inner pace and secret wounds.

It couldn't last, could it?

Through my window, I catch a last glimpse of sunset.

But I don't need the light switched on. I have got used to dimness – or, is it *dhimmitude*?

After the Flood, my faith was tried in so many ways, my strengths seemed so bitterly wasted and my prayers were kept unanswered for so long that I assumed God had relocated. Like the Pope who flew to Yamoussoukro when Rome fell.

After all, there must be many nicer galaxies than ours to which God might shift His attention. When did I stop believing – not in His existence, but in His care of us?

The little saint I once visited in Normandy captured my mood when she wrote: *"I get tired of the darkness all around me. The darkness itself seems to borrow, from the sinners who live in it, the gift of speech.*

I hear its mocking accents: 'It's all a dream, this talk of a heavenly country, of a God who made it all, who is to be your possession in eternity!

All right, go on longing for death! But death will make nonsense of your hopes; it will only mean a night darker than ever, the night of mere non-

existence!'"

Why keep this scrap in my wallet?

I must have written down this quote a long time ago. Can it count as a prayer? I know it by heart.

In that context, attending the First Mass tomorrow leaves me quite indifferent.

I'm glad for Fran... – for *Fr. Yusuf*. (I can't get used to calling him that.) The first priest ordained in Cairo since the liberation will offer Mass for the first time. It's an achievement for him and for the Bishop, after so much suffering. They turned a former prison into a seminary, he told me.

I will be polite with God. But I hope He won't mind if I don't stay very long after the ceremony.

In fact, I'd rather leave Cairo tomorrow afternoon.

There is work to be done. It's no secret that all must gather in Casablanca for the next decisive step in this war. Africa and Asia are liberated. But most of Europe is still occupied – and what of America? Doesn't *Casablanca* mean *White House*? In which case, I bet the ships won't aim for Lisbon but, via Cuba, for Washington.

While I'm here, the only question I find relevant is my responsibility in the war. Is there anything I could have done to prevent its outbreak, or at least to lessen its impact?

I lived in Egypt nearly two years, which I counted as the happiest in my life. And yet, when the horror begun, I was caught off guards.

These twenty-four hours in Cairo may be like a porthole through which I glance at what I used to be.

A young convert; a woman in love; a professional; a dancer; a bit of a thinker at times; a swimmer; a nun? – and eventually a...

No, this is too painful.

Why did the fairytale end so wickedly?

I feel like *Captain Nemo*, the submariner in the sci-fi story: after twenty thousand leagues under the sea, could I breathe the air of happiness past? Would my lungs and brains bear it? Could I ever meet up with the young and happy woman I once was, up on the surface?

Would we recognise each other?

If I look at her across the estuary of life and the gulf of war, if I try and remember how she felt, what she wore and how she spoke, it will be through my older lenses. I will project on her my broader experience, and my jadedness.

Can I resurrect her?

Can she help me carry my heavy present, and live through whatever sort of future is left for me?

Clara Cumberhart, where are you?

Where are we?

You, so candid, playful, fragile and yet empowered by a Love not of this world.

Through this porthole, will you let me see your face again, the lovely face that was mine before my soul withered?

But listen!
Oh no! I thought those were bombs again.
Why set off fireworks now?
I look at them through my window.
Yes, of course, victory.
Victory...
I hope it will end soon, because I want to sleep, and tomorrow will be another busy day.

PART ONE

Chapter 1

Out of Africa, and stranded in Europe!

I arrived safely from Cairo, only to find my connecting flight to Houston cancelled. So, here I am, trapped in glittering Paris-Orly Airport (like in the treasure cave of *Ali Baba and the Forty Thieves*), awaiting information which, we are told, will be displayed within two hours.

Why did I stupidly dump my fashion magazines in the recycling bin when walking out of the plane!

Only two hours...

It doesn't leave me enough time to venture downtown to the Champs-Elysées – and make Kitty and Raúl very jealous with an Eiffel Tower selfie (they deserve to be teased for letting me down)!

Like they say in the film: "We'll always have Paris." As Kitty's Maid of Honour, I should have suggested they came *here* on honeymoon. But it's a long way from Texas (and she couldn't fly, in her condition).

Thankfully, the wonderful Egyptian temples in Medinet Habu and Karnak are still vivid in my memory. And to be honest, not only the monuments, but also some of the inhabitants.

One inhabitant in particular?

Okay, I admit that I can't stop thinking of Azim.

But why on earth did he come and hug me just when it was too late! I can't believe that it was only five hours ago – or just three, with the time change?

I wish it were now.

Again.

I must try to forget.

The pictures on my phone are fascinating. Not this one with Azim at the Pyramids! Deleted. I looked awful on it. Unlike this Canadian family, handsome friends of his: what a cute little girl! She held my hand.

(An innocent hand, that one, not like the Gypsy fraud who charged me fifty Egyptian pounds to read my palm and swore that I "would soon find the great love!" My foot!)

More pyramids. A sphinx... Temple. Temple again. Who can believe that a civilisation designed those buildings with such skill and refinement, and more than thirty-five centuries ago? For what again? For worship. Well, that has ceased.

But all along the Nile, the buildings still stand, for the joy of tourists –

and for the prosperity of travel agents, including my boss (note: remember to mention the Aswan accommodation offer to confirm our better prospects in the South).

Prospects, did I say?

Love prospects?

I can't resist taking Azim's letter out of my bag. Several times on the plane I started reading it, and stopped.

To Clara, my beloved sister.

This letter, which I hope to hide in your bag before you take off, is my confession to you. Actually, it contains several confessions; and an invitation. I will start by confessing this.

This night is the most beautiful in my life, because I was with the person whom I have come to love more deeply than I had ever thought possible. I have only known her six days and I feel as if I had grown up with her. We had a drink on the terrace in the quiet of the evening.

The air was loaded with deep smells from the Nile, and the sky had put on brighter lights for the occasion. Red Moon Hotel boasts of five-*star rating – but one only dazzled me. She wore a blue silk blouse and a beige skirt smoothed around her knees.*

I wondered if her appearance in my interior firmament signalled an event of immense importance. Was she the heraldess of supreme joys? Was love imminently to be born in our hearts? Dearest Clara, this letter will explain.

Meanwhile, I will ever cherish this expression of your trust, when you pulled up your sleeve and unbuckled your leather watch band, allowing me to see the thin scar running across your wrist.

My beloved, my beautiful friend, the sight of this line pierced my soul. How could a young woman like you, so lavishly adorned by Almighty God both in body and soul, want to take her own life?

You said it was many years ago. I wished to fly across time and oceans and reach you just before the blade dared to touch your milky skin. I would have thrown my throat between knife and artery. Better, I would have arrived earlier, before any trial should have upset your treasured soul.

O God of our fathers, let all my blood be spilled rather than one of her eyelashes fall to the ground! And yet, Eternal One, You are the One who watches over us, even in our darkest hours. If only You once wished to use me for her fulfilment, in whatever degree or capacity, I would be the happiest man.

Then I did what under Sharia law should have cost me a hand: I stole – our first touch – and I assumed our last. If the penalty increases according to the value attached to the stolen good, I would have lost more than one hand indeed, but both – and feet and head (as to my heart, it wasn't mine to lose)!

My lips fell on that hated line drawn across a cherished limb, wishing to erase with a kiss the assault of the steel.

In that, they failed.

But not in the reward they earned for my eyes: a tear from yours falling upon my hand; and a smile opening across your brightening face a laughing "scar" that I wish would never heal again.

O mouth of my delight; O teeth, O tongue, O lips: what music you play to my ears as I rise and take my leave! Is sanity retained when a man loves his pains? Your voice, bidding farewell, is a kiss to my ears and a pang in my heart.

I stop reading.

His letter upsets me more than it thrills me.

Are these not mere words? What proves them true, Azim?

You said you loved me, and you ran away!

Chapter 2

In pink crocodile?

As a diversion, I just walked to the Louis Vuitton boutique near the bookshop to see their latest phone case, just released. It might fit mine.

But, in *pink* crocodile? I didn't see any of that colour crawling down the Nile (only sculpted ones in temples, brownish and harmless). Perhaps I would have, if I'd drunk a bit more. I should have accepted Azim's cocktail yesterday, but what if his mysterious "Katarina" had heard of it!

Sitting down again, I browse through the picture album on my screen.

I realise that we modern men and women don't need gods anymore, though we appreciate the zeal and the cultural achievements of long-gone believers.

Ruins are exotic, aren't they?

Think of the Valley of the Kings, with those amazing tombs! (And an air-conditioned ice-cream shop with genuine *Häagen-Dazs* on the way out...)

Of course no one manages to remember the names of the strange deities (all jackals, hawks and crocodiles) and even our guides knew little about the meaning of the rituals performed of old.

Actually, Azim seemed more interested in early Christian remains. (Must I *really* email him that picture of me he asked for yesterday? My dress was nothing very special. Just elegant, not special.)

But those beliefs, those words and gestures surely made sense at the time, and they were taken very seriously. From Pharaoh to the basest slave, all professed the same creed and abided by the prescribed ceremonies.

In fact, it looks as if religion was the heart and soul of the country.

And what a country: an empire rather!

My phone displays reconstructions of temple liturgies with various dignitaries and officials standing in line, while priests of different ranks sing sacred hymns.

Many of those rites, or formulas, were translated from hieroglyphs: formula for the oil-festival-perfume with honey (my favourite); formula for entering the temple; formula for going to the stairway; formula for entering the sanctuary of the deity; formula for incense, etc.

I can't help it...

My heart itches.

Much as I wish to ignore Azim, I feel compelled to read his letter further.

Where did I leave it?

Here...
Well past midnight...
Darling Clara, I had to come back.
I felt so silly, shaking hands with my sun, that is, with you. When all was calm and every light out, I made my way to the garden behind your room. Hiding against the purple bloom of the bougainvillea, I hoped that the wound in my soul would be less visible.
I saw you come through the curtains of your bedroom, barefoot, and kneel upon the grass, your gaze intent upon the moon, nearly full. I saw your shadow land amidst a silvery halo, and feared you would see mine, stretching in the same light.

My unease turned to bliss when I saw that the pace of the moon gradually led your shadow towards mine along the sloppy lawn.
My love left empty the mere muscle beating in my chest, and travelled to my outline spread out on the grass. My heart reached out to every herb and root, as if each one were my hair, my nerves and my fingers.
You were still kneeling in silence, looking to the heavens.
I wished to God that you might be praying. I prayed for you and me.

The moon gently drifted nearer to the river. The shadow of your arm, meanwhile, was touching that of my shoulder. As yours approached, my shadow shivered. The silhouette of your head came to rest on that of my chest, spread flat across the grass.
Over the river still and over this garden, O moon, suspend your dreamy pace!
That our shadows may share the secrets of our hearts.
O Clara beloved, radiant Habibah!
Did my shadow convey to yours my plea and my promise?
Did your shadow report to your heart and your soul?

But the moon knew better, and as it moved further, our two shadows melted into the blooming bush, while our bodies retained their postures far apart.
No two fingers had brushed, God knows; no limb had met living flesh. You rose and left.
And still, a kiss had been exchanged. While you were on your knees, I'd seen you slowly bring to your mouth the scarred wrist, still stripped from its watch, and apply to it your dear lips. As if mine had remained on that wound where they laid an hour earlier, I inhaled your chaste breath.
I gave thanks to the One who had granted our souls such a tender adieu, and went back to my room where my light shone all night.
So *utterly* insensitive!
He was *there* all along, then.
So close to me last night, and would not even let me *know*.

I can't bear it...

Just when I was begging for love, thinking myself alone in the garden, hoping for him to come and kiss me.

How could such a handsome man behave so selfishly?

Doesn't he know that Romeo is supposed to climb up to Juliet's balcony, rather than cowardly remain hidden behind the shrubs?

Enough of him!

Please, someone, show me true love!

Chapter 3

Still no update on my flight...
I really am bored to death now. Better bored than cross, though. Let me see what's up.
Nice website, this:
Paris, World Capital of Lovers. Choose how you love. Click. *Love and fashion. Love and cuisine. Love and culture. Love and sightseeing.* Click.
Take your Valentine to Sacré-Cœur. Enjoy the best view over Paris from the top of Montmartre. Click.
Love and Terror. Click.
Swinging Queen Marie-Antoinette and handsome Count Axel Fersen, hero of the American War of Independence. Deeply affectionate correspondence. Revolutionary tribunal found no ground for adultery. Finally, she was guillotined for treason. Count Fersen lynched by mob later in Stockholm. Click.
Charming and bloodthirsty Terror leader Louis-Antoine de Saint-Just, nicknamed "the Angel of Death." Had a young woman guillotined for rejecting him. Allegedly, had her skin tailored into breeches. Saint-Just died on the scaffold, aged twenty-seven. Click.
Is *that* Paris?
On second thoughts, it might be just as well if I don't venture outside of the airport!
Or, will the next entries be nicer?
Beautiful 25-year-old maiden Charlotte de Corday visited leading Terror propagandist Marat in his bathroom where he lay sick. He expected to receive names of suspects from her. Instead, she stabbed him to death in his bathtub with a kitchen knife concealed in her shirt. Said she'd killed one man to save a hundred thousand. Was guillotined. Click.
General Napoleon Bonaparte, aged twenty-nine, writes to Josephine as he sails back from Egypt to Paris: I'm coming: don't w... Click. Click. Click.
Exit.

Well, well... I didn't know all this!
Pretty grim, and gory... I should have clicked first on "Love and cuisine!" I hope that, since the French Revolution, there have been meeker and happier lovers in Paris!
I adore the *Amélie* film. *That* is a nice one; a *happy* one! Although I must admit, *tragic* love is more attractive.
I remember Azim's letter.
Should I read on?

Will it not upset me even more?

Perhaps he will explain *why* he didn't join me... I decide to give him a last chance, and unfold the sheets again.

My next confession is this: Clara, you saw me last night as a Muslim, and you were right, because I still look like one.

I have been very committed to my religion in the past. I trained with other radical young men. To tell you the truth, I joined the "Scimitars of Islam."

What!

In shock, I avert my eyes from his letter.

Did I innocently flirt with a religious fanatic? Well, I've had a narrow escape then.

What do you have to say for yourself, Mr Assassin?

(And *why* are you *so* attractive?)

Thank God I never killed, or even attacked anyone.

But I knew that I would have to, some day. I wasn't afraid of doing so. I killed many infidels on my plasma screen. We used to play violent video games for hours. They were not allowed, unless for a religious purpose.

"Righteous Rage" was our favourite. Life was easily taken, lost, and redeemed.

As I studied my religion, I became less convinced that violence was the best way to promote it.

Most of my comrades were rather aggressive. They'd been brought up that way, or not much educated at all, in fact. I have always loved to understand the reasons for our decisions.

I'm not an intellectual, but God gave me a brain and I try to use it. I have read books and surfed the Internet. My father, a schoolteacher, encouraged me.

While training to become a guide for English-speaking tourists, I discovered that Islam had arrived fairly recently in my country.

The greatness of Egypt pre-dated the conquest by millennia. Our ancient dynasties came first, of course, but also the Jews, the Greeks, the Romans, and Christianity.

I became ashamed when I read that in 641, the fall of Alexandria to the Arabs precipitated the downfall of intellectual life in the whole Mediterranean.

I'm naturally proud of our having founded the Al-Azhar community of Islamic study in Cairo as early as 970, and I used to wish I could have studied there.

But overall I deplore the fact that my religion hasn't favoured much intellectual achievement and has frowned upon theological debate.

Sorry, my beloved! You can find all this in books, and this letter isn't the proper place.

But I feel you should know.

Many times in the history of Muslim expansion, violence was used in the name of my religion. This escalated in recent decades. I was merely twenty. I had to distance myself from my radical companions.

They didn't like it and started suspecting me.

I shaved off my long dark beard and started wearing jeans and t-shirts again. It was three years ago.

I was a certified guide by then, and I met Mansur and his wife. You know their little daughter Talitha (she found you "very sweet and nearly as pretty as Mummy").

I take my eyes off Azim's letter, allowing recent memories to awake, although they feel so distant already.

Yes, I remember that nice family...

Tapping on my phone, I scroll through my albums to find their picture again.

There! How photogenic!

Difficult to tell which of the dad, mum or daughter I like more. And yet, I never really knew them, and most likely will never meet them again.

Was Azim more than a guide to them?

Tell me, Gypsy fraud, when will *I* have a family?

A family for Clara?

Perhaps, but you *can't* marry a terrorist – did you not read that he was one of those dreadful *Scimitars*?

Sure, he's really too extreme, for now. But I could persuade him to support democracy. I could make him change, couldn't I?

No, it would be madness!

Madness?

Yes, madly *romantic...*

Chapter 4

Frankly Clara, is it *wise* to read any further?

Should you not report him to the police, rather? Working as a *westernised* tourist guide will make him less conspicuous, but more dangerous as a fundamentalist.

And what if he *kills* anyone? You'll have their blood on your hands.

I know; perhaps I should drop him. But he can't be a bad person if he likes *me*, can he?

Let me read further – just *a little* (nobody's looking).

Of Muslim Lebanese descent, Mansur grew up in Canada and England.

However, he doesn't consider himself a Muslim. He works in real estate and construction in the Middle-East for his father's firm and comes regularly to Cairo.

Incredible: he knows the owner of the Chelsea Football Club and will ask him about flying his players here for a one-off game. Of course, we in Egypt have the most successful national team in Africa.

His wife Nour doesn't care much about football.

She's a Maronite Catholic, also from Lebanon, although her parents moved with her to America when she was still a teenager.

You should see Mansur's boat!

It's a floating office with all the facilities you can dream of, and also extremely fast. Her triple water-jets generate seven thousand, seven hundred horse power to give her a top speed of forty-eight knots!

Can you imagine?

That's eighty-eight kilometres or fifty five miles per hour, on water! It took us a full night to reach Lebanon when we travelled there once, but in optimal weather conditions, his boat could cover the distance between Port Said and Beirut in less than five *hours!*

The three of us had long conversations about God.

I admired Nour's faith in particular.

She had a deep relationship with her God, Isa ibn Maryām, Jesus Son of Myriam (blessed be their names forever); and with Myriam herself (blessed be her name forever).

She said that what makes Catholicism unique is that in it, God has come closer to suffering men than any religion has ever claimed or envisaged. But when she insisted that Jesus (blessed be his name forever) was truly God, I was deeply shocked.

We hold him as a prophet, nothing more.

She took me once to a convent in Cairo, where religious females spend their lives.

In their chapel, I attended a ritual they call "Adoration of Jesus in the Host."

At first sight, I wasn't impressed. I saw a mere disc of white bread displayed in a gilded showcase, set upon an altar. All fell on their knees before it.

The place was dark, with only candles lit. I waited out of politeness, expecting something to happen. But all they did was to burn a little incense before the device.

Silence went on.

Nour didn't seem to want to go. I stayed because of her.

I don't know why, but suddenly, as I looked again at this round glass amidst a few candles, like through a small porthole against the dark wall, I felt like Howard Carter peeping through the pierced door of Tutankhamun's tomb in 1922 (the most spectacular discovery in modern archaeology, you remember) after years of fruitless digging.

With feverish anticipation, Carter's patron Lord Carnarvon asked him: "Can you see anything?"

More than Carter, I could have replied: "Yes, it is wonderful."

My sacred peephole in the sisters' chapel revealed another *king.*

Unlike the royal mummy, it wasn't surrounded with splendid treasures and regalia.

But this King in the convent wasn't *dead, was he?*

What if Jesus Son of Myriam (blessed be their names forever) was truly *present in there, and alive? What if he were more than a prophet?*

As Nour and I were leaving, I felt uncomfortable, because for the first time I was afraid of asking the imam something.

Dear Clara, I see that I can't share this with you now.

It's too intimate and personal to put in words on paper. And also, my beloved sister, despite your being a Christian and, as Nour suspects, a Catholic, you aren't committed to those mysteries.

Clara, since I first saw you with the group at the airport a week ago, how much I have dreamed of discussing those things with you. I hoped for an opportunity. Did I miss it? Was I shy? I feared that my ignorance would make you laugh.

From the first moment my eyes met your face, my heart leaped in my chest.

You appeared to me as the perfect embodiment of what a woman should ever be (despite not being a Muslim). As a pilgrim lost in the desert unexpectedly reaches an oasis, I dived into your eyes and I drank your smile, never tiring of it. To me the desert winds never had any other purpose than to make your beautiful hair float and dance in the sun.

I stop reading and close my eyes for a while, as the generous praise, offered by my friend, unfolds in my mind.

Taking the mini beauty case out of my bag, I look at my face in the mirror.

It *isn't* vanity!

I'm merely trying to see *what* had met Azim's eyes to deserve such compliments.

I find my features to be rather in need of rejuvenating cream, while my hair looks flat and could do with a dry blow to regain volume.

A bit like my heart.

I don't feel like reading more of his letter just now. I see that my Egyptian guide isn't a terrorist. It's reassuring.

Let me buy some makeup (surely he wouldn't mind).

Chapter 5

As I walk out of the shop, I check that I still have ninety minutes to wait – so they say!
 I badly need some distraction – anything.
 Look over there, this sign: "Fast cabs to the city centre!"

 Too risky, time-wise – but I would *love* to stand by that bridge where poor Princess Diana met her end. People still leave flowers there, apparently. She must have been so wounded by life to run away with an Egyptian millionaire.
 I read that she was buried holding in her hands rosary beads given her by Mother Teresa of Calcutta. They were great pals. To think that she would have become Queen...
 What a fashion icon she was!

 That reminds me of that (expensive) hat that I bought for Kitty at Cairo Airport. I *had* to find a way to stop thinking of... him. Not sure it worked.
 What if I took it out of the bag?
 Just to take a look at it again... in case it isn't *exactly* the right thing.
 So much paper around it...
 It's simply *exquisite*!

 See this small floppy straw bucket hat, with its long white gauze scarf floating behind, to protect the neck and shoulders against the sun – can also be tightened over the mouth and nose in case of sandstorm (this is a *burka* I would gladly wear, if Azim asked me)!
 Note the delicate bordeaux velvet strap which will produce a very fine contrast against the fair chin and throat of the lady.
 This is too much! I *must* put it on...
 I know it's meant to be a *gift*, but on my head it's safe; whereas if hanging in a bag it's likely to be crushed between two suitcases. Every traveller knows that. And my main wedding gift is in my suitcase anyway (that was kind of Azim to show me the right place to buy this icon for Kitty).
 Also, I'll keep the wrapping.
 There... I can see myself reflected in this display.
 How perfectly it matches my Egyptian cotton dress and my smart linen jacket. And now with my oversize retro sunglasses on.
 Dearest, you look simply *gorgeous*! Typical 1920's "Death on the Nile" fashion, or Grace Kelly (or is it Kate Middleton?).
 Anyway girls, *this* is what I call style. And wait until you see my

darling Kitty wear this hat. She's three times more attractive than I – even when sitting (but only twice as slim). I hope that she will like it. Well, if she doesn't, I won't mind keeping it.

Dear me, enough frivolity!

End of catwalk and back to work, children: somebody has a presentation on Egypt to put together for her boss (my best chance to be sent back to Cairo soon). And it must be tourist-friendly. So, back to typing, browsing and pasting.

Click. *Today, 1ˢᵗ June: Feast of the Entry of the Lord into Egypt, according to the Coptic calendar.* Click. Further down, this website mentions Moses and the Exodus. I like those stories. They make the best movies. Who was that actor again who won an Oscar for playing King Ramses... Stuart Wattles?

Scrolling down I read that *the Son of God went out of Bethlehem and flew to Egypt: "And the idols of Egypt shall be moved at his presence, and the heart of Egypt shall melt in the midst thereof" (Isaiah 19:1).*

Indeed, it says, *the true God had visited Egypt, and Egypt had converted*. But since then, only the shrinking Coptic minority over there still believes that God became Man to save humanity. Muslims find it scandalous, and Westerners think it absurd.

I find it... Well, I wish it were still true.

I still owe Kitty a reply. Her voice message would not tell me what the "great news" was. But what an email later on! *Pregnant*! Just like that. As if getting married wasn't enough.

Actually, reading the news just as I was boarding in Vancouver for a business trip to Egypt was bad timing. I texted her that I was *delighted* and would want to hear all about it right after landing.

But I *didn't* ring her from Egypt. There will be time to talk it all through when we meet this evening and until the wedding.

In truth, I think it's wrong.

Not only the news, but the *fact*, is bad timing. It's too early or too late for her to have a child. What about her illness? And the stress of the wedding! So many things to prepare, and the guests, etc.

I will arrive a week earlier to help, but I can't do everything. And a lot must be done *afterwards*: to thank everyone; to sort out pictures; and so on and so forth.

Why not simply *wait*? It's only been three months, after all.

If I ever marry, I will want at least a few years in peace with my husband, before any children come between us. I know that she trusts me. I think it my duty to deter her. She won't like it, but once it's done, she will see the wisdom, and thank me for it.

- Ah, yes, there is *Raúl*.

But that's easy for *him*. He isn't the one with a debilitating disease. He isn't the one who will have morning sickness for months and who will then wake up every night for years, for feeding, nightmares, toothaches and the like. Men sleep and go to work (returning home only *after* nappies are changed, conveniently).

Precisely! What about Kitty's *career*?
Getting married is fine, why not? – almost trendy actually. But she's doing well as an accountant and is just about to be made partner.
Maternity leave would *abort* it all.

Chapter 6

Take courage, Clara!
    Only an hour to wait and then, *up* into the sky at last!
    No, I don't want to be brave. Now I'm in self-pitying mode.
    I feel jaded. Miserable me...
    What a life.
    Where *am I going? What am I doing, and all that?*
    Who cares for me – and what matters to me? Unlike Kitty, I'm not pregnant, and not even engaged. I did get hugged at an airport by a terrorist – but that doesn't count.
    He wrote to me, but that doesn't count either.

    Just for fun, though... *Could* it be that I carry a prospective husband in my bag? I mean, could Azim's letter really change my life – our lives? It's a one in a million chance. Try it?
    Okay... What more does he have to say? Still a few pages left!
    Actually, this might be the first *handwritten* letter I've received in years. I admit that it looks nicer than text messages. For instance, I like the way he draws the *C* for my name.
    There, down on the third sheet, his handwriting seems to become hastier. Was he in a hurry? Or is it *passion*? For *me*?
    He puzzles me now. Let me read further...

    I remember that afternoon when our group had arrived at the hotel after the visit to Isis Island.
    Everyone was resting and the waters of the Nile magnificently mirrored the sun, slowly lowering upon the palm trees. The vast swimming pool by the river seemed to be part of it. That's when I saw you come out, after swimming.
    You were wearing this cherry swimdress, and over it a kimono.
    No birds could be heard, as if silenced by your beauty.
    A hot wind was blowing across the lawn. The sun wasn't yet setting and its burning light gilded the river ... and you. I saw you walk towards me as if emerging from the Nile, with the temple in the background. You were all floating gold. I thought I was watching the goddess Isis.
    A dog started barking madly. I suddenly felt ashamed. If you were Isis, then I wasn't the loving Osiris but Sobek, the crocodile god.

    The gentle face of the holy man Yusuf (blessed be his name forever) shone in my heart, casting away Sobek!
    Nour had taught me to ask for his help in such cases, and I found him

always quick and powerful. After all, Yusuf (blessed be his name forever) had walked along the same river – my Nile, our Nile – with Isa ibn Maryām, Jesus Son of Myriam (blessed be their names forever) and with Myriam herself (blessed be her name forever).

He may have stood exactly where I stood, and may have watched his immaculate wife walk back from the water with the God-Child. He could look at her beauty and simply give thanks to God for it.

He would have known to ask for God's help if ever tempted, as the young man Tobiyah had done for the sake of Sarah, his betrothed one, whom Archangel Israfil saved from the demon Ashmedai, binding him in Upper Egypt!

I know that many men my age, Westerners and Muslims alike, would laugh at me for this.
They would consider me weak.
What is manly, Clara?
If it's courage, I have my share of it.
When the S.A.S. of your monarch came for training, on their way to Syria, and needed English-speaking scouts – I volunteered with four other men from my town. But I was the only one who dared to accept the challenge of the British to bite off the head of a horned viper.
One per fighter. Of medium size.
It's standard practice to overcome their fear.
They said I should enlist.
I won't do it again, dearest. There is more to manliness than this.

A real man I found, in the person of our holy patriarch Anthony, the father of all monks, who lived in solitude in the Middle-Egypt in the fourth century, long before Islam even existed.
He sold his estates and distributed everything to the poor, and lived by a cave in the desert, praying, fasting and fighting evil spirits. I'm so glad to have Anthony with us, in this my country!
Dear Clara, I wonder if I should write any further on this topic. In my first letter to you, I would wish to refer only to beautiful and happy things. You are so innocent and pure, my beloved sister.

Lifting my eyes from Azim's letter, I catch my reflection in the display opposite.
Can I see what Azim saw?
Is the girl on that bench, yes, *this one* with the smart linen jacket, innocent and pure?
Does she even care?
In fact, what boxes does she tick?
Fashionable, she is.
Good-looking, she – well, yes, clearly she is.
Brainy? (*Philosophy* led me nowhere – so glad I changed to *Tourism*

Management.)

In love? With a snake-beheader?

Now *that* would impress Sally, back home! She was already thrilled when I emailed her Azim's picture, asking if I'd ridden behind him, the day of the camel trek (I hadn't: a red-haired girl had got up there before I could think of it).

I look at the handwritten sheets spread on my lap.

Handwritten means no copy; no backup. If I *lost* his letter, no one would ever know his thoughts. His confidences remind me of a certain evening, only two days ago. We were alone in that other garden. He shared with me something intimate and I – *stupid* as I am – I laughed.

If I hadn't...

If instead I had shown respect, would he have come earlier to the airport?

Would he have let me know of his presence yesterday night in the garden, so close to me and yet, invisible?

Chapter 7

How very strange ... Have I been gazing into space for several minutes?
I put Azim's letter back in my bag. What's the time? Half an hour later. I feel as if I'd been gently *struck*. What will Kitty think of me? (What *Raúl* may think, I don't care *at all*.) Let me remember. Where am I? Yes, Paris Airport. Everything looks normal.

In my range of vision, many passengers and staff are walking across the terminal, queuing at the nearest gates, buying things from shops or staring at flight information screens.
Why? Obviously, they mean to fly somewhere.
Yes, but why?
Well, for studies or romance.
Romance probably (where again is that paper with Azim's email address?)
Or war?
Or leisure, or business; or because of family commitments, like this bridal shower, if only the plane shows up.
Again, *why*?

How can I put it? That's when a contrast occurred to me, between... Between the huge diversity of our particular destinations and the singleness of our common destiny.
Wherever we all fly, might we not all end up in the same place? At the end of history, aren't all women and men likely to stand together before some deity (preferably not a *crocodile*-god)?
It would make sense, for those who see God as their creator, their saviour or their judge.
Such would be everybody's final destination then. "Terminates here: all change!" Everything in between would appear as steps towards it. Whoa! Very few of my fellow-travellers would agree, I assume. Even fewer may presently be thinking about it.

And yet, could it be that we are all on a journey towards God?
Even *I*?
Nonsense! What am I thinking!
I'm not that kind of person. I've simply spent too much time in those Egyptian temples. Godless temples.
Still...
The whole terminal has become loaded with... how can I put it? – with

something spiritual. (I really sound like a *believer*.) Whereas a moment earlier it was captivatingly profane, now all those people seemed to be performing some ritual.

No, Clara, you're making this up. Or you're simply tired. *What* ritual anyway?

The ritual of... moving around. The ritual of... motion?

Yes! That's it! The ritual of motion. They are motion adepts. All *Motion* worshippers (sounds a bit like devotees of *Ammon* – the Egyptian god of the air).

Can't you see? This whole place, the airport, the escalators, the gates, the terminals, even the restaurants are all designed for one purpose, that is, to foster motion. Motion must be diverse, constant, efficient, comfortable... And, like in any serious form of worship, orderly.

Now Clara, have you just read that in your Egyptian guidebook? When on earth did *you* become an expert in worship? When was the last time you went to church anyway?

I know; it must have been for my Confirmation, since I stopped going when Mum left Vancouver to go back to Seoul.

You were about fourteen then. So, that's ten years ago.

Yes, but I'm getting side-tracked. Look at this long queue for Security. What I'm asking is: what are they standing there for?

One after the other, they are conscientiously submitting themselves to a scan of their belongings and even of their bodies, leaving behind any obstacle to motion. That is, any substance that could be used as a weapon or an explosive to radically interrupt the motion of the aircraft.

I can't believe my eyes: this woman is actually getting rid of a fairly large Chanel spray (I see the two interlocked Cs – same initials as mine) that must have cost an arm and a leg! I wish I could go and grab it! Could she not remember the hand luggage regulations: *Liquids are allowed in containers up to 100 ml. No larger containers will be permitted.*

Wait...

Why did this cause a little flash in my memory?

Something about it... the rhythm of the words... It felt like something I'd heard many years ago. But when and where had my attention been drawn to access regulations in such a momentous way? I didn't travel much by plane as a child...

There! I remember – but it seems a bit far-fetched...

Still, it must have been at Catechism class in Vancouver, soon after we left Montreal then.

What was that sister called again?

Sister Marie-Thérèse.

She was sweet and demanding.

I can hear her insist, with her strong accent: "Venial sins only: one may walk to the Communion rail. Any mortal sins: one must go to Confession first."

That makes sense.

Some impediments are small enough to be tolerated as they won't hinder motion. Others are simply too heavy or toxic to be kept at hand. We children understood that very well. I don't think we had very big sins to confess anyway, but we would want to be sure and would readily go to Confession.

I used to go, until I became a teenager.

One felt so relieved when walking out.

Forgiven. Pacified. Loved.

In their own way, all these passengers in the queue are *confessing*... to the scanner.

Or to *Motion*? As if saying: "O *Motion*, this is what I have done against you: I have caused potential deceleration. Please, spare your sluggish worshipper!"

And no one argues. They know the rules.

But *what* will be left of this poor man!

He's already got rid of his coat and jacket, and boots and belt, and scarf and hat (ugly: please burn it).

Now he's standing in the glass cylinder of the body scanner with his feet slightly apart and his arms arched up overhead (like a ballet dancer in fifth position).

All this, to prove that he's no skyjacker!

It's embarrassing to be seen like this by everyone.

At church, confessions were not performed in public, but behind a screen; and one would only expose one's *soul*.

Chapter 8

Houston, can you hear me? Need permission to take off!
No, they don't hear me... Still no update on my flight... But why on earth does Kitty have to get married in Texas! Or married at all, in fact. Could we not remain together, just my sister and I, like when we were five?

As I stand near the flight information display – childhood and teenage memories start flowing back to me.
That isn't so good, since I am feeling a bit emotional.
Anyway, by association, those nice hymns taught us by Sister Marie-Thérèse come back to my mind. "Litanies," they were called.
Two women or girls (often Kitty and Sister, seldom Kitty and I) would start singing a petition, and the whole congregation would continue.

There could be many such petitions to various saints, or to God, or to the "Blessed Virgin Mary." They were sorted according to their common theme, and the congregation's answer would change at each new section, as well as the melody.
It was something like: "Lord, have mercy on us. Christ, have mercy on us. Holy Mary, pray for us." There were other responses, I recall, such as: "We beseech Thee, hear us;" or "Deliver us, O Lord."

Here at the airport, we are about fifty passengers standing with our eyes fixed on the wide display board hanging from the ceiling. At a small distance behind the main group, I am struck again.
Again I know that pattern from the past... Much as I try to dismiss it, I cannot help noticing a parallel between the flight information display and the "Litanies."
This is so silly! But true, I feel.
The tune playing in my mind is the same as in my youth at church – only the words are different.
Let me sing it for you: *Tokyo – Landed. Bombay – Landed. Cairo – Landed* (I knew that). *Lisbon – Delayed. Toulouse – Delayed. Rome – Delayed.*
Other sections have other themes and receive different responses: *Brussels, Houston, Manchester – Cancelled* (that I also knew).
And further down: *Istanbul, Reykjavík, Washington – En Route.*

All of us standing there are united in expectation.
In hope, one could say. Hope to see the plane land safely, or take off.
Our hearts are following in spirit the hundreds of aircraft turning

around the globe like seagulls. We watch them slowly slide through the night, leaving behind pale streaks across the sky at dawn, like shining musical notes moving along white scores in this hymn to *Motion*.

Is this all *Motion* worship then?

I glance at my fellow travellers. Single men (and women); families with pushchairs; tourists and professionals. They all look like pretty decent folk. Are they all taking part in some sort of worship, and am I the only one unaware of it? Are they all devoutly focussed on their *Motion* deity and I, the only unbeliever?

I feel uncomfortable, as a foreigner might be at an Egyptian ritual in a temple, where she would have sneaked in uninvited. What if they find out? What will happen when they realise that I don't belong to their religion?

Wait a minute: who said you don't belong to it! What is your *religion anyway?*

Do I have one at all?

I glide through life without considering the ultimate landing place... The universal encounter, with God? Is that being a *Motion* worshipper like all others? Then I suppose, it matters little what planes I sit in; what I studied; what nice travelling job I found and whatever husb... (yes, even that).

As long as I am not doing it all for *God*, in *God*'s company and in preparation for *God*'s embrace after judgment (so Sister assured)... I worship *Motion*?

Indeed?

So be it.

I don't care!

God is long gone from my life – as are Sister and Confession. Whatever slows us down displeases *Motion*.

Including Kitty's pregnancy?

Leave me alone! Speed is all I need – and *perfume*...

I take my mini beauty bag out (I'm one for very discreet and top quality makeup) and say to a rather pretty tanned face in the tiny mirror: "Hello lovely *Motion* worshipper!"

Presently, Pretty Face's cheeks and ears turn pretty red!

Chapter 9

Let me go back to one who knows I'm worth it.
    Let me read further what my awesome *assassin* has in store for me.
    Which page was it again? There...

    Clara dearest, I want you to know everything *about me.*
    Because I love you so much, and because I trust you, I want to share with you what matters to me most. And so that you might understand what I'm about to reveal, I thought I should first explain where I come from.
    So now, dear sister, here's my secret!
    You heard me refer to my beloved Katarina. Yes, I'm deeply in love with her!
    She changed my life. She displayed before my eyes such a fascinating example of purity and intellectual honesty that I was conquered – or freed rather. Do you mind if I tell you a bit about her?
    Some girls don't like hearing others praised. But you are generous, and my friend. Also, I think she likes you.

Monster! How *dare* you!
At this stage, I nearly fold his letter back in its envelope.
But I am curious, and keep reading:

    So, Katarina grew up by the sea, not here in Cairo.
    I went to her place – Alexandria: oh! you would love it there. Our backgrounds are quite different. Nobody knows my family, and we scrape a living. Not so with her people – the affluent and mighty kind. Surprisingly for them, Katarina became a Christian at the age of fourteen, despite much danger and opposition from the government.
    Brainy and sharp, she got involved in debates about the official religion and the Christian faith. You can find a lot online about her (she's not on Facebook, though). She was unafraid to address panels of experts with PhDs etc., and many of them were actually convinced by her arguments and embraced Christianity.
    That didn't at all please the Governor, who tried to entice her, even offering to make her his wife if she renounced her faith. Now, she was stunningly beautiful (as you could see when we went into that antique store). She refused of course. Thank God, or I would have lost her!

Oh no! – Azim truly loves *that* girl!
I've no time to ponder this unwelcome news, as loud exclamations by

the flight information board catch my attention. Finally! – news has come for passengers on the cancelled Houston flight to go to the airline desk! In haste, I push Azim's letter back into my bag while hurrying toward the desk, with my fellow-passengers.

The good news is that we are on the move again (in two and a half hours according to my watch), taking off at 15:05 (loud cheers among our group as our *Motion* deity is revered again).

The bad news is that we will land at one of the regional airports nearest Houston, "either CRP or SAT", where we will be fetched by bus for a mere three-hour journey (loud moaning from our group: *Motion* is deeply offended by this further delay).

And the reason for it?

The airline representative solemnly announces that half of the Houston air traffic-controllers are on strike to protest against the insufficient increase in salaries in the unveiled "Spaceport" plans, an endeavour "to establish Houston as a key player within the commercial spaceflight industry".

There is silence then, our group not being sure whether to cheer or to moan, since this immediate delay in our intercontinental flight is perhaps a necessary sacrifice for the sake of future interplanetary flights.

Flying to the Moon! Flying to Venus! Flying to Mars! Now, *that* is motion in earnest, with a capital M!

Meanwhile, San Antonio is confirmed as our airport of destination, and updated boarding cards are printed and distributed.

Chapter 10

I am starting to feel pretty tired and, having booked no villa on Mars (check that), or on Venus (don't check), I decide to go and rest (sorry *Motion!*) anywhere quiet, until boarding.

First, I order a cappuccino and a cake.

Then, sitting in a corner of the cafeteria, I confront the loss of my illusions about Azim's interest in me. Just how much more do I need to *admit* the truth – and my defeat? Am I eager to learn whether they first kissed by her parents' swimming pool, perhaps, or even on that bench in the garden where he took me the other night?

He. Does. Not. Love. You. The woman he loves is that witty beauty! (What is that shop where he said I met her? I should remember.)

No wonder he didn't want me, whether this morning, or yesterday night. I should praise him rather, for having been faithful to that other girl, whoever she is! She had nothing to fear. That's why he stayed aloof. I feel so slighted.

In truth, I suspected it from the start. It wasn't normal. No man in his right mind would have spent so much time with an attractive foreigner (that's *me*!) and tried nothing, unless he'd *a lot* to lose. She's rich, he said. She certainly would hear if he betrayed her.

But why write to *me* about her? I won't be their chaperone! What is it to me – I've my own life to get on with, thank you. My fling is over... Or rather, has it not been all in my head from the start?

I feel a bit dizzy (and lonely).

All I want by now is simply to be carried to my destination. I will do my job as Kitty's Maid of Honour. I will be dedicated and cheerful. I will not resent Raúl for stealing my beloved sister from me (check: is Raúl an only son?) Neither will I resent Kitty for deserting Vancouver and for having dug up behind my back such a lovable Texican lawyer in faraway Houston (does that place really exist!).

And what else? – no, I will surely not email this selfie to an Egyptian guide whose warm eyes will never meet mine again, as we both know. A cowardly farewell, dear Azim, to invite me "to a very special place this afternoon" if I'd "remained in Cairo longer" – when you knew well I could not!

Too late. Why did you come too late?

And would not even kiss me! Why did you come at all! And why load me with sheets of far-fetched praises and abstract thoughts? Is *that* a love letter? Handwritten or not, I've read enough to know the answer. Leave me alone, all of you; that's all I ask.

Walking along the shining displays of duty free shops, and made weary by the heavy fragrances and the music on the loudspeakers, I soon realise that shade and silence aren't easily found in this City of Lights.

I'm feeling a bit dizzy, when I *jump*.

Over there, at the end of the main corridor, I can see a hieroglyph. Am I back in Luxor? Have I dreamed it all? It looks like the sitting-owl figure but, on closer inspection, it proves to be a human character, half-kneeling, half-sitting. Not in any temple nor in any tomb have I ever encountered this particular sign. Set out of its context, it could mean anything. Probably a logo for yet another fashion shop!

Then I laugh as, next to it, is the alphabetical translation: "Prayer Room."

What a surprise. I hadn't realised that such places existed in airports. At least, I've never thought of visiting any. It has simply never been on my radar when travelling. But now, it's just my chance to find somewhere quiet! Surely they won't want to sell me perfume in that place. And the sound of the loudspeakers won't reach that far.

I follow the arrow down the side-staircase.

It reminds me of my descent to the tomb of Tutankhamun, just a few days earlier. How moving to see the place where the young king had laid for millennia, whose beautiful gilded face I had admired at the Egyptian Museum.

But his tomb was crowded with tourists. I hope for no throngs in this Prayer Room.

Just to be alone...

Chapter 11

Two hours later! – on the runway, from my seat in the plane off to Texas, in haste before takeoff I type on my phone:

If I should ever die, let it be known that I found love!

Chapter 12

Three weeks later.
I have just read the epitaph I wrote on my phone.
I'm still alive.
And still stunned by love, if a girl ever was.
Was the Gypsy in Cairo not a fraud after all, when she said: "You shall soon find the great love?" Could she *really* have seen it in my hand? Was it a well spent Egyptian fifty-pound note?

Well, the wedding is done, now. Mum flew from Seoul and met with Dad for the first time in twelve years. It was awkward for the four of us to be together again.
Kitty was beautiful and Raúl is kind; so are his two brothers (even the rodeo cowboy one who knows about bullfighting). I wish Granddad had been there.
The ceremony didn't go so well for *me* though.
I found it difficult to focus on Kitty and on my duties as Maid of Honour. My thoughts and my eyes were always drawn to another place in the church.

Had I ever been in love? I'm not sure now. And what happened to me at the airport was so unexpected, and so intense as well, that I have needed time to process it all.
The bridal shower wasn't a success, alas. I was supposed to set a cheerful tone and, for all my efforts, my heart was grave.
Poor Kitty! Sorry, my darling, I just couldn't help it.
Not that I was sad or jealous. Actually, I was deeply happy for my sister. But suddenly, you see, I realised the seriousness of a loving relationship, and its splendour, in a way yet unknown to me.
It hurt me to have to try to be funny or lively about Kitty's imminent commitment, when I just wished to meditate upon it in silence.

My heart felt pregnant. As I suppose young mothers do, I'd started living at a deeper level, as in silent conversation with a new, unseen life.
Actually, I'm not sure even *now* that I want to name it. It's all too precious and too real for words.
Should I not wait? Should I ever say it? What use?
Here I am, back in Vancouver and back to work. Perhaps later.
Perhaps.
God Knows.

Chapter 13

Half a year later...
A mere few weeks until Christmas. The past six months were a busy time in my life. Kitty's baby boy is so cute, and I'm to be his godmother.
Although I'm very much still the same old girl, the things I went through have changed me. For better, I hope.
I now feel settled enough to relive it again. This is to help me understand better what happened; and to fix it in my mind, while my memory is still fresh.
Oh, yes, strikingly fresh.

I see the Paris airport lounge. I see the relief airport confirmed: San Antonio, Texas, instead of Houston, and I remember sliding the updated boarding pass into my passport. San Antonio: let it be.
I see the *hieroglyph* (the "kneeling man" prayer sign) and the narrow staircase down to the Prayer Room in the basement. I meant to spend time in silence before takeoff.
I couldn't see a lift and was glad only to have a small bag to carry down (my main luggage was checked-in), wondering how people with heavy suitcases could access that Prayer Room, let alone passengers in wheelchairs.
Down the staircase, all was quiet; not a soul around. I was so glad. It smelled of bleach, a bit like in a swimming pool or a maternity ward, as if the floor had been freshly mopped.
At a distance I saw my *hieroglyph* again, presumably set above the entrance to the Room. There were no windows along that corridor, and not much light came from the lamps on the ceiling.
I suddenly felt apprehensive. Was it not *too* calm? A bit too solitary for a girl on her own?
I pulled myself together and walked towards my goal, with my fist tightly closed around the handle of my bag. Pushing open a door which bore the sign "Chapel," I nearly bumped into a cleaner's cart, left in the vestibule. I would have preferred to wait until the staff had finished their work, but not hearing anything, I stepped into the main room.
It was empty. I felt relieved.

In the dim light, all I could see were a few rows of modern chairs upon a dull carpet. Much like a waiting room, if it were not for what looked like a surgical table, made of steel and concrete, standing at the front. I wouldn't want to be carried upon it, even if wounded.
A book lay on it, next to a green pot plant.

By a frame on the wall flickered a candle, through a plain red glass holder.

I dropped my bag and sat down on a chair at the rear, resting my head against the wall behind me.

What bliss! This was exactly what I'd come for. I loved music and dancing, and chatting and shopping but, once in a while, the supreme luxury was to do away with all that and just stay still.

To disconnect.

Spontaneously I checked my phone and was surprised to find that I had nearly no signal. Again I became slightly apprehensive, knowing that I couldn't call for help if assaulted in that remote area. But I decided to do what I had intended to, and closed my eyes to rest.

For some reason, they kept opening again, looking at the room around me.

Surely, this wasn't Tutankhamun's tomb. No mummy.

It was cool and empty. No gold here, no jewels.

Actually, the place could do with a little decorating. After all, they'd written "Chapel" on the door, not merely "Prayer Room" like upstairs. Some display of sacredness, even modest, might be fitting down here.

By the way, which denomination was it? Most likely Christian...

I started dozing.

After about twenty minutes, I became faintly conscious of a presence in the room. I sat upright again, trying to discern any threat, but in vain.

All was still, apart from the distant sound of footsteps over the ceiling, rolling like waves from one end to the other, as groups of passengers walked across the hall upstairs to their gates or to shops.

I felt unusually relaxed.

I didn't even really mind the flight delay and the change of airport; neither Kitty's choice to marry a Texan – half Mexican in truth, and earning good money. Raúl's firm had been involved in the legal settlement following the Deepwater Horizon oil spill in the Gulf of Mexico.

The picture of a brown pelican coated in oil, trying in vain to open its wings, flashed into my memory – poor birds...

Ugh! Over there: something moved!

My heart started beating violently.

Chapter 14

Behind the thick table, I saw for the first time a shape. A horizontal shape now gently shaking.

I was petrified and, although pretty safe on my chair by the exit door, I didn't dare to move. The shape was silent, and was growing taller, still shaking slightly. It looked very much like the sitting-owl figure of the hieroglyph.

But it seemed to be human; a kneeling body. Kneeling and... sobbing.

The person stood up, genuflected, and turning towards the door, saw me. I felt like stone. A man in his sixties wearing some uniform, he slowly walked towards the glass door into the vestibule. His brown face was tearful and beaming, as he caressed mine with his gaze. Why did he look familiar?

I heard him wheel out what I realised was the cleaner's cart. So much for my fear! I laughed in relief. This man was a member of the airport staff, a cleaner who had come here to...

Only at that moment did I realise the strangeness of the situation. What had that cleaner been doing here for the past half hour since my arrival? Not cleaning. Doing *what*, then?

I knew the word, but was reluctant to utter it in my heart.

Something warned me that it would sound like a reproach, and would cast upon my life an unwelcome hue. But I couldn't avoid the mental emergence of the word in my conscience.

This cleaner was... *praying*.

This old man had spent the last thirty minutes, if not much longer, prostrate on the floor of the chapel, apparently not sleeping (unlike me), but praying. Why not sit on a chair then (like me)? Why was he hiding at the front, by the wall? His posture mattered very little – I knew that I was unconsciously eluding the true question: *Why* was he praying?

Why pray?

Pray. I came to look at the place where he'd been crouching. Right above it was the cheap red glass candle-holder, whose flickering flame was mirrored as sparks in the brass frame next to it.

I started to feel afraid. Not in the same way as before, though.

Not fearing danger. Fearing love.

My inner senses were informing my heart about a reality in the slow process of unveiling itself.

It was ineluctable.

It came unhurried.

It felt desirable, supremely.

There was still time to escape; but the mere thought of it sounded too shamefully offensive. As my eyes started to feel tenderly directed to that gleaming frame, so my mind was led as if by an invisible and friendly hand to consider the square shape; the smooth surface surrounded by the frame, with an embossed crucifix bearing by its side – like a wound – a tiny keyhole.

A strange word blossomed in my memory... a forgotten word shone forth as a winter sun in my mind... a forbidden word unfolded in my heart as a phoenix opening its wings and I pronounced that word, very slowly, as if repeating it after someone else: "Tabernacle."

This brass on the wall was no mere frame. It was a *door* concealing the sacred cavity in which the faith of my childhood and early adolescence used to take for granted the true presence of a God.

But I was a child no more. With gusto I had tasted the sweet recipes of belief; I had enjoyed the comfort of religion until, becoming an adult, I had grown out of those nursery garments.

And yet, in that moment, I witnessed the unthinkable exchange of my previous certainties. What I definitively held as real, proven and honourable was losing consistency at high speed, soon to merely float in the air like a familiar cloud; while amidst that cloud the sweet myths of my youth precipitated into a solid substance.

I felt as one standing at Ground Zero, watching a reverse video of 9/11.

Dust and fragments of concrete and glass all upwardly assembled until, within a few seconds, the Towers were standing again firm and secure!

I was like a mum by her young girl's bed, reading to her child the tale of *Ali Baba and the Forty Thieves*, and being struck in awe when, having said the words "Open Sesame!" – she finds the bedroom wall ajar.

It wasn't planned.

Chapter 15

It didn't come as a voice.

Neither mine, nor anyone else's. But it did communicate – through ideas, pictures, and emotions. Even that is altogether too abstract. It was more like spiritual touches, like the beginning of a very slow dance with my soul.

A presence was making itself identifiable.

Strange paradox: it was gigantically powerful and supremely respectful.

It was totally invisible and ravishingly beautiful.

The more the presence disclosed itself, the more I trusted it.

I knew all along that I could choose to interrupt the process, at any time. I was by no means bound.

But I also knew that its occurring and unfolding were gratuitously given to me, as a royal and unmasterable grace. The presence became obvious.

It simply was.

There was nothing to say about it, any more than stating that there is a sun when you look into the sky on a clear summer morning.

My knees met with the carpet, between the wall and the table, as my gaze reached the framed door, with its crucifix and keyhole.

And my lips responded to the presence: "You've been here all along... And I didn't know it... I'd forgotten... I'd busied my soul with anger, with doubt, with achievements. I let the world lay its hands on me, wrapping my heart in linen cloths: my heart embalmed and buried deep in the sarcophagus of pride.

"If my past and present selves were two different persons; if the twelve-year-old that I was could read my soul as a woman, nearly old enough to be her mother, the girl would rightly have mourned her *mummy*, knowing me to be so busily dead!

"But you found where I lay and with divine patience you hallowed me back to life. From the tomb of unbelief, you unburied me."

My hands caressed the wall under the door as I spoke on in deep silence: "I can now feel that in my breast, the girl of twelve who beamed with faith was kept alive through your mercy."

Warmth breathed upon my body and through my soul as time faded away.

Daughter shone in my mind as a picture more than a word, filling me with unprecedented gratitude.

It later turned into *Sister*, which gave me the humble pride of an indescribable joy. I tried to dwell on it for as long as possible, as I feared a new stage in this revelation, which would take me too far... which would fill me with light when I deserved ashes, I who was but dust, or even mud!

The word came as a balm applied to my soul through almighty healing: *Bride*.
Tears flowed down my cheeks and chin as never in my life (with much sniffling). Unworthy, unworthy, so radically unworthy!
And yet fulfilled, fulfilled, so intimately fulfilled...
My heart exhaled gratitude as a holy smoke of incense.

Chapter 16

Objections rose like dancing blades around my joy, only to reveal its inner strength as they melted away one after the other.

Did I know what *was behind that door? What was I besotted with! Would I dare to say it, and see how miserably it failed the test of reason for any educated mind – nay, of mere common sense! Come on! Say it.*

Bread.

A piece of bread.

More than that? All right: make it two, three, or twenty flat discs of white bread in a vessel. Is that not the bare truth? Did your tongue as a child ever taste anything but bread when that food was stuffed down your throat, like a French goose?

Bread it tasted; food it was; but freely swallowed.

Did your eyes ever catch anything of that object but its whiteness and circular shape; just the way it looked in the plastic bag on the sacristy shelf before Mass!

What a blessing: I had long forgotten the words *Sacristy* and *Holy Mass* and how much I loved them. We also had *State of grace*: ... mysterious and beautiful.

Enough! Just because a man in a robe whispers magic *words over that bread, will it turn into... into anything else? Do men have such power?*

It has pleased God indeed to grant it to His priests!

Let us not get heated, dear girl.

You know that you can trust me: I'm your better judgment. And I'm sorry to say that your current experience is caused by fatigue; by the emotional shock of losing your sister to that Texan lawyer; and by the empty clasp of this Egyptian rogue.

Stronger women than you would react exactly the same way.

When you come back to your true self, you will admit that your shaken psyche simply made up this weird hunger for "sacred" bread, because just now you can't cope with your want of a loving companion.

If your mother had stayed with your dad, of course you wouldn't have this inhibition. That's what religion is about: helping you to ignore life's sufferings, until nature rebuilds within you the strength you need to stand up again as a responsible citizen.

Can't you see?

That last objection shook me badly. It rang true, so true. So far, the unsuccessful attempts of my "better judgment" had only increased my joy.

But now my tears were flowing again as I pressed my cheek against the glittering frame, begging for help.

Instead, doubt tightened its persuasive grip around my soul. Was it all in my mind? Was I making it up? It went on...

Back in the real world, pretty girl as you are, you will soon meet a handsome partner.

What about a banker?

An athlete?

An actor?

And true bliss will start, and you will gladly throw away these dirty crutches, borrowed from the weakest of this world, the wounded, the fallen!

That was a mistake.

Rather than being a *coup de grâce*, this finale set me free.

It revealed to me the great truth about my new love. That it appealed and applied precisely to the weakest of this world, to the wounded, the falling ones!

Because only *they* had known their dependence, their shame and their loss and thus, only they could ask for protection, forgiveness and redemption.

Between two sobs I heard my tongue utter: "Lord, have mercy on me, a poor sinner."

Chapter 17

Suddenly, a great stillness settled over my mind, while pictures started flashing like lightning through my mental landscape, carrying with them complex information, instantaneously displayed.

To my shame, I had never paid any particular attention to such news items.

My memory must have automatically archived them somewhere, until this moment when a mysterious force made them flare up before my eyes as "news icons."

They unfolded at once, one after the other, like allied parachutes whitening the dark sky on the night of D-Day. An army of facts was flying to my rescue, proving my newborn faith true, its object real and its effects verifiable!

Here are some I recall: friars in Colombian slum risking their lives to protect teenage girls from gang; tortured catechist in China; parents smiling at their baby with Down's Syndrome; grandparents and children gassed by riot squads at a peaceful protest for family rights in Paris; Padre kneeling by a dying soldier in Iraq; parish volunteers climbing up to the eighth floor to visit a lonely paraplegic; British midwives before a tribunal being denied the right to conscientious objection.

And, as the grand finale to these sacred fireworks: an immense crowd of young adults kneeling at night in front of a monstrance held before them by a frail white silhouette...

My Lord's *paratroopers*!

In different ways, they were all falling.

Falling to save us: the secure, the complacent, the busy.

Falling for justice; falling on their knees. Only by falling can we meet the arms of the Rising One. Through a leap of faith and humility – no recklessness here, nor presumption.

Falling in love, then?

One love only could catch and rescue all the falling ones across history.

And It lived in a vessel behind that door, where an infinite God gave Himself as Food. As was later explained to me, true human love was ultimately fulfilled in the Eucharist, the divine keystone of the human *cathedral*, bringing together all our charitable initiatives and our loving concerns, giving them coherence and bringing them to completion.

In that love, I fell.

It wasn't a myth. Not a sensation, nor an ideal. It was a Person. It was God made Man for my salvation.

The book open on the altar behind me was indeed a bible. My finger fell at random on this paragraph: "And I will espouse thee to me forever: and I will espouse thee to me in justice, and judgment, and in mercy, and in commiserations. And I will espouse thee to me in faith: and thou shalt know that I am the Lord."

I turned towards the tabernacle door upon which the embossed crucifix shone and, still weeping, I kissed its feet of brass with all the passion, respect and faith that I could muster.

Like my "news icons" earlier, church hymns from my youth unfolded in my memory, where they'd been stored mysteriously all that time:

*If I love Him I shall be chaste,
if I touch Him I shall be clean.
He hath espoused me with a betrothal ring,
and adorned me with a necklace of great price.
My Lord Jesus Christ hath espoused me with His ring,
and hath set on my head a crown as the crown of a bride.*

Never had His presence felt so clear; and yet, it was surprisingly discreet, unobtrusive.

In an instant, I knew myself secured, forgiven, embraced, loved, enlightened and glorified. I lay prostrate in thanksgiving for some time, motionless.

Eventually, my senses started interacting again with my mind.

I listened. The sound of footsteps still reverberated across the ceiling.

Later on, a priest told me that an international airport might be the best location for a tabernacle: "Nowhere is the contrast more striking between man's busy flutter and God's focused omnipotence," he said.

At that moment, in that airport chapel, I felt just *that*. We walk and run and fly in every direction, little knowing that our Beginning and our End awaits us right under our feet. Like bees overlooking the hive, we breeze over the One Who is.

My eyes found my watch, and I registered that I still had ample time to proceed to Security and to the gate for my connecting flight.

Wherever I flew, would I ever leave His loving embrace?

Chapter 18

I smelt a long forgotten fragrance... Incense!
 I sat back on my heels and looked around.
 Through the open door of the vestibule, I saw a man on his knees, like me.
 A thin thread of smoke rose from a bowl at his side.
 Perhaps it was now time for me to go. Streaks of makeup from my eyes, cheeks and lips had painted across my palms the picture of the past hour. On that occasion, abstract art was plainly readable. I could not imagine what my face looked like! But my bag wasn't at hand to make me presentable.
 I knelt with recollection before the tabernacle, uncomfortably having to turn my back on it as I went. Then I walked, with another kind of embarrassment, towards the door where my bag lay on the chair upon which I had first sat, looking at my feet so as to avoid crossing the gaze of the visitor.

A paper tissue appeared in my range of vision, held out to me at the end of an arm.
 Still on his knees the man assured me that it was "never used before: straight out of the pack." I thanked him and took the tissue. As I started cleaning my face, I heard him add: "Should buy L'Oréal: best waterproof brand."
 Puzzled, I asked if he worked in cosmetics.
 "Not bodily ones," he replied. "I help enhance souls instead," and standing up with a groan, he took off his scarf, revealing a Roman collar.
 I was speechless.
 He was a congenial plump little man in his fifties, smelling of tobacco, a bit bald and well under my height (even when standing): "Good afternoon Clara, I'm Father Paul. I assume that this belongs to you. I found it on the floor."
 It was my boarding card from the Cairo flight. "Thank you, Father."
 He replied: "You look much better now. Found what you had lost, there by the altar? I'm only asking because if you need more time I'm happy to wait: Mass won't start for another hour – Sunday schedule."

I felt encouraged by his pleasant take on my awkward situation and thought I would skip preliminaries. "Father, I just found God again, here in your chapel."
 "But," he replied, "isn't God everywhere?"
 "Not physically. I mean, not as the Lord is in the tabernacle... in the Host."
 "Well, I couldn't agree more. That's why I come here and offer Mass: that He may be found by all those who seek."
 "But Father, after what happened, I can't think of leaving Him now."
 "You'll find Him where you go. If you want my advice, Clara: don't talk

about what you've just found. Ponder it all, until it's time. And log onto this website," he handed me a flyer, "where you will find enough food for thought about the ways and means of His presence, and the consequences."

"Thank you, Father Paul, and also for the incense."

"That? Was for Him, as He spoke to you. And also for you, secondarily, to listen to Him. And perhaps as well, against another."

"I don't understand."

"The Bishop sends people to me, who need special prayers to quiet a certain *mad dog* (no need to speak the name of the evil spirit, he doesn't deserve attention). I found that blessed incense can help. And Holy Water."

"Were you praying for me then?"

He looked at me with affection: "Child, I have prayed for you since my very first Mass, twenty-one years ago, and even earlier. But more precisely, an hour ago as I was parking, good Nepomucen texted me... let me find it... this..."

He showed me his phone and I read: *Backup needed underground*.

"I'm glad I came straight away," he added, "and I surely prayed."

"Who is Nepomucen?" I asked.

"Landed from Khartoum a few years ago. Cleaning agent around here, as a hobby of course. His real business is prayer. Top professional. He has intuition. We complement each other well, since I pray poorly and I "clean" by trade. I always trust him."

"Thank God for Nepomucen! Am I safe to go, Father?"

"Do as we all do: make a thorough and humble confession to a priest; prepare for a good Holy Communion; and stay connected." He handed me a small plastic cord with blue beads attached to it. "Here's your direct line to our heavenly Mother."

Accepting the rosary I replied: "Father Paul, I don't know how to thank you for all that you've done!"

"Say a prayer for Nepomucen's wife: terminal cancer. And another one for me to smoke less (*incense* smoke is safe). And for this chapel to last. Sounds as if the Muslim prayer room is getting too small. I have fears."

I looked with increased interest at the rather plain face of small Fr. Paul, at his shabby jacket generously perfumed with the smell of pipe tobacco, as his words revealed an unexpectedly acute mind and heart.

If it hadn't been for my connecting flight, I would have stayed longer, and perhaps gone to Confession with him. What he'd just said encouraged me. I mean, not to fear the truth about myself, when I would be ready.

He went on: "And the last prayer, Clara (this is pure guesswork on my part, so don't take it too seriously): for your friend *Azim*."

Chapter 19

"What! How can *you* know?"

Looking embarrassed, he smiled apologetically: "Oh, well. Just a few thoughts I had while waiting at the back. I wouldn't share them, unless you insisted. Please, don't think me intrusive: deduction is one of my hobbies."

"I beg you, Father, tell me *everything!*"

"Fine. Only because you ask me, then. Here's where I started.

"Azim's email address is pencilled on your boarding card, rather hastily as the handwriting shows. Now, this puzzled me.

"If he'd turned up earlier, you would have taken time to enter his address in your phone, rather than on your precious title of admission through Security and onto the aircraft.

"So, it must have been the only paper at hand, literally, which suggests that he reached you in the queue just as you were about to walk through the metal detector."

That priest was astonishing: *card* reading, instead of *palm* reading like my Gypsy woman!

He continued: "On the other hand, if seeing him then hadn't mattered to *you*, you wouldn't have taken the time to write down his address in such inconvenient circumstances, with the whole queue waiting behind you.

"Now if you mattered to *him*, why would he not have come along with you to the airport and spent five minutes at the cafeteria (where you ate your cookie alone, before Security, perhaps waiting for someone)?

"But if you *didn't* matter to him, *why* would he inconvenience you by showing up at the very last moment, when you could give him no time at all – a hug at best?"

I meant to interrupt him and find out how he could see everything just as if he'd been present in Cairo.

But he went on, "Furthermore, if you don't mind my showing you, over his address on the boarding card, lipstick traces show – with a tiny crumb of white cookie, stuck there for good measure. (I have developed a particular attention to misplaced crumbs in recent years.)

"However, only the upper lip is visible, while the lower appears on the back of the card, indicating that you were holding it in your mouth. But since you carried only a small backpack (plus perhaps your light hat in a bag, if not bought at duty free after Security), you had both hands *free* to keep the card and passport in.

"Unless, just before walking through the gate, your arms happened to be clasped around... Well, dear child, I've no intel, but Azim should feel special, and he deserves a prayer from a friend. Sorry for showing off: I notice things onl when it might help a soul.

"Off you go now, Miss Nefertiti. Lift to departure gates in the corridor to your right. And remember next time: waterproof makeup!"

Stepping aside with a gentle smile, he opened the door into the corridor.

As I bent to take my bag and hat, I felt on my forehead some instrument loosely drawing a... small cross; while before my eyes, blue plastic beads swayed. My rosary! I'd let it fall onto the floor and Fr. Paul had picked it up for me.

No Queen of Egypt bore on her tiara the rearing cobra with more confidence than I wore the sign of our redemption, sketched across my brow by the little priest with the crucifix of my rosary!

I feared no more, knowing what love accompanied my steps, guided my thoughts, and sustained my breath.

Chapter 20

So there *was* a lift down here after all – and up again (I was glad for wheelchair users, and cleaning staff).

On pressing the button, I wondered if the world would know the change in me. "Will they look at me as a new creature?" I asked the lift mirror, while wiping away the last streaks of melted makeup (there, at the corners of my mouth).

Checking my watch I found that I still had more than an hour before takeoff. No time to lose, but I would be fine. As I walked out, all was as I'd left it. Although it seemed to me that I'd been away for a thousand years.

Would they remember me?

They *did*: "Final call for flight AA2300 to San Antonio, Texas: Passenger Clara Cumberhart, please proceed immediately to Gate 62."

I couldn't believe it! My watch still showed over an hour before takeoff!

"Passenger Clara Cumberhart, please proceed immediately to Gate 62."

My phone started beeping repeatedly.

With horror I realised that I'd meant to adjust to French time on landing and, instead of moving my watch backward by one hour for Paris, I'd moved it by two. I was in fact on Greenwich Meridian Time, that is, one hour late.

My stomach shrank to a small knot and my mouth went dry. And still Security to go through! *It's too late!* I cried out silently. *I've lost it all. Please, dear Lord, don't let me miss that flight! I must go to Kitty at once!*

Immediately a miracle occurred, as a member of staff shouted along the Security queue: "Cairo passengers, please follow me through now!"

Not knowing what explained this favour, I waved my boarding pass from Cairo and, beating a long queue, I was through Security in no time, having just a small backpack.

But my gate was in a distant satellite; surely ten minutes' walk from us. Apparently not all my tears had flown in the chapel, since I managed to cover my face again with new ones, sobbing: "This is all my fault! Too late, too late!"

A security agent came to ask what the matter was.

I explained in broken French that I (sob) was going to my (sob) sister's wedding in Texas and (sob) couldn't make it (sob) on time to the gate.

Thinking that *I* was the one about to get married, he was touched and shouted (as far as my childhood French let me understand) to a French African driver on an electric cart: "Look here, Rob, this beautiful American lady is getting married, can you take her at once to Gate 62?"

"Rob" saw me and laughed (I'd never seen such a wide smile and splendid white teeth!): "You getting married? You bride? This very wonderful! Me taking you now to gate! You jump in! Go, go, go!"

He dragged me on the seat next to him and started at full speed, with flashing lights and warning beeps, shouting as we slalomed along the carpeted corridors through frightened groups and falling bags: "Make place! Make place for bride! Place for very beautiful American bride!"

Thinking it not the best time to mention that I was actually Canadian, I put my hat on (sorry, *Kitty's* gift-hat) to free my hands and held onto the handles by my seat. People started cheering as we rushed by; some were clapping; others asking if it was a flashmob.

Our speed increasing, the long white gauze scarf attached to the hat floated behind us, like a wedding veil indeed. Children started running behind the cart, while further ahead a man was taking a fiddle out of its case and played at our approach. I'd never dreamed of such a nuptial cortege! Was I not Someone's bride after all?

Romantic but practical, my driver said: "Gate near now. When we there, you jump out very fast with bag. You don't say thank you – and no kiss! You go now! Jump! And lucky fiancé!"

I ran to the desk with my passport and boarding card, which a (pierced-eared) steward took off me and read, adding in a very kind voice: "You are too late Miss. Your seat was allocated to the last standby passenger. I'm extremely sorry."

I said instinctively: "But I have come from Cairo! I was delayed."

He took up his phone and I heard him state my case to a colleague.

Then he waited in silence.

It felt like hours!

I was about to collapse, when the jet-bridge door opened and a stewardess called: "Miss Cumberhart, do come in at once: you're upgraded to Business Class."

Ecstatic, I thought: *The miracle goes on!* and I flew, rather than walked, into the aircraft. With utter disbelief, I let myself be guided to a wide leather seat where I fell, crying and laughing: *Lord, you took me through it all!*

My phone displayed several text messages from Kitty, asking if I was safe. How kind of her to enquire! Yes, I was safely through, but what a race it had been! I texted back, assuring her that, thank God, I'd boarded all right and would land at San Antonio TX at 20:10, to be driven by bus to Houston.

I had good network coverage, and several emails from Kitty and my boss automatically downloaded into my inbox. He also was asking whether I was safe. And Sally too, and even Dad; and Mum as well! How could they all know of my latest adventure?

I quickly texted back to all that I was fine, and on my way home. I was feeling so weary by then. Other emails and texts could wait. (That was just as well, or I wouldn't have slept.)

In thanksgiving for the love I had found underground, I jotted my "epitaph" into my phone, as a prayer and, having wrapped myself in a cashmere blanket and tightened my eye-mask, I fell asleep as we took off.

Paris was gone with all its bright delights, but its purest light – that poor candle in the red glass lamp of a deserted underground chapel – shone forth in my heart.

Chapter 21

Food!

Shamefully, I remember that my very first thought, even before opening my eyes was: "Have I missed breakfast?"

Several hours had passed since takeoff when the smell of hot croissants activated my brain, teasing me out of my sleep, as a corn kernel thrown into a deep pond might hit a dormant carp at the bottom.

Waking up, I remembered the miracle of my boarding, my unexpected upgrade to Business Class, and found that breakfast wasn't easily missed when sitting where I was.

A hostess came immediately to offer me a range of delicious options including a full dinner or a lighter breakfast with Danish pastries, croissants, gazelle horns, muffins, seasonal fruits, and several kinds of tea and coffee.

I selected the spicy tomato juice with ice cubes.

Truly, these girls looked *so* stylish in those well-cut uniforms. I should ask them where the airline got them from. Still, their pillbox hat didn't match my straw bucket – ahem, Kitty's.

I had never been happier to see a face care wipe; and the ones in Business Class were so refreshing, and perfumed. Applying one to my cheeks and nose; then another on my eyelids and mouth, I felt reborn.

It also brought back to my memory the spiritual rebirth I'd been so fortunate to experience in the chapel, at the end of which I'd got rid of another tissue, coloured with my melted makeup. My redundant shroud...

I didn't dare visit my own heart to check if a certain flame still burned in it, or if it had vanished like a sweet dream over the Atlantic.

I vaguely feared waking up as from a fairy tale.

Surely the singular depth of my experience couldn't have been a product of my imagination. It was too real not to have left traces outside the underground chapel, which would appear in due course.

But, if patients are reluctant to set foot on the floor again after an operation on their legs, what in the case of a *heart* transplant?

How hesitantly would they try to *love*?

They might give it more time, so that the anaesthesia could wear off.

Perhaps I was simply shy, as in meeting a boy again after a very first kiss.

I hoped that the veiled Object of my love would not take offence, if His bride took time to adjust to her new condition.

I would now look at my emails.

Searching my bag for my phone, my fingers got entangled in a cord, felt beads... and extracted a blue rosary. I was like an archaeologist digging up her first tangible evidence from a lost site. I could have sung with joy: *You see: it wasn't a dream! Dreams don't leave rosary beads behind them!*

I looked at the little blue spheres of plastic, evenly spaced along the white thread. My "direct line to our heavenly Mother," as Fr. Paul had said.

How did it work again?

I proudly remembered that there were five groups of prayers, and a few others at the beginning, and some at the end.

But how did it start? My recollection of the Apostles' Creed was very hazy. Should I begin with the Our Father? I was at a loss.

Closing my eyes, I asked my Love for inspiration, if it pleased Him that I should... *pray.*

"Hey, Mary! Look, down there: this must be Lake Michigan!"

The passengers behind me had been very quiet up to then, but I gave thanks for that man's exclamation (immediately hushed by his wife). By association, it had prompted in the depths of my childhood memories the words of the *Hail Mary*. I would skip the Creed, and the Our Father.

My Love would hear my praise to his Mother. This indirect approach comforted me. Mary was less daunting. In a way, we were among women, despite my shame at not having spoken to Her for so long.

I started slowly: "Hail Mary, full of grace, the Lord is with Thee..." How incredibly soothing this address. And beautiful. I recalled that an angel had first spoken it.

An angel? So, *angels* had to be involved in all this as well? Not only my Love, but also His Mother, and now their angels? And more still? Like the Pope, the Swiss Guards (so smart!) and the Sistine Chapel? And even more, like... wait until marriage, give to the poor, forgive your enemies and protect the vulnerable?

I was reticent and thrilled at the same time.

A stewardess was coming down my way. I realised that she would see me holding the rosary beads. Watch this pair of guilty *squirrels*! Hiding their nuts away under the tray table: my hands with the blue beads...

The woman walked by. I confronted my uneasy conscience. No, letting it be seen was *not* showing off. Nor was it imposing my religion on others. On the contrary, hiding the beads was cowardice. It meant that I didn't acknowledge my religious identity. Could it not also deprive this stewardess of a modest testimony of faith?

With a little sigh, I lifted the beads out of my lap, back into the open.

Suddenly I felt happy and proud of them, as if each plastic sphere were a child of mine. Better accustomed to them now, I was able to pray several Hail Marys without distraction. Such were the first steps of my soul away from the surgical table. I could walk. Frail and slow, still I loved, and praised God for it.

I had slept undisturbed and now felt revitalized. On the screen before me, I saw that we were less than two hours from our destination. I should catch up with the world. Television first, and then emails. I put those Bose headphones on (amazing stuff – yet another Business Class privilege!) and I turned on the news.

"Latest on the terror attack in Egypt. 'Scimitars of Islam,' the Islamist terrorist group, has just claimed responsibility for the attack, warning Westerners and Egyptians that 'more punishments will occur unless all infidels convert.'

"Air traffic has now returned to normal at Cairo Airport after most flights were delayed for enhanced security checks, while several incoming flights were cancelled or rerouted. The CIA Director congratulated the Mukhabarat – the Egyptian Intelligence Agency – for sharing the details of all passengers flying from Cairo that day: such prompt international cooperation, it is hoped, will help identify the terrorists.

"The attack occurred in Cairo at 3 p.m. local time, killing four.

"Witnesses and security sources confirm that masked men on a motorcycle stood for about a minute in front of the local Coptic Catholic church in the deprived neighbourhood of al-Warraq as a few worshippers were going in.

"One of the masked men opened fire with a handgun, killing and injuring a number of those gathered close to the church door. Then both men fled the scene.

"Three of the victims were Egyptian and one American.

"The U.S. President condemned this barbarous act of violence and sent his condolences to the families, in particular the one of the deceased American woman.

"Her husband, Canadian tycoon Mansur Al-Khoury, was also injured and is in critical condition in hospital.

"The couple's young daughter was saved through the courageous intervention of their Egyptian guide, who shielded the child with his own body, and tragically lost his life."

The newscaster's voice continued – but I could barely understand what he was saying.

I can't.
I cannot.
Help.
Calling...
Calling Him. Calling You... Naming You. Help... Lord Jesus, my God and my Saviour!

I saw myself. I saw my hands shaking as I wondered why the pilot had chosen just that moment to dive into an abysmal air pocket.

Not only my hands were shaking, but also my arms, shoulders and legs. I grabbed my empty glass and attempted to vomit into it, but nothing came out. And why had the steward now switched off all heating – or had they just opened the aircraft doors? I froze, and I sweated, while my heartbeat accelerated, in fierce competition with the quickest techno music hits. My teeth joined in the orchestra, chattering.

The headphones slipped off my head.

As I seemed to fall, I saw my fingers clutch the rosary beads on the tray.
Falling.
Lord... Love, have mercy on Your falling bride...

Chapter 22

My eyes are still closed as I become aware of a familiar smell.

Not of croissants this time, merely Chanel N°5.

The first thing I see on opening my eyes again is a pearl necklace, and right above it, the friendly face of a middle-aged Indian-looking woman, smiling at me.

She's the medical doctor whom the staff called to assist me. Whatever she did to me was successful. I feel much more at peace now.

She tells me about herself. In Pakistan where she comes from, half the women doctors graduating can't find work. So she made her way to America where she was granted citizenship.

Her name is Dr. Nasreen Fatimah Yasir. She just happened to be sitting two rows ahead of me. She must be a good doctor, I tell myself (thinking of her pearls), or her husband is a maharajah – or both (some people have it all).

She asks me if I was in Paris only on transit. She says she has come from Geneva, where she attended a U.N. conference. I'm pretty sure that the staff has told her the first leg of my journey, but I appreciate the fact that she helps me recall only by stages the recent news which I will soon have to confront emotionally.

I tell her that I just saw on the news that a friend of mine was shot in Cairo, with a family I'd met.

She knows about it. She asks if I'm positive that the victims are the same people I knew. I try to remember and, alas, must admit that the brief description given on the news leaves no room for doubt. She answers that, as a Muslim herself, she's deeply shocked by the murder of innocent people in the name of her religion.

I notice that she's wearing (very smart) trousers.

I guess that she wonders if I'm also a Muslim. Apart from the recent incident of the rosary beads, this is the first time that I find myself in the situation of verbally expressing my religious identity. I'm a bit apprehensive, having only started to come to terms with what happened to me a few hours earlier, in the underground chapel.

I simply state that, until that afternoon, I had no belief.

Dr. Yasir smiles and kisses my forehead.

This unexpected part of the treatment makes me vaguely blush, or at least I feel myself doing so. I thank her for her kindness. She gives me water to drink, adding that she will accompany me on arrival and make sure that I'm taken care of. She adds that we will land in an hour and offers to remain sitting next to me, which I readily accept.

While she goes to fetch her handbag, the same steward who had taken my card at the desk (I hadn't seen him earlier on this flight) kneels before me. His badge reads "Oscar," but I fail to put a name to his fragrance.

Oscar furtively lays in my hand what I immediately feel to be my rosary beads, as he whispers apologetically that he found them on the floor at my feet.

It's the second time this day – and in my life – that a man hands a rosary to me.

I thank him and notice that he wants to say something more. I give him my warmest smile (although looking fairly weary, I'm sure) and he boldly ventures, in his very kind voice: "Miss Cumberhart, will you please pray to Him for me as well? I know He's the One who really loves me."

And immediately, Oscar moves away to let Dr. Yasir sit by my side.

On my palm I see a shape impressed in my skin, neat and deep. It looks like the impact of hail or of frozen green peas. But in the middle, the outline of a cross distinctly shows. I must have been holding my rosary very tightly when I lost consciousness.

Glancing at the beautiful necklace of my considerate neighbour, I decide to put my beads around my neck. At least I won't lose them again so soon.

Dr. Yasir sees me, and smiles in silence.

By now, I think I'm a Catholic; as my Love wishes.

Azim.

Azim. Where are you? Where *were* you?

What have you done! Where have you been!

What a tragedy. What a shock. You've broken my heart. My friend, my dear Egyptian friend. And this poor family, those acquaintances of yours... The mere thought of it!

Feeling cold, I button my jacket and open my bag to take my scarf, only to find a familiar envelope with my name on it. Azim's letter!

With all that had occurred since, I'd forgotten about it. I know where I stopped reading... His secret love for the rich girl from Alexandria. I don't know yet how it ends. I feel so weak. Could this not wait? On the other hand, it's vital that I should be apprised, if possible.

I caress the brown envelope and read as with new eyes my handwritten name and the words "Open only after takeoff." I'd done as he'd asked, after leaving Cairo.

It feels as if in another life. With awe, this time, I slowly draw the sheets out again. Unfolding the last two, yet unread, I find a smaller envelope taped in the middle. It's well sealed and, as I tear it open, a few purple petals fall over my lap.

Quite a surprise! Where did he pick them? They look very similar to those on the shrub outside my window, at the hotel. More of them remain inside the envelope. I will count them later, in memory of him. Having put them all back in safety, I resume my reading.

„Unknown Katarina, our friend is dead...

Chapter 23

She wasn't afraid to address panels of experts with PhDs etc.
Many of them were actually convinced by her arguments and embraced Christianity.
That didn't at all please the Governor, who tried to entice her, even offering to make her his wife if she renounced her faith.
Now, she was stunningly beautiful (as you could see when we went into that antique store). She refused, of course. Thank God, or I would have lost her!
They stretched her upon a spiked wheel, and when the wheel broke, she was beheaded, aged only eighteen.
Her glorious martyrdom occurred in 305 A.D. in Alexandria!

I read again the dreaded paragraph, not knowing whether I should laugh or cry.
What?
Azim had no girlfriend? He'd never met that girl!
Not that it changed things much, after the tragedy. But it revealed how foolish I'd been! How self-centred, rather.
Forgive me, dear friend...

She gave up her life for religious truth and moral purity.
Her sacred body is venerated on the top of Mount Sinai. This all took place a long time ago, as you can see. Many times I went to Alexandria to pray where she'd suffered and triumphed. I also went to Mount Sinai and stayed next to the great monastery where she sleeps.
I know that you may think me weird.
How on earth could a dead Christian girl from early antiquity have any impact on me, a fairly competent Muslim guide in Third Millennium Cairo? I'm sorry – I don't know how she did it, but... She inspired me and gave me courage to examine my religion critically.
I didn't mean to challenge my faith. Just the opposite: I hoped to understand it better, so as to become a more committed believer.

Later, I heard that the Christian sacred writings state that: 'In the beginning was the reason (or word) and the reason was God. In him was life, and the life was the light of men. That was the true light, which enlightens every man that comes into this world.'
According to that statement, not only was God intelligible, but He wanted to communicate Himself as Truth to my little created brain. It seemed to meet my deepest aspirations, although I was ashamed of admitting it.

I was also afraid, knowing that I would be in real trouble if my family and my teachers knew that I enquired about Christianity.
Whom could I turn to?
I'm convinced that Katarina is the one who sent Mansur and Nour to me.
It happened purely by chance – or so it seemed.
They'd asked my agency for an English-speaking guide to take care of a group of their foreign friends who were shortly to visit Egypt. They noticed that I didn't shun discussion on matters of religion.
Although Mansur is theoretically a Muslim, they encouraged me in my quest. Anthony was also involved (I told you about him, the hermit). And many others, like Athanasius; and Aristotle, who lived in Greece four centuries before Christ (blessed be He forever), but whose philosophical writings had been kept a long time in Alexandria.

I take my eyes off Azim's letter and look around me as the cabin loudspeakers attract my attention.

It takes me a few seconds to remember that I'm aboard a plane. On the seat next to me – yes, Dr. Yasir must be asleep.

But I've just heard a voice speak like an *echo* of what I was reading.

It was the Captain: "Ladies and gentlemen, you can see the lights of Alexandria L.A. to our left. We are beginning our descent to San Antonio, circling north of Houston. The weather in San Antonio is fine, with only a light breeze. We hope that..."

I switch back to my own train of thoughts. What a disconcerting coincidence: "Alexandria," "Antonio" (or Anthony)... I feel as if the outside world reflected the very private confidences shared in Azim's letter.

It gives me the strange impression that our personal journeys unfold on a wider scope than we think; as if all were somehow connected.

Chapter 24

So, nearly thirty minutes to landing.
Landing.
How will I face it all? How will I cope and adjust again to my life? What I have just learned from Azim changes my perception of him.
It's too soon for me to decide whether I'm less sad, or more. Why this trick with "Katarina"? Did he do it on purpose to make me feel jealous? Was he making excuses for staying aloof?

Azim... My dear, dear Azim. *What* did you mean? Was there a problem with you; something you were ashamed of? Was it not crystal clear to you that I would have said *yes*! That I expected it?
Why all these explanations to a very simple question?
You know which one.
Why did you not simply *kiss* me?
And I was wearing the linen dress and jacket you like most... Or rather, those you *liked* most, alas. You called me *Beloved* and you called me *Sister*. I don't understand.
Or do I?
There is little time for me to finish reading. I must continue to the end. I owe it to him. Where had I left it? Where had I left *you*? Here:

Dearest Clara, would it not have been too short, if God had come all the way down from heaven for our sake, and hadn't stayed with us and among us for as long as we live here on earth?
Such is the treasure I found in Cairo, at the convent where Nour took me.
I found the Holy Eucharist.
He is truly there in the Host. The Host is Him, God made Man for the remission of my sins.
I believed, Clara.
Dear soul, please forgive my lengthy presentation!
But how could you like me if you don't know me? And how could you know me if you don't know my soul and the faith that makes me love you? O Clara: I believed in Him. My fear was remitted; I submitted to Love.
In my heart, then, I became a Catholic.
Over the past two years, in secret, I received instruction from a Catholic priest in Cairo. I'm what they call a catechumen. But, dearest, beloved Clara, this is what this letter is all about and what I most wanted to share with you! Today... I will receive Holy Baptism!
"Anthony" will be my new name in Christ.

Today I will be truly a member of my God, Jesus (blessed be his name forever)! Today I will belong to Him forever through His beautiful Church. Today, I will be made so intimately close to you, in Him.

I know that you won't be there. I thought for a long time of telling you. But your flight back to America was booked for your sister's wedding, and I feared that you might have been embarrassed, had I asked you... Had I asked you to be my godmother.

Beloved, I would so much have loved to be led to Him by your hand! Nour wouldn't have minded swapping, surely. Several months ago, she'd agreed to do it for me.

But the priest told me that godparents really must be practising Catholics. Hence my not asking you.

Beloved, your safety also concerned me. I know that my former comrades have heard of my conversion. They call it apostasy. *In fact, I was threatened. I tried to explain to the ones they sent last month, that I retain all my love for my former fellow Muslims, especially my family and friends. But they wouldn't accept it.*

If they ever harmed me, I would be so sad for them, as they would have truly submitted to hatred; but I would pray that their sin be remitted and that they would find Jesus (blessed be his name forever)! I was pretty certain that they'd followed me on several occasions. But now I'm sure.

Last night, after saying goodbye to you, back in my room I found my email account hacked, and a warning from them if I mentioned to anyone something which... Well, I can't write it down, it would be unsafe. They know I'm about to forestall one of their next plots. They aren't sure exactly which one will be leaked to me.

A picture of you and me, by the George Hotel in Aswan, was attached to their message. My heart froze in my chest when I saw it!

Beloved, I rushed back to the garden outside your room and decided to wait, in case they attempted anything. I described at the beginning of this letter my delight in seeing you come, and the bliss of our shadows meeting. You walked back into your room and I heard you lock your sliding door, as I had advised you to do.

But some time after, another shadow hovered along the bush and landed on the lawn.

I thought some jinn had come! Sobek can't be very pleased with me for certain things I have done – and for others I have resisted doing. He hadn't seen me. I left him to sneak towards your door, as I needed to be sure. He seemed to be holding a weapon. I ran to the viper and we fought. I didn't bite off his head, but he stung my side slightly, and left.

I'm fine though, don't you worry, love. I was very angry that he should have dared to crawl across the very place where our shadows had met. That place of our farewell is sacred to me.

I took off my shoes and knelt, watching the sun rise behind the bougainvillea, whose purple flowers were turning to gold.

I extended my hand to caress the fiery shrub gently moving in the breeze of dawn. Some petals fell in my hand.

As I picked some more, by now lying safe against you (I hope they don't fly across the cabin!), I gave thanks to my Lord for all his bounties: for my faith and for you.

Chapter 25

Taking my eyes off the page again, I reach for the envelope.

Through the paper, my fingers feel the little heap of petals. Yes, they're safe. They won't get scattered now.

There's so little time left, and I don't want to rush the reading of such an important message. His testament.

But I need to know, in case a clue can help explain the tragedy, and perhaps lead to apprehending the perpetrators.

I read further:

I have just strapped up that wound again, with whatever I have at my disposal here (no time to visit a chemist). I dread what could happen to you on my account. They can't know that you are departing today.

But I won't let you leave this morning without seeing you one last time! I need to hold you tight against my heart at least once. I will come at the last minute, just before you walk through Security, so that no harm will come to you, my beloved sister.

At the airport I will see my informant and I will learn exactly what next evil trick they are plotting. I know the number of expected targets, but not yet where and when those evil men will strike.

I may counter them if I find a way to send information without their knowledge. But emails are now unsafe and I fear that they may have tapped my phone (they've accomplices in the administration).

I thought of using Mansur's floating office, but it will be too late. I wouldn't have him or his family involved anyway. I asked Katarina for advice, and I think that we've now found a way to inform a contact of mine who helped me in the past in similar circumstances. There might be a price to pay, but Katarina and Anthony think it worth trying.

So, be at peace my darling. All shall be well.

I told Mansur and Nour about the threat. They're fully aware of the risk they run if remaining connected with me while staying in Cairo, or in Egypt. Next week they will be safe, though, since I will be gone; I am to begin a new job for Mansur's firm, as coordinator for charitable schools he builds abroad.

Meanwhile, for their sake, I decided that they shouldn't attend my Baptism, as the godparents' presence (local parishioners who stepped in) will suffice, with the priest's.

But the mere thought made dear little Talitha cry! Mansur can't see her unhappy, so he opposed me, saying that the three of them would come anyway. I begged them not to, and I think they understand. We will meet after, on his boat, and celebrate.

In that same shop where I took you to buy your sister's present, Nour found a beautiful icon of our holy hermit Anthony, my patron saint as of this afternoon. It's meant to be a surprise for my Baptism, but Talitha couldn't wait to tell me ('It's a secret!'), so excited she was!

I wish you knew her better. Did you know that she was adopted? (Nour can't have children apparently.)

So, dearest, be tranquil.

No one in the parish or among my acquaintances knows where and when the ceremony is scheduled. It will take place in secret, but Myriam the Mother of my Lord will come (blessed be her name forever).

And with her many angels and saints.

Be sure that Anthony and Katarina won't miss the occasion.

Neither will Athanasius, nor his predecessor, the glorious Evangelist Mark and our first holy bishop of Alexandria, the scribe of Kephas.

As to you, darling Clara, at 3 p.m. this Sunday afternoon, on the most beautiful day of my life, I will carry you deep in my heart when I receive the water of remission; the water of life; the water of love.

If you read this in time, will you please say a prayer for me?

Oh, love! Meet me in His Heart! Meet me in the Host!

Azim – Poor Egyptian guide following his star to the rising Sun.

Chapter 26

I rest my head against the pillow and close my eyes.
But my eyelids fail to contain my tears. I feel them run down my cheeks. At my side, I sense that Dr. Yasir isn't sleeping anymore.
I'm not surprised when I feel her hand come and rest upon mine. I expected it. It's strange how even a total stranger can touch our heart. Compassion needs no introduction. I'm also grateful to her for keeping silent.

After a while, I open my eyes and turn my face toward her with a smile. She smiles back. I feel like telling her. Should I?
I speak: "My friend Azim wrote this letter to me, just a few hours before he was killed. I thought we were just friends. But now I have found out that he loved me deeply..." I pause. I'm talking to myself just as much as to my considerate listener.
I find it helpful to put into words the confused state of my heart. It's like a Russian doll – or a sarcophagus!
Its outer layer is mere surprise: how could my romantic story with this charming young Muslim end so abruptly?
The second layer is anger: I feel let down by him twice, through his conversion... and through his death.
The third layer is shame: how could I have remained so superficial, when he was travelling so deep!
The fourth layer is gratitude: for his witness, strangely glowing in me.
The fifth layer is stupor: as I realise that his death may well have been a deliberate sacrifice.
The sixth layer is fear: what will the One Who took my friend ask *me* to do, or to give up?
The seventh layer is...
Well, there's no seventh layer, or not of gilded wood at least, but one of flesh inside my chest, beating with love. Love for my God and for His holy will, whatever happens, whatever it takes.

I speak further to Dr. Yasir. "I also realise that I loved him. But my love wasn't like his. My love was more about me. About wanting to be loved. And now that he's dead, I feel my love for him tragically growing. Oh, Dr. Yasir, I love him so much now! I miss him so much!"
She takes me against her and soothes me with her hands. We remain like this, until a steward bows to her ear, asking her to follow him. What can that mean?
On her return, she says that I must be strong, and that she trusts me. She

adds that on arrival (as she was just told) I will need to answer a few questions from the C.I.A.

On hearing this I jump, and my heart beats violently.

They can't possibly suspect me of complicity in the shooting... I was already in Paris when it occurred! She says that they need to examine some evidence about the attack and that my testimony could be crucial. I give her an anxious look. Dr. Yasir says that I must do it, for Azim's sake.

I would laugh at this unexpected spy-movie turn in my story, if it weren't so tragic. I feel hot now and take off my jacket.

After a pause, Dr. Yasir adds that she will remain with me all along, even for hours, and will take me home directly after. I feel a bit relieved. She smiles again protectively.

Suddenly, I become anxious again as I realise that the C.I.A. will surely want to see Azim's *letter*. What if they take it from me? No, *that* I cannot allow.

I instinctively press the envelope against my heart; with the little bump made by our petals. This letter is my last glimpse of him. In a way, that letter *is* him. I must find a way. Yes, I know what to do!

I ask Dr. Yasir whether she would keep Azim's letter in her bag, for fear that the C.I.A. might not give it back. It's so precious to me. I will tell the authorities all the relevant information learned from it, but they mustn't get hold of it.

She answers that, as long as the envelope contains only ink and paper, she will keep it for me. I add that there are also petals in it. She smiles and slides my treasure in her (*Hermès!*) handbag.

I remember that I meant to check my emails.

What a joy! A message from Kitty.

Like a fresh breath from a forgotten land, I read the surprise my sister has for me. On learning of my change of flight and the Cairo ordeal, she asked Raúl to drive her to San Antonio, and they are already there, waiting for me!

I can't believe it! Kitty! Kitty! Kitty!

I will see her again! After all my pains and joys, I will eventually be able to let go, and cry and laugh with the sister who knows me so well! Thank you dear Lord for this present!

I email her back that I'm so happy, and that I will see her as soon as the authorities let me through.

Chapter 27

America again.

Here we are, landed on schedule at 20:10, and disembarking. As I get out of my seat and stand, I realise that I must have spilled some of my tomato juice when I fainted earlier: a trace clearly shows on my dress.

How annoying! And no time to wash it. I button my light linen jacket to hide the stain underneath.

After thanking the crew and waving at a blushing Oscar, I walk out of the plane and feel my own ears turn red in front of other Business Class passengers, as two C.I.A agents meet me, a woman and a man. They speak in a professional and reasonably kind way.

On entering the room where they mean to interrogate me, they ask Dr. Yasir to stay outside. She insists on coming in, as the medical doctor assigned by the crew to assist me after the shock I have just suffered. Before they can object, she promises absolute discretion, as is habitually required of her as a doctor and a diplomat.

Producing her American passport, she adds that her husband is the General Consul of Pakistan in Houston (so, not a maharajah after all!). The male agent having spoken with his boss over the phone, Dr. Yasir is *invited* to wait outside, until possibly being let in later on.

I feel vulnerable without my guardian and resent their decision.

By way of introduction, they inform me that they've been sent from the local C.I.A. base in Lackland (I don't care where that is) to ask me questions about *Agent Nebankh*. I'm confused, thinking they wanted to know about Azim.

It appears that both are – or were – the same person! (I'd forgotten his surname.) I'm taken aback and start shivering again. Azim can't have been working for the C.I.A.! Linking my Egyptian flirt with the U.S. spy machine sounds so utterly implausible!

Well, C.I.A. he wasn't, as Agent N'Guyen explains (she looks a bit Asian, like me). "Miss Cumberhart, all this will come as a surprise to you, and perhaps, I'm sorry to say, as a further shock. We thank you in advance for your cooperation.

"Your friend was an informant for British Intelligence. Voluntary.

"We had been monitoring communications of his former comrades, the Scimitars of Islam, and found that over the past months, two of their planned attacks against girls' schools in Sudan had been counteracted by units of the British SAS, unofficially present in that area.

"The Scimitars were very upset and suspected a mole in their ranks. The name of Azim Nebankh came up several times on their suspect list, but little was done as he'd left them more than two years earlier and was thought unable to access sensitive information."

I am dumbfounded. How unexpected... Feeling thirsty, I swallow some juice as she goes on: "In the last three years, the Scimitars have abducted girls, including Muslim ones, in Chad, Sudan and Eritrea. The alleged purpose is to enforce Female Genital Mutilation in villages where the custom is ignored.

"In reality, few of those girls ever return, as most are sold across the Middle-East as sex slaves via the *Sobek* network. This isn't the Scimitars' main activity by the way, although a lucrative one.

"We don't know through which channel Agent Nebankh acted, but we are certain that his intervention led to the failure of two recent attacks in Sudan. A third one was scheduled for yesterday afternoon at 3 p.m., Sudan time, against a Muslim school near the town of Osly, four hours north of Khartoum down the Nile. It failed.

"An SAS unit showed up by the ford just as the Scimitars were stopping the school bus, whose driver they'd already shot. They had boats to take the girls away, as they managed to do last year. All their men were shot or taken prisoner. We need further intel, but it looks as if the main cell has been decapitated.

"The Sobek network isn't dead yet, however. The attack in Cairo just an hour later was an act of retaliation on their part. We saw their text message giving the order. Agent Nebankh was definitely aware of possible reprisal. He chose to take the risk.

"Of course, I haven't even mentioned it yet: at Osly, all forty-eight girls were saved."

I'm stunned. Again. I wish Dr. Yasir were sitting next to me, holding my hand. I can't bear it anymore. Dear Lord, through how many such tsunamis will You take me? First, Azim's last-minute hug at the airport, when I thought it was all over – or had never started but in my silly head. Then, Your revelation to me, against all odds, in the underground chapel at Paris Airport. Next, in the plane, the double shock of learning Azim's death, and of reading his letter. And now, this...

I'm beyond exhaustion. I seem not to care anymore if I'm dreaming or not. Kitty. I want Kitty. She's real. She knows me. I need her arms to stabilise the world around me. I must simply get out of here, and go to her. I just want to go to my sister. *Let me go. Just let me go...*

"Miss Cumberhart... Can you hear me? Miss Cumberhart, when you've finished your juice, we are going to need all your attention. As Agent N'Guyen was saying, we need to know how Agent Nebankh sent information. We need his contact.

"We traced the transit of information up to him; and from the Apostolic

Nunciature in Khartoum to London and the SAS. But we still need the missing link, between Agent Nebankh and the Nunciature.

"His email account was hacked and he didn't use his mobile phone, as our monitoring shows. He was unaware of the location and time of the attack until he reached the airport yesterday morning.

"To meet the rather tight seven-hour deadline until the attack and to avoid any risk of his message being intercepted by the Scimitars, it's very likely that he chose to convey the intel to his contact only face to face, or written by hand.

"Hence my asking you: did he share any sensitive information with you? Have you forwarded any message to his contact? We know that you were on very intimate terms with him, and it would be in your interests, and in those of democracy, to let us know of any data received from him...

"Miss Cumberhart, are you able to answer me, please?"

This man is getting on my nerves – but he won't put his paws on Azim's testament. I'm so glad that the letter is safe outside this room with Dr. Yasir. After a silence, I reply coldly: "Agent Bloomen, Azim and I were just friends. Whatever he gave me is buried in my soul, with no threat to democracy, I can assure you. He never told me of his connections with any intelligence agency.

"As far as I'm aware, he died for his faith, not for a government. You can search me and my luggage, and check my phone log – but I imagine that you've already done that! You won't find anything from him."

I can't help adding, "And since you were so well informed of what that gang was planning, I wonder why you didn't prevent their attacks, and why you let my friend die!"

I nearly smile inside, imagining Dr. Yasir's look if she'd heard me, a bit like a drama teacher at a talented schoolgirl playing *Juliet*, as she unexpectedly starts improvising on stage at the end-of-year show, with all the parents and governors watching.

Agent N'Guyen pours more juice into my glass, while Agent Bloomen looks at me in silence.

Agent N'Guyen then asks if I could sit next to her in front of the computer screen. She explains: "Miss Cumberhart, we would like to show you some CCTV footage that we have received from Cairo and Paris Airport. We realise that you've been travelling for nearly a day now and must be very tired. We also sympathise with your loss.

"As a Canadian citizen, you are under no obligation to watch the videos, but as you surely understand, more people could be saved if Agent Nebankh's contact and murderers are identified. It would help us if you could look for any person you know either as a friend or as an enemy of yours, or of Agent Nebankh's."

I look at her straight in the eyes, determined to reach her soul if she has one. She doesn't object. Well, there *is* a soul in there. I begin to like her. Perhaps after all, even this Agent Bloomen chap has a soul. Perhaps I'm just very tired.

I ask her to play the film.

Chapter 28

The first piece of footage is from Cairo Airport.
I see myself enter the departure hall amidst a stream of tourists. I check in my large suitcase and look around for Azim. I check the time on my watch. I kiss the scar on my wrist under the band, as *we* had done the night before (this is a bit embarrassing, with those two C.I.A agents watching, but they can't know what it means).

The next sequence is at the cafeteria, probably from another camera. I still look at my watch. I finish my coffee and walk to Security, still eating my chocolate biscuit. I stand in the queue.
The next footage from a different camera shows Azim walking to a newsagent, at the end of the hall. Oh, *Azim*... To see him alive, moving, breathing... He utters something as he pays for his newspaper; could that employee be his informant? Are they exchanging vital information?
He then looks towards the cafeteria. He must be watching *me*. He sees me walk to Security. Just before I step through the detector, he runs towards me. No, no, I can't watch this... And, not with those strangers around me...

But it's too late. Azim has reached me now. I see his lips speak my name and I smile. I see myself weep. There's no sound, which makes the film even more poignant. He brings one knee down but, filmed from behind, one can't see that he's writing on his other knee. Rather, it looks as if he's proposing to me! (I remember now *what* he's jotting down, and upon which rectangular piece of paper!)
I tighten my backpack. Unexpectedly, he starts hugging me. He hugs me. Azim hugs me... In my surprise and unbelief, I let my arms float in the air at a square angle, as if I were a scarecrow, or a figurehead at the *Titanic*'s bow: *I'm flying*.
There's no music playing along with those pictures, but I can hear the tune, so vivid in my heart! I'm taken aback, holding my boarding card in my mouth (silly me: he might have dared to kiss me if my lips had been free).
I see my arms slowly, very slowly come around him. Scarecrow no longer, and not yet shipwrecked: I see a woman, in love with a man. Passengers in the queue behind us start showing signs of impatience. Security staff make signs for me to walk through or go back.
He hugs me still while we turn slightly, as if drunk or waltzing.
No kiss.
He goes.
I drown.

Agent N'Guyen presses the pause button and asks me if I anything suspicious struck me. Feeling hot in that room – don't they have air conditioning in Texas? – I open my jacket and remain silent for a while. I say that I saw Azim wait at a distance before approaching me at the last minute.

She asks if I didn't notice the two bearded men watching him from afar, and later taking a picture of him and me with their phone. I didn't. She says that they are most probably members of the Scimitars, following him. (I don't dare to suggest that they simply found me – or us – beautifully romantic ...)

Did I see Azim put something into my backpack as he was hugging me? No, I didn't, or didn't care. (How could I mind my bag when my heart was melting against his?)

Have I found anything in my bag since then? Nothing that didn't belong to me or could be a threat.

Agent Bloomen looks at me in a strange way and asks if I was *wounded* in any way. I say that I'm feeling very well. He points to the stain on my side, and suggests it is blood. I blush and explain how I spilled tomato juice when I collapsed on the plane.

Agent N'Guyen kneels down to take a closer look at the mark and, looking at me, confirms that it does look like dried blood. I'm astonished. She asks if I would be so kind as to accompany her to the bathroom next door and check me for wounds. This is becoming very awkward, but I don't have the strength to resist.

In the corridor, Dr. Yasir is speaking over her phone. It sounds like Arabic. She smiles at me encouragingly as we walk by. At that moment, a face from the Cairo CCTV footage suddenly flashes back in my memory. There *was* at Cairo Airport a woman in the queue behind me, who was wearing a shawl and no pearl necklace, but who looked just like... Dr. Yasir!

Within seconds, my brain tries to enfold the consequences of that hypothesis. Could *she* be Azim's contact? Surely not, or why would she not have told me? Then, could she be... I feel an icy sweat down my spine as I reach the bathroom door. Could she be an accomplice, on the murderers' side?

That large Hermès handbag of hers – unsearched, thanks to her diplomatic status – could easily conceal a weapon. After all, I know nothing about her, and befriending me in her motherly way might be just the best trick to get information out of me and identify the moles within their gang. If true, how wicked!

What a blessing in disguise, then, that Dr. Yasir wasn't allowed to accompany me. I feel relieved as Agent N'Guyen leads me into the bathroom. (But, through what strange association of ideas does the thought pop up in my mind of... a pregnancy scan? Unlike Kitty, I never needed any, thank God.)

The Agent looks at my side. It's indeed unscathed; but not unstained. To my surprise, through the light cotton of my dress, blood had stained my skin at the level of my left bottom rib. What a mystery!

Back in the other room, Agent N'Guyen reports on our discovery. Agent

Bloomen asks us to watch the next piece of footage in which he thinks he's found the answer. On the screen, I see Azim walk away from Security, while on his white shirt a dark spot shows, which wasn't there previously.

Agent N'Guyen says that Azim seems to have been shot or stabbed under his right bottom rib, just after leaving me, unless he was already wounded, and the dressing on his side got loosened while we were hugging, causing blood to leak slightly.

Then I recall the part of his letter, when he mentioned a fight against an aggressor by my window last night. He wrote that his wound was superficial. Still, it had occurred only a few hours earlier, so that even a shallow cut might still bleed. And what if it was deeper?

Should I not show Azim's letter to the Agents, then? Might they not find in it information which I missed out?

The letter! *She* has it! Dr. Yasir might have read it all by now, and texted her accomplices all they needed to know. *Why* did I entrust her with it?

Agent Bloomen says that the pictures show no sign of Agent Nebankh having been attacked before or after meeting me. I decide to tell them what I know about his wound, received the previous night. My information confirms their theory.

Agent N'Guyen asks me if I feel strong enough to watch the Paris footage at Orly Airport. Oh no! Will my whole life have to unfold on screen? When will it end, dear Lord!

And Kitty waiting for me, in the Arrivals Hall...

Well, let us go through it all and leave, and get to Kitty as soon as possible.

The next film must have been taken by a camera inside the jet-bridge. First Class passengers walk out (I wasn't upgraded that time). They drop newspapers and magazines in the recycle bin presented by cleaning staff.

Economy passengers follow soon after. Again that woman, who really looks like Dr. Yasir. She walks in front of me. Why did I put my unread magazines in the bin – silly me! I see myself walk further. Thankfully, the bloodstain is hidden under my buttoned jacket. Actually, I look rather stylish.

Next view: facing the flight information display, amidst hundreds of passengers. No one seems to be watching me, and Dr. Yasir's mysterious double has vanished. Me sitting among hundreds; me reading the letter; me typing; me yawning...

Now my hat fashion show (why is Agent Bloomen smiling now!); flights display again; and out through the exit door, following my hieroglyph down to the underground chapel.

Agent Bloomen announces with great disappointment that, due to French privacy regulations on worship, the footage resumes only when I walk out of the chapel. It's my turn to smile. There are things that even the C.I.A won't see.

Agent N'Guyen asks me how I spent nearly two hours underground, and if I noticed anything suspicious. I say that I went to rest in a quiet area, and didn't meet anyone *threatening*. Indeed.

We watch visitors walking in and out of the chapel... This is when it suddenly *hits* me.
Of course!
How could I forget?

Chapter 29

There *was* indeed someone else who took particular interest in me.

Someone who described my last meeting with Azim as if he'd literally just *watched* the footage.

As if he could have guessed all that simply from reading my boarding card... Someone who looked beyond suspicion. I can't believe it. Not *Fr. Paul*!

But again, how do I know that he was a priest in the first place, and not a terrorist in disguise, cleverly drawing information out of me, with my Cairo boarding card as bait?

It reminds me that, with all that has occurred to me, I didn't really pay attention to what Azim wrote on that boarding card. An email address, I had assumed? But since his usual one had been hacked the night before, he would have had to get a new one by the time he met me. And how could he do that, if he felt it too risky to connect to the Internet?

Where did I put that boarding card anyway? I look into my bag in vain; then in my pockets. I search my bag again, only to find in it the Eucharistic flyer which Fr. Paul had handed to me.

I unfold it and, with emotion, find my Cairo boarding card inside. I see Azim's handwriting. I see my upper lip printed in light Lancôme purple shade (the cookie crumb is long gone), my lipstick covering my friend's last word like a petal. And I read this unusual email address...

ClarAzims48pearls@OslyFord1500.
My hands are shaking as I read it again; and again.
ClarAzims48pearls@OslyFord1500.
And again.
ClarAzims48pearls@OslyFord1500.
I'm fascinated by this cryptic sequence of letters and numbers. Paradoxically, they beam at me as a decoding of our relationship.

I hand it to Agent N'Guyen, explaining: "This is what Azim was writing on his knee just before leaving me. I hadn't taken time to consider it until now. At first glance, I thought that it referred to the *Ford* Car Rental at Orly Airport. The Catholic chaplain at Orly looked at it with particular attention. He introduced himself to me as *Fr. Paul*."

Agent Bloomen immediately looks him up on his system, while Agent N'Guyen confirms my conclusion. It's clearly not an email address. In reality, it rather plainly indicates the number of girls to be abducted; the location by the Nile; and the time scheduled for the attack yesterday.

I ponder in silence, and soon I feel tears rolling down my cheeks again (I never thought human eyes could be so generous). I understand that his message wasn't only meant for his contact, but also for me. He wanted me to be a loving associate – albeit unaware – in the sacrifice of his life.

And for what? To save forty-eight Muslim schoolgirls from abduction by his merciless former comrades. He chose to begin the message with our two names united, as if the forty-eight precious "pearls" stemmed from our... union. Yes, I feel that my dead friend has begotten life. By giving up his own existence, he awakened me to a deeper life and shared the fruitfulness of his sacrifice with me.

ClarAzims48pearls@OslyFord1500...

I feel so deeply honoured and humbled. I understand now the bougainvillea petals enclosed in his letter. When I get a chance alone, I'm sure to count forty-eight of them. One for each of "our" children. I would never have thought of such a way to conceive.

Despite the apparent ubiquity of the C.I.A., Agent Bloomen is disappointed again (but this time I'm not smiling). He's simply unable to link Fr. Paul with any of the threads in the attack, or with the Scimitars, or even with the Khartoum Nunciature.

Fr. Paul is just what he appears to be. Born in the Channel Islands at St. Helier, Jersey. Studied in Paris and Rome. A dedicated Catholic priest with good exorcist credentials and a bad lung history.

His phone record shows no sign of suspicious activity in recent weeks; apart from, perhaps, his last text received before meeting me: *Backup needed underground* – which sounds ominous, but is probably harmless. I begin smiling, and stop as I recall...

Remembering is such a strange process.

But, I've just found *him*! I've just found the missing link in the transmission of Azim's vital information. Well, *that* was clever! Who would have ever suspected *him*!

I remember how he announced as I walked out of the plane: "Paper recycle for Children Charity: magazines, newspapers, tissues, boarding cards." I spontaneously gave my boarding card with my magazines.

He took it from me, looked at it on both sides in two seconds and said: "You might need it again Miss – your luggage tag is stuck on it; but thank you for the magazines." He must have been surprised to see me in the chapel an hour later. Or was he expecting me?

I recall his face as he walked past me... Brown, tearful and beaming... Of course. He knew. He knew that forty-eight Muslim girls in his country had just been rescued from rape or slavery, at the likely cost of the life of his friend and fellow Catholic – or soon to be.

He may have known that Azim was also sacrificing his love for me. That prostrated shape by the altar was weeping and rejoicing... For me. For the girls. For his friend. Should I tell them about *him*? Is there any use, or any duty, in my revealing the name of...

"Nepomucen!" Agent Bloomen now looks very pleased, as he explains: "I've just traced the number which sent the text to Fr. Paul. It's a French mobile registered as "Orly Airport Cleaning Staff 07." Only a few text messages are sent every week with it, and mostly to Fr. Paul.

"No calls or messages were received in the last two days, until this morning, when a public phone booth in Egypt sent the following text: *Asian Star CC on Cairo 1132 requires boarding card recycling.*" Here Agent Bloomen smiles. I take it as a compliment.

"The booth is located near the Business Lounge at Cairo Airport. At 11:45., the same Cleaning Staff French mobile sent a text to a mobile in Sudan, registered under the name of Lewis Kanisah, living in Khartoum.

"A man with just the same name happens to be the driver at the Papal Nunciature in Khartoum. The message was: *Sobek hungry again. Swift backup needed for 48 pearls at Osly Ford by 15:00 Sudan Time.*

"Less than fifteen minutes later, at 13:58 local time (11:58 Paris Time), the Khartoum Nunciature sent an encrypted message to the MoD in London. I can only guess its content. But within an hour, British SAS were at Osly Ford.

"Back to Paris now: out of seventy-three cleaning staff at Orly Airport, four arrived from Africa in the last two years. One was granted refugee status, from Sudan. His name is Nepomucen Kanisah."

Agent N'Guyen looks at her colleague with a hint of admiration. Although I'm impressed as well, I don't want to let it show. I would have been just as efficient as Agent Bloomen if I had had immediate access to all the mobile and Internet logs on the planet!

Still, I'm glad that I wasn't the one who revealed the name of Nepomucen.

Well, can I go now?

Not quite. The last piece of CCTV footage they were expecting has just finished downloading.

Agent N'Guyen warns me: "Miss Cumberhart, we are truly grateful for your time and cooperation. The third piece of footage has arrived. But it's likely to add to your distress, as it was sent to us by the Coptic Catholic parish of the Risen Christ, via Al-Warraq Police City Council in Cairo.

"It's the film of the attack which caused the death of Agent Nebankh.

"You don't have to watch it now, if you would rather rest. But it would be very helpful if you did, as the Cairo police have been working nonstop to trace the perpetrators (it's now 5 a.m. in Cairo) and your input could prove crucial to identify them."

I need to think. I walk to the window to gain time.

The wide open space. Along the tarmac, in the distance, a few trees are swaying in the wind. It must be warm as it's now June. Still June the first actually, like yesterday. My longest day...

Swallows fly across the two terminals. I so much wish I had wings to fly away. To fly back. Here the sun is still visible. It has long set over Cairo.

Over the blood of my friends.

For the first time, I think of Mansur, Nour and Talitha. What a lovely family they were. And now... Dear God, this is too awful. How could it happen? What can I do? In my heart I know that I must watch this last video. I owe it to my friends.

But I *need* comforting.

Kitty can't access this side of Security. I can only think of Dr.Yasir. But isn't she a terrorist? Please, dear God – how can I know?

Surely, if they let her in, she must be safe. If not... Let *this* be the test.

I tell Agent N'Guyen that I don't feel strong enough to watch yet another video. Unless she allows my friend Dr. Yasir in, to stand by me.

She whispers with Agent Bloomen in a corner of the room. Finally, she lets Dr. Yasir in.

I smile to both women and, in silence, I go and sit in front of the screen.

Chapter 30

Agent N'Guyen presses the button.
I see the Church of the Risen Christ. It looks rather poor, as do the buildings around it. This is clearly not the city centre. A working class suburb, at best. A dog lies against the wall, by the fence.

Cars are parked along the street and by the Post Office. A few Egyptians wearing grey djellabas walk through the pillars of cracked concrete. I know none of them, I'm sure.

Here he comes. It's *him*. He must have changed his shirt as I see no blood on it. My hand instinctively comes to rest against my left side, where his blood still shows.

How handsome is his young tanned face... I look at those strong arms which held me tight at the airport, just a few hours earlier. I have the strange sensation of seeing my own heart in a white shirt on this computer screen.

Azim walks up the concrete steps. He's only halfway when he stops, as a group walks out of the church down towards him. It's Mansur and his family.

Little Talitha waves at him, shouting joyfully. Mansur carries against his chest a voluminous parcel in gold wrapping. Nour is beautifully dressed, with a light yellow veil around her shoulders. She holds Talitha's hand.

Azim frowns. He's angry. He looks to the side and into the street. He makes gestures and must be speaking loudly, but I can't hear, for want of sound. Poor Mansur looks embarrassed. He seems to explain that they wanted to surprise him and couldn't miss his Baptism.

He points at a posh car parked across the street. I suppose it's his. The chauffeur waits outside, briefly waving at them. Azim nods and glances behind him.

Two men arrive on a motorbike. They wear black scarves on their faces. The dog by the grill starts barking furiously. Birds fly away. The man at the rear of the motorbike takes a handgun out of a bag and aims at the group. He begins shooting. There isn't a sound.

Nour falls. Three dark flowers quickly bloom through the folds of her lovely dress. Mansur moves to catch her but falls in his turn, still holding his parcel.

Azim leaps like a panther upon Talitha. He presses her frail body down, against the concrete steps. His cheek is very tight against hers. Spots appear on his back. Three. Now two more appear.

Oh no! I can't see that! Azim! My love! They are taking our life! They are killing our love!

Mansur's driver shoots at the killers – so, he was armed – but misses. They go on firing. To the left, two other Egyptians fall. A man and a woman. Were they Azim's godparents or proxies? A smoke of dust. The motorbike is gone.

I swallow.

People run out of the church. The priest is among them and rushes first to Azim, holding him as his face turns towards us.

Someone speaks on his mobile phone, surely calling the ambulance.

The priest runs to the church with Azim's blood upon him and comes back immediately, bringing water in his palms. He pours the water gently upon Azim's brow, speaking to him. What is he doing!

No, actually, he...

He must be baptising him! Yes, that *is* what he's doing! He's baptising my friend! He makes the sign of the cross upon him.

O dear God, I can't believe this! Azim seems to look at something. He stares intently at the camera. He can't be inspecting the bracket where the CCTV is mounted! He's looking... at us.

He sees *me*.

But... He's *smiling*. He smiles, so beautifully, like a victorious prince! His head falls back against the child.

You've conquered, my beloved. You've crossed the sea of hatred and death, and you've led me to God! I'm so moved. Things unfold, in my soul...

I found a friend in Africa, at the foot of the Risen Christ...

Little Talitha is dragged from under Azim. The blood all over her little dress isn't *hers* – thank God. She seems unharmed.

She runs to her Mum and holds her, while parishioners carry the body inside the church, her yellow veil turned dark and dripping, feebly floating in the wind like a broken wing.

Dear Nour, how much I would have *loved* you!

Two policemen run through the gates. They give orders.

Mansur still lies on the steps. His left arm holds his parcel. His right arm is moving in the air, as if calling for help. But his driver kneels next to him; what more can be done? This is awful!

The priest reaches him. He brings his ear near Mansur's mouth. Mansur whispers something. The priest goes to the church again, covered with even more blood, and immediately brings back water and pours it on Mansur's forehead, again speaking slowly. This is extraordinary: he's also baptising him!

Mansur is being baptised! He wants to die a Catholic, like his wife and friend. He's dying with Jesus.

The priest goes to the Egyptian victims. He blesses them.

The ambulance arrives. Paramedics run up the steps. They assess the situation and try to stabilise those still breathing.

More Egyptians flock outside the gates. Women are in tears. They must be crying very loud – I can't hear.

Yes, I *can* hear them now.

Or rather, I think I hear *a* woman. At my side, with dignity, Dr. Yasir is weeping... It's my turn to take her hand and hold it in mine.

Agent N'Guyen has moist eyes when she presses the pause button. Agent Bloomen clears his throat. They are nice people. I come to like them after all.

I answer questions, as in a dream.

No, I haven't identified anyone else.

No, it didn't strike me that the driver was very slow in intervening, considering that he was armed and, standing by the car, was well positioned to stop the attackers.

Yes, apart from his employer and Azim, he might have been the only one aware of the time and place of the event, and could have leaked the information. They will look him up. An American citizen was killed – not to mention the other victims, of course.

They take my details.

They print a copy of my passport, and of my boarding card with Azim's email address. Dr. Yasir also answers questions.

They take my fingerprints.

They even take a small sample of Azim's blood from my dress, on wet cotton, and a piece of my hair, "with my permission". (So much for my initial boast of having upon me no DNA of Azim.)

Yes, I permit.

Let them take all that they wish. I've just seen my *life* taken, my love – what could I ever wish to retain?

I'm not here, in fact, in this office. I'm spread upon the cracked concrete steps of a poor Egyptian suburban church.

Agent N'Guyen takes me aside and asks a few personal questions. It isn't confession but I tell her the truth anyway. I've nothing to hide.

Come down, tender swallow; stop whirling about in the warm afternoon breeze... Come back, sweet lark, and quench your thirst with my love, spilled as blood across the Cairo dust. O please, drink my life; that it may not be lost to the desert sands, but may benefit the living.

Around us, the valleys bow as the sun goes down. Two larks soar upwards dreamily into the light air. But we haven't lost our way. We are meeting in His pierced Heart.

We shake hands with the Agents. They thank me cordially. May they always use their powers, their network, their system for truth and good.

It's 9:30 p.m. when I eventually walk through Customs with Dr. Yasir and a member of staff wheeling my main luggage for me. I vaguely fear that journalists will await me, if they've traced me across the Atlantic...

Doors.

No paparazzi, no CNN!

I couldn't have stood another wave of questions. But my heart expects *another* meeting. Eventually, I will see *her*. In a few seconds, I will see Kitty!

There... Oh, this is a *new* wheelchair – an electric one. And this must be Raúl, standing behind her. I run to her and kneel by her wheel, and hug her as if, lost at sea and tossed for hours by furious waves, I had providentially met a floating mast. I've been up for twenty-four hours.

It's been a long day.

Dr. Yasir asks if we need a lift. But Raúl declines. She tells Kitty that I should rest for a long time before doing anything else. "If you ever need me Clara, you will find my details enclosed." She hands the envelope with Azim's letter to me, kisses my cheek and goes.

So, she didn't harm me after all.

Chapter 31

In the car, I sit at the back near Kitty. I think I literally cover her with kisses!

She laughs and cuddles me. Before she could mention "my" beautiful hat, I hasten to set it on her head, with the lovely gauze around her shoulders. (I kept the wrapping for her.) There! She's so pretty! And she's *my* sister. She laughs again and thanks me for the present.

She looks well enough. I'm so glad that her multiple sclerosis seems very much under control.

I glance at her stomach – yes, it *is* swollen! Better not mention her pregnancy now.

I compliment her on the new electric wheelchair, which collapsed into the boot. She says that it's her engagement *ring*! I see Raúl's arm come from the front seat towards us and rest on her knee.

I hold her hand.

Raúl explains that my arrival airport was confirmed only late on the airline's website: "It changed twice between '*CC*' and San Antonio; both are relief airports for the Houston hub, three hours' drive west." I ask what "*Sissy*" refers to.

He laughs: "*C.C.*? What, you don't know *Corpus Christi*? Of course, seen from Vancouver – or from Egypt! It's the main city down by the coast. Not the size of Houston of course, but still a third of a million inhabitants. My firm has a branch there. It's a booming Texas oil port."

Corpus Christi? I heard those words before. Is it not Latin for "Body of Christ"? I think to myself that, even though I haven't landed there, I have truly been introduced to its beauty over the past twenty-four hours.

We are staying at Raúl's parents, west of Houston. His own apartment is in town, where Kitty moved in a few months ago. (At the time, I didn't see the problem.) What a warm family they are! Rather old-fashioned though: it looks as if Raúl and Kitty don't share the same room here, but it might be a matter of space, for the wheelchair.

Raúl is of a teasing nature: "Make sure to keep your bedroom door shut at night," he warned me, "for fear of Blackie dropping a freshly beheaded lizard on your bed – his favourite breakfast – as a welcome present!"

"Poor Kitty wasn't so impressed on her first morning. Mummy heard her yell and rushed into her room, only to find that she didn't want to share Blackie's breakfast. You delicate Canadian girls! But we also have toasted bread and cereals on offer!"

He *isn't* strikingly handsome or even athletic, but I quite like him. In ten years, I may decide to forgive him for stealing my sister. His brothers haven't showed up yet...

Well, no surprise on waking up in the morning (*Blackie* kept out).

I must have slept an entire week! I feel so much better now. I didn't even have the courage to wash last night and threw myself straight under the duvet. But sitting now on the edge of my bed, I realise that my left side still bears a particular stain... Its colour is subdued, but I know *what* it is.

And *whose*.

Dear God, what a strange situation. Is this part of being a Catholic? *How* does one wash a martyr's blood away from one's tummy?

I pause, realising that for the first time I referred to Azim as a... a *martyr*. All the gravity and sacredness of what I have been involved with rise afresh in my memory.

Azim told me once that "hieroglyph" literally means "sacred writing." I feel that the stain on my stomach is more of a *hieroglyph*, then, than all the signs on those famous tombs we visited. It's written with a holy pigment, and not upon a *tomb*, please God. My finger travels around its contours, calling him back to life or rather, connecting with him; alive.

Which Egyptologist will ever read so fine a hieroglyph? Who can ever name it, Azim? It isn't "sitting-owl." It is certainly not "sitting-duck" either. Only *I* can fully decipher it!

It's "leaping-panther." You are "leaping-panther," my friend. Only *I* know it.

You live on.

Still, I can't keep your blood on me. But I can't use a sponge or anything artificial to remove it either, can I? I know what I will use: *flower power*. In my bag I find Azim's envelope returned to me by Dr. Yasir. It feels thicker than before. There is a smaller envelope inside, which I open.

Oh, dear Lord... What a beautiful pearl necklace, wrapped in a sheet of paper, soon unfolded. How is this possible! This sheet is a screenshot from the first CCTV footage we watched yesterday, with a close-up on Azim and me, hugging before Security...

On the back of the sheet are the words: "Dear Clara, I fear that there aren't enough pearls here for Christian prayer beads, but I'm sure that you will find a good use for them. You are welcome to sell them.

"They are natural pearls: you may receive enough in exchange for any journey to Egypt and, who knows, for providing assistance to some of the forty-eight girls saved by your courageous friend. *Insha'Allah!* Yours affectionately, Nasreen (contact details enclosed)."

I'm flabbergasted. That woman isn't only kind. She's compassionate and generous. I can't believe that I suspected her.

Should I try her necklace on? My hand discovers around my neck the plastic beads, which I'd completely forgotten. Well, I'm already wearing Our Lady's necklace. It should suffice for now.

God bless Nasreen. I look at the screenshot with Azim and me at Cairo Airport. Azim... My dear brother Azim. Please, hold me tight in my new faith.

Please never let me be separated from Christ Our Lord.

And how could Dr. Yasir – that is, Nasreen – obtain this printout from the agents? So, that was what she was asking at the end, while I answered the officer's last few questions. Issuing ghost copies of confidential footage can't be very much by the book for the C.I.A! Unless it's not confidential: after all, hundreds of passengers at Cairo Airport saw us hug! Or perhaps, she's C.I.A herself?

Whatever, it's very considerate. I will have it framed.

Meanwhile, I open Azim's letter and spread upon the bed... bougainvillea petals. One by one, very gently, I lift them out of the envelope. I feel like a midwife.

I was wrong. There are actually *fifty* of them, not forty-eight. I counted twice.

Eventually, the sight of my duvet covered with those flowery spots awakens something buried very deep within me. Each petal is the size and almost the colour of...

Why don't I dare to utter it? I suppose it looks not much bigger than this on a scanner screen. Perhaps one month old. Or two... Younger than Kitty's. I remember that each petal refers to a genuine human life, saved through Azim's sacrifice.

Who are they? Real young girls back from school, possibly singing songs and laughing mischievously. I wonder, do they wear school uniforms in Sudan? Do they go swimming? Do they learn ballet dancing, as I did? Or some type of dancing...

Little girls with eyes, lips and arms, as I have. Girls with a heart and a soul, with hopes and desires, like mine. Girls with sisters, brothers and parents. Girls with a future. Girls with a God Who made them out of love. Like me... Girls whose lives would have been destroyed only yesterday, by the Nile.

I remember that Azim wished to achieve this with my help. I look at the petals scattered across my bed; so fresh, so innocent, resting in a circle, all around the picture of Azim and I, hugging.

Am I not making that up? Is it not silly romanticism?

Still, I can't help allowing the thought of "family" to cross my mind. This is mere paper and plants, ink and sap; I know it. But I can't ignore the actual relationship they have with each other, any more than if they were blood relations.

So, parents and children? My children? Ours? I've never seen them – yet. But they *are* blood related. *We* are blood related. That truth is tattooed on my skin with Azim's blood.

I remember my tears falling on Azim's cheek. This is real. We shed blood and tears, and because true love, sacrificial love, inspired our gift, it bore lasting fruit.

I kiss a petal and gently rub it against my stained skin. The petal is still fresh with sap and smells nice. I don't want to destroy it; or any of them. Ever. I will scatter them in the wind at Osly, in the desert, when I visit *our* girls.

After creasing a few of them, enough of the blood has gone and I feel able to use ordinary body wash. Yes, I can wash now.

Something in my heart has been cleansed as well.

Chapter 32

I *had* to fly back. I couldn't leave them all in Cairo, in hospitals and morgues.

My boss understood and granted me compassionate leave. It was considerate of him. Actually, many people showed kindness towards me; starting with Kitty of course, once I'd made up my mind to tell her everything about Azim and the rest.

Ah, the wedding... She'll be very happy. They'll love her. And what a bonus that Raúl's mother – Pilar – is a nurse, even though she's retired. She twice helped me wash and dress poor Kitty, when her illness and pregnancy combined hadn't left her enough strength to take care of herself.

The last time I had to help, before I left, was on her wedding day. As her Maid of Honour, I would have assisted her anyway with putting on her wedding dress. But on that solemn morning, it was especially moving.

She hadn't slept well and was feeling very weak, poor darling. As I was drying her hair with a towel I whispered in her ear: "You are a living temple. You carry life. You are sacred. And you will be the loveliest bride. Thank you for being my sister." Later, the hairdresser came. He made her look beautiful – I mean, even more than usual.

After she'd eaten a bit and rested, she was able to stand on her own. I fitted around her the timeless white dress. It was "Empire" style, made of satin and organza, with a high waist hitting just below the bust to leave her swollen stomach all the space it needed, without drawing attention to it.

Oh my beautiful princess, standing alone! And how she smiled at me as I was on my knees, arranging the folds.

The day before, Pilar remarked to me that in her time a pregnant bride would not have worn white... I found her insensitive. Although deep down I felt that there was perhaps more to all this than I then understood.

And to be fair, Kitty probably agreed, since earlier that day, at her request, I'd wheeled her all the way to the confessional at the nearby church. I hope I'm not being nosy, but after some time I wondered whether she'd fainted. But no: she finally opened the door, looking rejuvenated instead.

Back in my room that night, after the ceremony and the reception, I again visited Fr. Paul's website. He'd written most of it, he said. It was very late, but I longed to know more about the Eucharist.

A host showed on the screen. The whiteness of the thin disc brought to my mind that of a wedding dress. On the page, Fr. Paul stated that from our perspective, believing Christ to be hidden under the externals of bread, as behind a thin veil, can be difficult and sometimes frustrating. Fair enough.

It occurred to me then that any veil has *two* sides, doesn't it? – not *one* side only. How do *we* look, I thought, seen from *Christ*'s side of the Eucharist? What does *He* see of us, when our eyes see bread and our soul sees God?

Well, I felt that He must perceive just what a bridegroom would see. He sees the beauty of His bride enhanced by the refinement of her dress. I found that every "Yes" that our soul utters to Christ hidden in the Host, further adorns our nuptial dress in His eyes. For every act of faith we make in Him as hidden behind the Eucharistic veil, He sees one more appliqué sown upon our wedding garment.

When we meet Him after death, Christ desires our soul in proportion to the variety and wealth of the materials invisibly stitched upon the background fabric of our soul: tulle, crochet, lace, taffeta, damask, brocade, velvet or satin of every cut and harmoniously assembled, with threads of gold and little gems!

This is how I would want Him to see me, when I die. What a beautiful dress! And one that costs no money, but only love, through faith in Him. And then, faith will be no more, as I will *see* Him. When my soul is made forever His, I will know Him as He knows me, without intermediary.

I felt that I should start receiving Holy Communion again. But first I had to go to Confession – as Raúl in Houston (why did Kitty mention this to me by the way, if not as an encouragement?)

At the church, Kitty stood! And Dad could walk her down the aisle. Her wheelchair was at hand, just in case. I was so proud of her; and so happy for both of them. My bitterness seemed to melt away.

There were few guests on our side of the family, but they had plenty of cousins and uncles and aunts. Mum didn't stay long and, in fact, I wasn't in the best state of mind to talk with her in depth. My heart wasn't at peace. It was longing for another place.

Raúl took Clara on honeymoon to Mexico. He's fond of the national shrine of Guadalajara (or is it Guadalcanal?) and wants me to visit it as soon as possible. I don't mind, but it will have to wait.

I felt that I was needed elsewhere.

Chapter 33

Back in Cairo, I went straight to the Coptic parish.

It was strange to see for the first time in real life a place I knew so vividly through the CCTV footage. It was as if I'd come there daily for years. The dog was still there, quietly lying by the wall. I'm normally afraid of dogs, but that one wagged its tail in a friendly manner as I walked by, so I dared to stroke it.

Up on the wall, I noticed the camera. Right above its bracket stands a statue of the Risen Christ, Patron of that church. It was outside the range of the camera. That's why it hadn't showed up on the footage. The C.I.A. would have found that information irrelevant, but it was essential to me. It meant that the last gaze and smile of my beloved friend was for the statue of Our Saviour.

And perhaps also, as first seemed, for those who would watch the film taken from that angle.

For *me*?

A guard asked for my documents and looked inside my suitcase before letting me in. Understandably, the parish now had to take extra precautions. I walked up the steps, very slowly. They were still stained in many places, particularly within the chalk outlines left by investigators. I knelt down first by the one I remembered to have been that of Azim holding Talitha.

Dear friend, I can see you resting in your humble halo of chalk. I kiss the cracked concrete, where your heart last beat. On that very spot, a little girl was spared. My Egyptian prince, you saved her through your panther's leap when other men, as you knew too well, had just jumped on forty-eight others, all claws and fangs out. But they'd jumped in vain – thanks to you!

It struck me that in fact, *two* little girls rather than *one* had been saved within that whitish silhouette. There was Talitha. But was *I* not the other one? Wasn't the faith I'd lost when I was about twelve resuscitated in direct connection with this spot? Was that by any chance why Azim had picked *fifty* petals instead of forty-eight?

But how could he have guessed? Had his angel told him?

The C.I.A's fascinating network was surely very little compared with the interaction of souls in God. Not in jest did Azim refer to Katarina, Anthony and others in his letter as to actual protagonists in his needs, in his life, in his choices – even the most crucial ones.

There *was* a network indeed, spreading far wider and deeper than any CCTV or phone log would ever allow. It encompassed this world and the next; the living and the dead; those who seemed to be gone but, in fact, were all the more active and helpful.

Here on earth, humble refugees like Nepomucen were part of it. And Fr.

Paul of course. And, as she followed God's charitable inspiration, why not Dr. Yasir too? Communication took place across space and time, from our loving God to every soul, and among souls; not to forget angels.

And I'd been invited in. Back in. And they were no dreamers. *They were the strong, the generous, the truthful, the chaste, the merciful, the fruitful, the meek, the beautiful and the tender. They truly loved. They lived.*

Members of the parish were standing next to me. They must have been watching as I was lost in my meditation, still on my knees by Azim's chalk outline. I felt proud of my tears. When they greeted me, I said that I was a close friend of Azim's, and they took me to the priest.

He spoke to me very gently. I doubt he was over fifty, although his long beard made him look older. He wore a sort of dark grey djellaba and a skull cap like a date palm seller. But his profile reminded me of a statue of Amenhotep III (without the tiara), which I saw in Luxor. They call him Abu Ephrem.

I had brought along in my bag the dress I had been wearing that fatal day, which I chose not to clean. The priest said that it should soon be established that Azim had been killed in hatred of the Catholic faith, and that he was thus a martyr.

He added that the dress stained with his blood would then be considered a sacred *relic*, and that at least the stained part of the material should be kept for veneration, if I permitted. I was moved.

He asked me if I would like to accompany him to the As-Salam International Hospital, located in Cairo's Maadi district, since he was on his way to visit Mansur who had just emerged from his coma.

So Mansur was alive! Thank God! I was so glad, for him and for little Talitha.

I accepted the offer.

In the car, Abu Ephrem said that, on hearing news of the attack, Mansur's parents had flown from Beirut immediately and were still in Cairo. Talitha was with them. She'd already attended several meetings with a psychologist to help her deal with the trauma. Thankfully, she seemed to be doing rather well.

In the hospital corridor, two guards prevented us from entering the room. Abu Ephrem introduced me to one of them (with stunning steel-blue eyes) who went inside briefly and, coming back, scanned my body, took my ten fingerprints on a portable touchscreen and a picture of my face.

A fairly handsome third man came out of the room to meet us, introducing himself as the personal assistant of Mr. Al-Khoury.

The family were gathered around Mansur's bed as the priest led me in. Talitha saw me first and ran into me, throwing her arms around my waist. She was half crying, half laughing.

She said that Azim was my friend and her friend, and Daddy and Mummy's friend, and that he wasn't gone for real, and did *I* think he was gone?

I said I knew he was with us.

Mansur wasn't fully conscious yet. He *was* so handsome, just as I remembered him (although I shouldn't notice such things). He spoke –

apparently his very first word: "Nour?"

No one knew what to answer. The only audible sounds were the regular beeps of the cardiac monitor and those, no less frequent, of incoming emails somewhere near Mr Al-Khoury's personal assistant. We were all looking at each other, when Talitha led me to her dad. She gently put his hand in mine.

His eyes were still shut, but he repeated: "Nour?"

I was very embarrassed. It wasn't for me to tell him of his beloved wife's death. I held his hand between both of mine, still standing by his bed, and whispered in his ear: "Mansur, we're all here with you, and we love you."

A smile seemed to appear on his face. His parents were looking at me intently, suffering visible on their tired faces. Talitha kissed her father's cheek. I came to his parents and said that I was a close friend of Azim.

Mansur's father stood up and embraced me with great emotion, not saying a word. He is rather tall and looks powerful.

I sat next to his mother. She had prayer beads in her hand, but I couldn't see if a cross hung at the end.

A large icon stood on the shelf opposite Mansur. It was very badly damaged, and stained. I wondered why it hadn't been restored... then I realised its likely history.

Several bullet impacts showed. The nose and most of the saint's halo were barely visible.

Abu Ephrem confirmed to me that Mansur had been holding it, wrapped as a present for Azim's Baptism, when standing on the steps during the attack. Because of its antiquity – a sixteenth century Coptic depiction of St. Anthony – the very dense cedar wood was framed in metal surrounds and fitted at the back with a steel sheet to protect it.

It had saved Mansur's life. Four bullets from the handgun had ricocheted off the icon, while only one had reached his stomach. St. Anthony had definitely shielded him.

How could I but marvel at this unexpected revelation? The man just baptised as "Anthony" had died as a living shield for a little girl, while his patron saint extended an armour of wood and steel upon her father, also baptised *in extremis*. I went to the icon and reverently kissed it, signing myself afterwards.

I was relieved when we left the hospital again. As we walked to the car park, a helicopter landed on the hospital roof. I was so glad that patients could be brought in so quickly now, and hopefully be saved. I would have loved being offered a sightseeing flight around Cairo, with the Pyramids at my feet. But that was unlikely to happen.

I fancied a stroll, and some time on my own.

Abu Ephrem had loaded my suitcase in the boot of his car when leaving the parish and suggested that, if I had no better plan, he could arrange for me to stay at a convent in town where the nuns had a few rooms for female guests.

Although I had booked a cheap hotel, I found his offer attractive and I accepted.

On our way there, I discovered that he wasn't Egyptian but Libyan, from Maltese parents, although he spoke English with an American accent. I asked him what he meant by 'bi-ritual', as he described himself. He explained that he had trained at a traditional Latin Rite seminary in America, but also ministered to the Catholic Coptic community. I didn't really grasp the differences – but I liked him all the same.

He dropped me at the convent and introduced me to the nun in charge. She was very friendly and took me to the third floor (no lift). After a few practicalities, she left and I found myself alone in a plain little cell.

A very deep sensation of *peace* took possession of me. Looking at my suitcase on the white tiled floor, I felt as if I'd been carrying it on my back for a long time and hadn't noticed until then what a difference it made to take it down. For the first time in weeks (or decades?), I was given a chance to stop.

To rest.

To think.

A small crucifix hung on the wall. The bed was very simple. Through the window, I could see a few buildings, some trees and perhaps a glimpse of the Nile. I could also see the roof of the convent church next door.

It struck me that *He* was there below: Jesus my Love. Just down there; so close to me. I would go and visit Him. Already, my mind travelled through the roof of the chapel to the tabernacle.

I walked downstairs and got slightly lost in the building.

But, making my way out into a small garden, to my amazement I *recognised* it.

Chapter 34

I had been there before, in another life. It felt so, in a way. I had sat on that bench with Azim at the end of my week in Egypt.

On two consecutive evenings while in Cairo, after the excursions, we'd left the hotel and the group of my fellow tourists, and had walked around the block and further away, chatting.

He had pushed an iron gate and introduced me to what he called his "private oasis." Against a high white wall stood a bench, under a large fig-tree. There we'd sat, in the warm shade, saturated with the sugary smell of ripening figs.

We had first talked about my professional expectations. He was enthusiastic about my boss's plans to start bringing groups from Vancouver. He wanted to give us all his contacts, which would greatly facilitate our first attempt since, as a young woman visiting Egypt for the first time, I was very much aware of my lack of experience and of clout.

Our conversations gradually shifted to anything and everything. On one occasion Azim had remained silent for some period of time. He seemed to be thinking of something else. Or of *someone* else. I'd felt slightly puzzled, wondering whether he was attracted to me, and was struggling with his loyalty to the mysterious "Katarina!"

Was she real, though, or had he invented her? I wasn't sure then. Unless that point had been clarified, I shouldn't have hoped for a love relationship with Azim. It was unfair of me. But I only admitted that in retrospect.

The street was quiet; the sound of traffic on the main avenue subdued. There was no one around to be seen. We were sitting at some distance from each other on the bench, with my handbag between us.

I hoped his hand would move over and land on mine. I expected his arm to slide behind my back and to settle around my shoulders. But nothing happened. Until, from the corner of my eyes I saw him move – but upward, not sideward! – to pick a fig...

He bit into it and presented the open fruit to me saying: "It's already ripe, because of the warmer temperature in this enclosed garden."

I dipped my finger in it, while Azim boasted of the beauty of this "typical Egyptian jewel," with its sweet texture. He asked me as I swallowed a mouthful, if I felt the chewiness of the flesh combined with the smoothness of the skin, and the crunchiness of the seeds.

In truth, I would have much preferred to share a chocolate cookie!

My disappointment, though, wasn't of a culinary nature. Resenting what I took as a cowardly diversion on his part, I remember grumbling in my mind that he seemed to pay more attention to a piece of fruit than to me. And was *I* not more attractive?

Or was it perhaps my task to be his guide in flirting, as he'd been mine in temples and tombs? Azim was clearly not one of those Egyptian men who hung around hotels, making a living out of supposedly spontaneous "romantic encounters"' with female tourists.

Maybe he was shy, or simply had no idea what a young Western woman expected when sitting as a couple, on a bench, in the evening.

That was just a week earlier! He'd vanished. I now stood alone under the fig-tree.

Azim was dead.

I sat on the empty bench, looking at the other end, where his body had rested, full of life.

His words came back to me: "Clara, I'm so glad that you could come with me to my private oasis. This is a special place for me, and sharing it with you will make it even more precious. There is something sacred about it.

"I wish I could tell you more, but perhaps it's too soon. You know, this is where I first found love. Real, true, substantial love. I sat here with the woman who introduced me to love. I'm indebted to her forever. I would so much wish to share more with you.

"Believe me, this savoury fig is *nothing* compared to it."

I didn't understand.

I actually found him pretty rude telling me about another love when my hope should have been clear to him. And how dared he bring up the memory of his Katarina sitting on this stupid bench! If he loved *her*, then he shouldn't have come here with me.

But, finding him attractive and funny, I decided not to risk everything by making a fuss.

We walked back to the hotel and he wished me sweet dreams.

Looking in the bathroom mirror, I confessed to myself that I was, well... very pretty! That's what not a few men say, and what (unbiased) women admit, and I couldn't deny it, could I? So, the problem lay not with *me*.

Suddenly, a thought crossed my mind. Of course! Azim was simply attracted to *men*!

He enjoyed my company, but was incapable of meeting me sentimentally. The story of the invisible Katarina was just a screen. Yes, it all made sense. Silly me: how could I not have seen it sooner! The day after, our group was to visit Giza. I would observe Azim, and the most obvious reason for his strange behaviour towards me would surely be confirmed.

However, that next day, I failed to detect any gestures or words of Azim's substantiating my guess.

On the other hand, that red-haired American girl in our group was clearly sending him signals. She was pretty and possibly younger than I; less tall as well. What was she thinking of! But her baseball cap would *never* do! Pathetic...

Thankfully, Azim was busy lecturing on the Pyramids (we were not spared the number, weight and size of stones). Looking at the nearby Sphinx, I felt that our young guide was an enigma to me.

I left the group and went to stand in between the gigantic paws of the sculpture, half-man half-lion. It was quite daunting to find myself so close to the monster, its threatening jaw hanging high above me. It would seem the risk of the Sphinx jumping on me was *greater* than that of Azim moving a finger in my direction.

We would see!

Having lost his nose, the Sphinx couldn't smell a woman – but he still had eyes. I started dancing – rather attractively, I hoped – in between the monstrous paws, challenging the beast. I loved classical dance and had trained for a few years at basic-level ballet.

But my improvisation by the Sphinx was definitely contemporary! To no avail, alas – all I managed to do was to attract a guide from the other group, who filmed me with his phone; while the red-haired girl watched scornfully. Azim didn't look at me once.

So, what was that love he'd mentioned, and wished to share with me? It couldn't be soccer! Was it the love of archaeology? I had no objection to that. Or, was he hoping to turn me into a Muslim?

That might be more challenging, although I didn't mind wearing veils on occasions, and I could go as far as burkinis, if he insisted. But I wouldn't be his jihadi bride! That is, unless he asked *very* nicely.

I decided to put him to the test that evening.

It was the eve of our last day, and my final chance to have our peculiar friendship bear fruit. Indeed, he would not get away with a fig this time. I would make sure that nothing got in between our lips!

As we walked out of the hotel for our now familiar stroll, I appeared to myself as a masterpiece of subtly tantalizing femininity. There was nothing out of place in my clothes and makeup; neither in my hair and perfume. I earned appreciative glances from Azim's colleagues, drinking in the hotel lobby as we walked by. Success!

I looked rather casual, but it was all craftily designed to attract a man's heart – if there was a man indeed, or a heart.

Chapter 35

The "private oasis" was empty again.

We sat on the bench in our usual places – with no handbag between us this time (I would take no chances). I slowly shifted our conversation to the question of cultural differences between Islam and the West, bluntly stating that same-sex relations for instance were frowned upon in his culture.

He agreed, without seeming at all upset, adding that he personally couldn't imagine finding happiness in sexual intimacy, but with someone of the *opposite* sex (I sighed, relieved).

I teased him on his use of the word *imagine*, having seen how the other girls in our group eyed him up. I said that I was sure that, with so many obvious opportunities, he had little left to "imagine."

How I was so bold, even forceful, surprises me now. It didn't sound like me. I must have felt quite frustrated by his lack of attention to my charms over the previous days.

Furthermore, the brotherly intimacy which he'd allowed to develop between us was unknown to me and unsettled me. I simultaneously relished it and regretted it, not knowing what to make of it.

There was a little silence.

Taking the lead, I was the one who picked a fig, bit it and gave some to him. Azim looked at me in a strange manner, under the sugary shade. I thought that, eventually, *something* was going to happen; although somehow, I also wished *nothing* would (are men as complex as we women?).

Everything was quiet.

I could only hear distant cars and music; and a boat horn by the Nile; and more distinctly, *isha*, that is, the muezzin's last call, through a loudspeaker across the street.

Azim swallowed the fruit and remained silent for a while, like the evening before, as if listening to something; or to someone. To the muezzin perhaps: after all, was it not prayer time for Muslims?

Eventually, he answered very plainly (as one would answer "I don't smoke, thank you"): "I'm a virgin, Clara."

I don't know what surprised me more: that he was actually a virgin, or that he would tell me so. In my embarrassment, I did something that I might regret for the rest of my life. I laughed.

I laughed as if he'd said something silly. But in my heart, I was touched by his confidence. Or wounded? Sitting next to me, his entire person, his body and his soul, became loaded in my eyes with a very particular significance, as if sacred. Like when I first saw Kitty pregnant.

And yet, he hadn't moved. His voice was just the same as a minute earlier.

He hadn't changed. But for me, he had. He had shared a very intimate dimension of his past life and of his present condition. I felt unworthy of his trust.

All of a sudden, I realised that we had been moving on two different levels; and mine was rather low, and selfish. I was ashamed. I apologised for my reaction and said that I admired him. He smiled as if there was nothing to worry about, answering that he'd learnt to value virginity only three years earlier: "Before, I used to find it burdensome, almost shameful," he added.

In such a situation, another man would have felt entitled to ask me in return if *I* had anything left to "imagine." Not Azim. I was grateful for his discretion which, as was becoming clearer to me, was no lack of interest but rather expressed a very delicate affection and a manly respect.

My thoughts were interrupted by a faint greenish spark flitting in the shade, near the trunk of the fig tree. But the *spark* was alive. A firefly! It rested on Azim's shoulder, and soon flew away. He hadn't noticed, apparently. I would have loved to take the shining insect home with me – or even better, to *become* the firefly and accompany my friend wherever he went.

We remained silent. But this time, it was a peaceful silence. A fruitful quietness, if I may say. Unlike before, it didn't affect me as a delay, as an obstacle. I knew that our relationship was deepening through that silence, rather than being hindered by it.

Actually, I could almost physically feel the increase of my affection for my young *Sphinx* (he was only twenty-three, one year younger than I). I acknowledged that, if anyone was leading the other, it was him, not me. And I was glad for it. Yes, I was deeply pleased to be led.

That's when my body betrayed me. Most unexpectedly, tears started to roll down my cheeks! The last thing I wanted. I tried very hard not to sniff, which would have alerted him. He didn't notice at first, as he was looking in front of him, as he often did.

Also, thank God, there was very little daylight left, especially under our tree. At some point he turned his handsome face towards me. I was amazed by his beauty. The way I had been planning things, it should have been the other way round. Too bad for me!

But the beauty I saw in him was much more than harmonious features – deep brown eyes, aquiline nose, firm lips opening into a vigorous smile, very masculine cheekbones and lush dark hair. No, what struck me through those qualities was that particular radiance of purity, which I had encountered in some children, but could not recall seeing in men (or women) up to then, or not as clearly.

He asked me why I was crying.

I said that I wasn't sure, but that I wouldn't want to be anywhere else in the world than on this bench, with him.

He said that my tears were beautiful, adding that he also cried sometimes, in moments of deep happiness. I was touched that he didn't tell me to stop, neither did he hand me a handkerchief. He seemed to find this all entirely normal.

I felt that his straightforward reaction strengthened our intimacy. Only people very close to me – like Kitty – could look at my tears without any embarrassment or superficial concern. I wished we could have stayed there all night, side by side.

I now hoped that no physical desire would interfere and spoil what was my first exposure to genuine intimacy with a man: that of two souls. But we had another busy day ahead and he stood up, inviting me with a smile to go back.

As I was drying my eyes, I saw him touch the high white wall behind us and, to my surprise, briefly kiss it. Did he care for *bricks* now? Having had sufficient proof of my ignorance of higher levels of love, I refrained from saying anything and followed him into the street.

As we walked back through the lobby at the hotel, we saw Azim's colleagues still busy drinking. One of them waved a smartphone with a video playing on it. I wondered if he wasn't the same man who had filmed me dancing in front of the Sphinx earlier that afternoon. He said something loudly in Arabic, of which I only understood the words "American" and "gazelle."

Azim stopped and looked at him as if he was about to kill a noisy wasp. Seeing his clenching fists and fearing there would be trouble, I said: "Azim, should we not get back to our rooms?"

His hands eased and he walked along with me, briefly responding to the other in Arabic.

Next to my door, I asked him what his colleague had shouted. He said that it was better not to repeat it. I asked whether it was about *me*.

He smiled.

I smiled.

We laughed.

We were alone by my door in the empty corridor.

I thought I saw a tiny fig seed at the corner of his mouth and...

Of his *beautiful* mouth and...

Suddenly perceiving that I was in great danger (or should I say *pharaonic* danger?) of ruining the whole evening by an irrepressible expression of my tenderness for him, I whispered in great haste: "Thank you and good night!" and rushed into my room, locking the door behind me.

Cinderella wouldn't have been quicker to disappear from the sight of her prince when midnight struck.

Kneeling on the floor, my elbows on my bed, I felt rejuvenated. I greatly wanted to thank someone, but I didn't know whom.

I slept very well that night.

Chapter 36

I stood by the empty bench. Azim was no more.
Or rather, he lived forever. I looked at the tall white wall behind. I laid my hand where Azim did. I pressed my lips to it as Azim did. Now I knew for *Whom* his kiss was meant.
You couldn't tell from the garden that this wall was actually the back of the church. Literally behind the bench, on the other side of the wall, stood the tabernacle. So I found as I entered the chapel, having walked along the building.

In the sanctuary, the little red lamp shined dimly by the tabernacle. I genuflected in its direction. I put myself in the presence of God. I had learned from Fr. Paul's website that this kind of presence is the most real on earth. God is present there as our Friend; as our Saviour; almighty; all forgiving; all loving; all focused on each one of us.

I told Him that I loved Him with all my heart. I thanked Him for the faith of my youth recovered and improved. I blessed Him for having sent me such an angel as Azim, the unexpected messenger of His Love.

Now I knew *which* Love Azim was talking about. This was the chapel where Nour had taken him. This was where he'd first witnessed the presence of God in the Eucharist. So, *Nour* had been the woman on the bench, not Katarina, even though his beloved Katarina had been there invisibly, as he had assured me.

I spent a long time on my kneeler, until the sisters came in to pray. After, I followed them and shared their silent supper. A bit later, Mother Joan-Maria, the superior, knocked at my door and asked me if I was comfortable. I assured her that I felt at home. She smiled and put a Visitors' book in my hands, adding that I could bring it back down to the chapel in the morning.

I was inspired to ask her about life at the convent. She looked at me. Amidst her tanned, old and deeply wrinkled face, her beautiful eyes reached my heart. She explained.

It's very simple.

The sisters sleep little, pray in the chapel nearly half the time, and the other half they do manual labour; even outside the convent. Daily, two of them bring help to the poor people in the slums at Ezbet El Nakhl and Mokattam.

They come from various parts of the world.

Sister was sitting on the only chair, and I at the end of the bed. Just a little light was still coming through the window: "Sister, I sat in your garden twice before, without knowing it belonged to a convent."

She smiled tenderly at me, saying nothing. I went on: "Sister, I was thinking today, in your chapel. I wonder if... Sister, what would be needed for a girl my age to stay longer. I mean, to remain here."

She kindly helped me: "To join the community, you mean, not just as a visitor?" I nodded timidly and joyfully, like a child whose Mum asked her if she'd done well at school that day – and she had.

Sister replied: "Postulants must have a very strong love for Jesus. Especially Jesus in the Sacred Host, as we spend several hours a day adoring Him in the monstrance. They must be Catholic virgins in good physical health. They must desire a life of self-effacement and of service. They must learn some Latin.

"Following the spirituality of Blessed Charles de Foucauld, our main inspiration, they must pray earnestly that our Muslim brothers and sisters will discover the love of God, offered to all men in the Person of Jesus."

I couldn't believe what I was hearing. It all matched my aspirations perfectly, as if Sister had been reading in my soul things that I wasn't even aware of. In truth, I had never considered becoming a *nun*. But to find myself in that place, after having spent those two evenings in the garden with my martyred brother, seemed too meaningful not to inquire seriously.

Then something Sister had mentioned struck me. I didn't dare ask the question. It wasn't about *Latin*... But I prayed in my heart for the answer to be given, whatever it might be: "Sister, what if a girl met all those requirements, but wasn't *really* a virgin?"

She wasn't embarrassed at all by my question – I noticed the same very straightforward outlook as Azim's concerning these matters: "My child, virginity is principally in the will. Virgins follow God's inspiration to give themselves totally to God. We have had sisters in the South who were victims of violence from soldiers. Even if bodily integrity is no more, they remain virgins."

I wasn't a victim. But was I a *virgin*? I wanted to be sure: "Sister, I've had three boyfriends, whom I allowed to become intimate with me, but never to the point of... In my heart, I don't think I really wanted it. I just wanted to be loved."

The night was falling, and Sister switched on the light. She put her wrinkled finger (with the nail cut very short – and not painted!) on one of the books laid on the table and suggested I should read it when I had time. She bid me good night and said we could talk again the next day if I wished. I took her motherly smile as an encouragement.

As she left, she dipped her fingers in the small holy water stoup by the door but, finding it empty, she filled it from a plastic bottle (marked with a large cross) on the shelf, saying: "God bless you Clara, and Our Lady keep you safe."

I stayed for a while immobile, thinking.

It was getting late and I thought that I should sign the Visitors' Book before reading a bit and then go to sleep. I opened it on my bed and found that it was more a register of prayer intentions than a Visitors' Book. There were many since last week, most of them in Arabic. Actually, most of those in Arabic – which I could not understand – seemed to bear exactly the same words, as if different hands had copied each other down the page.

Browsing backward, I came across the first entry on Sunday 1st June: *That my sister Clara may kneel in this chapel – Azim.*

His handwriting ran further down the page, in Arabic, with the same characters which apparently had been repeated many times down that page and the next. It looked as if, after Azim's martyrdom, local parishioners had piously echoed his last petition, on behalf of Clara, a girl whom they didn't even know.

Or *did* they know me? I was so moved...

I cried peacefully, looking at the little crucifix up on the wall. I felt it was time to prepare for my confession.

It would be the first in nearly twelve years.

Chapter 37

A list of sins isn't something one types.
Instead, taking a piece of paper and a pen, I started revisiting the second half of my life, asking God the Holy Ghost for light and contrition.

I couldn't find many sins; or too many.
I wasn't always sure of the malice of certain actions, words, thoughts and omissions. There were so many things I'd done through ignorance, or in a desperate attempt to protect myself emotionally.
When Mum wished to separate from Dad and was denied the right to take us back to Seoul with her... The horror of her departure... when we accompanied her to *YVR* (my aversion to that airport remained for years), and Granddad taking us back home.
Soon after, having to accept Abigail, our *stepmother*, into our own house. I started getting a bit wild. Not *very* wild though, compared with many girls at my school.
My best friends were Emma and Sally. Their parents also separated, and we shared a lot. Sally wondered if I wasn't becoming anorexic (she was bulimic). I looked for protection, and Kitty gave me a lot.
Dear Kitty! Beloved Kitty... What would I have become without you?
But I also felt angry at God and at the adults, and I wilfully exposed myself. That's perhaps where sin was involved.

Daniel... my first boyfriend. That was simply to show off and to prove to my schoolmates that I was capable of it. Our relationship didn't last long and he wasn't daring; were we just fourteen?
Still, he was the one who convinced me to have my shoulder tattooed with that silly symbol, and to pierce my left earlobe for a triple ring (I didn't have the guts for *gauging*, which would have stretched the smaller punctures).
Dad was furious! That was just what I intended. I regret it now.
After, there were a few kisses with boys at parties. Nothing serious.
Until my first year at University. I can't even remember the guy's name (a chemistry student?), which is just as well. There was truly no love. I had drunk too much, and I agreed to go for a ride in his car. He soon parked...
I don't want to think of it, but I suppose that confession should cover everything. I believed him when he said that if I was a woman, I had to act as one, or else he would shame me all around the Campus.
I didn't want to be mocked on Facebook. But I resisted him, somehow.
He threw me on the pavement outside my hall of residence, calling me "frigid," and drove away. I was so distressed that I took the pill (my only time),

even though I knew that there was *zero* risk of conception. Perhaps he was right – I mean, do I have a problem, compared with other girls?

I did stay away from men for a while.

Later on I met Khal, a fashion photographer, originally from Jordan. Sally used to ask: "And where is your *Lawrence of Arabia*?" He was kind. He loved taking outdoor pictures of me wearing smart clothes (a few got published) and said I should start modelling.

We nearly moved in together. But he gave up, as I was taking my time, and he still felt unfulfilled by our relationship, understandably. I wanted coddling, and he expected more.

Sally was genuinely concerned for me. Putting her arm around my shoulders as I was crying, she enquired plainly: "Clarry, *why* can't you do what it takes to keep a man? Don't tell me that you don't know the basics. Obviously, you've heard before that men's physical needs are simply greater, more quickly fulfilled and more frequent than ours, haven't you?

"The marks of tenderness *we* would expect as an essential stage in the encounter, *they* often see as wasted time. They don't *mean* to be insensitive when skipping them on occasions."

Proudly pointing at her new dress (a new soft jersey fabric by *Kayamashi*, I recall, with a pattern of purple petals tastefully spread against a yellow background), she suggested with a smile: "Look, it's like *shopping frenzy* for us: when it seizes us, we simply *must* buy the latest skirt, mustn't we? – come what may. We may regret it after, but what is done is done."

She went on: "I'm sorry to have to tell you this, Clara, but you really *do* need some sort of an electroshock. As your friend, I *must* save you from spinsterhood! So, do you know *what* Khal answered me right after you separated (I was merely asking him why he couldn't be more patient)? This is literally what he said: "Clara's got soft feathers, long legs and a lovely neck, but I can't live with an ostrich! Whenever I mention real-life sex, she buries her head into the sand. Perhaps she genuinely *can't* fly after all."

Needless to say, Sally's confidence didn't make me very happy – neither with her, nor with Khal, nor with myself. But it *did* work as an electroshock though, as for the first time I became *aware* of aspiring to something... different. To something more.

They were right, my *head* was in another dimension than my body, but rather than down into the sand, it was up in the air, I felt. If they wanted to compare me with a bird, then I was a *penguin* swimming upwards: light above attracted me and my head was already outside the cold water, as I jumped through the ice hole – into sunshine.

Why was that?
Why had I not given in, so far? Or, not completely? I didn't know.
I suppose that, at the time, unless I felt it were love with a capital "L," I just couldn't go ahead. But since then, with what Azim had shared with me, I

knew that waiting for my *husband* was the right thing to do.

And by the way, Sally's boyfriends didn't tend to stay very long with her anyway.

Oh! I just realised that Khal was *also* a Middle Eastern man... That's strange, as if I had a particular attraction to them.

Now *this* next sin is the most embarrassing one. But I *must* add it to the list...

Fine: I read Kitty's *diary*! Not all of it. Only a dozen pages. I knew where she kept it. It was on an occasion when I thought she was in love with a boy we knew, and I feared she might not love me anymore (I was thirteen). My indiscretion haunted me for years, and even now, I have the greatest difficulty admitting it.

Meanwhile, there was hatred in my heart, against my father. And I couldn't forgive Mum's absence. The worst thing was when I wilfully stopped praying.

I remember when I coldly decided that God had let me down. I was inspired to go and ask Sister Marie-Thérèse for assistance. She was sweet. But standing outside her office, I felt as if it was all too easy. Too easy for them, the adults. I found them all to be accomplices in my parents' split and concluded that they deserved my trust no more. "*My* God" had become "*their* God."

Without knocking, I walked away from Sister's office and from then on, I stopped listening to her. And to any adults, in fact, apart from my university professors, later on.

I cheated twice at some minor exams. That was ridiculous. I knew I didn't need to, in order to graduate with honours. Still, I'm sorry for it.

I was also vain, many times. In fact, to be very honest, I still am. But should a woman not try to dress well and be nice to look at?

Then I started working, and found myself to be one of *them*: an adult, whatever that meant.

And not to forget: I like gossip; cheese in excess; and white chocolate cookies (not all three at the same time, though).

The moon was casting its milky light into my little cell.

The small crucifix still hung above the bed.

I took it down and laid it in my palms.

Dear Jesus... What have I done all these years? You were there with me day and night, and I didn't care. I chose not to listen to You. I chose not to ask. Please, forgive me. Forgive a poor silly and proud and wounded girl. I so much want to be Yours now!

I was still kneeling on the floor by my bed. I rested my head in my hands, pressing the crucifix against my brow for a long time; then against my chest; then against my lips.

Please, take me as Your little bride. I'll do anything You want. If You are with me, I shall fear nothing, and all will be joy to me.

In the morning, Abu Ephrem heard my confession.

I felt so relieved when he said in Latin (the translation was displayed to my side): "And I absolve you from your sins in the name of the Father, and of the Son, and of the Holy Spirit."

You see, it's one thing to regret your sins and tell God so; but it's another to hear God's minister unbind your soul with the authority he has received from Christ, through the unbroken chain of apostolic succession in Christ's Church.

And yet, I had spent a dozen years without caring about it.

Abu Ephrem said that I was ready to receive Holy Communion again.

It had been eight years. I was in awe.

I had desired it since my "reconversion" in the underground chapel at Orly airport a week earlier. But I had postponed it as, even at Kitty's wedding, I hadn't felt sufficiently at peace to look into my soul and confess; and to meditate on what Holy Communion would mean to me. But on that morning I understood that there was no reason to delay further.

Having prayed the penance given by the priest during my confession, I stayed on my knees all the way through Holy Mass.

It wasn't said the way I remembered it from my teens. Rather than facing the congregation, the priest was standing on *our* side of the altar, turning towards us only on a few occasions.

He didn't greet us, or chat, or joke. He spoke in Latin, when not praying in silence. No one was asked to do the readings – Father read, as if he was speaking to God and the saints, rather than instructing those in the pews.

I was a bit overwhelmed at first. But I found it much easier to immerse myself in the mystery of Christ's sacrifice (Holy Mass is Calvary made present again, according to Fr. Paul's website).

It also made Christ's presence in the sacrament more manifest. In fact, it was all about Christ rather than about *me*. And yet, I didn't feel ignored at all, but valued and embraced in a way I hadn't experienced at previous Masses. '*You* aren't the centre,' it gently told me, '*Christ* is'.

I loved it!

When the time came, I followed the sisters and, after them, knelt at the Communion rail to receive my Saviour. The priest laid the Host on my tongue and I swallowed it reverently.

It was so simple. Just a little child being fed by her Father.

Just a little bride being met by her divine Spouse.

Of course, I cried. Silently, peacefully.

I recalled that a week earlier, outside that very wall, I had already cried before Azim, not knowing then what Love was promised to my heart.

Faith is such a mystery. I had spent so many years estranged from this treasure, my Eucharistic God. And now I knew that I could simply not live without it.

Could I *die* for it? Please God... yes.

How had it all happened? How had I been brought to this new perception of reality? Had my freedom been harmed in any way?

I knew which powerful "network" had been involved in my change. I'd had a glimpse of its ramifications across space and time. And still, I knew that they'd cast no spell upon me.

Rather, one had shed his own blood (and spread some on my skin). They hadn't brainwashed me. Actually, no one had even *spoken* to me about the faith. Not even Azim.

It had all occurred silently, like a flower blossoms. That flower was no lie, and no threat. I felt alive as never before.

At the end of Mass, after giving thanks to God, I put the book with the prayer intentions back before the Sacred Heart statue and read again, under Sunday 1st June: *That my sister Clara may kneel in this chapel – Azim.*

Two pages down, I wrote a new entry: *She knelt, and lives – Clara.*

Chapter 38

After his Mass and thanksgiving, Abu Ephrem had his breakfast, which the sisters prepared for him. It didn't last long.

Afterwards, he found me at the back of the church: "The police and intelligence have finished with the bodies of the victims. But Azim's family declined to take charge of his. They said that since he died a Christian, there's nothing they can do for him. Between us, they fear retaliation (in particular his younger sister Jamila, who shared a lot with him).

"So, my parish becomes Azim's next of kin. The morgue rang me yesterday afternoon, asking when we could come and fetch the bodies. I'm going there now to meet with some women skilled in embalming before transferring the mortal remains to our church, where they will lie in repose overnight.

"Burial in our crypt will follow tomorrow. Most people consider Azim a martyr, like his two godparents and dear Nour, whom I think you knew."

I remembered beautiful Nour very well, although I'd met her only a couple of times with Mansur and Talitha. But the essential role she'd played in Azim's conversion (with its subsequent impact on my life) made her very dear to me.

I asked if there was anything I could do to assist.

Abu Ephrem answered that if I was free now, I could come along and pray during the embalming.

I hadn't yet had any breakfast, but the prospect of praying by Azim's body in such privileged circumstances allowed no hindrances and, after two figs and a glass of milk (which I drank in haste, standing in the kitchen), Abu Ephrem and I drove off to the morgue.

We didn't talk, at first. I was deep in my thoughts, beginning to wonder if I was meant to go there at all. It would certainly be extremely difficult, psychologically.

After a while, Abu Ephrem said that, sadly, he'd become accustomed to this sort of tragedy. He tried to look at it supernaturally, of course doing his best to console and encourage the relatives and friends of those assassinated.

As we arrived, a black van was parked outside the morgue, with another large car. Three women were there, holding bags. To my surprise, I recognised Mansur's own mother among them. Could she be a Christian, then? She came to me and, catching me unawares, hugged me in silence.

I asked how Mansur was doing. She said: "My son spoke and is now fully conscious. I broke to him the news of Nour's death. He's deeply shocked, but I know him: he will fight to recover, in memory of his wife, and for the love of his daughter.

"The doctor hopes that he may be able to start walking again in three to five weeks. I came this morning to help with Nour's embalming. My husband ordered special items to make the funeral very beautiful."

I realised then that more than one body was to be taken to the parish. The five of us walked downstairs, led by an officer. The staircase smelt of bleach. The door was opened and Azim's body was wheeled out in the middle of the room. Then Nour's, next to him. Then the two godparents'.

This was going to be even more challenging than I had anticipated. I considered leaving. But it was too late. The mere thought of it made me feel ashamed.

I looked at the first shape covered by the white sheet. So, was this... *him*? Was the man I loved too late, truly under this veil?

The two other women were unpacking their bags while Mrs Al-Khoury pulled his light shroud down to the waist. I was on my knees, not daring to look. Then I raised my eyes, and saw.

A man's body. Terribly wounded. My friend's body. Azim's body. Dead. The post-mortem carers before our visit must have been instructed to position the arms in a prayer posture, with hands joined upon the chest.

The skin was torn to shreds. But the limbs had retained their elegance and still conveyed an impression of strength. The face was beautifully serene. The officer said that five bullets had been found in him.

I came to kneel closer while the women started preparing the bodies of the godparents. A deep wound gaped across the side of Azim, to the right. Certainly the one he'd received during his last night – *our* last night – when fighting against my likely aggressor. No wonder that it bled again at the airport.

Still holding my rosary beads, I put my fingers to my left side, remembering. Memories streamed back, of so many happy moments with him; and of the utter sorrow that had followed; and of the rebirth that had taken place at the end.

Azim's mouth was silent for now, but the side of my martyred friend had other lips, singing a soundless hymn of love, more eloquent than any words.

I stood up at last and only then noticed the many other scars that marked him. I failed to locate the impacts of the five bullets and realised that they would probably show only on his back, due to his posture when shielding little Talitha with his own body.

So what were these many, many scars all across his shoulders and his torso, down to his waist? Two very fresh ones must have resulted from the autopsy. But all the others were much older.

I felt sweat trickle down my brow, as my mind led me to the only explanation possible.

Whip lashes...

I could not believe my eyes. What could have caused such a terrible punishment? I had to know. I walked towards the officer sitting at a desk: "Sir, what caused the long thin marks on the young man's body?"

He was visibly embarrassed as he murmured: "Flogging."

Chapter 39

Flogging? Had I heard him correctly?
There was silence. I looked intently at him. He went on, alternatively reading from a paper and looking towards the door: "The post-mortem established that the deceased was flogged by... by someone, about six weeks before his death.

"The wounds had nearly healed, but some on the side of his stomach were reopened by a recent blow with a sharp blade, about twelve hours before he was shot. The back of the deceased shows many more such scars. There are forty in total."

I was outraged. Admittedly, flogging a man was little compared with killing him. But it was Azim's humiliation that I loathed. And the officer clearly knew the cause, but would say no more. Azim was no adulterer or drunkard, that such a penalty should have been inflicted on him!

A hand gently weighed on my shoulder: Abu Ephrem's.

He spoke gravely: "My child, this is a most hurtful sight, especially for you. But those dreadful scars, I can assure you, are no marks of dishonour. Just the opposite. Azim received them from his former comrades who were trying to deter him from becoming a Christian.

"He told me about what he unassumingly called their 'visit.' His sister Jamila took a great risk when she alerted me. I found a discreet place, managed by one of my parishioners, for his convalescence. Azim suffered greatly in his flesh as a confessor of the faith, even before he died a martyr."

Then I remembered the mention of this criminal "visit" in Azim's letter. And all that time, while I was chatting with him, he hadn't once expressed bodily pain or bitterness! And yet, throughout that last week spent with me, he must still have endured dire discomfort all over his body.

I was full of shame, thinking how I teased him and so superficially tried to flirt with him, while he bore in secret the glorious marks of his greater Love.

That afternoon at the hotel after the visit of Isis Island, I had even imagined that, due to some secret deformity, he was ashamed of being seen in public wearing a bathing suit. In fact, I was just frustrated that he wouldn't join me in the pool, when I had put on an elegant red swimdress, mostly to attract his attention.

Well, now I *was* seeing him.

Mrs. Al-Khoury interrupted my thoughts: "My son could be lying here... And my granddaughter as well, if it hadn't been for Azim. Now, come and see Mansur's wife. Come and see my daughter, the luminous Nour. Come and pray for her with me."

I left Azim, and walked to Nour.

Yes, even now she was beautiful, with her hands joined together, resting upon her breast. The women had finished preparing the two other bodies, now clad in long red robes, and had started washing Nour's.

One of them gave me a sponge filled with warm water. I felt that it was a sign of trust and an honour. Hesitantly, I accepted it and started washing – very gently – the lovely face and neck. It reminded me of Kitty and me, just a couple of days earlier, when on her wedding day I had taken care of her. Although, *she* was alive.

With shaking hands, Mrs. Al-Khoury gently pulled down the shroud. They poured unguents all over her skin; they combed her long brown hair; they spread costly perfume on her body and clothed her with splendid red silk, all gold-embroidered.

Mrs. Al-Khoury could not bring herself to lay the crown of flowers upon the head of her daughter-in-law. I felt so sorry for her grief. Coming nearer, I guided her hands and, together, we tightened the crown around Nour's lovely brow.

As a farewell I touched the feet which had shown our dead friend the way to the Church; to Christ. According to Azim, Nour couldn't have children. But had she not given life, in a different way?

Oh yes, she *had*.

I went to kneel by Abu Ephrem, still praying with his eyes closed, near Azim's godparents, as the women took care of the last body. My friend's body. His godparents were a married couple from the parish. They had died... for the spiritual welcome they had offered him. Did they have any children, or grandchildren?

Some men carried in four coffins of matted reed, perhaps from the Nile. The bodies were lovingly laid inside them. When everything was completed, Abu Ephrem took out of the bag four gilded crucifixes which he inserted under the joined hands of each martyr. They looked like kings and queens.

The men carried them up via a lift to the van outside, while we all followed in the large car. Several police vehicles and motorbikes escorted us to the church. As we arrived, we found that the street by the entrance was crowded with mourners, men in uniforms and journalists (even a CNN crew).

We made our way in, as the coffins were being set in the nave to lie in repose overnight.

Mr Al-Khoury was already there, giving orders for huge quantities of lotus flowers to be set around each coffin. Azim and Nour were laid side by side nearest the altar rail, with the godparents side by side in line with them. Incense was burning, as well as many candles. It was an extremely beautiful and moving sight.

We all knelt with the parishioners and prayed for a long time.

Chapter 40

Mr. Al-Khoury stood up, asking me to follow him.

Perplexed, I walked out of the church with him and his wife.

He said that Talitha was with her father at the hospital. He didn't know whether she should come to the funeral, especially without him, as Mansur was totally unable to attend the ceremony.

If I wanted to accompany them to the hospital, I could have lunch with them on the way and discuss the best plan to follow. I wasn't sure why he would think *me*, a stranger, qualified to advise them on this delicate family decision. But having come back to Cairo to mourn and to support fellow mourners, I accepted his offer of a meal (realising later on that I had eaten almost nothing since the evening before).

We were driven in a huge car to a marina on the Nile, near the business district. The car doors were opened for us and Mr. Al-Khoury escorted his wife and I towards a...

So, *that* was the ship Azim had mentioned! Well, she wasn't the tallest of those moored around, but she *did* look magnificent. And no other carried a helicopter! Yes! A real helicopter!

When we stepped onto the immaculate deck after crossing the bridge boat, I was so taken aback by the opulence that surrounded me that my hands actually shook slightly from sheer nervous excitement. Soon we were seated in a beautiful cedar-panelled dining room. Despite the air-conditioning and the low ceiling, it felt like an English manor as seen on TV series.

After some melon soaked in port, the main course was game: perhaps pheasant, I wasn't sure. Our conversation avoided painful topics.

My host described for me the ancient Phoenician civilisation and people – I think he used the word *thalassocracy* (I only knew of *thalassotherapy*!) – of which he was proud to be the heir: "We Phoenicians ran trade routes all across the Mediterranean two-thousand years before Christ, when Rome was at best a herd of goats grazing around a few huts! We created the first book ever, at our capital Byblos. Carthage was our proud daughter, but alas, jealousy killed her."

There was a silence, as the three of us realised that history had brought us back onto emotionally shaky ground.

Mrs. Al-Khoury rang for the waiter. I'll never forget the pudding! I was a warm upside-down chocolate cake. Its molten centre was topped with caramelized pineapple. They served it with raspberry sauce and fresh island fruit.

As the waiter brought coffee, Mrs. Al-Khoury said that she would go and rest a bit. The poor woman looked exhausted. And no wonder, after what we had just been through!

Mr. Al-Khoury led me to a small lounge and, as we sat down, he thanked me for assisting his wife at the morgue. He asked me if I would mind if he smoked – as though I would object, here in his own palace... that is, on his boat!

He then enquired how well acquainted I had been with Nour and Azim. He didn't know Azim much better than I, he added, but had offered him a job working for his family, shortly before he was shot.

I was struck by Mr. Al-Khoury's ability to shift from very emotional topics to very practical ones – and by the surprisingly modest size of his cigar.

Puffing, he went on: "I know that the C.I.A. spoke to you. That Agent Bloomen is efficient. I like that. They've confirmed that my son's driver leaked the time and place of the ceremony to the assassins. He's now in prison.

"He isn't a religious man. Mansur's assistant had hired him a few days earlier, through an agency. My competitors bribed him. We were just about to get the contract for the new terminal at Dubai Airport. Mansur was in charge.

"I met the Interior Minister last week and all looks clear to me now. Those so-called 'Scimitars of Islam' are petty assassins, messy improvisers, compared to certain firms I know. They surely wanted to get rid of Azim, as he'd hindered their sex-trafficking.

"But their religious fanaticism also offered my competitors the perfect cover to eliminate my son and to have our firm lose the Dubai Airport deal, and other markets."

As if thinking aloud, rather than talking to me, he went on: "However, they didn't know that St. Anthony's icon would save my heir's life. Mansur is my heir. My *heir*, you see? And little Talitha, after him – although in our culture, a *male* heir would be easier. Who knows, if he marries again... But who could replace Nour? If his new wife didn't produce a son, however, they could always adopt one."

I was beginning to feel embarrassed by his confidences. On the other hand, I was willing to listen further, since it clearly helped him after a week spent in agony.

"My son will live. The doctor expects him to walk in a month. That physician was highly recommended. I had him flown in especially from Switzerland last week. And believe me, I will find those killers, *insh'allah*.

"But enough of that. My question to you, Miss Cumberhart, is...

"Would you like more coffee? No?

"Sparkling water? There.

"My question to you is: can you step in for Azim Nebankh?"

Chapter 41

I choked slightly on the sparkling water still in my throat, and must have looked flabbergasted.

He smiled: "Of course, I haven't told you what the position is. Two years ago, Mansur wished to dedicate some of our charitable funding to the building of schools in Egypt, as we had done earlier in Lebanon.

"It was in fact Nour's suggestion; after long discussions with Azim, I assume. Mansur appointed someone to supervise the building and subsequent operating of three schools near the Sudan border, with plans afoot for two more in Sudan and Eritrea. Mansur, Nour and Azim went there together several times last year.

"That project was very dear to my daughter-in-law, and will be even dearer to my son now, as her legacy. Mansur felt that Azim, although a tourist guide by training, had rare qualities of dedication, of reliability, and a sense of initiative which would make him a good coordinator. He also spoke fluent English.

"With Mansur currently out of action, I must urgently take steps for this pet project to go on, and to flourish. I owe it to Nour, whom I cherished."

There was silence.
I could see that this strong man was revisiting very happy memories.
He must have *loved* Nour. Ah, if only I had known her better!
Now gazing at me, as if remembering my presence, he went on: "You wouldn't have to worry about fundraising. As I said, this project is part of our well-endowed Al-Khoury's Charitable Trust.

"Azim loved you. And I saw yesterday that Talitha likes you very much – which speaks loudly in your favour. Also, since as a businessman I can't rely on feelings as my sole evidence, allow me to mention the fact that Agent Bloomen didn't flag up any difficulties when he referred to you. Naturally, I prefer not to hire a jihadi bride.

"I can easily offer your manager compensation for a three-month trial period, after which you would either sign a permanent contract with us, or be taken back by your travel agency.

"Your salary would be twice what you currently earn and you would be based in Cairo, with a secure pied-à-terre in the South, where the three main schools are.

"Don't answer now. Think about it for a day; talk to your family.

"Now, might I suggest that you relax for half an hour under the shade over there, while I catch up with a few business matters, before we go to the hospital?"

There wasn't much I could say.

I thanked him for the offer and walked outside the cool dining room, into the hot afternoon breeze. Leaning against the deck banister, over the murky waters of the Nile, I looked at the high towers of the business district rising above the palm trees, against the backdrop of poorer areas and dusty streets, stretching into the distance.

Over there, was it perhaps the Ezbet El Nakhl and Mokattam slums? Were the sisters on their way there, carrying heavy baskets of food and clean clothes? And I, on the threshold of wealth and prestige...

How many girls my age would jump at such an offer! I was so taken aback that I didn't know what to think. It was all going so fast! I needed time.

Meanwhile, at the parish, the number of mourners must have increased around the four coffins. I wished to go back there in the evening. Azim. Azim; Nour. What do *you* want me to do? And what about my tiny cell at the convent? What about our fig-tree in the little garden?

Breaking my resolution to leave her in *peace* during her honeymoon, I texted Kitty. The network coverage was excellent – not like at the convent.

Then, lying down in a reclining chair, I dozed off happily.

A steward gently woke me up (named Frank, according to his badge, and with no pierced ear), saying that our party would depart shortly. Reaching for the bottle of sparkling water, I suddenly heard a deafening engine noise at the rear.

What was *that*?

Mrs. Al-Khoury arrived behind me and, smiling, led me towards... the helicopter, speaking very loud: "I hope you don't get air sick! My husband insists on flying rather than taking the car. He flies it himself. I think it helps him relax."

Keeping our dresses tightly against our legs and holding our scarves and sunhats, we boarded the aircraft, helped in by the handsome personal assistant. What was his name again? Jonathan, that was it.

Mr. Al-Khoury was already strapped up, headphones and sunglasses on, ready to take off. Within minutes, we were flying high over the Nile and I could see Giza in the distance, with the Pyramids and, to their side, "my" Sphinx.

Azim! Into what sort of adventure have you led me? Tell me that you are with me! Tell me that you are the invisible pilot of my life, by divine appointment. I know that, being so close to Jesus now, even more than before, you will lead me safely. My friend, my beloved friend, what shall I do?

We landed on the roof of the hospital, with Cairo at our feet and the wind in our face. Checking my inbox as we walked to the staircase, I felt like a top businesswoman!

On another continent, Kitty was up and had already texted back: *Dear Clara, I'm fine, thank you, and yes, Mexico is splendid! In brief, regarding your would-be boss: what a surprise offer!*

Raúl looked them up and says: 'Beware when you next lift little Talitha up in your arms, as she is heir to 2.1 billion dollars, her family ranking 849th among the world richest according to Forbes (it was 843rd last month).'

Now Clarry, listen to sister. I say: Don't get excited. Whichever way you decide, take your time. Let's chat soon. I need you.

I had to read the figure three times (making sure no one could see my phone screen).

No, Kitty couldn't have mistyped it. Standing in the lift between Mr. and Mrs. Al-Khoury and the (rather handsome) personal assistant and the (less handsome but steel-blue-eyed) bodyguard, I felt like an alien, a fraud.

What was I *doing* there? Could they not see that I didn't belong to the same world as them?

I know that a person is more than what she owns. But my sole fortune consisted in a second hand ivory Nissan in Vancouver (truly a prehistoric car, with no Bluetooth and not even a USB port); nice dresses and lovely shoes (my Bauer Vapor skates don't count, I suppose); a brand new hyper-light tablet and, when my parents die, an apartment in the same city and another in Seoul, to be shared with Kitty.

And, yes, a pearl necklace!

Which reminded me that I meant to ask Jonathan (the personal assistant) if he could help me sell Dr. Yasir's gift, as she expected.

Chapter 42

Our group arrived at Mansur's door.

I could not repress a bantering smile as I walked between the two guards without having to show my fingerprints this time. Talitha greeted us warmly, although the emotional toll was now showing on her face and in her behaviour.

She clearly was very close to "Jed" and "Jeda," her grandparents, who loved her deeply in return. But I was glad to see that she hadn't forgotten me. After kissing them, she actually jumped into my arms.

As I hugged her, I couldn't help remembering Raúl's warning. It seemed so surreal – almost crude – to make any connection between this half-orphaned six-year-old girl and one of the world's largest fortunes.

I then looked at her wounded father. What an amazing face – and what a tragedy. The shelves around him were covered with greetings cards and flowers. Mansur's eyes were still shut, but he could hear and speak.

His parents were describing to him the preparation for the prayer vigil at the church. They spoke in French, probably to avoid upsetting Talitha – with a Lebanese accent, rather than French-Canadian.

I understood most of it.

They couldn't decide whether it would be better or worse for the little girl to attend the funeral in the morning. Mansur was very moved. It grieved him not to be able to go with her. He was grateful for the live coverage which would allow him to follow the ceremony from his bedroom; but of course, it wasn't the same.

After some silence, he thought it best to ask Talitha what *she* preferred to do and said in English: "Talitha... You know that Mummy will be buried tomorrow at the church. With Azim. Her body was prepared this morning. Jeda says that Mummy is wearing a beautiful red robe, specially ordered by Jed, and a crown of flowers. And..."

He started sobbing. I couldn't recall having seen a grown man cry. I was so sorry for them all. I whispered to Jonathan that I would wait for a while in the corridor, and walked towards the door.

"Please, don't go!"

Talitha followed me, padlocking my waist with her little arms. "I don't want you to go!"

Mansur asked her to whom she was speaking. She was in tears.

Mrs Al-Khoury answered in French: "It's Clara, Mansur. Azim's friend. She helped me this morning... With Nour. She was here yesterday when you first spoke."

Mansur turned his head in our direction and opened his eyes, blinking:

"Ah... Yes, I think I remember. Azim's Canadian friend. We had lunch together in Luxor last week, didn't we? It seems like a previous life..."

"Thank you, Miss... Clara?... for your support. We are all very grateful."

"Now Talitha, you must be strong. For me; for Mummy. For Jed and Jeda. For Azim."

A doctor and a nurse walked into the room. Mansur went on: "You must be a big girl. Do you *want* to go to Mummy's funeral tomorrow? Or would you rather watch it here with me on television? You don't have to decide today. You can wait until tomorrow. Whatever you prefer will be the best thing, my darling.

"Come and kiss me now, because Dr. Schtreuli wants to see me, and you've been with me all day, and need to take some exercise at the Cairo Beach Club, with Jed and Jeda. You like the Beach Club, don't you? And today you may *dive* if you wish."

She let herself be led away by her grandparents after they'd kissed him. I gave Mansur a little head bow and followed with the personal assistant, when his voice stopped us: "And Jonathan: will you please make sure that Miss Clara – sorry, I can't remember your surname – is driven safely back to her hotel? Thank you."

That's how I ended up sitting in the back of the beautiful limousine, with Jonathan, as the Al-Khourys were flying back to the yacht. We didn't speak much during the drive to the convent, but enough for me to find out who he was: a refined Briton – Oxford educated – in his late twenties.

Mostly, though, Jonathan was occupied with the abundant incoming mail on his phone, which I had once again heard beeping persistently in his pocket in the hospital room. With a thrill, I realised that the interests of a two point one billion dollar fortune were transiting through the white hands of this nice Englishman (excellent taste, these cufflinks).

On arrival, he insisted on taking me all the way to the entrance door: "As you heard, Miss Cumberhart" – so *he* knew my surname! – "your safety was entrusted to me." He looked rather serious, but still very nice.

It was past 4 p.m. by then and, although I meant to rest and pray, I thought it polite to ask him if he wished to see the garden, being sure that such a busy man would graciously decline the offer. To my surprise, he accepted. It was too late when I realised what was going to happen. As it did.

After showing him the various bushes, trimmed since last week, and after having explained that the white wall was actually that of the sisters' church, it felt too early to part and too late to remain standing in the sun, so that, trying to prevent a slightly uncomfortable silence looming ahead, I was left with no other option than to suggest we sit in the shade under the fig-tree upon... the bench.

Except that wasn't *any* bench. It was a sacred place, hallowed by the moments of spiritual intimacy that a future martyr had shared with me. Azim... My Azim, not even buried yet! And I, so superficially oblivious, was about to violate this sanctuary and have a stranger sit on it with me!

I was mortified. I had to fight against a surge of hate towards poor Jonathan, as he chose the very place where Azim had sat. For a moment, I truly saw him as a desecrator.

He must have sensed that something was wrong since, after complimenting me on the inspiring quiet of the garden amid noisy Cairo, he seized the pretext of a further beep from his phone to rise and take leave. We shook hands. As I was opening the convent door, he read aloud on his phone that Mr Al-Khoury meant to send me a car, in case I wished to come and pray at the vigil later that evening.

I felt a bit awkward, as I had already spent a little more time than I thought befitting with their family. After all, I was my own woman and had come chiefly to mourn my friend Azim. I asked Jonathan to thank Mr. Al-Khoury on my behalf, but to tell that I planned to go separately, probably with some of the sisters.

He bid me farewell and left.

I sighed with contentment on shutting the thick door behind me!

Chapter 43

Alone with God, at last!

I put the set of keys back in my bag, only to feel the smoothness of a velvet pouch, much to my annoyance, as it contained the pearl necklace I'd meant to show Jonathan and hoped to sell with his help. *You silly girl!* I thought. *Instead of wasting time in the garden talking idly, could you not remember something far more important?*

I knelt in the chapel before the altar, only for a short while, thanking God for a momentous day, starting with my first confession and reception of Holy Communion in years. For some reason smiling, I went up to my room and laid down for a well-earned siesta.

But I found it difficult to fall asleep. It wasn't the heat. My arms crossed behind my neck, I looked at the ceiling, through the slow ballet of the hanging fan. The events of the past few days had unfolded so unexpectedly... They'd followed each other so quickly.

I was a girl of twenty-four on a business trip across Egypt. My aim was to identify the best options for my travel agency to launch its first Egyptian package. I had applied myself seriously to the task in hand. I had taken notes and many pictures.

I had emailed my boss daily and sent suggestions. I had been introduced to several subcontractors, hotel managers and entertainers. I had spent half the time with a regular tourist group, so as to observe efficient supervision in an Egyptian context.

It so happened that the guide assigned to the group was friendly.
And handsome.
And funny.
And in fact, very attractive.
But brotherly. *Too* brotherly?

Let me be frank: after two days, I simply couldn't get him out of my mind. Thinking about him had become my main business – when I wasn't in his presence – while my professional endeavour had fallen into the background.

Had I allowed things to happen that way? Had I *consented*?

I didn't know. I wanted to be loved. And my beloved sister was getting married, and obviously would need me less, and would have less time for me. And when would *I* find a husband? I wanted to be hugged by Azim, and he would not!

But he had given me so much more. He had enriched me deeply with his brotherly trust and tenderness. And I had understood so little of it. Until it was too late.

It was all in retrospect. I had unwrapped a pile of precious treasures, long after the one who had given them could be thanked. I was like a child on Christmas morning, opening her parcels as the bell tolls for Santa Claus, fallen from the chimney!

No; not quite. Because Santa doesn't *exist* (oops, sorry kids) – but Azim was real and, even now, he could hear me. He's alive in God (I was sure of that, back then).

I had also suffered a lot. But through my ordeal, I had learned much about the true meaning of love. I was still exhausted; and I felt rejuvenated. The last forty-eight hours had brought my initiation to a climax.

I would recapitulate.

On the steps of the church, I had wept by the chalk outline of my dead brother.

I had visited his widowed friend and mourning family in hospital.

By the bench, I had explored in my memory the revelation of fecund chastity.

Last night, I had been enlightened by Sister's explanations, while chatting in this little cell.

In the morning, God had cleansed me through His mercy in Confession.

God had fed me with His Sacred Body and Blood in Holy Communion.

Down at the morgue, I had seen martyred chests and limbs... I had read scars on skins... as words in a love letter.

I had followed my friends' coffins to the church and publicly venerated their remains at the very place where they had borne witness to their faith with their blood.

In a mysterious shift, emerging from the land of shadows, I had entered the world of the ultra-rich, and been invited to remain among them. But I knew where the true Light shone forth. And I had witnessed how suffering could hit the wealthy, just as much as the poor.

Finally, there I was, happily lying on my back, aware of my recently acquired depth, and asking God for light to find and do His Will.

Jesus! Mary! How happy you make me!

Chapter 44

A large crowd attended the prayer vigil, spent mostly in silence.

The four bodies lay symmetrically in their reed coffins, robed in red satin and surrounded with a profusion of lotus flowers, like immaculate and fragrant halos. The flickering lights of many candles projected playful shadows on the dead faces and bodies, conveying a vague illusion of life.

As I was kneeling at equal distance from Azim and Nour, I felt that their sacrifice had given me life. Only then did the simultaneity strike me, between my unexpected revelation in the Orly chapel and their death at the church.

It had happened *just* at the same time.

Of course, I was totally unaware of the tragedy at that moment. I had only learned about it in the plane, over the Atlantic. This deepened my faith in the reality of what I had perceived in the underground chapel.

Had my mystical experience at the airport occurred *after* I'd heard of Azim's and Nour's tragic deaths, I could have ascribed it to the emotional shock. But that wasn't the case.

I was, at the time, I remembered clearly, extremely far from any spiritual preoccupations.

From the moment I had left Cairo, after Azim had hugged me by surprise, I was simply cherishing that last-minute fulfilment of my expectation; but also moaning in frustration that he should have expressed his feelings so late, when I was flying back to a faraway continent, with nearly no hope, realistically, of further developing our relationship.

The conflict between thrill and bitterness had made my heart feel busy, but superficially. Deeper inside me, my soul wasn't reached yet. I wasn't spiritually engaged.

That had come as a total surprise, greater than Azim's hug *in extremis*. But how could I deny Azim's and Nour's sacrifice any influence upon my sudden change of soul?

How could such a deep restoration of my relationship with God (Lord, long may it continue!) have happened *out of the blue*, when just at the same time, these two souls deeply in love with God were giving up their lives?

How could I not believe that they had embraced, in their last prayer sent to God from this earth, even the spiritual welfare of the sorry *bimbo* that I was?

Both coffins lay side by side before me on this Wednesday night, exactly ten days after the murder. I felt that I could visualise the bonds of love, of which my presence there and then was an unexpected fruit, like a grape on a vine in winter. Yes, it looked like a vine, whose frail and torn branches nonetheless stretched far across time and space.

Nour had led Azim to God, whom he had discovered in the Holy Eucharist, at the sisters' chapel.

Abu Ephrem had catechised Azim for two years, and had taken care of him after his dreadful flogging.

Ultimately, Nour had accompanied Azim to Holy Baptism.

Here in Cairo, at the very moment when he was formally becoming a Christian, Azim had put his life at risk out of love for the forty-eight Muslim girls at Osly Ford in Sudan, whom he couldn't protect in any other way.

In France, from Orly Airport, Nepomucen had asked his brother for help in Khartoum.

With diplomatic courage, the Papal Nuncio had begged assistance from the MoD in London.

Back in Sudan, the SAS had risked their own lives.

The school bus driver had lost his life in Osly.

An hour later, the Scimitars had retaliated in Cairo, as Azim anticipated.

Out of love for him in such an important step as Holy Baptism, Mansur, Nour and Talitha had come to the church, despite Azim's prudent decision.

When the shooting had started, Azim had given up his life to save Talitha.

Mansur converted at the last minute – as he believed it to be – prompted by the love for his wife and by the sacrifice of his friend.

He was saved through the token of spiritual affection that he was carrying for Azim, St. Anthony's icon.

Abu Ephrem had taken a risk, baptising the two dying men so soon after the last bullets had flown.

And at the same moment, thousands of miles away, as I was *dozing* in the Orly Airport underground chapel, irreverently using it as a waiting lounge – grace had touched me!

Grace had touched me...

God had gently knocked on my soul, asking permission to be let in again.

And, overwhelmed by such generosity, I had opened my soul wide to His mercy.

Where was it going to end? Had I spread love further? Knowingly or not? I wasn't sure. It was still so early.

I had started making peace in my heart with Kitty and Raúl.

I had spoken again with Mum and Dad – that was an achievement.

I had tried to show compassion to Mansur's family and to the parishioners.

Azim had meant the saving of the forty-eight girls to be our joint achievement. Well, my part in this heroic act had been merely instrumental: I had unknowingly transmitted Azim's cryptic email address with the place and time of the attack.

Still, I found that accepting Azim's plan, even *after* it had been fulfilled, was my calling to greater love.

It was an invitation I felt free either to turn down in anger and frustration, or to accept with supernatural generosity. I could bitterly mourn my lost flirt, or offer up my loss in a sisterly way.

By God's grace, and through the merits of Azim and Nour's sacrifice, I found myself capable of the latter, somewhat to my surprise.

I meant to assist those poor girls in need, as soon as the pearls from Dr. Yasir could be sold.

Now, *she* was another person who had been very kind. I had emailed my gratitude for her gift before flying back to Cairo. But I needed to contact her and thank her properly. Who knew, she might even have good advice about this decision I had to make?

So, there I was, incorporated into a network of love; the Lord's mysterious *vine*. *Upstream* from me, so to speak, I was indebted to many who had risked or spent much for divine love to reach and heal me. *Downstream*, I felt called to let love flow freely through every faculty of my body and soul, if it pleased God to use my weakness to console or warm anyone up.

Azim. Nour. Azim and Nour. Praise to you my beloved ones: side by side in your reed coffins, like baskets for an adult Moses and his bride, floating down the Nile, almost hand in hand upon waves of lotus flowers!

I see you now, saintly lovers. I see you stand ten days ago on the steps outside. I know the love that brought you there. I feel the pulse of your godly embrace as you risk your lives and give all that you are.

I sense the bullets entering your flesh, whence life had so far never sprung: O virgin Azim, O barren Nour! But through the mercy of the Almighty, the lead of hate piercing your skins has made your souls fertile and... here I am!

On my knees before you this evening, I know that you've given me life; that is, God through you. With all my heart, as the child of your shed blood, I thank you.

For Mansur also, baptised in the wake of your deaths, I thank you. Please, make us faithful. Please, support us and obtain for us light and courage to do God's will.

Chapter 45

I realised that it was past midnight on my watch.
 I didn't mean to remain for so long in thanksgiving and intercession upon the hard (but cool) tiles.
 I genuflected towards the tabernacle and left, thinking of walking home to enjoy some exercise and further time to think. But the late hour and the remoteness of the suburb made a stroll unadvisable.

 As I looked in vain for a taxi, I saw someone wave at me from a car, parked down the steps. He walked up to me. *Mr. Jonathan*? There. After midnight. Hum, personal assistants don't seem to be kept very busy around here!
 Of course, I accepted his lift back.
 Instead of the Mercedes with leather seats, tinted glass and a chauffeur, the car was a rather battered Nissan: actually, the very *same* model as mine in Vancouver, (apart from the dark colour of this one)! Apologetically, he explained that it was his private vehicle while in town. The cufflinks were gone from his wrists, I noticed, as his hands hold the wheel. Plain buttoned cuffs: oh dear, how *shocking*!
 I smiled at myself, for there was surely nothing strange about a man changing shirts within just eight hours in mid-June in Cairo.
 Furthermore, the Al-Khoury empire not being quite the CIA, he couldn't have accessed such "sensitive" data as the brand of *my* car, left in an unknown cark park in Vancouver! His humble Nissan downgrade was a mere coincidence, nothing else. I was just happy to see him, and dismissed the thought that he had intentionally chosen a "low-key approach" to put me more at ease...
 I was (mildly) hungry, yes – how thoughtful of him to ask – and wouldn't mind stopping on the way in that quiet and stylish bar-restaurant, over there by the Nile. Jonathan was apparently well known in that place and they agreed to serve us despite the very late hour.
 I bet they knew *whom* he worked for!
 We sat down like friends, enjoying lark pâté and marvellous skillet-roasted chicken thighs with olives and rosemary – and an amazing bottle of Chardonnay! I slyly waited a few minutes before inviting him to drop the "Miss" and simply call me Clara, since I enjoyed his formal style, straight out of a British period film.
 But I was wrong about him. He had lived in England for years, but is Danish! He generously agreed to take care of my pearls and to find a buyer. He found it kind of me to want to help those unknown girls in Sudan. I was relieved when I laid the velvet pouch in his palm.
 My next guess proved wrong as well, as Musicology is what he read at

Oxford, not Management (although he had done so later on in London, on a crash course).

His first passion was choreography: one of his amateur ballets, *Ganymede*, had even been performed in his country. I was impressed, since the peak of my career as a teenage ballerina had been to dance in *Swan Lake* among another twenty schoolgirls, at the end-of-year school show (I wouldn't tell him *that*).

No, I forget: the year after, I had also danced in *Cinderella* – but that was figure skating. I loved to spring up in the air like a little angel, or a little bird, and move my limbs with grace. I thought I looked very pretty in my tutu! And – yes – I would *love* another glass of Chardonnay, thank you.

At Oxford, Jonathan met Mansur who was doing a postgraduate at the Saïd Business School, the business department of the University – 'near the railway station' (not that it helped me much to visualise the place).

He added that Mansur was a great polo player, but also loved classical music, which his firm sponsored generously. At the time, Jonathan was completing his PhD on Thomas Tallis (I had never heard of that apparently famous English composer – pre-*Beatles*, categorically).

I asked him how he had ended up working for the Al-Khoury's empire. Helping himself to wine again (*I* had had enough, thanks), he smiled, as if wondering whether he should share the story with me.

After a brief silence, he confessed: "This is somewhat confidential, Clara. But I trust you, and it may help you to know more about how things work around here.

"*Why* do you think Mansur's father approved of my becoming his personal assistant, ignoring applicants better qualified and more experienced than I? Because I got into the old man's good graces.

"You want to know *how*? I couldn't impress him with money, for sure; and he doesn't care much for music, between ourselves. But I soon found out his weak spot – even great men have one. His is *lost ethnic pride* (one day you may thank me for the tip, as it's worth a lot if you're clever).

"As a Lebanese, he's infatuated with ancient *Phoenicia*, that joke! So, my master stroke took place in London. I had invited Mansur and his parents to Covent Garden for a performance of *Dido and Aeneas*."

To my embarrassment, I had no idea who *Dido* and *Aeneas* were: obviously some talented musicians. I resolved to look them up the following day, in case Jonathan asked me in the future.

He went on: "As we were having a drink afterwards, I suggested that *Purcell's genius made the loss of the Phoenician civilisation feel all the more tragic*. I knew this would strike a chord with Jed (Mr Al-Khoury's pet name). He declared that 'Purcell was definitely better than Mozart' (as if they compared).

"I went further, stating that his ancestors' civilisation deserved greater recognition. Modern technology and scholarship should secure it. It was just a matter of hiring the right people, as they had done in France with that now world-renowned theme park on Gallic culture.

"I saw from Jed's look that he was hooked.

"'Of course,' I concluded, 'two millennia later, *my* Viking forbears tried to imitate the Phoenicians of old, running trade routes all across the Northern Sea, the Mediterranean and even the Atlantic. But they were mere marauders in comparison with the ancient and illustrious Punics. What was Viking Dublin compared with Carthage, or even with Marseille!'

"With friendly condescension, Jed insisted on the *nearly* equivalent greatness of the Vikings, 'whose Valkyries and all that had inspired Wagner, hadn't they?'

"The following week, my contract was signed."

Chapter 46

Jonathan's quick and subtle brains impressed me.

Back home, I knew that Emma and Sally would be thrilled when I told them all about him! I was flattered by his confidence, and glad to have made such an intelligent friend (I could call him a *friend*, couldn't I?).

Only jealous people, I told myself, might take offence at his innocent scheme.

By then warming to each other, we shared some further anecdotes about our respective lives. In fact, he was the one doing most of the talking, and about Mansur rather than about himself.

He told me how Mansur had met his wife.

One day at Oxford, Jonathan and Mansur attended a performance of *Hope In None Other* (I liked the title, even though I didn't know the music), one of Tallis' "most complex polyphonic compositions," said Jonathan.

It was performed by a visiting group from America selected by Jonathan – at the Oratory Church "on Woodstock Road" ("pretty decent worship there, musically speaking," he explained).

During the reception at the end, the singers were introduced to Mansur, since he was the main sponsor of the event.

Nour was one of them – forty in total.

Jonathan said that he'd never believed in love at first sight, until that evening.

It had been mutual and definitive.

Five months later, they were married.

We remained silent for a while. The beautiful couple was taking life again in my memory. Mansur and Nour. And little Talitha, who had grabbed my hand on our first encounter in Luxor.

I was surprised and pleased to hear that Jonathan's connection with them as a friend had preceded his professional involvement. He could be an even stronger support to Mansur and his family in the current circumstances.

He laid his phone on the table before me. I realised that I hadn't heard it beep once that evening! I thought that he meant to get back to work – or to bed. But instead, he displayed on the screen a picture of Mansur, Nour and Talitha. What an amazing-looking family they were! And now...

Now...

He said that he had a picture from their first encounter at the concert in Oxford. In fact, the screen displayed a close-up of Nour – looking so radiant in her black dress – singing on stage among the thirty-nine others.

So, Jonathan had noticed her even *before* she was introduced to Mansur?

The phone vibrated in his open palm. But his *hand* was shaking, not the device.

Was someone sending a signal – from very far away? When hearing Jonathan speak of love at first sight just now, I had assumed that he only meant love between *Mansur* and Nour... And perhaps that was indeed the case.

Perhaps.

I laid my hand upon the phone and his palm, and looked at him with affection, saying: "Jonathan, in the title of that piece of music you mentioned, *who* is the person outside of whom no hope is found?"

He remained silent, not looking at me; not withdrawing his hand either, its mild tremor subdued. We kept that posture for a while, moving neither a finger nor an eyelash.

His hand was now still.

Each of us knew that it was a very precious and important moment; one of those which shine in a man or a woman's memory even after the loss of youth and health.

Then he looked at me in the eyes, smiling, and answered: "God."

Was he a believer? If not, I so much wanted him to convert! But he'd expressed no interest in the Christian faith. I wondered how I could encourage him.

He was drinking his Chardonnay in silence, gazing at me.

After a while, he was the one who brought up the topic, as if reading my mind: "You know, Clara, if there is one thing that would attract me to the Church – apart from sacred music of course – it would be Confession.

"I can't imagine anything greater than knowing for *certain* that one's sins are forgiven. As many times as one needs. As many times... It's on my mind *a lot*. I could surprise you.

"If you want to know what I think – and I *don't* care if it sounds foolish – tonight, I see that *you* are just the woman I would want to confess to, if I ever needed. Because..."

As he spoke, I was praying for him to be relieved of whatever burden he carried. He stopped for a few seconds and asked: "Please, don't look at me like that. Don't look into my soul. You're too... pure."

He helped himself to another glass of wine, before adding: "I would confess to you because you... *you* wouldn't condemn me. Would you?"

"Jonathan," I answered, "of course I wouldn't condemn you. No more than God would condemn any of us, if we're sorry for what we've done wrong."

He blinked, then smiled dismissively. "Thank you. Not that I *do* need Confession, surely."

I was touched by his confidence, but felt that it was time to wish the Chardonnay bottle *good night*!

Jonathan drove me home in his Nissan and I bolted the convent door behind me, not knowing exactly why I was laughing.

Chapter 47

Hundreds attended the funeral in the morning, with portable air-conditioners making the heat more bearable.

The local bishop officiated. I was moved by the sight of that man, realising that he was a direct successor of the Apostles appointed by Christ Himself, two thousand years ago.

Civil authorities were represented, including some members of the Egyptian government and even the American Ambassador. Although Nour had been born in the Middle-East, she was a U.S. citizen; and her widowed husband, as well as her father-in-law, carried considerable weight also in America.

As it happened, little Talitha had come. But not alone.

To my astonishment, Mansur was with her.

I hadn't seen them at first. Mrs. Al-Khoury led me out of the nave through a door into the adjacent presbytery. On the first floor was a room with a window opening into the church. That's where her dear son had been carried up, on a stretcher.

The room now looked more like an intensive care unit, with a real hospital bed, bottles of oxygen, a drip and monitors. There was also an air-conditioner.

Dr. Schtreuli and the nurse were standing at the back, looking rather concerned, if not upset. It became clear to me that this move was against their wishes and advice.

Talitha hugged me as I walked in. She looked so cute in her long blue dress. Like most women downstairs, she was wearing a chapel veil. (I was grateful to the sisters for having lent me one.)

Mansur looked at the two of us with an expression of mingled gratitude and pain. I guessed why, and hoped to make myself as discreet as possible. Actually, I intended to greet him and walk back down into the nave, where his father was standing with the V.I.P.s.

I came to stand by his bed, assuring him of all my sympathy, and of my prayer for him and all those he loved.

He answered: "Miss Cumberhart, your presence here is a *great* comfort to me and my family, since you had met my dear wife and were close to my treasured friend Azim. Thank you."

I kissed Talitha and walked back to the nave downstairs.

During Mass, I heard for the first time *Hope in None Other*, Thomas Tallis' polyphonic piece. It sounded even better in Latin: *Spem in alium*.

That was Mansur's *only* requirement for the whole ceremony. His father had arranged for the forty singers to be flown from Europe and a few from America! Several of them knew Nour from when she used to sing, I was told.

Later on in my life, I learned at length about that amazing piece of Renaissance music, a forty-voice motet for eight five-part choirs.

Very soon after the beginning, a high-pitched note arose, which a soprano kept for a long time, while other voices gradually joined in at different pitches.

Their lines would meet with the soprano's and somehow cover it.

Then one would hear the soprano again; and lose it again.

It was like a lantern carried through vast orchards at dawn, and intermittently glimpsed at, from a distance, across flowery trees.

I pictured myself walking across downtown Vancouver, or in Manhattan, each block turned into a thousand giant cherry trees in bloom, still separated by wide avenues through which the lantern could be seen now and then.

What the music sounded like was the opposite of a competition or a struggle.

There was no fear or violence.

Rather, the voices met, as if helping and even embracing each other.

Sometimes, one or two voices were given clear prominence; while at other moments, the full blast of various choirs would take over, conveying a strong impression of power and confident vitality.

It sounded like choreography for the ear, or architecture for the soul.

Sitting in my pew in that Cairo church, with the four open coffins in front of me, I tried to identify *what* that very intricate but harmonious pattern reminded me of.

It felt familiar, and yet mysterious.

Was it a place I had visited? Was it an event I had attended? Or was it a person I had met?

I couldn't recall...

Until all of a sudden, the light flashed. I *knew*! It was...

Chapter 48

It was the *network* – the network of love. The *vine*.
It was that complex and living structure, or, more precisely, that spiritual organism where each voice – each person – was cherished for his or her individuality and yet, was fulfilled through free interaction with other people; often sacrificially, as I had experienced.
It was the network; called by experts *The Church*. What Tallis was to his ten-minute composition, God was to his network, or "love-net."

But God being more potent and loving than the best human composer, He had endowed each voice with *freedom*, so that none ever felt *forced* to sing this or that note. On the contrary, the more faithfully they followed the score, the freer they sung, the more tuned in they were, and the more harmonious the general impression.
Clouds of incense were rising at the altar and by the coffins as the music went on.
The soprano was heard again.
It sounded so full of momentum, and yet so humble. It was like a butterfly *caressing* my ear-drums, and soon reaching my heart. Or rather, it felt as if the membrane inside my ears *was* literally my heart!
How dearly my soul wished to follow *that* particular voice in its mysterious dance; until it was welcomed with a fiery finale as in a family of princes and angels...
Nour had sung *that* voice. That evening in Oxford, *she* was the leading soprano.
I started to understand better why *a man* could be transfixed by it. Especially when the man was a music expert and heard in advance in his mind every note sung by the forty voices, like a chess champion anticipating the best combination of the thirty-two pieces across the black and white squares.
And even more so, when the voice had the face and demeanour of *Nour*...
My eyes rested upon her, lying peacefully in her open reed coffin. Filled with respect, I kissed in spirit her comely brow crowned with immaculate roses, recalling under the red robe the tortured skin I had washed and perfumed only a day earlier.
Dear Nour, I hear in my heart the gracious voice of your soul, leading us all indeed, through a harmony reaching deeper and further than that which our ears and minds can presently detect.
Help us, dear friend!
Help us trust in the beloved Composer.
Help us avoid the false notes of despair and selfishness, of impurity and

deceit.
Lead us through the woods, to the light of true love...

I read again in my order of service the lyrics (a quote from the Holy Bible) translated from the Latin:

*Hope in none other –
have I had ever,
but in Thou Saviour,
O God of Israel,
Who can show anger
both and graciousness;
Who absolve the sins
of suffering man.
Lord God, Creator
of Heaven and Earth,
be mindful of our lowliness.*

Praying that Mansur and Talitha (and Jonathan) would be comforted by that saving *hope*, I walked to the bishop to receive Holy Communion: My Lord and my God!

After the ceremony, Nour's body was temporarily kept in the crypt. The Al-Khourys were not certain where they wanted her to be buried.

She seemed to have little family on her side. Her cousin, Vardah Wattles (whoa! the famous interior designer herself...), was apparently present, but I didn't see her. I only met Nour's parents from America. She was an only child, and so talented. What is grief? How to share it? I felt inadequate, but said I would pray for them and her.

Azim's body was kept next to hers, for the same reasons. His family had left him under the responsibility of the parish, and Mansur needed more time to think where he would like him buried. He considered the decision to be his.

I managed to slip from the church unnoticed, in case Mr. Al-Khoury asked me if I accepted his offer of a job.

I knew that he had many *more* important things to think about on such a day. But he had also shared with me the emotional significance of the school project for his son, in memory of Nour and Azim.

Consequently, he was likely to wish to hear from me, before I disappeared and possibly flew back to Canada, as should be my next step, whatever I chose.

I also preferred to avoid meeting Jonathan again *alone*; and Talitha.

I felt my love for them increase, but I didn't trust my heart. I had learned not to be led by my emotions. I would write to them all. They had been so welcoming and generous.

I accepted a lift from the sisters and, with a surprisingly deep sensation of liberation, I sat on my chair in my tiny cell, looking at my crucifix on the white wall.

Chapter 49

Departure Hall – this way.
How strange it was, the next morning, to find myself again walking to Security at Cairo Airport, just twelve days after the fatal date.

I felt as if I had lived ten lives since. Being early, I went to the same coffee shop, ordering my usual (large latte and white chocolate cookie).

I relished the sensation of revisiting the sequence of events that had unfolded from that moment onwards, but now with full knowledge of their succession and consequences. I wasn't to be taken by surprise, this time.

I could *see* things come, and ponder.

I was carrying only my light backpack and my sunhat.

Something deep in my soul shyly wished to do again *exactly* the same gestures as last time, as if to resuscitate past memories. I aspired to follow an intimate protocol.

But I also felt in my conscience that it could be a risk, a temptation. The past, after all, is meant to help us serve God better in the present and the future. It shouldn't be a luxury to indulge in, or a sanctuary.

I couldn't help glance at the CCTVs. How many lovers, how many spies, how many innocents and terrorists in this vast departure hall were being filmed unnoticed? My heart was beating fast as I approached the metal detector.

I felt ridiculous, putting in my mouth my boarding card as though it would make a prince charming appear, just like a dozen days earlier! – as if I were Aladdin rubbing his lamp to summon his genie!

Fairy tales may reveal deeper truths than we think. Or are certain gestures endowed with magical powers – I mean, for real? As a child of God, I don't believe in magic – but in Providence, yes.

So, here he was, materialising, as if out of a cloud. A genie with *cufflinks*! Jonathan caught my backpack as I was walking towards the detector. I came back, slightly annoyed – and strangely pleased.

I wanted no hugging.
I wanted no bloodstain.
I wanted no murder and no secret agents.
I wanted no repetition.
And yet, this nice man seemed to care for me.
I was a tourism executive from Canada, on her way home. End of story.
I was touched that Jonathan had come all the way to see me, though.
He apologised for his unexpected arrival, and said that he would not delay me.

He handed me an envelope, asking me to open it. It contained a 12,141.97 Canadian dollar bank draft! Jonathan said that he'd found a buyer who had paid slightly above market rate for my pearls. I thanked him warmly for his trouble. I was rich!

There was a brief silence – while the queue behind me started overtaking us...

He looked grave and asked if he could request my prayers. That didn't sound like him.

He confided: "Mansur is paraplegic.

"Dr. Schtreuli issued this morning a formal diagnosis of spinal cord injury. He says that the imprudence of yesterday – attending the funeral – is unlikely to have worsened his condition.

"It was caused by the fall on his back against the edge of the concrete steps at the church, during the attack. The bullet made the injury worse and the paramedics didn't handle him properly when moving him into the ambulance, which increased the damage.

"He had an operation last week, which they hoped had worked. But one couldn't be sure, as long as Mansur was unconscious. Dr. Schtreuli affirms that by now, he should be capable of moving his legs. However, the contrary is true: he doesn't even feel his toes, or knees, or thighs.

"In fact, he's completely paralysed from the waist down. His spinal cord is seventy percent severed, with low expectations of recovery, even with transplant. His condition will be definitively confirmed in five weeks."

I was horrified. I didn't know what to say. But *why* was my first reaction so brutally insensitive, as I asked without thinking: "And, does that mean that he can't have children either, in the future?"

Jonathan kept silent, thinking. I wished now I could brush off my stupid question – but it would have sounded even worse.

Then he whispered: "Strictly between us: not outside a fertility lab."

His phone was beeping again. He added: "Truly, I wish you *could* stay. It would help us. It would help *me*."

I looked at Jonathan and deeply felt as if I should stay, as he hoped. In the past few days, affection towards him had been rising in my heart. I wasn't sure I wanted to know if my love for this charming companion was that of a sister, of a friend or of a...

I *had* to go. I *wanted* to go. I thanked him for sharing the sad news – and for selling my pearls: "Please assure Mr. Al-Khoury that I will pray for him, whatever that means to him. And also for you, if you wish."

Holding my hand, he was about to answer. I prayed he would speak his heart. But he remained silent and let me go, watching me walk through Security. From a distance he waved at me, adding: "Mansur just texted me: *Sell my horses*."

And so we parted.

That was a *poor* metal detector. For the second time in twelve days, I had walked through it with thick needles piercing my heart, and it hadn't beeped.

Sitting in the lounge by my departure gate, I felt badly the need to think about something else. Or someone else. I wouldn't buy another lovely sunhat, like I had done last time. I felt empty.

What about checking my emails? Kitty had sent me pictures from Mexico. Just the cheer-up I needed! Oh, she was standing! And so lovely with her sombrero on! Now, what had she done with my Egyptian hat?

Anyhow – and so tanned... and, yes, that bump was *definitely* bigger. Less than six months to go! I emailed her that I was on my way back to Vancouver (eighteen hours, but via London, not Paris!) and would call her the day after.

My boss had also emailed me. How kind; he was asking about the funeral, of which he'd watched a bit on CNN. He wrote that he'd spotted me! He also referred to the Al-Khoury family, pointing to the fact that, like us, they were Canadian citizens. And had I met them at all, by any chance?

I had, yes; by chance...

Chapter 50

Another message was from Dr. Yasir.
She thanked me for my email and wished me a fruitful visit to Egypt. Well, it was over. I emailed back that her pearls had been sold for a good price, and asked if she knew how I could help some poor girls in Sudan or elsewhere.

I didn't tell her yet about Mr. Al-Khoury's offer to work for him in his charitable school project, as I preferred to use the money from the pearls without any input from his family. It was *my* story after all, and Azim's.

Meanwhile, I thought that I would look her up on the Internet. I discovered with awe that she was the UN Commissioner for Reproductive Health in Asia, the Middle-East and Africa:

Nasreen M. Yasir, Ph.D, earned her medical degree in obstetrics and gynaecology from Aga Khan University Medical College in Karachi.

She also completed a doctoral degree in Sociology at Yale University in the U.S.A.

After working as a medical doctor in Pakistan and America, Dr. Yasir joined the Reproductive Health Department of the United Nations where she has served in various capacities. At the last General Assembly in Geneva, Dr. Yazir stressed the fact that:

'It has been the constant effort of this Department to support surgically safe termination of unwanted pregnancy (TUP) and female genital mutilation (FGM).

'Though I have performed both in my career as a doctor, I believe that FGM in particular should never be coerced, whatever the cultural and religious motivations alleged.

'Later, as UN Commissioner, I saw many women and girls who underwent FGM sometimes bleed to death, or die of infection. Most are traumatised. Those who survive can suffer adverse health effects during marriage and pregnancy.

'Such risks to the patient made me become unsupportive of FGM in most circumstances.'

There was a nice picture of her (wearing no pearls) somewhere in Africa. The article quoted further: "*I am well aware of the positive sociological marker procured by FGM in some cultures. In the last five decades, TUP played a similar role for many culturally oppressed Western women. Admittedly, no woman should be deprived of either, if it is her choice.*

'I only call for the safe and acquiesced administering of FGM. In relation to FGM, under-developed countries are today in the same situation as Western countries were fifty years ago in relation to TUP.

'Safe and easy solutions were found in one case; they must be promoted in

the other as well.

'FGM normally occurs before first sexual intercourse; TUP, obviously after. However, whereas TUP does not affect irreversibly the sexual integrity of a woman, FGM does.

'That difference should not be underestimated.

'Every woman counts, rich or poor. But the poor are more vulnerable.'"

I was impressed.

Only, I wasn't sure why she called *TUP* – that meant *abortion*, right? – a "positive sociological marker." I would look online what the Church had to say about it.

In fact, at *what* stage of pregnancy does the child become a human person – and can we humans ever *not* be persons?

Dr. Yasir would know the answers, of course.

It felt strange to think that I had sat in the plane next to an important UN executive, whose voice spoke strongly in defence of powerless girls and women. And I knew how real the violence inflicted was. My friend Azim had died partly to save forty-eight girls from it.

How selfish and superficial my ordinary interests seemed in contrast! I didn't even mean fashion and make-up, but simply my job. *Tourism*... It sounded almost obscene, when so many women suffered in their flesh. Sure, but what could *I* do about it?

I took from my bag the brochure given me by Mother Superior, at the end of our last talk the evening before. Those sisters were so dedicated. They cared for the poor, the suffering.

But they did it the Christian way: all in the name of Christ, Whom they sought to serve in the person of His members in need.

Also, their Eucharistic devotion deeply attracted me. How much I would love to spend two hours every day in front of the monstrance, kneeling at the feet of my beloved Jesus!

And to pray for our Muslim brothers and sisters to find God made Man, Jesus Christ – Love incarnate.

On the other hand, might not Mr. Al-Khoury's offer be from my Lord?

Could it be my *calling*? I would have wonderful friends in Cairo: Mansour, Jonathan and, of course, Abu Ephrem.

Could I not do a lot for poor girls in Egypt, Sudan and elsewhere if I agreed to coordinate this charitable programme? I was thrilled by the challenge, and concerned about my lack of experience.

I would pray about it, and speak with Kitty, and perhaps with Dr. Yasir as well.

Our flight was boarding.

I stood up and produced my boarding card. It bore no scribbled email addresses.

PART TWO

Chapter 51

Happy feast, dear Saint Joseph!
I didn't know that May the first was a bank holiday also in Egypt. Today, everything is quiet (or nearly). This is my first opportunity to make a pause and just to think for a while.

I'm kneeling in my convent cell in Cairo, before a picture of St. Joseph walking near the pyramids, with Mary holding the Child Jesus, sitting on a donkey (I *love* its long ears and sweet eyes!).

I speak further to St. Joseph, Protector of the Holy Family: *So, you remember what I asked you five months ago, don't you, when I signed up for my new job here? To help me start a family...*

Well, it's taking longer than expected. I've seen many, many children, but what about a dad*? Saint Joseph, you know my secret inclination. But it seems so out of reach... does it not?*

Looking back, I realise that it's been eleven months since I left Egypt after the funeral of my friends. I spent half a year in Vancouver before accepting Mr. Al-Khoury's offer. Generously, it was still standing. I don't regret the delay. I preferred to wait until Kitty's child was born.

Little Javier is so cute: my baby nephew! Seeing Raúl and Kitty with their first child was very moving. As I looked at the little creature, I thanked God Who had been so generous. I watched my dear sister feed her baby and marvelled at the simple beauty of life.

Unexpectedly, both Mum and Dad travelled to Houston for the Baptism. Please God, a new chapter will begin, for all of us, now that they are grandparents – and I a godmother...

I moved to Egypt after that wonderful event, five months ago. Since then, I've visited *six* Middle-Eastern countries where the Al-Khoury charitable schools are located. I'm blessed with friendly colleagues and a very stimulating framework. Time literally flew since then.

Jonathan and I meet at least once a week, and not only for work. We also discuss music, and go to the ballet. I had no idea there was such a thing as the *Cairo Opera Ballet Company*! I haven't told him that I used to dance at school (he would laugh at me).

He wants me to learn classical singing. Azim once said that I sing well. Currently, we're working on *Douce Dame Jolie*, a love song by William of Machault (that's the name he mentioned, I think). Medieval French is tricky, but as an incentive, he sent me a video of Nour performing it. *She* really could sing. (I hope *Mansur* will never hear me, though.)

Jonathan has become a very dear friend. I keep telling him about God, and he keeps calling me his *confessor*. This is a private joke, as he hasn't disclosed any offence to me – if he even believes in sin.

When I'm in Cairo, I swim every morning at the nearby Red Moon Hotel; early, before the tourists wake up. One of the Al-Khoury bodyguards is always there even before me. *He*'s surely no tourist. His name is Luke.

I'm not sure he remembers me from my first visits to Mansur's hospital room nearly a year ago. But I haven't forgotten his steel-blue eyes. He swims like a shark (mind you, I've never seen sharks near me, thankfully).

Last month, Luke offered to show me how to improve my technique. I was trying to get too much propulsion from my leg kick, he noticed. His advice, instead, was that my kick should lift my legs up, and be a *low drag*. He was pleased with my progress, but I was exhausted.

He joined me for breakfast afterwards (our first time sitting together). He won't drink coffee though, and turned down my suggestion of bacon and eggs.

I couldn't feed on kiwi and açai palm (a fruit from Brazil, Luke says, that has thirty times the amount of antioxidants of red wine). I hope he's allowed a glass of Bourgogne on his day off.

It sounds silly, but I feel pleasantly safe in his presence! He's so strong and gentle that I know nothing can happen to me when he's around.

Yesterday, we tried rescue swimming (I can't remember who suggested it). He hasn't needed this skill for Mansur yet, but he's obviously *on his guards* (no pun intended) whenever they go swimming.

Well, I don't think there is a chance – I mean, a *risk* – that *I* would need to rescue a paraplegic billionaire any time soon.

I also spend time with Jeda, Mansur's mother.

We're quite close to each other now. She takes an interest in my job with the charitable schools, a project so dear to Nour. Among other things, talking about her late daughter-in-law with a young woman like me soothes her, she says.

She often wishes me to visit Mansur and Talitha at home, on their yacht.

I go, but am a bit uncomfortable. Mansur is my chief executive officer, and a wounded widower. We need clear boundaries – at least, *I* do.

Does *he*?

Talitha doesn't! The little darling keeps hugging me, whenever we meet. Mansur seems to like it, and yet he still calls me *Miss Cumberhart*...

It feels strange to hold his daughter on my lap while calling him in return *Mr. Al-Khoury*. Or are children more honest than us adults? I feel more comfortable when following her to the kitchen: she wants me to show her some (basic) recipes.

Two weeks ago, she heard that I swim daily and asked if she could swim with me. I said yes and we spent a lovely afternoon together. Her father didn't come, though. In truth, were I offered the chance to swap my current position with that of Litha's governess, I would gladly accept.

I exchanged emails with Fr. Paul, sporadically.

I first asked for his prayer after the attack. After all, on that 1st June, he'd been personally involved – with Nepomucen – in the tragic and providential conjunction of events between Cairo, Osly and Orly.

For that reason, I found particular solace in reading a few lines from him, although I tried not to take too much of his precious time. I considered him truly my father in Christ, as he was the priest present and interceding for me in the airport chapel, in Paris, when I was re-born to faith, through God's mercy. He had given my soul its (blue plastic) umbilical cord: my rosary beads!

I mostly asked him questions about his website.

It provided me with a wealth of information about my found-again Catholic faith. My greatest discovery was the Most Holy Eucharist! I was taken aback by the depth, the complexity and the coherence of our faith in that great sacrament. It made perfect sense to my *little* brain and inflamed my heart with love.

Yes, the Sacred Host *is* Jesus, the true God; really, not symbolically.

The Host is Jesus our Saviour, with His Sacred Body, with His beautiful eyes and adorable hands, truly present among us. Wishing I had learned these things as a teenager (or remembered them, if they'd been taught me!) – I resolved to share them with my friends in the future.

That would include other amazing truths like the communion of saints; the motherly mediation of the Blessed Virgin Mary; Holy Mother Church as the Bride of Christ; the virtue of purity, and the sanctity of marital fecundity. I wish all could discover the splendour of those doctrines.

Many think them boring, or illusory. So did *I*!

But now I've discovered that they are the real thing, and answer any girl's desire for true happiness – and surely any boy's! You can find it all online, and for free!

I'm so happy with my new faith. Thank you Lord!

Please, make it bear abundant fruit of love in my short life (and graciously remind St. Joseph to send me a dad – that is, a *husband* – if You want me to start a family).

Chapter 52

Don't think I haven't been *working* hard as well!
I've shared my time between Cairo and Upper Egypt, where the three main schools are, with occasional trips to Lebanon and Eritrea.

South of the border, in Sudan, the Osly school will soon be completed. It might be another half-year until we can open it, but the basic structure is off the ground. There will be space for seventy girls as a start, Muslim and Christian.
We're also to have a small hospital with an operating theatre, to answer the needs of the local population. A Sudanese intern, Arous, is about to complete her medical degree and will work for us.
At my suggestion, the architect located the theatre in the basement, to protect patients and staff from the heat and sand. At Osly once, I witnessed a sandstorm and regretted leaving my special hat in Cairo.
Being caught in it was quite impressive. You wouldn't believe how those tiny grains of sand managed to wend their way inside my suitcase (tightly shut) and would even end up in between the pages of a book stuck at the bottom!
I didn't mind. It made me think of God's promise to Abraham, who also travelled to Egypt: *I will multiply thy seed as the stars of heaven, and as the sand.*

Last but not least, after much debate, we decided in favour of building a chapel!
I have strong reasons for wishing God's Real Presence on that particular spot, where the forty-eight Muslim girls were saved by Azim's sacrifice.
I've spent some of the money from the pearl necklace in providing clothes and books for the girls at Osly (I haven't yet told them anything about the connection with Azim.)
I also gave money to the widow of the bus driver shot by the Scimitars during the attack (to think it's been nearly a year).
Whatever was left, I spent on many bougainvilleas to plant around the grounds.
My boss had been generous in allowing me to leave, even temporarily. On the other hand, Mr Al-Khoury's conditions were very advantageous for him. And, I vaguely suspect a deal for a tourism resort in Sharm el-Sheikh, to be built by Mr Al-Khoury's firm and managed by my boss. But I wouldn't put any pressure on Jonathan to find out and confirm my guess (even though I sense that he's more than willing to oblige).
I signed the permanent contract two months ago. My Nissan, left in Vancouver, I sold to Emma: there's no going back!

Dr. Yasir emailed me last week – for business!

She thinks that the Al-Khoury Charitable Trust (which runs our schools) may qualify to affiliate with her UN Department. She says that it would give our work wider recognition. All that she will need is to visit us and go through our school books on biology, sexual and religious education, gender equality and reproductive rights.

In case our resources didn't meet UN standards, she would provide purpose-made exercise books for our girls. I hope the books *I* purchased will pass the test though.

She may even bring a crew along and shoot a film! I'm quite excited! Filming *my* work at *my* schools with *my* pupils: it's like showing my baby to the world!

Unfortunately, I must admit that Nasreen's principles are at odds with what I have learned of the Catholic faith over the past eleven months. Does she intend to teach my girls to use *contraception*? And will she call *abortion* for what it is, or will she condone it as part of Reproductive Health?

I've read thoroughly about all this and I won't accept books or support a film undermining the Catholic position, even when offered by my doctor friend. To be consistent, the same would apply to a possible husband! I won't allow myself to become involved with a man who doesn't appreciate the Church's wisdom on bioethics.

I look at the whitewashed walls of my little convent cell; at the small crucifix; at the table where I sit. My table... The very one upon which Sister had showed me the books to read, on my first evening here last June, nearly a year ago.

I made the right choice. I mean, in requesting permission to keep my room at the convent as my base in Cairo, rather than accepting the much larger flat which the firm offered me. I tried not to be indebted to Mans... to my employer. Unclear boundaries call for trespassing and, well – never mind. I love to come back here every week – shaking the desert dust off my clothes – to share some of the life of the sisters.

They also kindly catechise *us*. There was true need for it, since neither I nor Mansur had much knowledge of the faith we had found again, or embraced *in extremis* in his case. It's strange to find myself in that parlour downstairs with Sister, Mansur (sorry: "Mr. Al-Khoury Jr.") and Talitha, as if we were all children again.

Sister has finished going through the basics of Catholicism, and we may soon change and go to Abu Ephrem for systematic adult catechism. I feel that Mansur would like a more intellectual approach. He's obviously bright and needs in-depth answers to his philosophical questions.

I also sense that he would relate better to a male teacher. What about sexual morality? I realise that he can't enquire about it in the presence of Talitha (I wouldn't be comfortable either). Talitha is quick; she often surprises me with her sharp grasp, like this morning, on the Holy Trinity.

This is our only occasion to meet once a week. I declined most invitations (not all) to have meals at the yacht, thinking it a bit unprofessional. While in Cairo, I work at my own office in the Al-Khoury building, not far from the marina.

Due to his condition Mansur – or "Mr. Al-Khoury Jr." – can't yet visit the schools (a real disappointment). He stays in Cairo most of the time, for his physical and psychological rehabilitation therapy.

No spectacular progress has been made with his spine as far as I'm aware, but he's in better spirits. He takes part in an online support forum with the Reeve Foundation Paralysis Community (his father knew Christopher Reeve).

Talitha worries me more, in fact. Our darling seems to be losing her gaiety. Spontaneous laughter is less frequent, whenever I see her. She still hugs me when we meet and part, but I feel a sort of unconscious helplessness, even in her tenderness towards me.

By the way, she left me a letter this morning. I should read it now, poor darling. What can she wish to tell me that she couldn't say in the parlour? I bet she's forgotten how much ground cinnamon she needs for the apple-crumble recipe I told her about ("a surprise for Daddy").

Let me open this envelope, with my very name on it: *Miss Clara Cumberhart, Sisters' Convent – bye hand.* Only *one* spelling mistake: well done. I love her child's handwriting. One can see that she has put all her care in shaping the characters properly – even with different colours for each!

And she's only six years and a half, I reckon.

Chapter 53

Miss Clara,
 Daddy says that I need a Mummy again, because he wants to see me happy again, and I don't no how. And Daddy isn't very happy either, and he says that Mum is in heaven and she's also with us.
 So Daddy says: If you find someone who can be a good Mummy for you and you like her very much, Mum won't be sad but very happy, and I will be happy as well.
 So Miss Clara, can you please be my new Mummy? Signed, Talitha Al-Khoury, Cedrus III Yacht (Deck 2, Cabin 17), Cairo Marina.

Am I weak? Am I a coward, and a heartless person? I read this letter again and again the next morning, sitting at the back of the sisters' Chapel. My taxi booked to the airport is on its way to fetch me.
 After much cogitation, and after praying, I popped round to the office last night to take my few personal belongings and purchased a *one-way* ticket to Houston.
 Forget the contract. Forget the schools. I can't. This is not the way people get married.
 And who says that I want to get married in the first place? I mean, who could know that I've been contemplating it? And to *Mansur*? Marriage implies reciprocity, and he never indicated any particular feelings towards me. He's always been very polite and courteous. Even friendly, although rather formal, calling me 'Miss Cumberhart'.
 I know, I call him "Mr. Al-Khoury," but that's because, after all, he's my boss, although not my line manager.
 He deals with much more important matters (he wouldn't even know my email address).
 Without boundaries, collaboration would become impossible. And I'm a professional woman. So, not a hint of reciprocity.

No. But... how could he *reciprocate* love, unless I... What? This is absurd!
 I? I, in love with Mansur? With Nour's widowed husband?
 I, married to a paraplegic billionaire?
 Well... Fine: I can't deny that the thought did cross my mind. On some occasions. Some rare occasions. Or, not very frequent ones.
 But I've always dismissed it! I'm not that kind of person. I'm not a vulture hen, preying on the remains of a massacred family! Furthermore, this is Egypt, not Austria: *The Sound of Music* upon-the-Nile won't do.
 My phone beeps. Good, that must be the taxi, right on time. It's already hot

outside, but the air is full of the scents of spring. The driver loads my luggage, and off we go. I watch the familiar streets disappear behind us, vanishing from my life, probably forever.

Sitting at the back, I check my features in my tiny mirror. I don't look *too* bad, considering the circumstances. Also, I like this dress I'm wearing. It's convenient when travelling as it doesn't crease, and weighs nothing. Just like my elegant Egyptian straw hat. I can call it *mine*, now that Kitty has given it (back) to me after the baptism. She guessed how much I loved it.

I read the letter again: *Miss Clara,*

Daddy says that I need a Mummy again, because he wants to see me happy again, and I don't no how. And Daddy isn't very happy either, and he says that Mum is in heaven and she's also with us.

So Daddy says: If you find someone who can be a good Mummy for you and you like her very much, Mum won't be sad but very happy, and I will be happy as well.

So Miss Clara, can you please be my new Mummy? Signed, Talitha Al-Khoury, Cedrus III Yacht (Deck 2, Cabin 17), Cairo Marina.

I'm pathetic.

Will I ever grow up? Why these tears now! Just a sleepless night.

Talitha... Mansur... Nour... Azim... What is this all about? In truth, nothing would make me happier than to hug Talitha and hear her call me "Mummy." I would do *anything* for that child. At the bottom of my heart, I know that Nour would like it. And she would approve as well, if I could help Mansur find happiness again. But what about him? Could *he* ever love me?

I feel that his wealth is a serious obstacle. How could my involvement not arouse suspicion, when I have so much to gain from it materially? On the other hand, his disability speaks favourably to my heart. Over the past couple of months, I've thought often of the coincidence of Mansur and Kitty being both in wheelchairs. I've smiled at the striking picture our two couples would make!

That is... If he... If he ever saw me not as an employee.

But... and the other question? Children. Jonathan shared the plain truth with me when I left, eleven months ago. And since then, Dr. Schtreuli's diagnosis has been confirmed, as far as I know. Mansur is paralysed from the waist down. So? Could I be his wife in such conditions? Could I renounce ever having children of my own?

There are methods... But I've been through this in my heart. I'm clear about it now. I would want to conceive through marital embrace – or not at all. I would want our children to be a gift of love from my husband, with no human intermediary – as our Creator designed it.

And I read that medical intervention raises morally questionable issues with fertilised eggs – *embryos*, new human beings – left unused, and frozen or discarded.

So, yes: I would be ready to give up conceiving, if I *had* to. That would be a sacrifice. A very big one, as I would so wish to hold in my arms children of our own flesh. But we would have Talitha; 'our' treasure. And perhaps we could adopt more children.

Besides, who knows if, over the past eleven months, his condition hasn't improved, even though he may not yet be able to stand?

I would love to give myself totally to him. To assist him in all his needs. I could train as a physical therapist; I'm sure I would be good at it. I've done it a bit for Kitty in the past.

I can't *bear* the sight of this superlatively accomplished man sitting in a wheelchair – my fallen Superman. If my presence at his side – my love – could bring a smile back to his face more often...

Dear God, what do *You* want me to do?

We've reached the terminal. I take my hat which was laid next to me on the seat, and find under it a large envelope with my name written on it (not in coloured pen). I don't recall having put it there. The driver says that he found it upon my suitcase at the chapel, and took it into the car.

I open it, being slightly apprehensive now, and too tired for another surprise. Nothing in the envelope, but... my velvet pouch. With no pearls inside.

How on earth has this item, sold *eleven* months ago, come back to me? Another Egyptian mystery. I walk into the departure hall, feeling very melancholic.

I have plenty of time.

Yes... I *will* do it. I *am* doing it. I sit at "my" coffee shop and order my usual. No, I'm *not* expecting any prince charming to materialise before I walk through Security.

Kitty's emailed back. Raúl and she will come and fetch me at Houston – with Baby Javier! Another message reached my inbox earlier. Now I'm shaking.

It's from *him*.

This is the *first* time Mansur has emailed me personally. He must be furious. It was sent twenty minutes ago. I suppose that I must read it.

I would rather wait. No, I must be brave.

But I'm weak... I leave the coffee shop and walk to Security.

Sweet Lord, why is escaping so painful – and staying even more?

Chapter 54

Access denied!

The customs officer stopped me: "We're sorry, Miss Cumberhart, there seems to be a problem. Could you wait here for a few minutes?" It's been a quarter of an hour, and I'm still sitting in that waiting room. I'm becoming anxious.

The officer comes back, without my passport. He says that my visa needs further verification. His colleague is on it, but it may take a while. How incredibly frustrating! Well, I might just as well read Mansur's message then.

Apprehensively, I reach for my phone.

Dear Miss Cumberhart,
Please excuse my contacting you directly, especially for a non-professional matter. But still confidential, as you will see.

My daughter Talitha has told me about her letter to you. I don't know how to apologise enough for her initiative. I would very much like you to believe me when I insist that I was totally unaware of it, until she asked me why you hadn't yet answered. She showed me the draft, which, as she said, she faithfully reproduced for you, only with coloured ink.

Being now informed, I'm at a loss to find a solution. I perfectly understand that Talitha's note must have made you extremely uncomfortable. It must be difficult for you not to think that her father suggested it to her. This would be totally unacceptable, coming from an employer, and you would be in your rights to take offense and make a drastic decision.

I was told of your visit to the office last evening, and of your missing belongings this morning. May I again appeal to your bounty on behalf of my little girl, and of me, begging that you may not act without hearing all parties involved.

Trusting in your comprehension, and forgiveness, I remain, yours faithfully
– Mansur Al-K.

I'm still shaking. He emailed me. For the first time. And he signed with his first name. He's right, I suppose.

I was too quick. I was rash. I freaked out. But I...

Oh no! Now I'm getting a second email from him! Please, sweet Lord, please, help me out of this situation.

Oh, there's a link to a *video* file. It's downloading. Now it's playing! There: it's him, looking at me, talking to *me*...

Dear Miss Cumberhart,

Dear Clara,

I will now truly cross a line, as they say. I saw your taxi go. I was in my van parked by the convent, the large dark one, equipped for the wheelchair.

I told my driver to leave that envelope on your suitcase at the back of the church, while you were hearing Mass. But in my first message, I lacked courage to explain what I meant.

This pouch came into my possession eleven months ago. I kept it as a memento of your generosity towards the poor girls in the Sudan. I'd woken up with no wife, but with a God. With no friend at my side, but with the icon of a saint in front of me.

I'd woken up with – to all intents and purposes – no legs. In those painful circumstances, the first words I recall were uttered by your good self. The first touch I felt was your hand taking mine. While my eyes were still shut, I called my wife, and your voice answered.

Mourning is an awkward journey. I tried to fight through it. For months, dire grief was engulfing my soul, and I don't know yet what fruit it will bear, good or bad. I'd lost all hope.

In my darkness, I laid your pearls by St Anthony's icon. Gradually, as I tried to pray, looking at them gave me some peace. Then I found myself looking more at the pearls than at the icon. Then I was looking at the pearls less for their sake, than for what they evoked. I should say, for whom *they evoked.*

I spoke a lot to my wife. I know that she's still with me. I asked her how long I should mourn. I asked her why I should live; and whether she wanted me to.

Then you came back to Cairo. It was all my father's initiative. I was too weak to take a hand in it. But I must admit – your return overjoyed me. Even though we would not meet, or so rarely, I loved to know that you were near, and were getting involved in the charitable work that was so dear to Nour, to Azim and to me. I wish my health had allowed me to visit the schools.

When I was well enough, we started catechism at the convent. I knew that I had to learn about being a Catholic, and every week I determined to attend, mainly for the sake of my faith. But the fact that I would see you there appealed to me more and more. Talitha may have perceived what I hadn't told her; which I hadn't even admitted to myself.

I see now that I must not blame myself for the death of Azim and of my beloved wife. I see that God saved my life for a purpose. So, live I must. Live I want to. But I also see that I live better when you are near.

My mother noticed it. She appreciated your kindness at the morgue, and your discretion at the funeral. My father also liked the fact that you were present but not forceful. I meant to address all this after the first anniversary, next month. But children are sometimes better inspired than us adults. Hence this message, Clara.

I interrupt my watching. The phone is shaking; I mean, my hand is, holding the device (like Jonathan's when we first met properly). The videos of Azim watched with the C.I.A in Texas (eleven months ago) spring back to my mind as well. But this man talking to me is *alive*...

Meanwhile, the customs officer reappears with my passport (good sign) – and with my checked-in suitcase (very bad sign). He explains that my visa couldn't be verified on their system and that I must seek assistance from my government's embassy. I'm free to return to town. A taxi is awaiting me and the fare to my domicile is already paid for.

I gasp internally: *Kitty! They won't let me come back to you. Now I've missed my plane for sure, and my ticket is wasted.* I would burst into tears, if it weren't for this officer watching me.

I'll show him that I don't care. I take my passport back, grumbling that I will go in a few minutes. With a brisk head bow, he leaves me alone in the room, with my suitcase. I breathe deeply, and watch further on my phone.

I'm a powerful man of thirty-two. I'm used to giving orders, and seeing them executed. I have many people working for me, and looking after me. I used to fly my own helicopter and my jet; I used to ride fast horses...

And yet, I feel powerless as I speak these words to you. I very much dread their impact. But whatever happens, I know that it's better to tell you the truth now. May God have mercy on us.

I come back to this velvet pouch. It's my heart. I'm not trying to be poetical. I'm stating a fact. You will find it empty. A treasure was in it: my love for Nour. Seeing my love enhance the beauty of my wife was my pride and my delight. Nour wore my love upon her as a queen. And I lived for her love.

While we now love each other even more deeply in God, I must confess my need for help granted by incarnate affection. In my situation, more than ever, I need to see the face of love; I need to hear its voice; I need to feel its hands.

In a way, my life changed when I made my First Holy Communion two months ago. I know that Christ, Our Saviour, takes me to Him in that sacrament. It gives my sufferings a depth and a price that I'm only beginning to understand.

But the state of my soul, it seems to me, would greatly improve if He made it possible for human hands visibly to reach out to my crippled body. I don't mean carers (I have dedicated ones). I mean a wife.

That pouch is in your hands as a symbol; the heart of a crippled widower. My heart was emptied once, when Nour disappeared, and I nearly died. So I send you the empty pouch, because its present content – the pearl necklace – is of no use to me now, unless I see it worn by you, at my side.

I must also confide to you that, should this message find in you benevolent dispositions, our union may not without difficulty bring about children, due to my current paralysis. But my doctor is confident, and my priest informed. This isn't easy for a man to write, even less so for one as proud as I. But I mean this message to be a proof of my sincerity.

Lastly, the deep affection of Talitha for you, since the first time she saw you at Luxor, is a necessary condition but not a sufficient one for my proposal to be sent, or accepted.

Fundamentally, the love of children must rest upon that of the spouses. It would not be fair on her, on me or on a prospective wife if she didn't choose to become my wife before accepting to become Talitha's mother.

I'm sending you this improvised speech from the sisters' Garden, behind the chapel, where I'll stay for a couple of hours, praying on my own.

If you've not yet taken off, as I assume you are about to, and if you're inspired to walk into that garden soon, please be assured that I won't resent it as an intrusion, but will welcome it with exultation.

Your fellow catechism student, Mansur.

Chapter 55

God bless all customs officers!

Cancel every visa, if such is the condition for bliss. To think I might have missed such a proposal! I'm not waiting.

Forget my airfare. If they call my name on the loudspeaker, say that I got lost. They can have my seat, aisle or window! It's a case of *force majeure* – an earthquake called love!

In the taxi (luxurious and mysteriously paid for), back to the convent, I'm watching his message again, trying to ignore the chaotic traffic and constant horning. Mansur... Husband? *My* husband? *His* wife? Mansur's wife?

But why is this driver *so* slow! Training for the slug Olympics?

Is the tarmac melting, that our tyres should be glued to it?

Two camels now, right in the middle of the road! I never *hated* camels so much in my life. Tell me, *why* do they exist?

Looking back, I start wondering if the thought of spending my life with Mansur hasn't been part of my mental framework for months, unconsciously.

Faster, please! Don't tell me I've got the *only* cabby in Cairo who cares about traffic lights, red or green! As if *anyone* around here does.

What if Mansur *leaves?*

Come on, driver! Watch this bus! Yes, fantastic! Brilliant bit of overtaking.

By now, my stomach is just one big knot. Will Mansur still be there? Will he wait for me? Did he say *two* hours? And I can't text him. It's not the way to answer a proposal.

He meant to talk to me next month, and spoke only when he felt he had no other choice.

Mansur. I'm ecstatic. I simply can't believe it's true. But yes, that's his van, still parked by the gate. Thank God!

I'm not waiting for the change! Thank you – *Shokran*.

I'm not waiting for my suitcase – drop it anywhere; sell it; give it away; burn it! Fine, leave it by the gate! Yes, peace be with you also – *Salaam alaikum*.

I try to catch my breath again.

I check my dress and hat.

I slow down as I push the garden gate.

The sun is still shining, but its light is subdued. I see a shape under the fig tree, against the white wall. By the bench. On his own chair. He's holding beads in his hands.

I stand inside the gate, as though in a *bridal* detector: it buzzes! (I know, it's only the sisters' bell, calling to prayer.)

He lifts up his head. He sees me. I see him. I don't move. He's only forty steps away. How far it seems; and how close... I start walking, very slowly.

His gaze is like a hand. One more step. One more. I stop, three steps away from him. We look at each other with deep attention, acute pain and triumphant exhilaration.

I take off my hat. I can't believe that I'm seeing the face of the man who wants to marry *me*! But does he? Have I not misinterpreted his words? He sees my anxiety. We look at each other again. So far, none of us has spoken a word.

He looks serious as he speaks first: "Before anything, I owe you the truth.

"*I*'m responsible for your missing your flight. *I* asked the airport not to let you through."

"It was a last resort. I'm sorry. I'd have died if you'd gone."

I'm taken aback. This is *so* romantic: better than *Beauty and the Beast*!

If I needed a further proof of his love for me, there it is. My prince's hand reached out for me as I was about to commit the biggest mistake in my life.

How can I tell him that I'm not offended, but honoured? I take my passport out of my pocket and hold it open before him at the visa page. With a smile, I throw it away (as a blind girl her white stick), far into a flowering bush.

This gesture should speak better than words. It means: "See, I surrender all for the love of you. I need no passport if your heart is mine."

We look at each other in silence. Is there a hint of sadness in his eyes? And in mine? Do we foresee the trials which every relationship has to overcome? Finally, he speaks.

"I would wish to kneel down; but I can't. Would you like to stand next to me?" I step forward. He takes my hands and asks: "Clara, will you marry me?"

I answer: "Yes, I will, Mansur, with all my heart."

He kisses my hands and dries a tear from his eye. I sit on the bench against his wheelchair and we kiss.

A rewarding kiss for those other kisses which could have taken place on this very bench with Azim and Jonathan, and for good reasons didn't.

Then he gently bends my head against his chest as I feel my scarf being taken away from my throat. Something cool and smooth travels upon my skin, encircling my neck and I hear the faint click of the clasp closing behind me.

It's my pearl necklace – the one I'd sold! With some additions... My fingers now count three strands, and feel some stones whose colour I can't yet see.

We remain in silence under the fig-tree, in the shade until sunset. I kiss the white wall as we go, in thanksgiving for love.

He leaves.

Back in my cell, I can't believe what has occurred.

Until in the mirror, above the small basin, I see a tearful face and under it... a *neck*, adorned with a triple strand of magnificent pearls, whose gleaming whiteness is enhanced by five large blood-red rubies.

Chapter 56

We both would have waited longer.

We knew that after such a tragedy, merely a year would seem a rather short amount of time to mourn and honour our beloved deceased. But we prayed about it. We tried to think what Nour and Azim would want for us, and for Talitha.

I rang Mum and Dad: out of respect more than for advice or permission, as their marital failure didn't commend them as very reliable guides in the choice of my spouse.

Of course, I spoke with Kitty. She first found Mansur's intervention to retain me at the airport *controlling*, rather than romantic. But after hearing my reasons, she supported my choice. Our respective families approved and thus, the date was set for July 1st, one full month after the anniversary!

Abu Ephrem was concerned with the short amount of time left for the doctrinal side of marriage preparation. He insisted on the fact that, marriage having become so little supported by modern society, prospective husbands and wives needed to be catechised at length and to fully grasp the purpose assigned by God to conjugal love, as well as the graces and the beauty embedded in it.

Due to the extraordinary circumstances, and since Mansur was a widower, familiar by definition with many aspects of married life, Abu Ephrem gave in, and generously set for us several two-hour sessions, tailored to our needs. He also spoke individually with Mansur, and with me.

He asked me if I felt sure of myself, of Mansur, and of my calling. Was I definitely *not* attracted to religious life, in Cairo or anywhere else? Would it not be too challenging for me to marry a former *Muslim*, and such a wealthy man? Even though his family was much westernised, one shouldn't underestimate cultural differences.

I answered as honestly as I could, and he gave me his blessing, saying: "After all, dear child, this may be the most beautiful way of turning last year's tragedy into life. You will need a lot of courage to assist your husband. In his case, wealth may be more of an obstacle than ill-health. Keep very close to the Sacred Heart of Jesus and to the Immaculate Heart of Mary, and you will flourish, you and your family."

I could have kissed him, as a daughter her father!

What Abu Ephrem told Mansur, I don't know. But all seemed to go well.

After that, we both talked to Talitha, separately. He saw her first; then I.

We were on the ship, in what used to be Nour's boudoir, indeed more of a private prayer room, with a beautiful ivory crucifix, and a picture of Our Lady (to whom Nour had a great devotion).

I entered the room to find Talitha in tears of joy. I cried as well. I took her on my lap and hugged her tightly saying: "Talitha, do you want me to be your mother?"

She answered: "Yes, very much."

Then I asked: "Do you want to be my daughter?"

She said: "Yes, please."

We had just adopted each other.

I went on: "Then my beloved little one, from the moment your father and I become husband and wife, I will also become your mother. And from that moment, you will be under my care. I will do all I can to make you happy, and holy. And I will alway, *always* protect you. Do you understand?"

She was looking at me in silence, visibly moved; then she nodded and said: "Thank you."

I concluded our mutual adoption saying: "Now my darling, let us kneel down before the crucifix. Your Mummy Nour prayed here every day. Let us ask her to pray for you and me, and for your daddy, that we may become a happy family with God's help."

Her little voice joined mine in a simple duet of love as we started: "Our Father, Who art in heaven, hallowed be Thy Name. Thy Kingdom come. Thy Will be done, on earth as it is in Heaven. Give us this day our daily bread. And forgive us our trespasses, as we forgive those who trespass against us. And lead us not into temptation, but deliver us from evil. Amen."

Then she looked at me, as if awaiting something. I kissed her and said: "Let us pray now to our Blessed Mother from heaven. You know, Talitha, she's the Mother of all of us, whether children or grown-ups: you, me and Mummy Nour. That makes us all sisters on earth in a way."

So we went on together: "Hail Mary, full of grace, the Lord is with thee. Blessed art thou among women, and blessed is the fruit of thy womb, Jesus. Holy Mary, Mother of God, pray for us sinners, now and at the hour of our death. Amen."

Mansur and I were to enter into this new relationship without looking back. Because of what we had been through, both of us having lost a treasured partner in the attack, we knew what a mistake it would be to look at each other as reincarnations. I could not be *Nour* for Mansur, and he must not be *Azim* for me. It had to be a new story, with new spouses – even though the child was the same.

This made me decide to choose Paris for the wedding. It wasn't too far for Mansur to travel and neither of us had acquaintances there. It wasn't even where I'd learned of Azim's death, since I'd taken off for Texas unawares. I admit that I liked the idea of a small wedding in a special place.

It took some insisting from Fr. Paul in Paris, as Archbishop's House stressed that airport chapels aren't equipped for weddings. They wanted us to book with the Lebanese parish instead. But Mansur's "people" – as he called them – were persuasive enough and so, I would get married in the very place where I'd found God again.

Breaking the news to my fellow staff was challenging. Like it or not, my new status radically altered my relationship with them. I was to become the wife of their top boss!

Somehow, I was feeling embarrassed to tell Jonathan. Thankfully, Mansur had already informed him. He texted me that he was less likely to "confess" to me now (this was our ongoing private joke).

Among various reactions, I particularly remembered how Luke, Mansur's head bodyguard, had looked at me the morning we met at the swimming pool, after my engagement was made known. He said: "Mr. Al-Khoury couldn't have chosen a better swimmer, Clara."

We were both aware of a hint of sadness in his voice. I replied that I was glad I would soon be under his expert protection as Mansur's wife. We were standing by our usual pool, looking at each other with deep affection, or mutual esteem. There was no one around, just a few birds. I felt sad as well when announcing that I might be coming less often to the pool now, or at another time.

This realisation seemed to hurt him – a man who could kill an enemy with one finger! I was sorry. After a silence, he said: "It will feel strange calling you *Mrs. Al-Khoury.*" I would still call him Luke. We smiled at each other and dived, drowning any possible regrets.

For the first time, I overtook him.

Chapter 57

Mansur wanted only the best.
There was a wedding dress I particularly liked, by Vera Wang. Mansur preferred Sarah Burton. I would have made it a surprise, but why not let him give his opinion, after all?
Sally *screamed* over the phone, warning me it was bad luck if the groom saw the dress before the wedding. But I'm not superstitious – although, admittedly, the Gypsy woman was right last year: I *had* found love.

After looking at many pictures, we chose Christian Dior. Their head seamstress flew from Paris for the final fitting in Cairo, on board the *Cedrus III*.
Kitty and Mum would only meet us in Paris, and I couldn't really ask the sisters to attend the fittings. I had female colleagues here in Egypt, but no one I felt close enough to invite to my fitting. (I also wished to avoid possible gossip and jealousy from the women at the office.)
Emma, Sally and Ashley were my three oldest and best school and university friends from Canada. But they would come straight to Paris. (I preferred them not to witness, here on the boat, the new status to which Mansur's wealth was raising me.) So, my future mother-in-law was to be my adviser, which suited me well.
My dress was nothing extravagant. I chose ivory rather than plain white. It had sleeves down to my elbows and concealed my shoulders (and back). The neckline was modest and there was a little train. And a beautiful veil!

Jeda and I had spent the morning with the seamstress in Nour's boudoir. Both looked at me, very pleased with the result, when somebody knocked at the door.
Mansur was asking if I would mind very much if he saw me wearing the dress. Really, was it not enough for him to have seen the pictures? Could the actual dress not remain a surprise? But after all, why deprive him of this simple joy?
So, he wheeled himself in with a large smile, despite a slight tension around his eyes, and helped himself to coffee from the guéridon. I hoped that he wasn't in pain. He looked jubilantly pleased.
After a long silence, as if lost in contemplation, he congratulated the seamstress and me, and his mother. I was so proud of his appreciation! I loved to turn on my heels and make the light material of the dress swirl around me, as my dear fiancé sat back and seemed to sip the sight of me with more delight than the contents of his cup.
His mother was stolen from the room by Talitha's governess, and the

seamstress was gathering some items in the next room (Nour's bedroom). Mansur told me that he had several destinations in mind for our honeymoon and would keep the one chosen a surprise, but he wanted to know my preference in terms of climate and cultural interests before making a decision.

I couldn't believe that this was true. An engagement necklace, a church in Paris, a dress, and now a honeymoon! It all seemed so sudden; like a dream. I thought the time had come to share with him my intimate desire.

I answered: "Darling, thank you so much for all that you're doing for me. Thank you for the great choices for our honeymoon. I would trust any of your ideas. But since you kindly ask me: there's a place I would love beyond everything to visit with you. But I can't dare to tell you, because it would cost you very m…"

He interrupted me, insisting that no expense would come in the way of our happiness, and that I had only to name the place, and he would arrange to travel there with me.

I believed him, answering: "Then, I would love the two of us to visit… Tora."

He looked puzzled and asked: "How do you spell the name of that place? Like "Tora Prison" in Cairo? Is it in Italy?"

I said: "Oh, darling, you've guessed. It *is* Tora Prison in Cairo."

His face turned white and his forearms begun to shake slightly. With a very calm voice, which sounded metallic, he replied: "Clara, are you speaking of our *honeymoon*? What on earth do you want me to do in Tora Prison? Thank God, I don't have *any* friends in there."

Feeling that he must know whom I meant, I answered: "Abu Ephrem has visited him several times. He tries to assist him."

By then, Mansur looked visibly upset; indeed, more than upset: "You… You be… very careful about what you mean to say. But wait just a minute; I need this seamstress to leave us alone."

I went next door and asked the woman if she would not mind leaving our rooms for a while – which she did. I wish she could have stayed! I foresaw a storm, and third parties might have lessened its impact.

But it was too late. I was alone – with my future husband. I walked back very slowly, praying that he would understand, and waited in front of him, standing in my beautiful wedding dress.

He was looking at me like a political commissar in North Korea.

A dreadful silence occurred, until I whispered: "Your former driver Ali's wife and children are destitute. No one will help them now. He said that he didn't know that they wanted to shoot anyone. They only told him that the targets were bad Muslims, who should be rebuked. Because you survived, they would not pay him; not even for his family.

"Last month during Lent, while praying, I was inspired to give Abu Ephrem some of my savings for Ali's family. They were grateful. They moved to the Mokattam slum. I visited them with the sisters. Please darling: I so much wish you would come with me and tell Ali that you forgive him! That would be the most precious wedding gift I can imagine."

I'd managed to speak my heart out, keeping my eyes away from his. I was waiting, still standing in the middle of the room as at a tribunal, knowing that I had said something of far-reaching consequence. Apparently, I had made a tragic mistake.

Mansur became almost mad. I had never seen him like that. He shouted: "How *dare* you! How dare you pronounce before me the name of the hyena that caused my wife to be butchered with such a dear friend, and with my little girl too if it hadn't been for Azim; and with Youssuf and Yasmina Helios, innocent parishioners!

"How can you even *think* of the devil I'd entrusted with the safety of my family; and who betrayed us for petty cash instead; who allowed them to be killed and stole half my body!"

After a brief silence, he sneered bitterly, as if suddenly inspired: "Let me call my tailor and cancel the trousers for my new wedding suit, since below the waist I'm nothing: a jacket will suffice – no need to waste the money! How can you think for one second that I could find myself in the same room as that traitor and not cut him into pieces!

"How can you be so wickedly insensitive as to suggest that I should assist the members of his loathed family, happily breathing, while through his fault, mine is rotting in a crypt! How is it possible! You!

"You, of all women! You, who were passionately in love with his victim, our friend Azim! You, speaking those horrors to me, your future husband and the only survivor of the slaughter – with my darling Talitha! You must be out of your mind! But *who* can you be!"

Still at some distance from his chair, I actually fell on my knees before him, seized by deep sobs, my veil and train spreading at my side, like an ivory tide across the dark carpet. But my abasement and vulnerability seemed to *excite* his anger instead of subduing it.

I later realised that the crucifix and the painting of Our Lady were visible to him, in the background behind me. Alas, the sight of them hadn't been enough to placate him. On the contrary, were they not pricking his conscience, enraging him further?

He went on, his voice less vociferous, but all the more threatening, now waving a pamphlet in his hand: "But that's not all. Actually, I've been meaning to speak to you about this since yesterday, when you left this brochure on my desk. I read it with great attention. Do you realise what it implies?

"It says bluntly that, according to the Church, I'm possibly not allowed to have children. They won't endorse any of the well established procedures that give millions of couples the joy of fostering life.

"What is this all about! When in my first video message I explained that due to my paralysis, our union might not bring about children, I had never ruled out having recourse to artificial insemination!

"I only meant to be fair, stating humbly my physical deficiency, as it has an obvious impact on conjugal life. But how can you expect me to marry you and not want to have children with you! When any doctor, any hospital would be able to perform the simple tasks required!

"Don't you know that I'm the heir to an empire! Don't you have eyes to see what my father built up, and does it not occur to you that I inherit this with the responsibility of passing it on!

"But in case you aren't aware, in our culture, my heads of departments won't gladly bow to Talitha, even though she may be bright and later on may earn all the business degrees required! I told Nour so, when we first contemplated adoption. But, like you, she wouldn't see it as an issue. She'd fallen for Talitha – *no wonder*. She said we could adopt a *boy* later on, as we meant to do."

His tone had softened but, as if remembering my presence (and my crime!), he vociferated: "Unless I have a *son*, or several sons, what we've achieved will go to the dogs. Are you hired by my enemies to deprive me of offspring, after they failed to kill me and my daughter?

"Before our honeymoon at Tora Prison, do you want a wedding picture of us in Giza by the Sphinx: I could buy it a hundred times, and yet I'm dust at its feet, for it lost only its *nose*, yet I can't be a man!"

Chapter 58

I lay prostrate on the floor, my knees and elbows on the carpet, before him.

He could only see the top of my hair and my back, I suppose. My veil had slipped back from my head down on my shoulders. I was listening, praying, fighting to breathe amidst the violence poured out upon me: *Kitty! Kitty! He's stabbing the bride in me!*

I could hear him browsing through the pages of the brochure: "Do you agree with that? Let me quote it for you in plain language. Enough poetry!

"Techniques involving only the married couple (homologous artificial insemination and fertilization) are perhaps less reprehensible, yet remain morally unacceptable. They dissociate the sexual act from the procreative act.

"The act which brings the child into existence is no longer an act by which two persons give themselves to one another, but one that 'entrusts the life and identity of the embryo into the power of doctors and biologists and establishes the domination of technology over the origin and destiny of the human person.'

"Such a relationship of domination is in itself contrary to the dignity and equality that must be common to parents and children."

The quote from the *Catechism* sounded a bit academic in the present context, I felt, even sententious. I wished he would stop, but he read further: "Under the moral aspect, procreation is deprived of its proper perfection when it is not willed as the fruit of the conjugal act, that is to say, of the specific act of the spouses' union...

"Only respect for the link between the meanings of the conjugal act and respect for the unity of the human being make possible procreation in conformity with the dignity of the person.

"Pope Paul VI said that there is an 'inseparable connection, willed by God, and unable to be broken by man on his own initiative, between the two ends of the conjugal act: the unitive end and the procreative end.'"

With scorn and anger, he added: "Finally they list practical issues. At least, this is plain speaking: 'The sperm used is usually obtained by masturbation, which the Church teaches is immoral. The sperm or eggs used may not come from the couple desiring the child; because one of the spouses may be infertile, it may be necessary to use the sperm or eggs from an outsider.'

"'More than one embryo must be conceived to achieve one implantation. All remaining embryos – which the Church holds should be respected as new human lives – die, are frozen indefinitely for later implantation, are used for research, or are discarded. Children conceived through IVF also have a greater incidence of birth defects.'"

As he wheeled closer to me, the brochure fell on my neck (I can't imagine that he would have thrown it at me) and slipped near my cheek on the carpet.

The pages must have had very sharp edges, as a sensation of tingling made me bring my finger to my nape, and a very thin trace of fresh blood showed on it.

There was a pause.

I sat on my heels, finding my breath again. For the first time he could see my red eyes, and my cheeks covered with tears, and more on my lips and chin which I tried to dry off with my bare forearms, not having a handkerchief at hand. I was conscious of having become a rather *unattractive* bride-to-be.

Ignoring my begging looks, he went on, still speaking harshly: "I could dwell at length on all those points. But the main pretence is that they want me to treat those fecundated cells as if they were human beings. This is taking too far the Church's concern for vulnerable ones.

"Let Her care for the poor, the refugees, the sick, the orphans, the prisoners, the persecuted, and I will support Her with all my strength – but for God's sake, what have our seed and eggs to do with anything! This is organic matter, and nothing else.

"Furthermore, it's a most intimate business, and the question should be settled between husband and wife, without interference from priests who, after all, have chosen celibacy, unlike us! So, since you say you love me, you will commit yourself to this procedure and bear me a son. End of the story."

He paused and added: "Did you say that Abu Ephrem went to see that man?"

I wasn't sure why his thoughts were led again to the visit to Tora Prison, which had unleashed his fury.

After a silence, as he was looking at me with hatred, and perhaps with disgust, he asked: "What do you respond! *Girl*?"

I burst into tears again, which must have confirmed him in his verdict that I was a pretty simpleton, following blindly what the first cleric put into her mind and *pathetically* devoid of any critical judgment. I managed to calm down and sat on a chair, asking if he could give me some water.

He rang and, one minute later, a member of staff in an apron and nurse cap opened the door. Her splendid red hair made her look familiar, I could not think why. She soon came back with a bottle of fresh water and a glass, which she put next to me on the tray table. She looked embarrassed, and with good reason.

I hoped nobody had heard the row. How would she and the other crew members look at me if I was to become his wife within weeks, and the mistress of this magnificent boat?

Still, the water did me good. As I drank, I prayed in my heart that God would not let me leave the room – it was high time I should – without offering the man I loved at least one word which could reconcile him with God and the Church.

And with himself. And with me.

But the words he spoke chilled my soul, more than the water had done my throat: "Well, you've nothing to say. Perhaps, after all, it was a good thing that we should clarify this matter. Perhaps I missed something, when Abu Ephrem first mentioned it…

"Perhaps we were about to make a mistake. Perhaps *I* was. And you also. It's not too late. I'm an invalid, and no one will comment if the date is *postponed*, until better advised. Now if you will excuse me, my business team is awaiting me in the office."

Each sentence penetrated my heart like a dagger. The commotion nearly made me faint. Thankfully, I wasn't standing. As he turned to withdraw towards the door (wheeling upon a fold of my veil), the side of his chair bumped slightly into the small table, and his coffee cup fell against my stomach and bounced on my lap.

It was half empty, but the brown liquid spread over the ivory fabric with the most shocking effect. We both looked at the dress in silent consternation.

He said: "I'm sorry."

I think he meant it.

Chapter 59

I stood up, checked my dress and spread my veil behind me.

The brown stain was dramatically conspicuous. It would have looked bad on any type of garment but, needless to say, on a wedding dress and after the way he'd treated me, the only word that came to mind was "desecration."

I opened my mouth for the first time: "Before you go Mansur, I beg you, please let me have your attention. I'm just a young woman in love. I've lived twelve years away from God and finding Him again has brought life back to me.

"I would so much have loved to bear your children. Welcoming the views of the Church, of God, hasn't been easy. It took me a year, passing through imperceptible stages.

"But now I understand. I thought that, together, we could be strong enough to offer up that sacrifice, and that in return, God would not leave us empty.

"In my distress, I confess that I trust in God as ever. He's life itself and love, and truth, and compassion. If we can't have children the normal way, He will still make us *fecund*, as a couple, in some *other* way.

"I'm certain of it. I *saw* it with Azim, whom you referred to, and with Nour. I saw it! I have touched it with my hands! Such was the way forty-eight innocent girls were saved from death, or worse.

"*I* didn't give birth to them, but through Azim and I, God saved their lives. There was a cost to this. Azim paid it. Will you say that he died childless, when those forty-eight girls are now freely moving on with their lives, and with the assistance of your family's charitable trust?

"I didn't bleed, but I wept. And his blood and my tears were made fecund again, for my benefit this time. God restored life to my soul, to me, the woman you asked to become your wife – through Azim's sacrifice! And through Nour's."

Mansur hadn't moved, and looked as tense as before. I went on:

"Why were they ever killed? They were killed because their lives were obstacles to other men's fulfilment, whether financial or religious. In the eyes of those men, the life of your wife, of your child, and of our friend – and your dear life as well – had lost their value.

"They weren't considered as *fully* human lives anymore. Their rights were cancelled. They could be disposed of. And so they died, defenceless, silently.

"Like *other* human lives conceived and sacrificed by fathers and mothers, by doctors and nurses, for higher motives. Even more defenceless; even more silent.

"I saw the chalk outlines on the steps of the church after the murder, and I wept. But who weeps for the *glass* outlines around tiny human beings in laboratories, frozen for experiment or merely destroyed, as happens after every IVF!

"Or, does *size* matter to qualify as human? Then, did Azim do something stupid when shielding your daughter with his life? Nour was twice as tall and three times heavier: was she more human than Talitha and thus, worthier of being saved?

"Or is *speaking* necessary to be human? Then on your hospital bed, during your coma, when you couldn't utter a word – looking brain-dead, in fact – should you have been disposed of, as not human?

"I would have stood against *anyone* attempting to disconnect your oxygen and water drip! Do you see now why I can't act in any other way for other human beings, much smaller and less articulate than you, but created by God like *you* were; and destined to reach the light of day and grace, like you?"

Still standing in my beautiful – and stained – ivory wedding dress, knowing that I might never wear it again, I was shaking. Not with anger, though. Not even with grief.

I felt a holy strength inspire me.

I didn't wish to win.

I didn't mean to hurt.

I felt as if I was giving birth, as I uttered the saving truth.

I concluded: "In that prison cell, across the river, there's a culprit. But his crime has incarcerated you as well.

"Your grief will turn into poison, unless you allow God to transform it, into *forgiveness*. You're incapable of it, like I was. But you belong to Christ, like I do.

"Such was your dying wish, Mansur, and so it was fulfilled. I saw you! My heart was there. I saw the priest baptise you.

"Mansur, ask God for help and He will make you rise. And your soul will stand, luminous and strong before His face, and mine."

He waited a moment, his hand on the door handle, then left in silence.

I undressed, washed the coffee off my skin (surely not with *petals*), put on my normal clothes and disembarked unseen.

It was warm outside.

High in the sky, I thought I saw a couple of storks. Swallows were flying over the water, passionately playing between the waves in the wind.

How easily those birds crossed the wide river!

What had happened to us? Could *we* not fly – or swim?

Sweet Jesus, mercy!

Chapter 60

Swimming was indeed the best thing I could do!
Back in my room, I felt strongly that the nervous storm that had just ended, or its aftermath, would wear me down unless I took some physical exercise.

I walked to my usual resort, the Red Moon hotel where I'd first stayed, then a mere tourist, with Azim. It's just three blocks away from the convent, by the Nile, and the staff is friendly.

I never could see that place again without remembering – the lobby where his guide friends had praised his "American gazelle"; the restaurant; the terrace where we'd sat; the garden where he'd watched me kneeling on our last night before fighting for me. It looked just like any comfortable hotel, only loaded with invaluable memories.

It was late morning and most groups were still out, probably at Giza. Diving into the huge pool felt wonderfully refreshing, even more mentally than physically.

I love to swim underwater, and can keep my breath for several minutes.
I remembered Luke explaining the process to me, in this very pool, a few weeks earlier: *Our bodies are so well designed that, as oxygen fails, our heart rate automatically lowers and our blood is directed to key organs.*

I felt so liberated, leaving the outside world to spend some of my life – however briefly – in another dimension.

What bliss it was!
After twenty minutes partly underwater, I got out of the pool.
Such a delight! Just to feel warm. Not to move. Not to think.
With no white dress on. No veil. No bodyguard. And no necklace.
I wouldn't go to the office. It stood too close to the *Cedrus*, and I didn't want to meet any colleagues just now. Things were awkward enough between us since the wedding announcement.

I checked my emails on my tablet and found that the work at Osly was going according to plan. The foundations had already been dug for our mini hospital. Good.

Normally, I would have travelled to one of our sites in the South, like most weeks. But I felt it timely to stay in Cairo, or nearby.

A thought crossed my mind. Yes, I hadn't yet taken even a day to visit *Alexandria*. There, by the sea, Azim's special friend, the young and beautiful Katarina, had died for love. A long time ago.

I had neglected her. What if I drove down there and asked for her advice?
Back at the convent, I knelt in the chapel. The sisters were having

Eucharistic adoration. I knew that my dear God was with me, whatever the outcome.

As my soul was adoring the white Disc, I felt that my Saviour was there, equally silent and vulnerable, truly present and humbly offered to our love and protection, like all the victims of the earth. He was *the* Victim.

Is this why the Church is the only voice consistently speaking up in defence of unborn human lives (let alone all other persecuted men, women and children)? Is it because in the Holy Eucharist, She has received as Her Heart a human, silent and vulnerable Presence?

As I was leaving the chapel, I saw Jeda praying at the back, near the door. I didn't want to disturb her and merely gave her a nod as I walked by.

Unexpectedly, she followed me into the vestibule: "My child, I came here to pray for you and Mansur. I heard about your row this morning. He shouldn't have treated you like that. No, please, let me explain to you. It isn't entirely his fault.

"You see, I've loved him too much. Not that a mother can ever love too much, of course. Rather, I have *praised* him too often. Did Mansur tell you that Jed and I had lost a baby? He was stillborn. The following year, Mansur's birth was such a consolation!

"We realised too late that, for his own good, we should have been more demanding – or *stricter*, as his father would say. Aunt Farah says we spoiled him; although she knows what losing children means."

Keeping silent for a little while, she avoided meeting my eyes. I felt sad, but I also admired her. For a woman in her position, admitting such things, and to *me*, required courage and humility.

She went on: "Mansur used to get very angry when things weren't going *his* way. He shouted on occasions. Marrying Nour did him a lot of good. His strong love for her improved his character. But her death left him without the guidance he still needs.

"We do our best as parents, but it isn't the same, and he's a grown man, very much in control of his own affairs. Perhaps I shouldn't speak like that. He may not approve – although I told him I was coming here to see you (*he* didn't send me). My son is a good man, Clara. He can do great things."

She then addressed a matter which I had never properly considered. It left me baffled at first. But I was glad she mentioned it: "In case you've… heard things… about how Muslim men sometimes treat their wives, I should add that he never resorted to physical violence when in anger.

"Not against his horses, and much less against his wife. In fact, Nour warned him before the wedding that if he *ever* raised his hand against her, she would leave the house – just as if he betrayed her. (She didn't say she wouldn't forgive in either case.)

"You see, Nour and I were very close. For his flaws, my son has one great quality. He says sorry, and *makes up* with generosity for any distress he may cause. Clara, may I speak to you as one old enough to be your mother? Take your time to make up your mind, and don't feel bound by your engagement.

"If you find that you still want to marry Mansur, don't do it out of pity. Don't marry him with the idea that you will change him, either. Marry him because you love him as he is, and because you trust that his love for you is greater than his flaws."

She embraced me and walked to her car.
I hadn't said a word.
She seemed frail when stepping into the huge Mercedes, its engine purring. The chauffeur closed her door and they glided away.

Chapter 61

I was grateful to Jeda.

She'd given me perspective, if not a solution. At least I knew better what to expect from Mansur. What was I to do? Should I leave Egypt – again? Unless Mansur changed his mind, I couldn't remain. I didn't care about apologies, although they would be welcomed. It wasn't so much about me as about him.

I grieved for his heart, for his peace, for his soul. For his salvation. I so much wanted him to know Christ and His Church better. If only he could experience the beauty and warmth of what I called the "network," he would see that it was actually much more than an *institution*.

A living *organism*, that's what it was. The Mystical Body of Christ, suffering and sanctifying.

The following day, I had a long conversation with Kitty on Skype, and another one with Abu Ephrem at the convent. Their advice provided me with new angles to consider. *She* was a married woman, and *he* knew Mansur's family well.

Kitty recommended that I should take this first clash very seriously. She feared it might reveal just who Mansur was and how he viewed me, deep inside. In which case, she urged me to extricate myself from the relationship with all speed.

Otherwise, after ten years and the first emotional flush of love fading, he might take me for granted and his attitude could all too easily become abusive.

I then mentioned Jeda's confidences. That made Kitty less concerned, as she could see like me that the issue was in the open and that Mansur, assisted by his family, had been working on it.

However, she insisted on the necessity of a sign of regret, with an act of reparation at least as spectacular as the offense had been. Otherwise, she commanded, I should board the very next plane and fly back to civilisation – billions or no billions!

Abu Ephrem is celibate. But his ministry to couples and families involves a lot of counselling, which gives him a wider experience than many married men. He confirmed that Mansur had a tendency to be domineering. Other men converting from Islam, he'd witnessed, did show the same bent in relation to their wives.

But, he added, the extreme violence inflicted on Mansur the previous year, both physical and moral, had certainly made him more aware of his limitations. He'd learned vulnerability the hard way.

Because he was of good will, he would put that painful experience to good use, for him and those he loved. Abu Ephrem agreed with Jeda that in any case, I shouldn't marry him out of pity.

They both said to pray, and wait. And hope. Both insisted that I was *not* to flee. Dear Kitty; dear Abu Ephrem. How much I would love those two wonderful friends of my soul to meet each other! I would have to organise that.

Meanwhile, I would go on my pilgrimage to Katarina's place. So, off I went, to the bus station. (It was by no means a form of escapism!)

Alexandria was terrific. And a mere ninety-minute bus ride from Cairo! Many French restaurants, but what a disappointment not to find the place where dear Katarina had offered up her life! There wasn't even a small shrine.

I sat at the ancient Roman amphitheatre, trying to connect with her in my heart. Her eyes would have seen that site, at least. Perhaps, she'd been tried there, as it was convenient for the crowd to watch. Ah, that I might have but a thousandth of her eloquence, to plead for the truth and convince those I loved most!

Failing that, I would joyfully offer up my limbs and give up my life, if it helped convince anyone! Like Katarina did. She would have seen the great lighthouse, guiding the many merchant ships back to safe haven – one of the Seven Wonders of the World. But the tower was no more, while Katarina's light still shone in many hearts.

And yet, there was so much darkness in other hearts. As there had been in mine. How could I have remained away from that Light for so many years? How patient God had been with me! And still was, as I surely didn't consider myself "arrived" yet.

It struck me that from the age of five, after leaving Montreal, I'd been raised in a large city by the sea, just like Katarina. The Vancouver skyline flashed through my memory. And my fear and thrill when Daddy and Mummy took me for the first time to the Jericho Sailing School! And my delight when the four of us sailed to the Gulf Islands. I stood under a warmer climate now.

I managed to pray in a church, before walking by the sea. How stunning the Mediterranean was. Oh to be there with... To be there with him! With Mansur! My love! My treasured friend! My husband-to-be! Where are you?

I went to bed early that night, putting on the cotton djellaba that I use as nightdress. It's blue with white Arabic patterns embroidered on the front and sleeves, and at the bottom as well, by my feet.

I bought it for very little at Khan el-Khalili. I must admit that I like it very much! I pulled the hood back upon my face against the moonlight, and fell asleep, feeling like a Bedouin or a monk.

I don't know what time it was, when something awoke me.

It sounded like an animal, rather heavy, slowly crawling on the landing by my cell. My heart started beating fast. I hadn't locked my door. Why would I? I live in the guest quarter on the third floor, where no other women than I currently live.

But the presence was coming nearer. I *had* to get up and lock up! On tiptoes, I threw my cream burnous (also purchased at the bazaar) over my shoulders for protection, in case anything jumped at me; and I reached for the door key.

I thought I was dreaming when I heard *my name* whispered. I knew that voice, even though it spoke so low! Opening the door, I couldn't believe it. No wild beast crawling to my threshold; no assassin either! But my beloved!

Mansur!

Chapter 62

I rushed to him, half crying and half laughing: "Mansur! How on earth did you get all the way up here! Where's your chair? Who helped you? And at this time of night?"

He lifted his face towards me. He was unshaven and looked very, very tired. He whispered: "I... I came alone. But please, don't look at me. I don't even know how to breathe in your presence..."

That was it? He was back? Back to me?

Kneeling by him on the landing, I answered: "My love, don't breathe at all then, I will do it for you!" And I kissed him, pouring all my soul into his.

He must have sweated out all the water from his body, lifting himself up the three floors by arms' strength! Lying on his back with wide open arms, he seemed like a drowning man just rescued from furious waves and tossed onto the shore. I added: "You can't stay out here."

I dragged him backwards into my tiny cell, like an army nurse sheltering a wounded soldier while bombs are falling. I hadn't realised how heavy a man can be: Kitty weighed nothing in comparison! He tried to rise on his knees, resting his elbows on my little table and chair, but even his strong arms wouldn't suffice to carry him.

I was heartbroken to see this powerful man reduced to so little. He'd flown jets across the sound barrier (or nearly), and tired nervous polo horses; he was the 849th richest man in the world – out of seven billion; and he could not even stand on his knees!

Shivering, he said: "I can't speak your name. I can't look at your face. I can't even ask for your forgiveness. Any right you had given me to be near you and seek access to your heart, I've turned against you with utter cruelty and arrogance."

I let him speak, as I thought it would help him.

He went on: "At the very bottom of my heart, I discerned that you were right. But I was shocked by the radical consequences to which such principles would lead us. I became tired, envisaging yet another sacrifice, when I felt that I'd consented to so many already.

"I meant to speak with you calmly, and ask earnestly for an explanation about the brochure. Only yesterday did Abu Ephrem inform me that you had merely passed it on to me on his behalf. He wanted to explain it to me at length later on, following up on his conversation with me."

He recalled: "I was annoyed that you were kept busy the whole morning by the seamstress and Mother. So I thought that I could just as well come into the boudoir and admire you. When I saw you in that stunning white dress, I felt immensely proud of you.

"But immediately, the thought of never having children with you, from you, sprung into my memory; and the anticipated frustration, with a feeling of dire injustice, made me see red.

"And then, when you mentioned Ali, I was taken aback and still knew you were right, but found that it was leading me too far, or too soon. I felt jealous of your moral superiority and I became angry at you! At you, whom I cherish!"

He paused, as if trying to repress a sob rising in his throat: "I gave in to a voice which wasn't mine. I fell into the horrible temptation of taking advantage of your vulnerable posture. My little bride-to-be, standing in shining ivory...

"Instead of agreeing, I humiliated you! Why did I not simply keep silent, waiting to calm down? The more I offended you, the more the abyss of my injustice captivated me, and I fell deep into it. Can you forgive me?"

We remained silent for a while. I was hurt again, but his confession was necessary, and I accepted it. Then I recalled how much this man had suffered over the past year. How he'd supported Azim in his conversion, while he wasn't even a Christian himself. How his affection had led him to the steps of the church at the fatal moment. How his own driver and bodyguard had betrayed his confidence. How he'd lost everything in an instant.

Had *I* not been horribly insensitive in suggesting the visit to Tora Prison, and in connection with our marriage? I had only meant to seal our love through a heroic act of forgiveness. What had *I* suffered? What had *I* endured? And if I had, what marks was I still bearing? Azim's blood wasn't tattooed on my stomach; and Nasreen's pearls had long been sold to good use...

Pearls? What had I done with the necklace? It obviously meant much more to Mansur than to me – I wasn't sure why. I decided to mention it as it would help balance a bit our respective guilts (a very tiny bit): "Mansur, in return I confess that I left the pearls in Nour's bathroom. I didn't do it on purpose."

He said: "I have them in my pocket. Would you... Would you mind wearing them again... One day? If you feel like it...You don't *have* to, of course."

Yes, he *really* liked those pearls. I smiled and whispered: "Please, will *you* put them around my neck, like the first time, in the garden? I would wear them with great joy, for the love of you."

I heard him sigh with relief, as if this truly liberated him. We were sitting side by side upon the carpet, our backs resting against my bed. But my untied hair and the hood of my djellaba hanging down my back were getting in his way (silly me, why not wear a normal *hoodless* nightdress!). He eventually managed to fasten the necklace.

I said gravely and distinctively: "I forgive you, Mansur."

Despite my precautions, the rescue from the landing and our conversation in my room must have been audible enough for the sisters downstairs to be alerted. One of them called out from the staircase: "Clara, is everything alright with you up there?"

Chapter 63

Thankfully, she wasn't behind the door! I was petrified. Mansur wasn't very composed either.

I walked to the landing and said: "Sister, I apologise: I've just woken up after a long nightmare. But I'm fine now. Sorry to have alarmed you. Good night."

As I tiptoed back and shut the door, Mansur whispered, still sitting on my carpet: "I heard what you told Sister. Was that not a lie?"

I buried him in my burnous, protesting in a low voice: "How *dare* you lecture me, sir! When *you* crept into my room in the middle of the night against convent rules; and I merely tried to save you from shameful expulsion. What's more, I didn't *lie*. I have been through a real nightmare, for two days! But thank God it's over now – is it not?"

He laughed silently and I felt as if I hadn't seen him smile or laugh for centuries.

I went on: "You can't stay here Mansur. No men are allowed under any circumstances, including on the guest floor. The sisters make no exception, even for Mr. Al-Khoury Jr. of the *Cedrus III*!"

He smiled and said: "My doctor could testify that I'm no threat. I thought that my physical condition would earn me a dispensation, merely to sit on your carpet!"

But I wouldn't have it: "No man can be trusted, sir, trust me. And even if things are as you say, one can't set a precedent, or hazard one's reputation. I will call your carers to come and get you. How did you enter anyway, the doors are locked at night?"

He answered: "I told my people to go home, and that I would pray at the convent – which I did. Then I hid in a corner and waited until it was all quiet."

Looking through the window down into the street, I saw two silhouettes standing by a large black van behind the garden hedge, one of them with a tiny red light by his face, smoking: "Well, your team has ignored your orders, or followed higher ones. I see them outside the garden, waiting for you. Sorry, sir, your last chance to stay is gone. I will go down and let them in."

He grabbed the hem of my djellaba: "Wait, please. Just a few minutes. Just resting here on the carpet for a moment, while you sit on your bed."

I didn't have the heart to say no... It was a pleasantly strange situation. Both of us were now lying on our backs, well apart, looking at the ceiling through the fan. Despite the gap between my bed and his carpet, I felt closer to him than I'd ever been while held in a man's arms.

He commented: "So, *this* is where you live? I often wondered what it looked like. It's so incredibly *small*. When I think of the four-room flat that was made available for you in town.

"This is just a cell, really. There isn't even a bathroom attached to it. Just a basin? And no Internet, surely. But I like it very much. I feel reborn, in your cell. It's been a long journey to find it."

There was a silence. A very peaceful silence.

"Clara, why do you not *stay* here? I mean, as a sister? What led you to agree to marry me?"

His question took me by surprise. He was right, why exactly had I chosen not to pursue a vocation here, despite having seriously contemplated it? I deeply meant to serve God. He was becoming day by day, more and more, the joy and centre of my life. I would continue to pray, even after moving out of here. But why move out, indeed?

Several factors were at stake. I wanted to help girls in dire need, as Azim's legacy. I also loved Talitha and felt responsible for her, to some extent – this time more as Nour's legacy. I'd been moved deeply by the sight of Kitty pregnant, later holding Javier, her baby boy. Her spiritual intimacy with Raúl had resonated in me as something I particularly wished I could share one day with a man.

Also, the complex mixture of power and vulnerability in Mansur's character and situation had struck a chord with me. Was I unconsciously trying to replicate my exclusive relationship with Kitty, of which her marriage had deprived me somehow, but which Mansur's paraplegia allowed anew?

One thing was certain, the tragedy of the past year had revealed to my heart and soul that love was much, much more than sex! Through peer example and a typically modern lifestyle in Vancouver, I'd grown up taking for granted that sexual activity was a prerequisite for any emotional fulfilment. I'd found the opposite to be true.

Such knowledge hadn't been *imposed* on me by contradictors, to prove right any ideology or creed. It had simply occurred through direct experience, with the shedding of blood and tears. I knew it. I'd learned it. That was all.

I had experienced firsthand how the meeting of souls, in God, secured genuine fecundity. And I remembered from my failed attempts, and from the confidences of my friends, how sex without God's blessing leaves us jaded, wounded and tarnished.

On the contrary, I had seen spiritual offspring granted by God in unforeseen ways, regardless of the social relationships among those involved. Friends, men and men, women and women, children and adults, even Catholics and non-Catholics concurred in fostering spiritual life around the world, through sacrificial love, at various levels.

The criterion was our desire to let God spread His love through us. In a way, hadn't little Talitha engendered Mansur and me to spousal love, when her ingenuous letter had set in motion our feelings and our wills? She'd unlocked our pride, our fear and our selfishness. Were we not the children of her candour?

In consequence, much as I longed to conceive, doing it on God's own terms as explained by His Church didn't cost me; on the contrary: it was the only possible way I could envisage. And if our union proved sterile, I would offer it up and would be fulfilled with Talitha; with helping poor schoolgirls; and with further adopted children, if Mansur wished a son, or several!

I turned my head down towards him. His eyes were shut.

Chapter 64

In the silence, the well-known sound of a mosquito interrupted my thoughts.

It was hovering over me, slowly, but couldn't find my skin, covered by the long djellaba. There was something almost dramatic in that very light music, which indicated so certainly the effusion of my blood. The insect would reach my skin. It would puncture me and would feed on my blood and after that, an itchy bump would appear.

When the music ceased, the sting would be felt.

There! On my toe. Just as I expected.

"Why don't you kill it!"

Mansur wasn't asleep and, hearing the sound, had pulled himself up against the bed and tried to wave the creature away from my foot. He kissed my bitten limb.

I smiled. Should I tell him? Was I not again about to cause an untimely shock between my soul and his? "They enter through the gap, at the side of the fly screen, which is loosened from the window frame. I let them in."

As I thought, Mansur objected: "Why! I will have the yacht handyman come and fix it first thing in the morning! You can't let yourself be bothered by those bloodsuckers. And I will buy you a repellent you can plug-in. I assume there is power in your cell? Don't you find the mere sound of them infuriating? *I couldn't sleep!*"

Right, I would tell him, if he asked: "My love, I have my reasons."

He protested: "What reason on earth can make you tolerate the utter discomfort of those micro-vampires, when you could so easily prevent their coming, and be left to sleep in peace! Furthermore, I strongly object to your beautiful smooth skin being perforated!"

I sat up on my bed and took his hand in mine, saying: "Darling, I do it for *you*."

He was flabbergasted. His look was almost comical.

I went on: "I read it in this book about early formation in the sisters' Congregation. The novices used to be asked to let mosquitoes bite them at night, as a penance for the will, even more than for the body. It was a very "natural" mortification. Very "green."

"They dropped that rule since. It was never strictly enforced anyway. But I thought I would try. I found it a good way of offering up tiny sacrifices for you.

"I wouldn't have mentioned it, of course – but then, I hadn't planned on your witnessing it, here in my cell in the middle of the night. And *you* asked about it. I checked online: here in town, the risk of them carrying malaria is practically nonexistent. However, I promise to stop as soon as I will be pregnant, please God. You aren't angry at me, are you?"

He looked at me in disbelief and, I thought, with admiration, answering: "You mysterious little woman! How far will you go to procure my happiness? I should try your method.

"But it would work only from my waist up, since below, I wouldn't feel the sting. Only, what could I offer the penance for, unless it were for myself? God knows that I can see nothing in *you* which would require improvement."

After a silence, he confided: "As to my paralysis: the doctor confirmed that the therapy is working. But he recommended patience, as we're still at an early stage. Abu Ephrem was relieved to know, as the marriage wouldn't be valid otherwise, he said! He probably mentioned to you the difference between consummation and fertility? The former being necessary and the latter not? Sorry for being specific."

I simply nodded. *What good news!*

He went on: "You know Clara, I have been thinking a lot, over the past two days. I realise that I've never really wanted doctors to be involved if conception were at stake. They're fine for any other business, including some forms of sexual treatment. But I now agree that life must be... How did you call it again? A gift of natural love, not a medical achievement."

But what of a male heir then, I wondered? A mere two days earlier, Mansur was so brutally intent on its necessity. Had his misogynist collaborators suddenly been subdued? Or was he contemplating adoption again, of a boy this time? My beloved's change of heart seemed so radical... I prayed that divine grace might have caused it, and no lesser factor.

"Also, as I mentioned in my initial email, the day I proposed to you... Well, I sometimes don't take opposition well. It may be the main flaw in my character. Nour was patient with me; and so is my entourage. But once I see I've done wrong, I do apologise. You can be sure of that! I thought you should know while there is still time."

After a silence, he added: "I must make up for the way I treated you last time on the *Cedrus*. Clara, we both know what first anniversary it is this coming day. A year ago, we were preparing for Azim's baptism, and you were about to fly back to America.

"As it happens, I spoke yesterday with the Minister of Justice. Although it was short notice, he granted me permission to visit Ali in Tora Prison tomorrow. That is, this morning at 10 a.m. Would you be free to come with me?"

What a joy! For a brief moment, I wished to dispense with convent rules and let him rest on my carpet! But remembering my commitment to the sisters as their trusted guest, and knowing well that we were not (yet) married, I checked my djellaba, stood up, and dipped my fingers in the holy water stoop by the door, marking his forehead and mine with a cross.

I knelt down and we turned towards the small crucifix hanging on the wall above my bed, whispering one Our Father, one Hail Mary and one Glory Be. I was glad to hear that he knew his prayers well enough. Perhaps, he'd been saying them with Nour and Talitha.

Then, realising that he must have been dehydrated, I gave Mansur a glass of water from the tap (I should have thought about it earlier!).

While he drunk, I put on my burnous again and tiptoed downstairs to let his carers in. They were discreet enough, or the sisters thought it better to ignore the incident.

Within a few minutes, my love was whisked out into his van, and to his *own* bed aboard the yacht!

I stayed a bit in the little garden, barefoot, looking at the bench under the fig-tree. A hand on my throat, I smiled at the contrast between my humble oriental clothes and the treasure hanging around my neck.

I wasn't Princess Badroulbadour though, since no oriental magic had procured my felicity. Rather, touching the white wall, I gave thanks to God for a treasure greater than gems, once lost, and now found again, increased.

Chapter 65

At 10 a.m., we were an impressive delegation getting out of two black vans, once the triple gates of Tora Prison had been shut behind us.

Jonathan walked with me (his friendly presence made me feel less uncomfortable), while two carers, two bodyguards and a lawyer followed Mansur and the Prison Governor.

Thanks to a special favour, I, a woman (and not even a relative of any prisoners), was allowed to be part of the group. I tried to be as inconspicuous as possible, wearing a long loose dark dress, a large black shawl around my shoulders and neck (concealing my necklace), and a veil over my head.

The place fitted the description I had just read online in the car: *Tora Prison is a vast complex in South Cairo and reserved for criminal and political detainees, including many who held office under the previous regime. It's one of the largest and oldest prisons in Egypt, and guards are notorious for torturing inmates. It's more like a city of prisons, each with its own walls and watchtowers.*

Taking no chances, I'd left even my rosary beads at home (I wouldn't be kicked out for carrying a visible Christian symbol). But I still had ten fingers to count the Hail Marys, for all those miserable souls detained, whatever crimes they'd committed, or been accused of.

After our documents had been checked twice – and our bodyguards disarmed – we walked into a large lift, and down into a basement, along a bleak corridor. Grills were unlocked before us, and slammed at our back with noisy clangs.

I was feeling slightly claustrophobic. How long could *I* survive, spiritually, in such an oppressive environment? Without even considering any direct violence inflicted upon me... And to whom could I turn if I needed help, let alone consolation?

O, dear Jesus, how can Your children end up in such places? But You were once a prisoner as well.

The cell we entered was small and smelled of damp cement and urine. I remained in the antechamber with Jonathan.

Mansur wheeled himself through the grills towards the back wall.

A rather tall and athletic-looking man was standing against it, his hands shackled in protruding heavy steel rings.

He only had trousers on (a dirty-looking inmate jacket lay by his bare feet). Dark patches showed on the wall and floor. Those were no hieroglyphs, although I felt as if we were in a tomb. I dreaded to think what liquid had impregnated the concrete, and by what process...

So, *that* was the chauffeur who had betrayed Mansur. He was the man who had leaked the time and place of Azim's Baptism, just a year ago. He was the one without whose complicity all our friends would still be alive. I didn't feel angry, but very sad. What a waste! What a waste it had been.

The man looked at Mansur in defiance.

"Should I not," thought I, "go and stay near my fiancé?"

This visit was *my* suggestion, and he had only accepted it as a very costly token of his love for me, on the occasion of our pending wedding.

"Should I not stand by him?" I looked at Jonathan, who gently put his hand on my arm.

I assumed that it was better for me to stay behind. I would pray, then.

The Governor spoke to Ali, formally introducing Mansur and his delegation.

Ali sneered, saying: "I know my former boss. And I know well why he's come just this very day. And why you let him in, with his guards. You can beat me to death, it won't change anything. Do it, if that's your way of celebrating a first anniversary. What can I expect anyway? I'm here for another twenty-one years, and my chances of survival in this hell are small."

A gaoler slapped him and he stopped talking, but he looked very intently at Mansur, whose face I couldn't see. There was silence. Ali seemed puzzled by what he saw in Mansur, who nodded eventually towards his lawyer.

The man opened a slim briefcase, adjusted his glasses, and started reading aloud in an impersonal voice: "Communication of status regarding Mrs. Kamilah Fawad and her children."

Ali jerked in his shackles and shouted: "Leave my family out of this! Don't you dare! They were *never* involved! They knew nothing! Nothing! Do you hear me?"

He was slapped again, and after another nod from Mansur, the lawyer went on.

Chapter 66

"Following the arrest, trial and sentencing of her husband, Detainee number 849 Ali Fawad..."

Ali's face looked horribly tense, as the lawyer referred to his wife Kamilah.

"...to twenty-two years of strict confinement for the following convictions: active complicity in the murder of Mrs. Nour Al-Khoury, aged twenty-seven, singer, an American citizen; active complicity in the murder of Mr. Youssuf Helios, Retired Shopkeeper, aged seventy-seven and an Egyptian citizen; active complicity in the murder of Mrs. Yasmina Helios, Housewife, wife of the aforementioned, aged seventy-two and an Egyptian citizen; active complicity in the murder of Mr. Azim Nebankh, Tourist Guide, aged twenty-three and an Egyptian citizen..."

Jonathan took my hand as the lawyer read further: "...active complicity in the attempted murder of Mr. Mansur Al-Khoury, left paralysed, CEO of Al-Khoury Construction Corporation, then aged thirty-two, a Canadian and Lebanese citizen, and husband of the aforementioned Mrs. Nour Al-Khoury; active complicity in the attempted murder of Miss Talitha Al-Khoury, daughter of the aforementioned couple, then aged five, a Canadian-American citizen; perpetrated by gunmen on the first of June last year at 3 p.m., outside Risen Christ Coptic Catholic Church, al-Warraq, Cairo, in the presence of the same Ali Fawad; as the said victims were on their way to attend peacefully a service of the Coptic Catholic Religion...

"...Following the sentencing of her husband for these offenses, Mrs. Kamilah Fawad and her three children (plus a fourth child born five months after that date) found themselves unable to pay the monthly rent for their two-bedroom flat located 24 Shagaret El Dor Street, Cairo Governorate, Egypt.

"Neither were they able to pay the debts incurred for food and electricity expenses over the fourteen months previous to the arrest of the aforementioned Ali Fawad on the fourth of June last."

I became a bit impatient.
Where was all this leading us?
Jonathan's face gave me no answer.
What was the point of listing the misfortunes of this poor family?
Mansur couldn't be doing this out of cruelty! Surely not. (I tried to dismiss the still very vivid memory of his ruthless behaviour towards me – from his own confession – just two days earlier.)
Ali was looking more and more pale and tense.
I could see his contracted jaw muscles and biceps, and I was glad (I hate to

say), that his shackles were heavy, since he could have struck down my beloved fiancé in his wheelchair with one fist.

The lawyer went on: "An order of eviction having been pronounced against the tenants, they were expelled from their domicile on January the seventh last, and chose to relocate to Mokattam slum in Cairo.

"Since then, evidence of any income received by Mrs. Kamilah Fawad and her four children, or of stable housing used by them, could not be gathered."

Please, sweet Jesus, this is *torture* for Ali!
Let it end soon.

The poor man was clearly in deep anguish, at hearing the destitution of his loved ones, when he knew that he wouldn't be able to assist them in any way until he got out of this hell, if he ever did!

Let this lawyer conclude! Was he heartless?
Did he not have children, or a wife!

I pressed Jonathan's hand in mine as the monotonous voice continued reading, with less emotion expressed than if it had been a weather forecast: "On the thirty-first of May last, the situation of distress of Mrs. Kamilah Fawad and her four children was brought to the attention of The Al-Khoury Charitable Trust, a division of Al-Khoury Construction Corporation.

"The same day, at 3 p.m., Mrs. Kamilah Fawad assented to being relocated with her four children to a four-bedroom flat at El Tahrir Sq., Downtown, Cairo, 11516, Egypt, a property part of a residence owned and administered by Al-Khoury Middle-East Real Estate Corporation; under the single condition that Mrs. Kamilah Fawad will act as caretaker to Number Thirty-Four block of flats, consisting of twelve separate apartments.

"The expected workload is eleven hours per week. Details of the working agreement are attached to this Statement for consultation."

I hardly dared to believe what was read out.

"This professional position and the use of the four-bedroom flat, or of another dwelling place of similar size and standing, are granted for the duration of the absence of Mr. Ali Fawad from home; or until his youngest child reaches the age of majority, should the detainee die in prison.

"The ordinary expenses incurred by Mrs. Kamilah Fawad and her children as regards food, clothing, health and education will be covered monthly by The Al-Khoury Charitable Trust for the duration of the present agreement.

"In addition, these dispositions will remain in force for the benefit of Mrs. Kamilah Fawad, should she find herself a widow and without adequate resources, even after all her children are no longer minors.

"The aforementioned Detainee number 849 Ali Fawad, as head of his family, is hereby apprised of these dispositions and requested kindly to approve them, signing and dating the present copy."

Chapter 67

Silence followed. Everywhere.
No doors were banging.
No shackles clanged.
No voice was heard.
Everything was still.
Suspended.
A blind person would have been unable to tell that at least *ten* of us were present in that small space. Everyone was looking at... Mansur.
It was an unprecedented occurrence.
The Governor seemed as taken aback as Ali. Were there any records of such a thing in the annals of Tora Prison? The lawyer was the only one who didn't seem surprised, or moved.
But he'd spelled it all out. It was clear. Set in writing with legal precision. I still couldn't believe my ears.

Now it was Jonathan's hand which pressed mine – actually *hurting* me! What was the matter with him? I hurt his hand in return!
How could Mansur have done *that*?
And he hadn't spoken a word of it the night before! When he knew, and had it all prepared... He hadn't referred to it once to secure my forgiveness, when that would have been a spectacular proof of his change of heart.
His terrible words two days earlier, in Nour's boudoir, burst back in my memory.
No, he hadn't spoken mildly then, about Ali and his family. His anger, his fury were not feigned. What could have caused such a radical transformation? Who had touched him so deeply?
I knew Who...
And I could still not see his face, as I stood far behind his wheelchair.
Let me go to him! He's *my* fiancé, nobody else's!
Let me go and hug him! I'd never thought of such a response to my prayer. I didn't anticipate the height, depth, breadth and width of the mercy that One had inspired him to show!
As I was about to move, silence ended abruptly.
It was Ali, desperately sobbing. I'd never witnessed such a sorrowful sight as this strong man, about the age of Mansur, hanging from his shackles little more than his skin, and pouring out through his tearful eyes the contrition for his crime; the relief for his family's future; and the stupefaction for the generosity which had secured it.
Mansur nodded to the gaoler, who looked at the Governor, then unfettered

Ali.

The poor man fell down on the concrete floor, at the feet of Mansur, still in his chair. He didn't move for a while and I feared that he might have fainted, or worse.

Then... he kissed Mansur's *shoes*.

Mansur nodded to his lawyer, who came to our antechamber and requested *me* to follow. I was shaking with emotion as I came to stand very close to my beloved.

Not looking at me, he seized my hand and kissed it. His voice hadn't been heard once so far in that room.

Only *then* did he speak to the prisoner: "Ali, two days ago, my fiancée asked me to forgive you. She said that, although *you* were the one in prison, only forgiveness could set *me* free from my resentment.

"I answered that if I were in the same room as you, I would rather tear you to pieces, and would wish your family every misfortune. I'm the one who would have needed your shackles, to keep you safe from my vengeance.

"She prayed to Jesus Christ, the God of mercy, for me as much as for you.

"Ali... I forgive you your crime.

"But it depends on you to be forgiven by *God*.

"Ask Him as I did, and you will be saved. And now, embrace me as a brother: I'm just a man like you, and a *sinner* before God."

The bodyguards had to lift Ali from the ground and carry him to be clasped by Mansur.

As Ali was now standing again, but still looked so piteous, I couldn't resist the urge to throw my ample shawl around his shoulders and chest.

While I was doing so, my veil slipped from my head and my face was caught in the light. Ali looked at me for the first time, and seemed shocked to *see* me.

He was obviously trying to connect the sight of me in that room with some earlier memories.

I had never met him before, surely.

Chapter 68

Still gazing at me, Ali asked Mansur: "Sir, is the lady called C.C.?"

I answered straight: "Yes, I *am* C.C.".

He looked at me again and said: "The lady's picture and initials were on the list of targets they showed me the day before. They said she should be punished. She wasn't at the church during the attack. But I feared that she might have been shot as well at another time, somewhere else."

There was another silence.

Everyone was now looking at *me*. Still holding my hand, but more strongly, Mansur nodded to his bodyguards and he was wheeled out. All followed, apart from the gaolers, Ali, and the lawyer, who helped him sign the copy of the agreement.

On stepping outside, I took a deep breath. I felt as if I'd lived ten lives underground! Jonathan was lagging behind, probably kept busy with administrative details.

Mansur and I got in our van and were off.

Only then, sitting beside my beloved, did I feel able to express my passionate gratitude. I found no words and simply fell upon his chest, sobbing in turn.

He took my head in his hands, caressing my hair. It felt so good to see his strength and might turned into heroic charity, after he'd used them *against* me two days earlier.

At his feet in Nour's boudoir, I'd felt his power and authority directed at me, like a giant truck at night on an empty motorway, with blaring horn and full lights on, would run at high speed towards a hapless squirrel!

And now, his beautiful hands were caressing my head, and he smelled nice and was smartly dressed; and he loved me.

He explained: "I asked the Minister of Justice if Ali's sentence could be reduced, in the event that I, as the only adult victim surviving, would request it.

"But the Minister advised against it, for fear that it would be interpreted by radical Muslims as Christian cowardice and weakness, which could make the situation even more difficult for Christians in Egypt.

"We will see. At least, I asked the Governor to protect Ali from any injustice during his time at Tora Prison."

We remained silent.

I let him rock me gently, enjoying every curve in the road and any acceleration of the van, as they caused my cheek to press even deeper against his chest. I could *sense*... Yes, no doubt: a *heart* was beating in there! A *man*'s heart, thank God.

I might have snoozed, as his voice woke me up, whispering into my ear: "Nour and Azim's anniversary Mass is at 6 p.m., isn't it? So, before we go to the church, I want to take you with me now, anywhere. Let's *escape* for the day..."

I was thrilled and asked: "Just the two of us?"

He said: "Yes, just you and me."

Knowing that the bodyguards were sitting behind us and the carers not far, I whispered back: "Can you take me to a desert island?"

He kissed my ear and said: "Of course, I know just the one we need. It's only forty-five minutes away. My flying carpet will take us there, if you can swim. *Can* you?"

Pretending to be offended, I boasted: "When *you* will swim underwater for three minutes, you might ask about my swimming!"

He laughed and said: "We will pop in at the convent for you to get your swimming costume; unless you don't mind using one of Nour's, since you are about the same size – in which case we could go straight to the yacht and disappear even more quickly?"

I hesitated for a brief instant, as the prospect of wearing his dead wife's clothes made me uncomfortable.

But I realised how long it would take to get to the convent, through all the traffic. So I replied, teasing him: "Only if she had nice swimdresses – I won't wear a burkini!"

He tickled me, while giving orders over the phone, so that on arriving at the yacht (yes, she *was* a magnificent ship), we only had to put on our beach gear. I managed to spend only ten minutes in Nour's impressive wardrobe (although Mansur said it had been half an hour!), and in no time we were in the air!

Bye-bye Cairo!

Chapter 69

However, I wasn't yet fluent in the Al-Khoury language.

Speaking English, I'd thought that "just you and me" meant "just you and me." I could have driven him anywhere in Jonathan's old Nissan. I used to own just the same car!

To my irritation, in *his* idiom, "just you and me" meant "you, me, one bodyguard sitting next to you, a pilot-bodyguard flying my helicopter, one carer next to him and – that truly was the last straw – the new nurse from America, very young and pretty with splendid red hair (but *who* selected his staff?) sitting next to me."

That is, next to *him*!

Why did she look slightly *familiar* to me? I expected that, at least, she wouldn't swim around him when we got there. I could take care of my fiancé, thank you!

When I'm in charge, I will have Kitty's mother-in-law hired as his exclusive nurse, and I won't be surprised if the therapy proves successful more quickly than predicted...

And where was Jonathan? Could *he* not swim? *He* was one I would have liked to come with us, if I couldn't be alone with Mansur.

I put on my stylish oversize sunglasses and looked through the window, sulkily. The huge city was long gone, and below us spread the desert (boring dunes, frankly), until in the distance I saw the blue sea line near Ain Sukhna, where we were heading.

We landed and got out at last.

Freedom! After the tension at the prison in the morning, I felt like a newly born person, as the warm wind blew against my dress and scarf, while my eyes were already diving into the blue immensity opening up before us.

There were many trees and a thick lawn. I wheeled Mansur at a distance, by the sea, while his retinue ate their lunch, further to the side. My love and I shared the nicest picnic ever. We were so lucky!

He pointed his finger towards a tiny rock, shaded by a grove, about eight-hundred yards from the shore, and said: "I promised you an island. Do you feel ready to swim all the way, or should we hire a boat?"

A bit concerned, I looked at him, not knowing how to raise the question of his *legs*. How could *he* swim that distance, moving only his arms? He said that, as far as he was concerned, he would be fine, only slower than me.

So we went down towards the water and took off our clothes. I must say that dear Nour had excellent taste! Her swimdress was an inspired balance between modesty and elegance. It had straps like small wings covering the shoulders (and my silly tattoo from teenage!) and a skirt with flowery folds that fell below the knee, but would still dry fast and offered full ease of movement to the legs.

Why had I waited until I would visit a Muslim country one year earlier to learn about this option! Don't flowers or butterflies look prettier with their petals or wings on, than without?

Actually, I *had* worn a similar outfit once, I recalled, at a skating competition. I would now perform before a much smaller audience, but one that mattered much more to me – my beloved (and his team).

From the corner of my eyes, I was pleased to see that the nurse was keeping *her* dress on. Great, she would not swim along with us. Actually, she was opening a book on conversational Arabic... Why would she learn that language: did she need that to impress my fiancé? I averted my eyes from her. I had dearer objects to look at, thank you!

However, seeing Mansur's chest for the first time gave me a slight shock. It was brown and muscular, but I'd almost forgotten that he'd been *shot* as well.

One impact showed. I felt culpably oblivious of that truth, whose consequences he had to bear, not only through the affective void of widowhood, but also through the physical pains endured daily.

The carer wheeled Mansur down the beach into the water, and he got out, floating. I suddenly realised what a relief it must have been to him not to feel his own weight press upon the numbed lower half of his body, but rather to feel the water carry all his limbs, restoring his unity of motion.

Why had I not thought of that sooner? I would have gone to swim with him daily. I was ashamed to admit how easily one can overlook the crosses of the sick and disabled. Their good humour may lead us to assume that they aren't as inconvenienced as we first thought, when in fact, their smile often expresses their heroic desire to put *us* at ease, in their crucified company.

I came to him and held his hands. We had water up to our chins, and laughed as children. What a miracle to see him *stand*! His whole body was upright before me. I'd mostly known him sitting or lying – or crawling. Our "vertical" encounters had occurred twice only, with his family and Azim, the week before the attack.

One bodyguard (my friend, steel-blue-eyed Luke) and the carer were already in the water. They weren't wearing coloured swimming trunks like Mansur, but full body swimsuits, with waterproof backpacks and dive knives...

What for? Surely, they wouldn't accompany us to the island! Please, let them not!

Thankfully, Mansur was quick to intervene: "Luke, I will paddle without your help today. I feel in very good shape and Miss Cumberhart is a good swimmer – *you* trained her, I've heard. We'll go to the little island over there, and back. We don't require any of you to attend. Of course, you all enjoy yourselves swimming along here, as much as you wish."

Mansur's order didn't seem to please them at all.

Luke answered: "With respect, sir, this is imprudent. May I stress that I'm under strict orders from Mr. Al-Khoury Senior to organise your safety? We're in an open area with unknown people around, and, meaning no offense, today's anniversary date increases the risk.

"I would much prefer if Bazam and I swam along with you, at a short distance. Also, health wise, it's quite a stretch to the island and back, with steep banks and possible undercurrents further off the beach."

Bazam nodded in assent.

I was a bit embarrassed, as those two men knew better how to assess the risks, but on the other hand, I saw that Mansur needed to assert his independence, for his own psychological recovery.

My beloved looked a bit upset, and finally replied ironically: "And you forgot the sharks! Mind you, I wouldn't feel it if they caught my legs."

Seeing my horrified look, he smiled at me: "I'm only kidding, darling. None have been spotted around here for years." Then, to his bodyguard: "Okay, Luke. Let's strike a deal: you find us two life jackets and we will wear them to the island, alone."

As Luke wasn't convinced, Mansur pulled out his joker – our last chance of enjoying time *on our own*. He said: "Fine, I'll tell you what: you see that motorboat by the restaurant? You hire it for the afternoon and keep an eye on us through your long-range binoculars while we swim. I promise to wave at you as soon as I feel tired. What about that?"

Luke nodded reluctantly and started walking towards the restaurant, suddenly turning back and shouting: "Sir, what if the boat isn't for hire?"

Mansur shouted back: "Then I'll buy it! And if it isn't for sale, I'll buy the restaurant. I *mean* it. Besides, you always have the helicopter to reach us in no time, if ever needed."

It seemed as if nothing would get in the way of our escape! Like defiant schoolchildren, we grudgingly reclined in the shallow water, our elbows in the sand, waiting for permission to swim away.

Chapter 70

At last, the boat was hired – or purchased with the restaurant as one package, I didn't ask.

Two huge fluorescent lifejackets were tied around our bodies. We looked like an Apollo space crew after sea landing. So much for my beach fashion show!

Never mind! Never mind in the slightest, provided we got our green light!

As soon as granted, we pushed off into the deep, and away we swam! What a pleasure! What an indescribable delight! I'd forgotten – since my previous dive only two days earlier. How can we spend most of our lives out of water, when we were formed in it?

Mansur swam faster than I had anticipated.

He had broad shoulders and, having used his arms intensively on his wheelchair, was in fact better trained than I. But I had *legs* – unfair... I caught up with him and we swam side by side, he on his back and I doing the sidestroke to keep watch on him.

Half-way between the beach and the island, we paused.

It was the most exhilarating sensation I had experienced in years, if not in all my life.

There I was, floating in the Red Sea, with dozens of yards of dark blue water under my feet – its depth enhanced by the silvery fish schools dancing in it; with the immense clear sky above me; with the man I loved and who wanted to marry me and, for the first time ever – listen everyone: *no one* around us!

No one, no one, no one but us! – and God.

We hugged – as much as our thick jackets allowed. I was thrilled by the sight of Mansur's body so comfortably upright. It was my delight, and I shared it with him.

Peace suffused the blue horizon, the little waves around us and our hearts.

A few storks flew over us, majestically.

Finally reaching our destination, we dragged ourselves onto the rocks. A mere islet it was, devoid of any human presence. There wasn't even a boat anchored with tourists listening to the radio, the usual *curse* of picturesque creeks.

We tore from our bodies the disgraceful jackets and threw them away, as the ultimate stage of our emancipation!

We were free.
We were *alone.*
We were happy.

Resting on our backs, exhausted and enchanted, we let our skins and hair dry under the sun. Mansur took my hand. We said nothing. It was one of those moments when words are superfluous.

Nature around us lent its manifold splendour, as the alphabet of our thanksgiving.

We only needed to look at the vast firmament above our heads, adorned with white and grey clouds, to be brought closer to each other in our hearts. The light sound of the waves and behind us, the rustling of eucalyptus leaves in the warm and salty breeze, and the distant call of seabirds... everything sang the praises of the Almighty, Who designed this complex and living harmony to tell our souls about His beauty and love.

Turning to the side, I rested on my elbow to behold my beloved.

His eyes were shut, but he was well awake, as I could see from his hand, swiftly squeezing a mosquito against his thigh: "Naughty insect: it has just bitten me! I'm surprised it would fly that distance from the shore."

As he begun scratching the tiny bump, I enquired: "Did you *feel* the bite? Is it itching?"

He answered: "Of course I did; and yes, it *does* itch, even on a billionaire's skin. It's annoying enough. I don't know how *you* manage to ignore them at night, up there in your cell."

For a moment I actually felt a slight dizziness, a bit like a scientist – a geneticist for instance, like Professor Lejeune – on the verge of proving a world-changing hypothesis. I asked, pointing at the small whitish spot: "Mansur, did you notice *where* the bite is located?"

He looked at it. Then stopped. Then looked at me.

There was a long silence. We looked at each other.

I moved to his feet and tickled his soles. That must have been an awkward sight (seen through long-range binoculars, for instance) as neither Mansur nor I was smiling. In fact, we were both deadly serious. He didn't laugh once at my tickling: "No, I feel absolutely nothing. Not the faintest stimulus. Sorry."

I tried again by his knee and thigh, only to receive the same answer. But above his waist, sensorial awareness occurred as normal. "False alarm, darling," he said. "Or false *joy*, rather. I'm just the same crippled swimmer.

"But that mosquito bite still puzzles me. How can I sense the itch, and no other signal? I was bitten before on my legs or feet, but it's the first time I recall perceiving the sensation. I'll ask my doctor when we get back."

Not *yet* though, please.

Let us *stay*...

Let us remain on this tiny island, *forever*.

We lay back again, smiling. In that escapade into a state of original innocence, our bliss had reached an unspoken climax.

So it must have been, before the first sin.

So they must have felt, before they lost grace.

The thought of sharing first parents made us brother and sister in a deep and fulfilling way.

As explained by Abu Ephrem during our marriage preparation, Adam of old would have been all to Eve, and she all to him, as far as human interaction was concerned.

They would have looked at each other as at complementary reflections of their divine Father, Who had created them as one single human race, male and female.

Sin had distorted their perception.

Mutual trust had turned into lust; and shared adoration of their Creator into domination of one by the other.

But the New Adam, Christ, had restored and even improved human affection, making His saving love for His Church – His immaculate Bride – the type and the program of conjugal love.

I reclined on my side again to look at Mansur. His eyes were shut, and his chest was moving up and down as he breathed, peacefully.

Words from the Bible quoted by Abu Ephrem the previous week came back to my mind: *The husband is the head of the wife, as Christ is the head of the Church. He is the Saviour of His Body. Therefore as the Church is subject to Christ, so also let the wives be to their husbands in all things.*

But the priest had insisted on reciprocity: *Husbands, love your wives, as Christ also loved the Church, and delivered Himself up for it: That He might sanctify it, cleansing it by the laver of water in the word of life.*

I so much wished to be just *that* to Mansur!

I wanted him to be proud of me, for no superficial or base reason, but for the beauty of my soul, through the mercy of God. I wanted to be for him a little mirror handed by God. I had spoken those words in my heart many times, and many more words which I didn't recall with precision, apart from those, I think: *He that loveth his wife, loveth himself.*

I lay closer to Mansur, and found myself whispering a spontaneous prayer: "Dear God, thank you for having created me. Thank you for having called me back to You. Thank you for having led me to such a generous and courageous man as Mansur.

"Please, help us prepare to enter Your great sacrament of matrimony with the best dispositions of heart and soul.

"Protect little Talitha, whom I'm honoured to receive soon from You and from him as my treasured *daughter*.

"And, if Your glory were better served that way, please grant Mansur complete healing of his wounded flesh. Amen."

My eyes were shut as I spoke, and I was surprised to feel my hand caressed by Mansur's. He wasn't asleep, and had certainly heard me. I was glad, because in a way, it could now be considered as my own declaration of love to him, which I might not have dared utter so freely if I had known he was awake.

Revealing the inside of my soul was the truest gift of intimacy I could offer my spouse-to-be. I saw that, without such a gift, bodily contact would remain superficial, and finally deceptive.

He opened his eyes and whispered in my ear: "Clara, I've never heard a more beautiful prayer. Thank you."

Chapter 71

We sat up, looking at the beautiful landscape.

The sky, uninterrupted by any buildings, and only by a few mountains; the yellow horizon of the desert; and below, the green belt of trees and the very few houses; and the sea; and our twenty toes.

Mansur said that he could see Luke on the beach, by the boat: "Armed with those long-range binoculars, my *chaperone* is surely keeping both eyes on me! And on you (although, I'd rather watch over you without *his* help.) He must be pleased that we haven't got ourselves into mischief."

He went on: "You know, I feel a bit guilty about them. Here I am, enjoying myself on a dream island in the company of the most perfect woman under the sun, while they wait in the heat, until we feel ready to swim back."

I pointed out that there were *worse* working conditions than being flown in a helicopter to eat and swim in the Red Sea, even if it meant looking after a wounded billionaire. He laughed and said that it was time to get back if we wantèd to arrive at the church on time.

With some regret, we moved down towards the water to put on our space equipment again. But, looking around, I couldn't see our lifejackets.

"Mansur, where did you put the jackets? I can't find them...

"Ah-ha!" I managed to rescue *one*, since its strap had caught in a branch immersed in the water. But the other was gone.

Mansur admitted: "We're in trouble, dear. Luke will be *furious* if we swim back with only one jacket on. It's my fault. I shouldn't have been in such a hurry to get rid of them."

I told Mansur to wear the jacket himself, while I would swim close by. I was fine and could cover that distance without any help... unless he wanted to wave at Luke and have him fetch us with the boat?

(I *admit* that I meant my suggestion to tease Mansur's manly pride...)

He looked at the beach with defiance.

After reflecting in silence for a moment, he announced: "I have a better idea. We're not going to use *any* jackets, this time! We aren't children after all. And if needs be, you stay close to me." He threw the jacket far away behind him.

We were soon in the water, and swimming back. Luke had taken the boat off the shore and was looking at us from a distance – not protesting though.

I swam ahead and playfully came back underwater. It was a wonderful sight to see my beloved moving his body freely.

He dived in turn and met me under the waves, where we exchanged a kiss, beyond the reach of any binoculars!

Back on the surface, I noticed after a while that the wind was stronger swimming back. I also suspected a contrary current. We were progressing rather slowly.

However, wishing to spare Mansur that little humiliation, I pretended not to see, or not to mind.

But he was getting tired and stopped, recalling an anecdote as he was catching his breath: "It reminds me of that time at the beach when I was a little boy. I didn't know how to swim yet, and my nanny carried me on her back as she swam to the raft away from the shore.

"I remember feeling quite afraid, as I realised how completely dependent on her I was, wondering: 'And what of me if she suddenly dived?' But I also liked her all the better, I suppose, for the higher sense of care and safety she offered. Later on though, I realised that Jed had fired her for her imprudence when taking me without my floats on.

"Dear Haifa... She would have been about *your* age. But now, I'm too big a boy for you to carry me on your back! Even though you're a trained rescue swimmer... And I'm delaying you. I will wave at Luke for them to fetch us with the boat."

I immediately opposed the suggestion. It would have been surrender.

I told Mansur that I would hold his hips while swimming with my legs, so that he would be kept horizontal on his back, and could put all his strength in striking the water with his arms. He agreed, and it worked very well.

After a perfectly honourable time we landed ashore – even escaping scolding for the loss of our jackets!

We rinsed the salt off ourselves at the beach shower and sat in the sand, our swimming costumes drying fast on our bodies. We looked at the tiny paradise where, with so few words spoken, we had just shared such wonderful moments.

Something fluorescent was hanging from one of the few trees on our insular Eden, slowly waving in the wind.

That thrown-away jacket reminded me of those crutches one sees tied to the vaults of shrines, as tokens of miraculous cures – and of thanksgiving.

Admittedly, we had thoughtlessly littered a beautiful island.

Still, oh yes, thank you dear God with all my heart for such a swim!

Chapter 72

We landed a bit late at the yacht.

With the dreadful Cairo traffic, there was too little time for me to go back to the convent and change if we wanted to get to Holy Mass on time. Mansur again suggested that I could wear some of Nour's clothes, if I didn't mind. Once more, I was slightly uncomfortable.

But Abu Ephrem's words about my dress stained with Azim's blood came back to my mind. Yes, that dress had become a relic, since it bore the blood of a martyr. Well, would not the same apply to all of Nour's clothes? Were they not a martyr's possessions?

I would wear them as suggested then, asking for her protection, as I endeavoured to succeed her in the love of her husband and daughter. On further reflection, I found that over the past year, Nour had become almost like a sister to me.

As I was checking my face and makeup in her bathroom, I saw that a proper relationship had developed between me and her, although we had only met twice while she breathed, and twice again after, at the morgue and at her funeral.

Was that the type of friendship which Azim repeatedly referred to, in relation to his martyred virgin Katarina, and his holy hermit Anthony? Did the dead truly live amongst us, in God? That hypothesis matched my experience. Hence, as if at her invitation, I walked into Nour's wardrobe, which was still half full.

Among many treasures, I found a long black dress of faultless quality and style, fitting enough for the occasion. It had folds and modest slits on both sides, allowing for long strides if one ever had to run, in the *very* unlikely event (please God!) of another attack on this anniversary. Under it, I wore an immaculate white gauze blouse, whose iridescent mother-of-pearl buttons (each of them engraved with a letter of the alphabet) it took me a while to fasten.

I heard Mansur enquire if I was ready. Well, I wasn't quite there: why are men always in a *hurry*?

Nour and I had about the same measurements. Even her shoes fitted my feet! Mid-heeled suede sandals and a yellow scarf wrapped around my neck and over my head completed this sober and elegant mourning outfit.

Mansur was awaiting me in Nour's boudoir. He looked at me with surprise and admiration as I walked in. I couldn't help recalling the very similar look on his face when, less than three days earlier, he'd watched me wear another dress, in that very room. But not a *black* one.

I felt a pang in my heart, when seeing him again in the boudoir, by the spot where I'd knelt on the carpet, in dire humiliation and helplessness.

The similarity must have struck him as well, since he wheeled towards me and, taking my hand to his lips, said: "Clara, although I don't deserve you, you make me the happiest man in the world."

That was enough to cast away our little cloud. Mansur looked very elegant in a black suit and tie. In the car taking us to church, little Talitha was sitting between us. What a joy to have her with us! A warm, motherly feeling awoke in my heart, soon pervading my whole body, as I put my arm around Mansur's lovely daughter.

I gave thanks for the building up of the small network of our mutual relationships. All had occurred rather suddenly, and so unexpectedly! And I still knew them so little, in fact.

But things seemed to be falling gently into place.

As if guided by a mysterious hand, the fragile threads of our lives were progressively intertwined, and woven into the intricate fabric of divine providence.

I'd come to identify certain patterns in God's beautiful tapestry: expiation, like two days earlier; consolation, as in the past twenty hours; and overall, redemption.

Praise be to God, Our Lord!

At the church, for want of a ramp, Mansur was carried in his wheelchair to the top of the steps. It was the first time since the funeral that we were present together in that tragic place.

Below us, the chalk outlines had long faded away. But flowers had been laid on the four areas where our friends had died. Nour, of course; Azim, my dear brother; and poor Youssuf and Yasmina Helios, his doomed godparents.

It struck me that, after all, Mansur was a victim as well and deserved to be commemorated. But there were no flowers where *he* lay, since he'd survived. I walked down to that empty spot, near Nour's flowers, and spread across it the yellow scarf I was wearing.

Only *then* did I remember that Nour had worn an identical one on that fatal day. In fact, it might be the very same one, but dry-cleaned, since not a single dark stain remained.

The CCTV pictures from the video I had watched at San Antonio Airport, with Agents Bloomen and N'Guyen, flashed back in my memory. It seemed so long ago...

Now why, in Nour's wardrobe, had I chosen precisely *that* scarf? Surely that's why Mansur had stared, on seeing me walk in... How inconsiderate of me.

I was kneeling on the step, trying to cover the area where Nour's widower and my future husband had lain, apparently dying, just a year earlier. I knew that he was watching me with Talitha from the top of the steps.

The scarf shone against the background of the grey concrete like a manifesto of hope and tenderness. I meant it to be a sign of Nour's continued love for him. That love had sprung from the love of God, and my aim as Mansur's new wife wasn't to replace it, but to continue it.

Let it not go, I prayed.
Rather, may it flow...
May it grow...

Please God. The yellow scarf was no shroud then. It was life. I leaned towards the centre of it and kissed it, as I would kiss Mansur's heart.

Before I stood up, I was joined by little Talitha who kissed it as well, before pressing her innocent lips against the four wreaths nearby.

Thank God for children.

Chapter 73

We were moving inside the church when a parishioner handed the scarf to me again, assuming I'd forgotten it.

As I turned back to thank her, I thought I saw Jonathan in the background, sitting in his car near the Post Office. Yes, it was a Nissan like my former one, and the same dark colour as his, with a silhouette very similar to his on the driver's seat.

I waved the scarf at him as an invitation.

Although he wasn't a believer, as far as I knew, his close relationship with Nour, with Mansur, with Talitha and me, would justify his presence. But the man didn't get out of the car.

Perhaps it wasn't him, or he hadn't seen me. Or possibly, he felt it too painful to commemorate the loss of a woman whom he had so passionately loved. I remembered his hand shaking with her picture in it, as he was showing me on his phone the depiction of their very first encounter at the concert in England. Poor Jonathan...

Suffering in silence all those years since Mansur and Nour's wedding; and even more so since her death. Why was life so difficult for him, when mine was turning to be so full of joy and hope? I would pray for him at church. If only he could find God!

Talitha was wheeling her father in. Although she wasn't really tall and strong enough to push and direct the chair, he let her do so, finding it a precious opportunity for both of them to bond, through grief and void. I assisted her efforts with one hand.

Abu Ephrem offered the Mass. There was no music. I was surprised to see so many parishioners. But my particular pleasure was that both Mansur's parents had come back from Beirut. I liked them and was grateful to them for having welcomed me as their future daughter-in-law. We embraced each other with emotion.

Other members of staff of the various Al-Khoury companies and of the *Cedrus* attended as well. The latter employees in particular had known Nour very well and held her memory in deep esteem and affection.

Abu Ephrem preached on self-denial, faithfulness and forgiveness. I felt inadequate, having so far in my life barely exercised any of those virtues. But I asked Azim and Nour again to intercede for me, so that I might improve with God's grace, and with their example and assistance.

I looked at Mansur, who had given me this morning such a moving proof of his moral strength at Tora Prison, when showing himself so generous to his assassin and to his family.

Oh yes, how inadequate *I* was! Nobody had really offended me yet. Or perhaps, I hadn't noticed? Or, had I forgotten? Did I have anything to forgive?

Images of my last twelve months kept appearing in my mind: my first encounter with Azim; the lunch in Luxor with Mansur and Nour; my conversations with Azim on the bench, in his "private oasis;" our last evening on the hotel terrace, with his kissing the scar on my wrist; my time alone, as I assumed, in the garden by my bedroom, not suspecting his presence; our last minute embrace at the airport; my totally unexpected re-birth in the underground chapel at Orly Airport; the shock of hearing news of the attack over the Atlantic...

Such a shock.

I still went cold remembering that moment.

...Dr. Yazir's help and my silly suspicion proven groundless when I unwrapped the pearl necklace in Houston; Kitty's wedding, and Kitty's pregnancy; the funeral, back here; my return to Vancouver; and then here, beginning work at the various schools, either run or being built by the Al-Khoury Charitable Trust; my first encounter with my dear Osly girls saved by Azim (and me), and my bougainvilleas planted on the school site down there; the catechism classes with Mansur and Talitha; Mansur's fairy tale proposal, and...

Another cold tremor went down my spine.

...And the *not-so-fairy* confrontation in my wedding dress, ending only yesterday night with our reconciliation; the terrible and wonderful scene at Tora Prison this morning; and lastly, our dream swim to *paradise island*, and back...

Events seemed to flow naturally, like movements in a melody. But I had no idea where it would end. I trusted in God, and in my beloved fiancé.

One month from then, I would be his *wife*!

Mansur and I were the first to go to Holy Communion. Jeda followed us. Thankfully she *was* a Catholic – but she had kept vague when asked about Jed's religion. Back at my seat, kneeling with the Blessed Sacrament still within me, I gave thanks to Jesus my Saviour, and I renewed in my heart the total abandonment of my body and soul to God, and a firm desire to fulfil His holy Will the best I could.

After Mass, we walked down to the crypt where the bodies had now been laid to rest permanently. The tombs of Youssuf and Yasmina Helios, Azim's godparents, had been decorated by their relatives.

Mansur had wanted a plain and beautiful design for the tombs of Nour and Azim.

Nour's bore the following epitaph: *Spem in alium* – that is: *Hope in none other*. On Azim's, I read: *Numquam habui* – or in English: *Have I had ever*. I didn't need to ask for a translation, as I remembered it from their funeral. I had long kept the Order of Service. The quotes on our friends' twin tombs were the first verse of the well-known Renaissance motet: *Hope in none other have I had ever, but in Thou Saviour.*

Jonathan and Mansur still loved that music, and the three of us had often discussed its structure, its meaning and that of similar compositions (I mean that *they* had discussed it, while I listened with admiration).

The idea of two quotes from the same work linking Nour's tomb to Azim's appealed to me very much.

I hoped that my life with Mansur would be so truly faithful and loving, that our tombs could bear similar epitaphs. Or rather, I would want to share one single tomb with him, with a sculpture of us lying side by side as in ancient monuments, he behind me, protecting me!

I knelt by the wall, resting my forehead against the cool marble slab, giving thanks for so much generosity shown to me, when I knew myself to be so undeserving of it.

The chauffeur drove us back to the convent and Mansur asked me if I wished to eat out. I answered that it had been a short night and a long day, so that I would be glad simply to stay at home.

He insisted on accompanying me to the front door and said: "I don't want you to feel abandoned, just because of my infirmity. Even though there's no lift, I could easily have my carers carry me up to your room and we can picnic there if you wish, before I go back."

There was a silence.

From behind his chair where I was standing, I stooped down against his shoulder and whispered in his ear: "Sir, we are sorry to announce that you've lost your claim to *conventual exemption*."

He turned his head towards me, trying to guess exactly what I meant, while the beginnings of a smile started to make his face shine. He asked: "But... how could *you* know?"

Our cheeks were against each other and my hands crossed over his chest, when I answered: "Blessed are the merciful: for they shall obtain mercy."

He was about to speak, when I put my finger on his lips and concluded: "Time to rest, my beloved; and soon my spouse. I will call you in half an hour, after my prayers."

He wheeled himself away towards the gate and to his van.

Was a man ever dismissed from the door of his belle with more exultation?

Chapter 74

I sat for a while upon the bench in the garden.

Was not my happiness supreme?

How could God be so concretely attentive to our needs, when He had so many billions of men, women and children to take care of? I felt as if it were almost too good and, for a moment, I feared that fate, which had struck us so brutally a year ago, might come back with a vengeance.

But my silly apprehension soon evaporated when a familiar silhouette appeared through the garden gate, moving behind a large flower bouquet. That was a nice surprise. One didn't see much of *him* around here these days. I guessed that he was kept very busy with Mansur's health issues, which must perturb the smooth running of business.

Watching him walk along the slab alley towards my bench, I rejoiced at his sight, grateful for his friendship. I would discreetly inquire why he hadn't attended the Mass. And yes, those flowers *were* bougainvilleas – my favourite ones! – although I'd only seen them as shrubs planted in soil.

"Clara! I'm so glad to find you. I wouldn't have left without seeing you again. These flowers are for you. I know you like them."

Puzzled, I took the bouquet from his hands. Where could Jonathan be going? "Oh, you're flying away again? You, important businessman! Is it to Beirut, or London this time?"

He sat on the bench next to me, looking pensive: "Neither, my dear friend. In fact, I will be gone for a while."

I was alarmed: "You mean, until the wedding? But you can't meet us directly in Paris: what about Mansur's bachelor party? Is it not the Best Man's job to lead it?"

He smiled: "Dear Clara, circumstances compel me to miss your wedding. I'm so terribly sorry. But it won't be a great loss for my speech as Best Man (although I'd already jotted down on paper a few funny ideas). As to the stag night, I won't let dear Mansur down."

I stood up, now very serious: "Jonathan, what circumstances on earth could ever make you go away when your best friend is getting married, in the difficult condition that you know better than anyone else, and needs your support more than ever!

"And, for what it's worth, his bride-to-be considers you as a *personal* friend, so that your absence would grieve her just as much."

I paused, trying to understand, worry growing inside me. "Is it your health? Did you get bad news from your doctor? Or have some of your close relatives died? Please, tell me. I need to know. Surely you owe me the truth?"

He was looking into the distance, as though beyond the hedge, still silent.

I sat down closer to him and took his hand: "Jonathan, what can have happened? There's nothing Mansur wouldn't fix for you... Or, don't tell me it's anything to do *with* Mansur... If it is, I will speak with him. Everything will be fine."

He gently took back his hand and said, still not looking at me: "Clara, I'm so grateful for your concern. But you know me. I'm a rather *discreet* sort of chap. Not one for great manifestations."

"People say it helps to speak and get things out of one's system."

"But what if it's really *bad*?"

"What if one is professionally bound to secrecy?"

"What if disclosing certain things may *hurt* the people one cherishes most?"

I was more and more astonished. What terrible truths could Jonathan's friendly heart be laden with?

He'd just described himself adequately: he was a discreet character. Actually, I would rather call him unassuming, modest, and humble. It was what made him so *special* – the fact that he was always in the background, available, competent, quick; but never overbearing.

My alarm had at least that advantage, that I was putting words on his qualities, taken for granted until now.

And if I could help him, I *would*. Perhaps, that was why he'd come to me. Perhaps, a female friend was just what he needed to unload whatever burden he was carrying, and to be happy again?

Sitting on our bench, with my heart so full of my own happiness, I felt a bit like his older sister (although he was nearer to Mansur's age) and I offered my assistance again: "Jonathan, I beg you to let me help you.

"I don't ask you now in relation to our wedding. If you can't come, you can't. But for your own sake now, and because of my affection for you, please let me know what this is all about. I promise to keep it secret, if it helps you."

He looked at me for the first time and sighed deeply: "Thank you so much, Clara. This is more than I'd hoped. Well... I must speak then. But remember, this is only in response to your request. Only because *you* begged me to tell you.

"So, this is the plain truth: yesterday afternoon, Mansur banished me.

"I must leave Cairo before sunrise tomorrow, and never see his face again."

Chapter 75

I couldn't believe my ears.

His elbows on his knees, he hid his face in his hands – or only his *nose*, in fact, since I could still see his moist eyes and cheeks. As he started sobbing, silently, his shiny cufflinks glittered at his wrists.

What he'd said was like a sword plunged into my heart.

How could the two men I... The men I liked – *loved* most... How could the two *living* men I loved most be separated? And in such anger?

Or, to be more accurate, how could my future husband be so inflexible as to "*banish* from his face" the one who had been such a long-time and faithful friend, and a loyal and efficient personal assistant?

"Jonathan, I know Mansur well enough. He would never intentionally hurt anyone." As I spoke, I tried to ignore the thought that the wedding dress incident didn't really bear this out.

"You must have misunderstood him. Please, tell me it isn't so!"

Still hiding his face, he murmured: "There's no room for mistake. It's all in writing, in full legalese. His lawyer convoked me this morning and read the document to me. I had to sign it, and kept a copy."

I started feeling tears come to my own eyes and asked: "But Jonathan, what on earth can have motivated such a terrible measure, and after all these years of intimate friendship? Please, *tell* me. Whatever you've done, I won't judge you."

I put my arm around his shoulders to express my sympathy. He rested his head against my neck (I'd always liked his aftershave) and said softly through his hands: "I... contradicted him. I dared to tell him what I found to be *wrong*. And it wasn't about the business."

I held him tighter and whispered back: "My dear, dear friend, if it wasn't business, *what* was it about?"

He answered *one* word, which hit me like a banderilla – those harpoon-pointed colourful sticks that are jabbed into the bull's back at corridas, as Raúl's brother once boasted to me, to tire the beast before using the sword.

The word he said was: "*You.*"

This was becoming much more serious than I had anticipated.

I had an unpleasant feeling of something *very* bad looming ahead; something hostile coming inexorably closer; as if my strength had been assessed in advance and my soul overpowered, even before the assault.

And my price set.

And my master or mistress satisfied; whoever he or she was.

But it was too late to stop now. I *had* to know, and if my suffering could help anyone – starting with my unfortunate friend on the bench – it wouldn't be completely wasted: "Jonathan, what could you have done against me? What could Mansur reproach you with? Whatever it is, I forgive you."

Still in the circle of my arm, as under my wing, he said: "It isn't something *I* did."

"It's something *he* did. It's things *he* does."

Then he suddenly stood up and walked a couple of steps away from me, adding: "No, forget what I've said. After all, I must still consider him as a friend. If that isn't what fidelity is about, then what is?

"And I don't want to be prosecuted. I don't want any trouble, and he's so powerful! What could I do against his lawyers? To my shame, I have no savings; or very little. I don't even own a flat.

"Clara, it's better for you, and for me, if we drop this topic now. I'd just come to say goodbye and wish you the best for the wedding, and after.

"You're such a wonderful woman, so worthy of every respect and honour. You're... *a lady*. Please forgive me for speaking so freely. I wouldn't, if we were to meet again.

"It's been my privilege to know you. It's been my... Clara, I don't know how I can go now, but I must. Please, forget me."

He shook my hand clumsily and walked away.

It took me a few seconds to recover and realise what he'd said, and what was happening.

With my mid-heeled sandals, running out of the garden was a bit tricky.

I left my flowers on the bench and made it out only as he was driving off; but I managed to catch his car door – the window was lowered – and he stopped, the engine still running.

I was by then in (moderate) tears and begged him: "Jonathan! You *can't* go away like that! You can't leave Cairo... You can't leave us... You can't leave *me* like that. Please stay on!

"Tell me what I need to know. I'm sure that this is a terrible misunderstanding. We *must* talk it through, and please God, we will find a way out, together. But I need your help, just as you need mine – if you wish to accept it."

He looked at me with an equally tearful face, although he dried his eyes briskly, as a man who doesn't want to show his emotions.

Without a smile or a word, he opened the passenger door and we ended up in that same elegant bar where we had sat by the Nile, nearly a year earlier, on our way back from the funeral.

The night had come.

Chapter 76

He ordered a bottle of *Potocki*, apologising:
"If you don't mind, this evening I need something a bit stronger than juice, and this is the most exclusive vodka. But if *you*'d prefer a soft drink..."
I assured him that vodka would be fine. In fact, I felt that I needed a fix at least as much as he! But first I went to the Ladies' Room.

I wished to stay alone for a short while, to think (and also, to check my face in the mirror).
Fr. Paul was right about L'Oréal: waterproof makeup *was* a good idea. This time, my eyelids, cheeks and lips didn't look like a battlefield. I set right the sleeves of my dress. But, feeling a bit hot, I took off my yellow scarf, letting my throat become visible, against which my beautiful necklace beamed with all its pearls and rubies. Suddenly, I wondered if the jewels didn't look slightly *over the top*. They surely clashed with my plastic rosary beads. Which of my two necklaces should I take off?
Never mind. I drank a glass of water and tried to think calmly.
This *had* to be a mistake. There could simply be no valid reason for Mansur to be angry, and Jonathan *was* to be rescued, not bullied.
My phone showed a text message from Mansur: "I can't find sleep on this empty boat. Is my dove still at chapel? She said she would call me..."
I wasn't in the mood for texting back and, switching off my phone, I returned to our table.
The waiter had brought the bottle and filled our glasses.
Jonathan stood up as I arrived and helped me sit down. I had always appreciated his utter courtesy, even though it sometimes felt a bit old-fashioned. But we don't live in a world where women are ordinarily paid much respect, and it was nice to receive it from him.
The vodka bottle was beautifully designed, like sculpted ice; but its emblem, a triple cross with its lower left arm broken, made me slightly uneasy. Jonathan explained that it wasn't a cross but an old Viking character called the *pilawa*.
I dipped my lips in the vodka as he spoke: "Clara, I've just been thinking about what you said earlier. I came to find wisdom in your words. Beauty... Thus, if you really, *really* want me to tell you, I will do so. Whatever it may cost me. I don't mind.
"Truth comes first, and by now, I know that your beautiful soul won't shun it, even though it may hurt you. I won't hide from you that I'm not a deep believer. I mean, nothing like you. But in my own way, I try to be an honest man. A decent fellow, despite my limitations."

These glasses were rather *small*. I'd felt nothing while swallowing the contents of mine. I put it back on the table, answering: "Jonathan, I want to face the truth with you. And we will carry it together."

He helped himself to another glass and put the bottle back on the table, when, noticing my empty glass, he apologised and filled it again.

Having swallowed the spirit, he replied: "I need courage. Please, Clara, first bear in mind that *we* and Mansur belong to very distinct cultures. This truth is essential for a fair consideration of the differences between *us* and *his* family. I know that he was brought up in a rather westernised way, but there are very deep aspects of one's personality which are embedded in one from early childhood, and that will influence one's behaviour for life.

"Up to a year ago, Mansur was a Middle-Eastern Muslim, like his father. His mother is a Catholic, as you know, but also a convert. The only son of Lebanese and Iranian parents, Mansur is necessarily conditioned by his upbringing. Add to that his financial background. As he likes to say, he's "heir to an empire."

"I never talk about those things, but some are in the public domain. So, you should know that your future husband is among the one-thousand richest people in the world.

"That has nurtured in him, from youth, a sense of almightiness that would be despicable when found in most men, but simply expresses the truth, when you belong to that category of wealth.

"In short, Mansur is a *god*, who can do anything he likes.

"I have lived with him long enough. He only needs to open his mouth – or even less – to *look* anywhere, and immediately, the thing or the person he wants or dislikes appears or vanishes at will.

"I learned this morning that his power knows *no* limits, and extends even to old friends. By sunrise, I will have evaporated, like a character from a fairy tale. I will disappear into thin air at Cairo Airport, just like he prevented *you* from flying away, the day he wanted you."

So, Jonathan knew *that*? I recalled how Mansur had managed to stop me going through customs, the day he proposed to me. Was Kitty right after all to find it controlling, rather than romantic?

Ignoring the more likely answer, I drank another (small) glass to hide my unease. I laid my hand on Jonathan's, keeping silent, but my eyes tried to convey as much affection and protection as I could.

He looked at me with gratitude, I felt, as he added: "Many times, I've been shocked or hurt by Mansur's actions or words. I coped with them the best I could, because I knew that his heart was *good*, and that I had to refrain from projecting our Western values onto him. And, to be honest, *Western* men are no angels either.

"So, I chose not to let my emotions lead me.

"That reasoned stance, and my knowledge of him as a friend from university, allowed me to work as his personal assistant for three years. Last year, of course, the tragedy of the attack changed many things. I was certain that, having lost his wife and nearly his daughter; and his friend Azim; and the lower half of his body – our dear Mansur would improve.

"But, I'm sorry to say, the opposite happened. It got *worse*."

There was a moment of silence, while he poured himself more vodka; and also in my very small empty glass. I picked it up and sipped automatically.

I was hurt, but I needed to hear it all. Let Jonathan be specific. General statements wouldn't help him or me.

I asked: "Jonathan, I thank you for your sincerity. But at this stage, should you not tell me the *facts*? I stress that *I* am the one asking.

"As Mansur's fiancée, I have a right to be informed of his whole personality, whatever it may cost me. And no one better than you is able and entitled to help me.

"So, please, *what* did he do?"

Chapter 77

He drank his glassful and, sighing and shaking a bit, went on:

"Fine, Clara. You've a right to the facts."

He showed me his phone. A picture appeared of ten magnificent rubies on a velvet tray.

I noticed: "They look similar to the ones he gave me, enshrined in my pearl necklace, look: one, two, three, four, five." I pointed at them, hanging around my neck.

Jonathan approved: "Yes, he sent me to that auction in Amsterdam. He was adamant that he would get the whole set of *ten*, and he did. I had to bid rather high on his behalf."

I was puzzled: "But I don't see the problem so far. Only, where are the five other rubies?"

He touched the screen, and another picture appeared. It was a young woman with a white dress to her knees and a cap on, at a beach that looked familiar – as did the woman. She was wearing a glittering belt around her waist.

She looked *magnificent*, with splendid red hair. That's when I gasped. She was Mansur's nurse! And, zooming in on the picture, the belt appeared to be gold, with five rubies enshrined in it.

I was shaking and put the phone back in his hand as if it were radioactive.

He explained: "I'm sorry that you had to see that. That's Ruth Sheehan, as you saw yourself. His new nurse. He wanted the stones to echo her hair. He designed the belt originally with ten stones. But she complained that it was embarrassing in public – and uncomfortable at night.

"He insisted that no one would think the belt genuine, and would simply assume it to be fancy attire found at the bazaar. All she could bargain for was for five gems to be taken out (you know where they ended up)."

Slamming my glass (empty again!) down on the table, I rose and asked defiantly: "Jonathan, what you are implying is extremely... extremely... *displeasing*.

"I should be grateful if you could provide evidence. After all, nurses may buy fancy jewels *anywhere*. Who can say that she hasn't ordered five fake stones precisely to match my genuine necklace!"

Noticing a couple of late customers turning their heads towards us with surprise, I realised that I'd probably spoken *much louder* than I thought... I felt dizzy standing and hoped no one noticed.

Jonathan looked as if I was asking him too much. Then standing up as well, he came just behind me. I could smell his nice scent. He searched on his phone again, tapped the screen, and a video started playing.

It was Ruth again, at the same beach, wearing around her waist the same belt with the five rubies. She was crouching at the feet of a man lying in the sand. She was facing the camera, but I could only see the man's back. She was pouring sunscreen (I assumed) on the man's ankles. I could hear the sound of waves, and seabirds, and some children laughing.

Looking at Jonathan, I said that it was inconclusive. He said nothing and the video played on. Ruth turned her head to the side and shouted: "Litha, come and help me rub Daddy now, and please take your toy back!"

Out of compassion (so I assumed), Jonathan switched off the sound, as I watched Talitha – for it was her – arrive and start smearing the man's legs with oil. Feeling nauseous, I sank down towards my chair, thankfully supported by Jonathan who anticipated my sudden weakness and caught me in time. I was so grateful for his good reflexes...

But the whole thing was so shocking. I found the strength to ask: "*When was this film taken?*"

He said: "Two days ago, at *Ain Sukhna*. There's a small island where he likes to rest. Never without his nurse, though."

I felt as if one more banderilla had just pierced my flesh. Surely, that's why the nurse wouldn't swim this afternoon, unlike the bodyguard and carers. *She* kept aside, not to have me see her belt – yet...

Jonathan helped me to another glass of vodka: "Clara, please don't jump to conclusions. And please, don't accuse Mansur, or Nurse Sheehan. *I* am the one to blame."

Putting my glass back on the table, I said firmly: "If anyone is innocent in this shameful story, it is *you* Jonathan. And *I*, I hope. And Talitha."

But he went on: "You don't understand. *I* hired Ruth; Mansur didn't. After the tragedy, I was desperate to find ways to foster his resilience. I thought that anything or anyone related even remotely with Nour and Azim, and with the time of their shared happiness before the attack, could help him enormously.

"I recalled that Azim had mentioned a girl who was a nurse, among his last group of American tourists. He'd said jokingly that having doctors or nurses in the group was always a bonus, in case of an emergency. I thought that Mansur would like to be cared for by someone who had known Azim in his last week.

"I was able to trace her via the travel agent and, with the approval of Mansur's father, our family head of staff offered her working conditions which she would have been foolish to turn down."

I started shaking again.
So *that* was where I'd seen that girl.
She was part of our group!
Yes, at Giza for instance.

I couldn't believe the cruel irony of it. She was the red-haired beauty who had unsuccessfully tried to lure Azim. And now, she...

I couldn't allow even the mere thought of it to unfold in my mind.

Chapter 78

How could dear Jonathan have been so stupidly *ignorant*!

Does he not have the slightest notion of what a young woman like Ruth Sheehan could want, and do?

He guessed my silent furore: "Clara, I see now that I was naive. Or rather, my desire to assist my friend at any cost made me blind to other issues."

I didn't answer, yet...

Was that not also why I had been hired? Because, even more than the red-haired nurse, I'd been associated with Azim, and with Nour and Mansur? Was I not also – to some extent – a voucher for Mansur's happy convalescing?

I looked in his eyes and dared to ask him: "But was it *you*, then, who chose *me*?"

He looked embarrassed, but nodded: "As I said, I was *desperate*. I was on the lookout for any chance, however small, to restore Mansur's hope. I wanted to provide continuity between his past and his future.

"And *you* appeared. I was in his hospital room when you first visited, less than ten days after the attack. I saw you walk in and, immediately, I felt that hope had entered the room.

"Then Mansur spoke for the first time, his eyes still shut. When Talitha led you to him, and put his hand in yours, and when you spoke so kindly to him, I became certain that destiny had sent us the ultimate cure, in your person. My eyes crossed those of Mansur's parents, and I detected the same hint in their look.

"You were a witness from our recent and bright past, materialising after the horror, and asserting in your very discreet way that there was a future for him, and for us. Clara, whatever happens to me, and to you, I will never forget it, and I will be grateful to you forever."

He'd taken my hand and was pressing it to his heart, in notable contrast with his customary shyness. I let him hold it, as he went on: "Mansur's father had come to like you, as an asset to his son's recovery.

"After I made hints that we should find some way to keep you around, *he* was the one who suggested that you should be given the position first offered to Azim as supervisor of the charitable schools. But you left us, taking your time.

"During the six months you spent in Canada, I referred to you regularly in Mansur's presence. Talitha also remembered you and I encouraged her to mention your name to her father, hoping that it would cheer him up.

"This is also why I told him about your pearls. He was still weak, but had been deeply touched by the fact that you wanted to sell them to assist the young girls, whose safety had cost the life of Azim, and indirectly of Nour.

"He paid a good price for them, but forbade me to let you know that *he* was the buyer. He was always interested in jewels, as much as in horses. When you came back and started working for his family, Mansur was deeply happy.

I kept silent, remembering my return to Cairo after Christmas, and my great expectations. Jonathan went on.

"However, a few weeks ago, Talitha confided in me that he wanted her to have a new mother. But she was spontaneously attracted to Nurse Sheehan. Please Clara, *don't* get upset. She's just a child, and she would see that young woman every day, taking care of her father, while you – with commendable discretion – would seldom come to the yacht, and would mostly meet once a week, for catechism class.

"Other women would visit sometimes, elegant ones, of a background more akin to Mansur's, like Nour's cousin, Vardah Wattles – the interior designer. She would have stood a good chance if she hadn't recently married that Scottish actor.

"But Talitha didn't feel particularly close to them.

"When I asked her whether she knew of any woman whom she would like to have as a mum, she thought for a little while and said "Nurse Sheehan." I must tell you that I was very disappointed, as I suspected the nurse to be slightly ambitious, and I wouldn't have her take advantage of her position to lure away *our* Mansur!

"On the contrary, I knew that *you* wouldn't marry him for his wealth. Unlike Ruth, you would be a devoted wife to him, and a dedicated mother to Talitha. I'm not ashamed of what I did: I persuaded Talitha to write to *you*.

"Actually, I almost dictated the letter, while maintaining her childlike phrasing. And I was right. Her petition matched Mansur's expectation, and now you will be his bride, and Talitha's mother.

"If I believed in God, I would say that it's a match *made in heaven!*"

I'd taken my hand back from Jonathan's chest and was now holding my glass – when had I emptied it again? – looking silently at the bottom of it.

Contradictory feelings were fighting in my heart.

On the one hand, I was grateful to know that my interests had been protected so successfully against that red-haired adventuress. But on the other hand, where I had assumed there was spontaneous affection, I now saw...

I didn't dare to acknowledge the word which, like a cancerous lump, was pushing under my swollen heart and trying to erupt in my mind.

I admitted it at last.

Manipulation.

With the best of intentions, Jonathan had just exposed the *artificial* roots of my current relationship.

Was it not clear now that Mansur had never truly loved me?

And that Talitha, innocent Talitha, had only spoken as advised to?

The human heart was an empty vessel – like this glass.

The room seemed to have taken on a strange ultra-sharpness and the background noise echoed in my ears – shock, maybe? – but I looked at Jonathan with anger and gratitude, like a child forced to walk her first steps towards adulthood.

As a true friend, as a more mature personality, had he not indirectly opened my eyes? Was it not now up to me, either to adopt his more experienced vision of love, or to revert to childish romanticism?

Jonathan had shown himself so ignorant of female psychology, and yet, he seemed to read my soul as he addressed precisely the issue which concerned me: "Clara, you'll be happy with Mansur.

"You just need to learn more about love, and particularly in a family like that of Mansur's. We Westerners tend to see love as passionate and one-to-one. But in the Middle-East, they love as a clan, as a *tribe*. That's why polygamy is approved of.

"The family, the group, is more important than the individual. And wives don't have any difficulty if their husband – their affectionate master – needs to show tenderness to more than one woman. That's how most men are. Provided the wives are blessed with children, especially with *sons*, everything's fine.

"I think you are strong enough now not to be scandalised by what you must know. Please, as I said from the start, if you love Mansur and his family, don't project our Western values on their behaviour."

He was about to fill my glass again, but I put my hand in the way, feeling my thirst gone. For some reason my palm missed the glass and landed on the table.

I let him pour vodka into the tiny glass again.

Why *resist*, after all?

I was bracing myself for the stripping of a deeper layer of my affections. It wasn't so much a banderilla this time. I saw my heart being unwrapped by Jonathan's friendly fingers, and despite my embarrassment, I was glad to grow up. There's a time for everything.

He went on: "*Azim* had become very close to Nour. Their shared interest in spiritual topics was an essential aspect of their relationship. She and Mansur loved each other very much, but in a very *free* way. It was understood that they wouldn't take offense if, occasionally, the other spouse found complementary happiness with other partners, provided husband and wife retained preferential love for each other.

"Mansur would never have tolerated her carrying another man's child. But, if I may suggest without detracting from his open-mindedness, his benign tolerance was perhaps eased by the fact that Nour was sterile. Various specialists had said so, and we all assumed she would never conceive.

"Adoption had been a last resort.

"When against all odds she got pregnant, I was informed before Mansur would be made privy to the great news: you will see why.

"I had to report to Mansur's father, who ordered a paternity test. But it was too early, as they apparently can't occur until the third month. Jed, as Talitha calls him, interrogated Nour in my presence and – this is strictly confidential, so please never tell *anyone* – it appeared that the genitor wasn't his son..."

He looked me in the eyes and, after a pause, concluded: "Nour confessed that the father wasn't Mansur...

"But *Azim*."

Chapter 79

I interrupted Jonathan, gasping in horror!
I was now the one hiding her face in her hands.
My mind couldn't connect the sound "Azim" perceived through my ears, and the cherished memory of the virgin man who had taught me the beauty of purity and chastity.
Azim... This was unbelievable.

Pictures of our conversation under the fig-tree flashed back. And of our brotherly friendship. And of his clear look, when candidly telling me that he was a *virgin*.
Could he have been lying?
Was he pretending?
On the other hand, Jonathan obviously had Nour's confidence, and what interest would she have had in involving Azim? In retrospect, could not their intimate friendship have led them one step too far?
I could picture them in the South, looking for suitable areas for the new school and sharing so much – unofficially – in that wonderful project.
Having stayed there myself (albeit single) so frequently in the past six months, I knew the beauty of starry nights in the desert, the deep silence all around... In situations of intense emotion, boundaries can be crossed with no bad intention; without fully *noticing*...
Could it be that my dear Azim had been too tender towards the lovely Nour?
Closing my eyes, I kept silent for a while.
After my first shock, and the pang in my heart, I was coming to discern some *beauty* in this accident. That surprised me, as only two hours earlier, I would have cast away the mere suggestion as repelling. Something in me felt pacified by the thought that, after all, Azim had tasted love with such a deserving creature as Nour, before dying.
After all... *a host of films and TV shows sped through my mind*... dying a virgin *was* sad, wasn't it? And if Azim had told me otherwise, I now understood that it had been to protect me.
But it still hurt.
Well aware of my dismay, Jonathan had remained silent. I was grateful for his discretion. When he saw me more composed, he asked me if I really wished to hear the end. I insisted that I *had* to.
He gave me a smile of admiration and sympathy, and went on: "So, on hearing that Azim was the father, Jed became absolutely furious.
"He was mortified to find out that sterility was not on Nour's side, but on

Mansur's. He couldn't believe that his son had failed to give him an heir, when a mere tourist guide, a schoolteacher's son, had been successful. Jed was convinced that the child would be a boy – which couldn't be ascertained at that early stage.

"I felt sorry for Nour, as her father-in-law had spoken to her rather harshly. But I took it for granted that the problem would very soon be solved in the customary way, since she'd conceived only three weeks earlier.

"Until she told us that she meant to *keep* the child! I was taken aback, and so was Jed.

"He offered Azim the very advantageous position of coordinator of the school branch of his charitable trust, on the condition that he would convince Nour to be reasonable. They had no intention of running away and actually, they agreed that they'd made a mistake. But neither of them could be persuaded to end the pregnancy.

"We were all in dire straits, as their decision could have a deep impact on the stability of the family business – if Mansur were to learn about it and react badly. No doubt he would ask for a paternity test. If you thought him violent, by the way, in the boudoir the other day, learn to bow under fiercer blows.

"The following morning – I was in Beirut on business, but I will always remember that fatal date, just one year ago – Jed spoke with me and assured me that Mansur *would* act brutally against Azim, no doubt, when hearing the news; and possibly against Nour, with traumatic psychological and legal consequences to be expected.

"We could see the headlines!

"Jed stressed that he would never allow anything, nor *anyone*, to frustrate his son and destabilize his empire. The same afternoon, the attack occurred at the church. It was a Sunday. Mansur and Talitha were *not* supposed to attend the Baptism, but only Nour, as Azim's godmother.

"On hearing the news, Jed suffered a stroke.

"Perhaps I should keep this to myself, but I still wonder if his shock might not have been caused by the unplanned presence and subsequent injury of his son and granddaughter, rather than by the death of Nour and Azim. I don't mean to cast suspicion on my employer, though, especially since I was away that day and didn't witness the attack by the Scimitars.

"It may all have been a tragic *coincidence*. However, the question of the pregnancy was solved, and Mansur never suspected anything."

That last revelation stunned me, if anything else could. I liked Jed, and I felt that my affection was reciprocated. But Jonathan clearly suspected that at the very least, he might have been able to prevent the assassination of his own daughter-in-law – not to mention Azim and his godparents.

I was out of my depth.

Jed was no murderer!

I recalled how, on the yacht, he'd told me that his competitors had bribed Ali into leaking to them the time and place of the Baptism.

There were so many suppositions... so many motives.

Had Jed guessed what was likely to happen? Had he simply let the sequence of events unfold? Not intervening was very different from killing, wasn't it?

And who was I to judge the fears and anxieties of a father and a successful businessman, I reasoned? He'd been humiliated by his son's dynastic failure: if *I* had built an empire such as his, would I not have felt the same? Something felt a little... *off*... about this argument, but somehow I couldn't seem to grasp *what* it was.

It seemed to make sense... Perfect sense...

My thoughts ran on, feeling very clear and confident.

Yes, it *was* tragic.

Yes, innocents had died.

But *good* had come out of it.

Mansur had been baptised.

Thousands of families among their employees had perhaps been spared redundancy through the secured stability of the Al-Khoury businesses.

And finally, I had met Mansur, and I was *about to*...

I could not manage to spell in my mind the happy completion of our pending wedding. The prospect was suddenly not so appealing to me after all.

In fact, I felt confused, as if my moral compass had entered a magnetic field or cloud, leaving me defenceless in front of options which, up to then, had appeared in sharp contrasts of true or false, and right or wrong.

Where was north?

Was there such a thing as *north*, anyway?

Had it not been a useful artifice, a convention all along? What I had learned during this rather trying evening was making the facts of life appear more complex and subtle than I had first thought.

I felt called to *grow up*, and to reason more in terms of sincerity, of opinions and circumstances. Absolute principles and lofty ideals were proving inadequate tools to embrace the reality of life as unfolded before my eyes by Jonathan.

The experience was a rather bitter one but, at the end of the day, a salutary cure.

Someday, the fairy tale has to stop.

And my initiation into greater moral flexibility didn't mean the end of compassion and love. It only made me more *humane* and less judgemental in my affections.

I looked at my dear guide across the little table, sipping his vodka.

He seemed so unassuming.

He was *nice*-looking, rather than *good*-looking.

Was he not the timely embodiment of an older and trusted companion; if not *more* than that? Was he even aware of the transformation that his painful disclosures were inducing in the depths of my soul?

Probably not: a man who could be so ingenuous as to hire Nurse Sheehan for my future husband and not foresee the likely gold-digging, wouldn't be able to read in me deeper than the tears or smiles appearing on my face. Still, I didn't resent the pain he had involuntarily caused me. He had meant well and I had to be grateful.

Furthermore – as I suddenly recalled – he was about to leave Cairo, and probably depart from my life, *forever*. He hadn't yet told me exactly why.

But it would not change our fate: by sunrise, my cufflinked genie would have vanished... It grieved me to think of it.

I was feeling a bit hot and wished to spend a moment on my own, to think.

I asked him to excuse me, pretending that I needed to visit the Ladies' Room.

Chapter 80

I went outside to breathe.
Everything wavered as I walked, as though a heat haze had entered the hotel despite the air conditioning.
Most customers had left the lounge and the terrace was empty.
Stars showed up better in the desert, I knew, but despite the bright lights of the city, I could see a few.
It felt even hotter outdoors. I tried to ignore the fact that I had drunk too much vodka, making things sway. A bit like being on a boat.

Speaking of boats…
Downstream, on the opposite bank, a helicopter was taking off from a yacht, guided through the night by searchlights. It was certainly the marina where the *Cedrus* was stationed. But was it her?
I examined the beautiful ship, trying to locate Mansur's windows. I saw a couple of tiny silhouettes on the deck, but the distance was much too great to tell if my future *husband* was there.
How strange it was to look from afar at what my life could have… At what my life was about to become.
I became conscious of a greater divide in my heart than the one gaping across the wide river between the terrace where I stood and my fiancé's yacht. I loved Mansur, but not as exclusively as earlier. I found myself to be an aloof sort of bride-to-be.
Had I just grown up? I wasn't even really sad, I think. My soul was simply numb.

Like my body? It didn't react when feeling Jonathan's chin over my shoulder. He was standing behind me and we looked at the dark and glittering streams for a moment, in silence. A few boats were moving against the current.
My friend whispered: "Rainer Maria Rilke (the Austrian poet, you know) says that his direction in life was revealed to him on this river. He was on board a large sailing vessel with sixteen oarsmen. They were going up the Nile to the Island of Philae. A mysterious boatman was singing at irregular intervals…
"Let me quote Rilke for you, if I remember correctly: 'Whilst those about him were always occupied with the most immediate actuality and the overcoming of it, his voice maintained contact with the farthest distance.'"
Jonathan stopped, adding no comment.
In fact, I didn't understand what it was about, but it sounded melodious to my mind. I liked that kind of smart quotations. It made me feel cleverer, and better esteemed.

The breeze was still rather hot upon my sticky skin.

I was feeling a bit somnolent, wondering as to myself, but aloud: "Jonathan, why do you have to go? What is it that caused Mansur to banish you by sunrise?"

Standing close to my back, he was keeping silent.

Until I heard his lips utter what sounded like a Greek tragedy: "I was the shadow of a god.

"Shadows don't speak. They follow; they project; they magnify."

"I had accepted many things and done my best to abide by the values of my god – like you did for yours. But seeing you treated with disrespect was more than I could endure.

"Two days ago, after that terrible clash in Nour's boudoir, I saw the coffee stain on your wedding dress. I was horrified and could have punched him. He was in a state that afternoon and, in the evening, we met in his study, as we often did – with a bottle of *Potocki*.

"I stayed up for his sake and yours (I don't live on the boat, as you know, although I have a cabin there). Showing me a brochure about bioethics, he asked my advice about your philosophical views on contraception.

"Frankly, I didn't give a damn; but I told him that on one occasion, when I was feeling very low, you had given me hope again, through one single gesture and word. I added that he would be the most *stupid* man in the world if he let you go.

"By then, we had drunk more than a few glasses. He promised me that he would make peace with you, on your own terms. I was relieved for you both, and drove back to my flat, keeping the brochure, out of interest.

"But before going to Tora Prison this morning, Nurse Sheehan reported that a different doctor had visited him. As my position required, I asked what sort of examination was needed.

"She was hesitant to answer, but I pressed her and she admitted that they'd collected a fresh sample of Mansur's sperm, which was immediately frozen and stored. I rushed into his office to confront him, as I suspected that he was breaking his promise to you.

"He laughed at me, saying that his promise committed him only from marriage *onwards*, and that you would surely become reasonable after remaining a childless wife for a while. He meant to prepare for that time and wouldn't take any chances with his health and posterity. Nour, he added, was unable to conceive (so he assumed), but hopefully *you* were not, and your reluctance would soon fade away.

"To shake him, I nearly threw in his face the whole secret of Nour's pregnancy by Azim, but I refrained. Still, I was furious and said that he was manipulating you in the most vile and arrogant manner.

"That's when I crossed a line."

Was it possible? Could my fiancé have spoken those terrible words, so soon after having made his peace with me? But then, no reconciliation would have been needed if, earlier, he hadn't treated me like his *slave*.

I saw myself in Nour's boudoir again, in my wedding dress, prostrate under the gale of Mansur's contempt. Had I not seen the *real* Mansur then, and tried to ignore it, because...

Because deep inside, I longed to become Mrs. Clara Al-Khoury – the mistress onboard?

After a silence, Jonathan went on: "The frustration that had accumulated in me over previous years burst open and I reproached him for many things. He remained silent for a while. I was standing on the other side of his desk – a frame with your picture stood on it – trembling with indignation.

"Then he asked if I would keep my mouth *shut* about the morning's sample collection.

"I said that before being the future wife of my boss, you were a close friend to me – a very *dear* friend in fact – and that in consequence, I couldn't promise to leave you in the dark regarding something I knew to be so important in your eyes. That's why I came to your convent this evening, but I lacked courage and would have left, if you hadn't run after me."

He gave a sad smile.

"I knew that my answer to a man like Mansur was tantamount to signing my resignation. I was right. As your van drove off from the prison, I was kept behind by Mansur's guards and his lawyer, and had to agree to the terms of my demise.

"From a professional point of view, I can't complain, as he has rewarded me generously for my three years of service. But our relationship was much deeper than that. I was profoundly hurt to see that he would terminate it in such a businesslike manner, without any qualms.

"However, what made me suffer most was to realise that his will would not even bend for a compromise with his own future wife. My god appeared to me like a tyrannical child, and I grieved to imagine that you would become his next *rattle*."

I was too horrified to consider Mansur's betrayal then and there. Later, I would have to confront it. But presently, I felt such warmth towards Jonathan, while a melancholy music could be heard, coming from the lounge now deserted.

In a silent avowal of our affection unexpectedly found to be deeper than that of mere friends, very slowly, we started dancing.

I didn't know where we were going, *if* we were going anywhere.

It was so good not to think, for a moment...

Looking back, I find that I hadn't the remotest idea of eloping with Jonathan! I only knew that I was weary of my past attempts to find happiness, and grateful for a diversion, even for a couple of hours, or days.

I was busy rowing in my heart; let *him* watch for us, and sing if he wanted, as his poet advised.

It was getting late, and we finally walked down to the underground car park where the valet had left his Nissan. Half an hour later, as I realised long after, Mansur's bodyguard, steel-blue-eyed Luke, came looking for us in the lounge, and was told that we had left already.

To think that I lay right under his feet...

Chapter 81

The engine wasn't running.

Sitting in silence, side by side inside his car, we were listening to a beautiful piece of music on the CD player. Jonathan said: "I'm glad you like it. Schubert's String Quartet number 14 – the *andante*. It was my deepest inspiration when I used to dance. You remember I was a dancer, don't you? That's what led me to try and design a few ballets – like some actors become film directors. But that was a while ago, in Oxford."

I smiled appreciatively and in return dared to mention my prowess as a schoolgirl ballerina. At fourteen, I shifted to figure skating... I should have kept both hobbies.

Jonathan looked at me with renewed interest: "Truly, you can dance? I mean, for real; not merely standing against each other like on the terrace?"

I proudly exhumed from my memory a few technical terms and was amazed to find wonderful pictures from my adolescence conjured up with them: *tours en l'air*, *arabesques*, fish dives...

As I uttered those words, the muscles in my arms and thighs seemed to awake, as if impatient to stretch.

And, what if...

A daily swimmer, I needed no physical preparation!

"If I *can*? Let me show you!"

Prompted by a sudden inspiration, I unstrapped my suede sandals and stepped out of the car. Nour's black dress would not hinder my movements in the least. There had been no shooting to run away from (thankfully). Now there would be dancing!

Jonathan looked a bit puzzled, until he saw me in "fifth position," my foot in front of the other, closed up, and my arms raised in a beautiful ballerina oval! He started playing the andante again and watched me from his seat.

During a few minutes, I improvised a sequence of rather creative steps, – more fun than style, to be honest – before getting back into the car. Schubert's andante must have been on replay mode, as we sat silently, listening to it again.

After a while, he spoke first: "You should have been a dancer, Clara. Your limbs seem surprisingly fit for one who doesn't practice, and I liked your balance and pace. Once or twice, you reminded me of Kang Sue-jin in *Madame Butterfly* – perhaps her most poignant ballet. You are indeed a graceful butterfly, attractively emerging from her chrysalis..."

"It may not be too late for you to take up dancing again, even though not at professional level. And, perhaps, *I* should return to choreography..."

We were silent again, looking through the windscreen at the thick concrete wall of the underground car park, as if trying to decipher what the future held in store for us. After a while, he said the dreaded words: "I must drive you home, Clara.

"It's well past midnight, and I must make sure to catch the 06:09 a.m. flight to Copenhagen. You've made my last evening in Cairo pure bliss. With such an unexpected farewell, I don't regret my banishment – if it weren't for the fact that I will lose you forever."

I detached his fingers from the handbrake and eventually spoke: "Jonathan... what if I didn't wish to remain *here*?

"What if my life were to be spent with... *another* man than Mansur?

"Two days ago, he shouted that marrying me was a terrible mistake. I wonder now whether he wasn't right."

He took my hand to his lips and said: "Dear Clara... If I didn't think it a dream beyond all my expectations that *I* could, perhaps, ever be that man, I would still say that you don't know what you're saying. I'm a pariah. Mansur is powerful and, wherever I went, he could ruin my reputation if I... If you... We..."

After a silence he went on: "I wouldn't make you happy. I'm poor and with no significant connections for a woman like you to develop her many talents. Believe me, better for you to go back to him, to whom you belong."

I started rebelling at the thought of it. I was merely *betrothed*, not yet married. Furthermore, I knew now that my future husband – still much-loved – had a very different conception of love from mine. I felt no animosity towards Mansur and his family, but I earnestly questioned our match.

There was no one in the car park, but us.

What lay *behind* that thick concrete wall in front of us? Probably the Nile!

Ah, to swim away... to let myself be carried by its powerful streams, down to the sea... Still, flying off with Jonathan was out of the question.

I *was* engaged.

But that memorable evening had opened *other* doors, and I felt a terrible lack of time to think and make a rational decision. I could never dance like that with Mansur. I loved him, but I couldn't see Jonathan go away without a further token of his affection.

I wished for a sign, a hint. Should we dance again, all night, and try to delay with airy steps and tender caper the rising of the sun over the Nile?

Why was I surprised to hear his words? How could I not have expected them? Perhaps, *friendship* means different things for women and for men.

"Clara, would you make me the happiest man in the world, before I vanish? I feel as on death row, and no mere cigarette will do. I need your love, if you love me."

I knew what he meant and found myself taken off guard. What could I answer? I didn't want to hurt him, after what we had just shared. And he'd become my best friend. He'd cured me of my romantic vision of love – and had unshackled me from a rigid conception of truth.

In retrospect, how simple it is to state the obvious, namely, that I should have slapped him in the face and got out of the car!

I was too slow.

Was I also, perhaps, vaguely curious to see how far he would dare to go? Did I seriously think it a game? Or was I ready to take a risk because I'd just learned that my dead friends and my future husband had been less *shy* than I?

Also, an element of shame led me to overlook my light inebriation, whereas increased caution was most needed. I had not eaten since the picnic on the beach and wasn't used to strong alcohol. In truth, looking back, it's clear enough that my judgment was increasingly impaired by the *many* – if small – glasses of vodka I'd drunk.

With any other man than Jonathan, I would have suspected a hidden agenda. But he had become such a trusted companion. We had shared so much since our first meeting in Mansur's hospital room a year ago... and he was in great trouble just now – and all because of *me!*

Yes, he'd confronted Mansur for *my* sake.

Yes, *that* was what had precipitated the crisis.

I bore responsibility for his fall.

He was very close to me now... winding my seat down flat...

Opening my eyes again, I saw on the ceiling of the car a spot of light moving like a signal. It might have been the reflection of Jonathan's cufflinks, or the light of a phone.

I now *had* to object, quickly, or my passivity would mean acceptance. He was trying to undo my upper button with one hand: it reminded me of the time it had taken me to button that shirt, in Nour's wardrobe.

Nour... In less than two seconds, her picture flashed into my mind, followed by a sequence of others. Nour coming out of the church with Mansur and Talitha, with her yellow scarf floating in the wind, waving at Azim and me. Could she not see the danger? Could she not run away?

Nour, beloved sister, *why* had you come? You meant well, but your affection for your dear brother made you imprudent! Nour falling on the steps of the church... Azim leaping on Talitha... Petrified passers-by, among the shops and cars along the street opposite the church square.

The Post Office...

My Nissan parked...

My Nissan?

No!

I put my hand on Jonathan's, still busy with the tiny mother-of-pearl button: "Wait!"

Chapter 82

Wait. Wait...
I will never know by what strange process my memory connected that particular image with my brain, at that particular moment.
I mean, I don't know the mental course.
But I know the supernatural one.
Oh, yes, I know it well.
Thank God! Nour had waved at me, across the valley of death. She'd warned me, in a sisterly way.
God had granted me life. Life for my soul!

But what a shock! What an awakening! I'd watched carefully the CCTV video with Agents Bloomen and N'Guyen at San Antonio Airport a year earlier but, obviously focusing on the cherished victims, I hadn't paid attention to the *cars* parked nearby.
However, a *knot* of secondary information had still been recorded by my memory.
I had unconsciously identified the familiar shape of a Nissan car, similar to mine in Vancouver. My eyes had automatically noticed, within its shade, the intermittent flashes of a small shiny item, and the brighter one of a bigger device.
In association with those meaningless details, my memory had also stored the profile of a *nice-looking* face, one never met in the flesh yet.
All of a sudden, those unconnected pieces of information, which had floated unbeknownst in my deeper memory, precipitated into a combination loaded with momentous meaning.
A man was sitting inside a Nissan during the attack a year ago; just like a few hours ago, during the anniversary Mass. That man was wearing cufflinks, which glittered in the sun. On neither occasion had he got out of his car. And the first time at least, during the shooting, he was using a mobile phone, the lit screen of which – or its mirroring of sunbeams? – contrasted with the shade inside the vehicle.
All this mental process of deduction occurred almost instantaneously.
It wasn't the product of my brain, but a gift of grace.
It was an emergency.
I knew who had sent an SOS, that so prompt an assistance should have reached me, so mysteriously.
And that time, no text message had been required. No boarding card either and no email address. Rescue had travelled straight from the Sacred Heart of my Love to the blinded soul of His brainless daughter.

Of His imprudent, and too humanly affectionate, and culpably inebriated daughter – but His daughter still. Of yes, *backup was needed underground*, most urgently, and backup had been sent, instantaneously!

My hand had just come to rest on Jonathan's, whose fingers still held my fastened button.

Shivering, I heard myself ask him in a cold, slow and less and less subdued voice: "Jonathan, *why* did you not get out of your car, during the attack?"

He didn't withdraw his hand; but mine, spread over his, registered its very slight wince. He was very much master of his voice, when he whispered in my ear: "Darling Clara, I told you that I was in Beirut that day."

I couldn't wait.

I *had* to confront him: "I saw you. I saw you sitting inside your Nissan, just like now.

"I *see* you parked by the Post Office, opposite the church.

"I see you film the attack with your phone, which catches the sunlight, as does your cufflink on your wrist; just like... What! Are you *filming* me now*?*"

I was *horrified*: "Were you filming me all along? Is it why you had only *one* hand free to try unbuttoning my shirt? Were you also recording our intimate conversation?

"Well, I don't care now. I see through you entirely! I see you there, a year ago. You are there, on that dreadful afternoon.

"I see you. I see you, Jonathan!

"*Why*?

"Why did you not get out of your car!

"Why did you not come to their rescue!

"Why did you leave them to die!

"Why did you not run after the murderers, who were standing so close to where you were parked, near Ali himself!

"Why did you not run to your best friend Mansur, fallen, to give him assistance even after the murder!

"Why? Why? For the love of God, answer me!"

He tapped on his phone and put it in his pocket. He *had* been filming and recording. He was still reclining on his seat, while I had brought mine back upright. He was smiling in silence, looking at the concrete wall.

Eventually, he said: "Clara, what a sudden change in your behaviour and affections! My word, you look like a Gypsy, a prophetess in a trance! Mind you, this is the country for it: Gypsies are originally from Egypt, aren't they?

"Please, calm down and let us chat. How can you see me *there*, when I'm *here*? I'm here with you, and I love you. And, I think I don't count for nothing in your heart, do I?

"I'm sorry. This is all my fault. We just had a fairly intense evening, and too much to drink. What with the emotion of our parting, on top of it!

"It's perfectly natural that the tragic events of last year should have impressed themselves into your memory. Now, memory and imagination are *twin* faculties. In situations of emotional distress, the distinction between them is easily blurred."

I interrupted him: "Like the distinction between right and wrong; and between true and false? Between good and evil! I feel I'm awakening, as from a nightmare. I can't believe that you could have had any unfriendly intentions towards me.

"Please, Jonathan, tell me that it *isn't* true. Tell me that throughout this very special evening, when I tried to support you in your alleged anguish, you were not merely, coldly, planning to... to *seduce* me."

I shivered at the thought of such a betrayal, and of such a convincing pretence... if it was true.

He yawned and repeated: "Clara, we're both very tired, which is only natural. I won't take offense at your hurtful suspicion, since I love you deeply and nothing from you will make me angry. Simply, what colour was that Nissan you said was parked outside the church?"

I tried to remember: "It was white, or of a very light colour, anyway."

Jonathan smiled and requested: "Please, would you get out of the car and describe what colour it is?"

I did as he said, and remained silent, standing on the concrete. Both of us waited, saying nothing. I felt confused and ridiculous.

And very rude.

And very ungrateful, and ashamed.

I got back in and sat beside him.

He enquired: "Are you alright, darling?"

I answered in a very low voice, trying to make it sound as sweet as I could: "Jonathan, I apologise. I don't know *what* happened to me. Your car is black, of course."

He brought me against his chest and we stayed immobile for a while, until his hands – both of them free now – started taking liberties with my dress.

I spoke loudly and firmly: "Jonathan, please leave me now. I must go home, and so must you. Remember your flight."

He asked with a smile: "Well, are you a hundred percent sure that you won't regret it, little ballerina?"

With a nod I confirmed: "I will never regret being true to my conscience, by the grace of my God."

I added mentally: *And true to my fiancé.*

Click.

Instead of switching on the engine, though, Jonathan had pressed the central locking button, by his window.

I was caught.

Chapter 83

I frantically tried to get out.
 But my door was definitely locked, window included. Not even a bird could have flown away.
 My captor spoke calmly: "You want to go home, Clara? Well, since you just boasted of making *truth* your home, consider yourself arrived at your destination. You shall know the truth, and although it will hurt, I bet you'll enjoy it.
 "You won't have me, Clara? But you shall *hear* me. You turned down my invitation. But you will hear my *confession*, whether you like it or not."

Left with no choice, I braced myself for more unsavoury revelations, crossing my arms and legs, and moving as far from him as I could.
 He took out of the glove compartment some printed material which he tore to tiny pieces, letting them fall on his lap. "These are the pictures of my dead love. I'm sorry about all this. It was meant to be a work of art – my masterpiece – and sadly, it will only appear to posterity as vengeance. How vulgar!
 "I hate bad taste, it's so banal.
 "What a waste.
 "I should be angry at you, my would-be *Cordelia* (not Lear's, that bore – Søren's, *she*'s fun).
 "You danced my ballet so perfectly...
 "It was a ballet for brains. The ballerina was your *will* and the stage was your *soul*. By slow and gentle steps, I had carefully guided your will out of its very archaic resolution of fidelity. For that, I needed to contrive a few things. Ignorant souls will say that I "lied" – when I merely enshrined facts in an imaginative setting, thus enriching your boring mind with true beauty, like Golovin's scenery for Stravinsky's *The Firebird*."

I was taken aback. So he had *lied* to me. Then, perhaps, my dear friends hadn't acted the way he'd said. Hopefully, they were just what I had believed them to be.
 Jonathan's fingers were still nervously tearing the pictures.
 I wondered if he was on drugs.
 He explained further: "I merely nurtured the thoughts I found in you, like a caring gardener. I found pride; I found jealousy; I found curiosity; and lastly, I found lust.
 "Why blush now: did you think yourself an angel?
 "Such are the four strings of my Clara *cello*. I played you with delight. Seldom has so great an artist met such a well-tuned instrument.

"You were a living cello, a dancing cello. I watched your thoughts, your answers and your gestures being performed like so many classical figures and poses, with the spontaneity and precision of a great ballerina. It was my most successful ballet ever.

"A pity that there was no audience. At least no *live* audience – because the little film I took with my phone, while you lay consenting under my fingers, will immortalise for further generations the sweet acquiescence of your will.

"You know what? – *that* is why crime will never count as a fine art. Criminals must do without an audience if they don't want to be caught, but artists can't. Unless, perhaps, when a crime is the final performance of a great artist."

Gooseflesh, it occurred to me, *is an awkward phenomenon. It starts with a stimulus such as cold, excitement or fear, causing the hair muscles to contract.* But I wasn't cold; rather the opposite – and I would have given all the excitements of the world to lay secure in my own little bed!

Jonathan went on: "But as always, lack of culture fosters ruin – that of an individual or of an empire. In your case, it will be both. Naughty Clara, could you be so shamefully ignorant of the title of Schubert's String Quartet number 14? Knowing it would have given you a timely clue: *Death and the Maiden*. I let you guess which part I play."

He started the andante again on his CD player. That music! It now sounded like a bell tolling.

My lips were dry as cardboard and my throat aching, as I tried to speak: "Jonathan, I know nothing of what you are saying. I repent of having danced tonight. It was untimely. Please forgive me and let me go."

Jonathan produced before my eyes the last intact photograph. Enough light reached us from the neon tubes on the car park ceiling for me to see.

He was on the picture, looking a bit younger, wearing a dance belt with red tights and ballet slippers. He was presenting a large gilded cup to a man dressed as an impressive brown bird, with a stunning feathered mask and magnificent wings, more like an angel.

I couldn't refrain from asking who the other man was – as if that information was likely to improve my situation!

"Poor Clara, you thought yourself very clever, didn't you, when you noticed my emotion a year ago, that evening when Nour's picture in Oxford showed on my phone? You rejoiced, thinking that my secret had become yours, thanks to "female intuition," no doubt.

"Love at first sight there was, between Mansur and her – but in my heart it was *hate* at first sight! I knew immediately that *he* was caught!

"She took my friend, my hero from me! She only needed to appear, to breathe, to look.

"My god, captured before my eyes by poisonous tentacles!
"Disgusting.
"When she started singing, all was over. Damned siren! Misery!

Treachery! Vulgarity!

"Why did I not hire *boys* rather than women to sing those voices, as was the norm in the old days! And now, you're wearing black like her that evening. You're the *new* Nour.

"Two years after their marriage, Mansur told me that Nour couldn't conceive. He looked heartbroken. I told him how I sympathised. I was sincere, but inside, I also felt relieved; or *avenged*."

What Jonathan had just said about his relationship to Mansur troubled me. I knew they were intimate friends from university, but... Was there *more* to it?

I *had* to know: "Jonathan, even though you didn't like Nour, and probably dislike me as well, please, tell me the truth now. Were Mansur and you... Were you both... ?"

He lit a cigarette (I refused the one he offered me!) and reclined on his seat, next to me, as if we were old chums sharing friendly memories.

That's when the thought first occurred to me that he might be *insane*. Not a happy prospect for one trapped in his car, but on the other hand, madmen have their own logic and, if you only identify it, they may cooperate. A good thing that he had no weapon.

He laughed: "Of course we were not! Or you wouldn't be here, about to become his *wife* – sorry for delaying you, by the way.

"And *I* would be with him! My dear Phoenician...

"I remember his arrival at Oxford, sent across the sea by his mighty father, like the Carthaginian of old: '*Missus Hannibal in Hispaniam, primo statim adventu*'... Sorry, I should quote Livy in English, for your sake: 'Hannibal was sent to Spain, where he was no sooner come than he won the favour of the entire army.'

"That *army* was the group of us, sharper students, as we admitted the superiority of Mansur in every field. He rowed down the Isis like a professional athlete. You should have seen those shoulders in action!

"But the 'army' was also my own inner world.

"I was never a strong character, and I used to feel rather weary of life in those years. His apparition unexpectedly provided my thoughts, my feelings and my dreams with a focus, a heart and a direction. One day, I realised that he was my god. So, what did I do? I put all my faith in him."

Jonathan seemed to have forgotten me. I wished it were the case.

He went on: "I decided to devote my life to his service, to his glory and exaltation. Not that he needed me for that. But I would make myself indispensable. And I would share in his power. I gained influence."

"You think I boast?"

"For instance, then, *who* do you think suggested to your friend Dr. Yasir to affiliate the Al-Khoury Charitable Trust to her UN Department? It would be done already if you hadn't dragged your feet, and I would have got you and Yasir a shared Nobel Peace Prize – with front cover picture on *Time Magazine*!

"But you will see... The shadow of a god can be greater than gods if it projects well; especially downhill."

This reminded me of another shadow meeting mine in the night: Azim!

Would my dead friend help me out of this unsolicited confession?

Chapter 84

"Nice blade. A gift from Mansur."

Taking out of the glove compartment a long and beautifully ornate knife with a snake-head hilt, Jonathan recalled: "I hoped to die like Mishima, disembowelling myself, before my best friend would cut off my head. Rather classy, hey? Don't pull such a face. You don't know who Mishima was, obviously. Some say that he was a deviant. Perhaps. Unhappy, though, he surely was.

"Now, you asked me earlier if *I* was...

"By the way, *why* do you all want me to be gay? And what if it isn't my cup of tea, so far! Friends of mine are, just like some are vegetarians, and nobody wonders if *I* eat meat.

"If *only* they didn't shout insanities on the day of their big parade. Wilde would have found it rather *unpalatable*, as any artist should.

"Apart from that, we get on well. They're people one can work with. Sex is only a means, or a bait. Remember after all, Clara, that what matters is dominating. Since dominating increases with isolating, natural bonds must be questioned, loosened, and broken."

Indeed, I wished such a one could have broken my window and carried me out of the car. But there was no one in sight to rescue me.

I ventured: "Jonathan, I'm sure that you've been a faithful friend to Mansur. He would not have kept you by his side in a trusted position if it hadn't been the case."

He became very sombre and I thought he was crying. After some time, he said, as if thinking aloud: "Clara, I'm not a murderer. Even though he'd left me for Nour... even though my loyalty seemed little rewarded, I didn't want them to *die*. I was still living in his company, and meant to remain as long as I could.

"But I was blackmailed by the competitors of his firm. It was about preventing Al-Khoury Construction Corporation from signing a crucial contract to build an airport terminal. They videoed me at *Tadzio's* during a men's party with...

"With not only *adult*... men."

This further revelation hurt me deeply. How can one fall *that* low?

Jonathan went on: "I'd gone along only for fun, as that isn't quite *my* thing.

"But it was enough to compromise me. It was a set-up by the rival firm.

"They told me that they only needed to know the outdoor locations and times when Mansur would be without his guards. If I didn't cooperate, they would send him the video. He would have cast me away at once, especially with

Talitha around!

"I was torn apart. I had to choose between his life and his esteem.

"I was weak. I could survive his death, but not his contempt.

"I told them what they wanted. But I'd resolved to die with him! I *swear* to you!

"However, at the yacht that afternoon, as we were about to get into the Mercedes, he said that I looked so terribly pale and shaky that he didn't want me to faint at the church. It's true that I hadn't slept that night, and had thrown up all the contents of my stomach. So, he ordered me to stay at the boat. From the car, Talitha waved at me as they left."

Jonathan kept silent for a little while, as if revisiting the scene.

Then he spoke further: "I couldn't allow it. I rushed to the church with my own car and got there a bit after them. You were right about the Nissan – I had it painted black after."

He looked round, and seized the long knife. The blade was bright, and glistened. Looking up, Jonathan pierced open the headliner, widened the slot in the fabric and pushed aside the foam underlayer, revealing the original colour of the metal roof: a pale streak, probably white.

So it *was* true...

Paint was speaking loudly to our eyes.

He suddenly took on an artificially posh voice as if trying to drown his shame in irony: "I suddenly realised how unbefitting it was to drive a *white* car, like driving a fridge! But buying a new one was so *bourgeois*. At the garage, they mentioned a paint called "carbon black shade."

"I liked its name: my soul in a single hue! Heavens, just like a burnt diamond! Let it be my coat of arms, painted on my carriage.

"It took less than an hour to dry. If any moron asked me why that change, I answered it was a *mourning* colour."

I felt disgust and pity for him.

After a silence, resuming his normal tone he went on: "Anyhow, let us go back to that fatal afternoon. I parked by the Post Office. I meant to get out and die as Mansur's improvised bodyguard. But the shooting begun. I was too late.

"I didn't know that they'd also secured Ali's cooperation. I was in a state. I'm not sure why, but I took my phone out and started filming. I guess that I unconsciously wished to keep him alive, at least on my screen.

"How many times have I watched that dreadful video! I know it by heart. A week after, my god was still breathing, but was crippled. The very worst scenario: a god not dead, but *dwarfed*!

"And my heart still beat. It had all turned out contrary to my expectations. I genuinely tried to assist him the best I could. I truly hoped that *you* could help him, and Talitha."

Jonathan sounded almost normal by then.

Until, after a silence, he smiled ironically: "You may as well know, since it doesn't matter now, that all I've said about the relationships between Mansur,

Nour and Azim; and Ruth, Jed, Talitha and you was... embellished by me (simpletons may call it *false*).

"Those people are what you thought they were; I mean, *dull*.

"But you are too naive to have ever tasted such rare aesthetic pleasure... Pouring droplets of doubts on a network of relationships – family is best – and watching them turn from faith to filth; until kin falls apart, each member under my sole control!

"That's true power, through isolating.

"Your love kept them embraced, so I watered you with acid – your soul, I mean. Death seed for my maiden."

Despite my unhappy situation, my heart leaped on hearing the truth set right.

Now I could *endure*, since the people I loved and trusted most were vindicated in my esteem. In that, at least, I hadn't been mistaken.

They *were* loving!
They *were* chaste!
They *were* truthful!
And even if they fell, right is *not* wrong!
And good is *not* evil!
And truth is *not* falsehood!

Jonathan spoke on, while caressing his cheeks with his knife: "I didn't know how to deal with my shame. I could see the anniversary of the attack drawing nearer, but I couldn't cope with pretending any longer.

"And the infamous video, which could be sent to Mansur at any time, hung over my head like a sword of Damocles: after all, my betrayal hadn't secured his death, as they wanted. Confessing wouldn't be so bad, I thought, as if he learnt it all from another source.

"So, the day after your row, I told him everything."

Jonathan paused, clearly recalling their dreadful meeting.

After a silence, he went on: "Mansur was absolutely devastated. I hadn't chosen my moment well, since he was already in a state, conscious of how badly he'd treated you the day before.

"If he hadn't been in his wheelchair, I wonder if he would not have beaten me. It would have been the least I deserved...

"We drank a lot of vodka. I collapsed on the ground, kneeling at a distance from him. For half an hour, neither of us spoke. I wonder if he wasn't praying, as I once glanced at his face and saw that his lips and fingers were moving, while his gaze was on the frame with your picture.

"Eventually, he said that he needed to think and be left alone. He only asked me to spend that night onboard.

"After the second worst night in my life, he convoked me this morning and said that he wouldn't have me prosecuted or arrested. But he couldn't see me again."

I jumped on hearing this latest revelation. So, the nurse allegedly visiting earlier today to collect and freeze a sample, before we met at the prison? That was one more lie!

I could have slapped him (but in my present situation, it would have been imprudent in the extreme).

Jonathan was still distractedly shaving himself with his knife, and I prayed that it might keep the blade busy with him forever, for fear that, finding itself idle, it might turn to another target.

Chapter 85

I listened to Jonathan with particular attention when he added:

"Mansur told me that I had to attend the visit at Tora Prison and that his will would be expressed to me there. After which, I was to leave Cairo by sunrise tomorrow, that is, in five hours from now.

"I was extremely tense during the visit, and made sure to remain at the back of the cell with you, not to be confronted with Ali, in case he knew anything about my complicity.

"Through the bars, suddenly," Jonathan went on, "light flashed in my soul. I'd forgotten that I had one – a soul! The sight of that strong man shackled onto the wall burned my conscience like a red iron.

"*I* was the one who should have been hanging over there! Ali had only betrayed a master whom he'd vaguely known for a week from the driver's seat. He'd done it as a desperate attempt to save his wife and children from misery and destitution.

"Of course, he'd acted wrongly. But *I*... I had sold the life of a long-time friend to protect my reputation after a shameful deed. I had betrayed one whom I knew so intimately. One who had put in me all his trust, and the secrets of his heart and the interests of his family – if those of his business were not enough!

"I could barely look at Ali falling unshackled, and at Mansur embracing him. I'm sure now that Mansur intended the display of his forgiveness of Ali to be a message for me. He wasn't able to speak the words to me, but in that striking scene, he was bidding me farewell."

Jonathan started crying.

I almost reproached myself for my softness, when I found that I pitied him! There I was, first nearly seduced and now kidnapped by him; and the future wife of his victim, Mansur, who had miraculously survived the shooting, after having lost Nour, his first beloved wife, and nearly his daughter – and I felt *sorry* for my captor!

Mysteries of the human heart... or, are *we* women truly designed for tenderness and compassion? Is that sheer weakness?

Please God, would Jonathan's confession soon be completed? What more could he add?

Not looking at me, not even frowning, he spoke on as in a dream: "In that stinky prison cell, I was first overwhelmed by Mansur's generosity. Then a voice shouted in my mind that, on the contrary, he was inflicting on me the worst punishment!

"I listened to that voice assuring me that, through his lordly mercy, Mansur had intended to lock me up in shame for my whole life; whereas trial and imprisonment would have been much easier to endure. I became convinced of it and started *hating* him more than I had ever loved him."

After a pause, he exclaimed: "Farewell? Exiled? Me? Never!

"Who does he think he is! We will see.

"Meanwhile I hold *you*, his heart, in my hand like..."

He lifted my chin with the flat of his blade, as if showing my head to an audience: "Like a ripe fig which I show the Senate of my heart. Against my Carthaginian foe I claim: *Delenda est Carthago*!"

I hadn't quite understood his last words. Spoken in Latin, they sounded vaguely to me like: "*Belinda's scared to go*". I remembered thinking that I was surely not "Belinda" (had I ever met her?) as *I* was scared to death – to *stay*. Whatever he meant, it was ominous enough.

He put away his blade, thankfully.

I had to listen further, though, as he explained: "That's when the idea for tonight's choreography arose in my mind. I meant to remain in his memory as long as he would live. The film of our intimate conversation will show to your husband that you chose *me* before him. At least, he will never be *quite* sure. Is it not an original present for his stag night?"

The arrival of a car interrupted him.

While it parked, Jonathan whispered in my ear: "I haven't finished my confession. If you shout, if you merely groan, I will unfasten your belly button, with this..."

Simultaneously, I felt the sharp end of Jonathan's dagger against my stomach, through my dress and shirt, while he leant against me to conceal the weapon in case the visitors walked by.

My heart beating frantically, I prayed: *Sweet Jesus, mercy!*

The other car parked.

Its engine was switched off.

A door slammed and no more footsteps were heard.

My last chance of escape had walked away.

The blade pressing into my navel prompted a strange revelation, what people call near-death experience, I suppose. The vision occurred instantaneously, in the twinkling of an eye.

Imprisoned in our common car, utterly vulnerable under my captor's weapon, I felt his long curved steel as the evil version of an umbilical cord. It was an *anti*-bond, connecting me to the Nissan as to a womb of metal, to carry death into me instead of life. In contrast, the sheer splendour of human gestation suddenly overwhelmed me.

My memory was unlocked and my mind realised how abysmally indebted I was to my own *mother*. Mother... She'd welcomed life and had made space for me within her. She'd carried me gratuitously; she'd unconditionally protected me, and fed me.

On this spot of my abdomen where a madman's blade now pressed, a cord of love used to join me to my mother, a mere twenty-five years earlier. Her body shielded me from the outside world, unlike Jonathan's. She meant to prepare me and, in due course, to introduce me to life outside, whereas my captor, like an evil twin in our shared womb, was about to... abort me.

"Oh, Mummy!"

The little cry escaped me.

I was in tears.

And suddenly... so was *he*! The friend who had turned against me was now weeping silently.

Gone was the blade. Sweating profusely, I could breathe again! Jonathan had fallen back upon his own seat, with tears rolling down his cheeks.

My heart was frantically beating but I kept silent, not knowing what he was capable of. Had a miracle just occurred?

He spoke with mere sadness in his voice: "You called your mum for help. *That* chain is stronger than expected. Perhaps you're right. To me, life is all ashes and blood. You and I, and all that exists, seems mere waste. We're just matter in motion, travelling fast to the drain. Life's a long miscarriage."

"No, that sounds already too consistent. Rather, life's painful diarrhoea."

There was a silence.

I vaguely remember praying, I'm not sure for whom.

Suddenly, he added: "There's no need to increase the mess, though. I've done quite enough already. Keep this, you've earned it. I'll turn it off here and now."

He switched his phone off and pushed it into my hand, concluding: "Don't turn it on again, just smash it – destroy it with the video. There's no signal down here, see, so nothing's saved to the *cloud*: it's *all* right there, in your hand.

"Your husband won't ever know that you danced for his betrayer.

"And now, let me take you home. My confession is ended."

After a moment he added, so softly that I almost didn't hear: "But who could absolve me?"

The car drove off and five minutes later, I staggered my way to the convent door and bolted it behind me, trembling.

Chapter 86

"Clara!"

Breathless, I jumped violently as a man's voice spoke right behind me. I nearly fainted against his chest, shouting: "Get away from me!" Then I recognised Luke, Mansur's head bodyguard!

He withdrew his arms, asking: "Miss Cumberhart... at last! But, are you all right?"

I sighed, sinking down on the first step of the staircase. The poor man looked most concerned. I assured him that I was fine, and reluctantly, he let me begin walking up the stairs without his assistance. It would take me a while before I allowed men to support me again – *friendly* ones in particular.

He insisted that I should call Mr. Al-Khoury without delay, as he was deeply worried about me. I heard him update Mansur on his mobile as I walked slowly to the first floor, then to the second. As I paused, Luke concluded his conversation with: "Yes, sir. Yes... Yes, sir, I will stay here."

It was a very tired little lark indeed, ascending the spiral stair.

But a *living* lark, thank God, whose feathered belly hadn't been torn open and whose blood still ran through her weary wings.

I eventually dragged myself up to the third floor and inside my room, collapsing in nervous sobs before my small crucifix.

Was this place heaven now, for real?

I had never imagined that hell was a mere car ride away from my cosy cell. In no tourist guide had I read that a victim, walled alive, ever escaped Pharaoh's tomb; but through the mercy of God, *I* had. Yes, I'd been plunged into the streams of death, and taken out.

It wasn't yet *my* time.

I looked at the crucifix: no stranger thing ever happened than on that hanging tree where love overcame death. I reiterated a humble, absolute and loving surrender to God, of my soul and all its faculties; of my body and all its powers; of all my relations and possessions, past, present and future.

The frail blue rosary was still hanging around my neck (as well as my other jewels). That (plastic) umbilical cord of my soul hadn't yet been cut. I kissed it with gratitude, thanking my Immaculate Mother for the protection which, I was now convinced, she'd deigned to extend over me, her foolish daughter, against the flames (or fireworks!) of evil.

Was I wounded though?

Literal navel-gazing (and uncomplacent) revealed an unscathed stomach. My badly scratched belly button was bleeding superficially, although still "buttoned-up," thank God. In the morning, I would see a nurse, just to get it checked.

Washing was such a relief (what cool water and body lotion can achieve!). But it would take longer for the filth of doubt and shame to disappear from my soul. Human fangs had injected it into me with such expertise that I hadn't felt it going in. Had I not even cooperated? I thanked God for the deeper cleansing that awaited my soul in the confessional, first thing in the morning.

Why this sensation of cold, strangely?
Over a pair of denim shorts and a t-shirt, I put on my djellaba with its cherished embroidery, and started to feel my old self again.

I dried my hair, soon admiring its restored dark brown shine and elegant volume. How pale I looked in the mirror: nothing powder couldn't fix, though, if still needed tomorrow!

On my table lay Jonathan's smartphone.

How much poison in images and words stagnated inside it? And yet, the device felt so light in my hand. I would dispose of it securely. The compromising video would never be disseminated. Thank you, Lord.

Jonathan...

Through the window, above the mosquito screen, I saw his Nissan still parked by the gate. Both front doors were open and a man was sitting on the grass, in the sisters' garden.

What was he waiting for? Not for me to wave goodbye!

He would miss his flight. Well, if he did, my fiancé would send him to *jail*, as he deserved!

But enough: that wasn't *my* problem! *I* was safe again. Let him wait as long as he pleased: why would *I* care?

As I walked away from the window, my bare feet trampled upon something soft on the floor. Nour's black dress lay in a heap, an ambivalent witness of my humiliation, and of my redemption. The shroud of my foolishness.

I felt around my neck the precious gems given by my beloved. There I stood, the betrothed one of the most merciful, generous and trustworthy man in Cairo, if not in the whole world. I was free, thank God – and in love.

I had to call him. Luke had said that he was very worried. If he feared the half of what I'd been through, he wouldn't be asleep, for sure. I took my mobile out of my bag and found several messages texted by him during that dreadful evening, expressing a growing anxiety.

One pierced my heart even deeper: "Please text back! Now! The sisters described the car in which you left, nearly an hour ago. It's Jonathan's. Whatever he tells you about me, or about anything, I beg you *not* to believe him!

"I meant to explain everything tomorrow. He's *very* dangerous. I send this from the helicopter as we take off, hoping to locate his Nissan by his usual restaurant or at his club."

I realised that from the terrace of the bar I had seen his helicopter fly across the river. At the moment when he was frantically looking for me, knowing what danger I was in, I'd started dancing with his enemy...

Feeling too weak to speak directly to him, I texted in haste: "BELOVED! Safe. All well. Sorry. Love you more than ever. Free tomorrow morning after 8 a.m. Mass here?

"Need you SO much!"

Chapter 87

I meant to thank my Saviour, downstairs.
Throwing my white cream burnous over my shoulders, my feet shod with sandals, I walked down to the chapel, ignoring my utter exhaustion.

The gleam of the little red light by the tabernacle filled me with joy.
He was there.
You were there, sweet Jesus.
I believed in a God Who loved me so much that He had embraced my human condition to get closer to me; had suffered and died, walking before me through any trial I might endure; and if it were not enough, was offering His Body, Blood, Soul and Divinity as Food for my soul, under the externals of bread!
He also gave me His own Mother and made me part of his Family.
He was calling all men and women to be saved by His Love. And my joy and fulfilment was to foster that love, universally.
Really, calling *all* men?
Yes, *all* men.
Even...
Not *him* – no way.
Could I really not try to reconcile *him* with God? Was it not the last chance before he would leave?
No – don't think of it.
And yet...
But, was it *prudent*? Had he not nearly stabbed me, half an hour earlier?
Was it *right*? What would my fiancé say?

I walked into the vestibule where the bodyguard was still waiting.
Would Mansur make him stay there all night? "Luke," I asked, "would you kindly stand outside by the door, while I go and speak with someone in the garden? I should be grateful if you could be ready to intervene; only if I call, though."
On second thought, I enquired: "Oh... you wouldn't use your *gun*, would you?"
He answered: "Clar... – Miss Cumberhart, I've already noticed the presence of Mr. Amlødi. With respect, he looks drunk to me, and potentially dangerous. I must mention that Mr. Al-Khoury forbids me to leave you alone with him."
I was embarrassed, as my conversation with Jonathan demanded privacy. On the other hand, I couldn't act imprudently – not again.

A godsend: Mother Joan-Maria entered the room. She took me in her arms, saying: "Clara! You are back! Thank God. We have been *so* worried about you since your fiancé Mr. Al-Khoury rang. And Luke here has kept watch all night, poor man!

"Are you all right? You must go and rest now. We can talk tomorrow, that is, after sunrise."

I wished to secure her approval, and asked: "Mother, I feel I must speak to the gentleman outside. His need is great, and I think the Lord has put it into my heart to try and help him.

"But he leaves Cairo in two hours, probably forever. With Luke standing by, would you let me out? Please."

She took my face in her wrinkled hands, those hands which had so often carried food to the poor in the slums, including Ali's family; those hands which had scrubbed many floors and held many rosary beads...

Those hands whose skin was once smooth and whose fingers may have worn fancy rings, long ago, as her feet walked to meet young friends in the village, perhaps, with her then unveiled hair floating in the breeze loaded with the fresh scents of spring in her native country, far away from Cairo...

I felt her wrinkled palms rest on my perfumed cheeks, my chin and ears, as if I were made of clay.

She said I looked feverish and should rest, or something to that effect. She was right: I was shivering.

Never mind – let her reshape all that I am, according to God's love and sanctity!

How incredibly young and fresh her gaze, when she brought her eyes close to mine, looking deep into my soul cupped between her hands.

We remained like that for a moment, while I prayed that it would never end, as I felt scanned and cleansed as if by a laser of love! She gently took my hand and led me to the glazed door of the chapel, right behind us.

We knelt down and prayed three Hail Marys, and invoked the Sacred Heart and the Immaculate Heart.

She stood up first and told Luke (her thumb reaching for his forehead to draw a sign of the cross – to my surprise and *his*, no doubt): "Everything shall be well, my son.

"Please watch over my child until she gets back in.

"And then, go and rest. Both of you."

Chapter 88

I opened the front door.
The fragrances of the flowers and shrubs hadn't evaporated. The night was still very dark. I saw the fig tree and, under it, the bench.
My bench.
Our bench.
But it was empty – apart from a bouquet of bougainvilleas.

Luke couldn't prevent me from walking out of my own house, especially with Sister's blessing. But he had set conditions. He would flash his handgun laser sight to warn me if he deemed me under threat. I had begged him to remain *hidden*, at least, unless I shouted. Pressing my hands, he'd replied ominously: "A word from you will be his death, Clara: just as if your mouth fired bullets." Dear Luke looked very tense and I felt that he would not hesitate for one second pulling the trigger.

He added: "Even if I were not under orders to protect you, I would rather die than let you be hurt." I was concerned that his sentiments towards me might lead him beyond what duty and prudence required. I needed to placate him and, with a sisterly smile, I whispered: "To die? Surely *neither* of you will die, Luke. Only, watch over me as your pupil, since I'm about to practise what *you* taught me once." Puzzled, he enquired: "What did I teach you?" Stepping away from him into the garden, I answered with a last glance at him: "Rescue diving."

Would he... would he come to the tree?
Where was he? Where was my kidnapper? Where was the man, once a trusted friend, who had kept me under duress, twisted my perception of truth, his blade piercing my very flesh?
Where was the faithful companion of my fiancé, whose frustrated worship had turned to crime, when he'd betrayed him and his family to save his good name?
And had he not deserved that shame!
Feeling secure under Luke's watch, I walked a bit further. Through the straps of my sandals my feet felt no dew yet upon the grass: it was too early.
Where was the gifted soul who designed ingenious choreographies, explained polyphonic masterpieces and quoted forgotten poets and dusty historians? Had he left and flown off?
Was I off the hook?
I sighed.
Looking further around, I saw at a distance, by the fence, a moonlit heap, slightly moving. As I walked closer, the whitish shade appeared to be the back

of a man. I realised that it was a body, curled up, lying on its side. Apart from the trousers and the unbuttoned shirt, it looked like a mature foetus, abandoned in the night.

As my shadow touched him, he whirled away, shaking. He soon turned his head towards me, looking like a hunted animal as he growled: "Leave me alone! Go away! Have you not seen enough of me?

"*You* have escaped the coffin of shame into which I tried to nail you beside me! But *I* am still in it: not so easily can *I* get out. No need of a coward's car – the *world* is my coffin. Go! And don't come any closer! Don't look at me!"

An empty bottle lay by him on the grass (I recognised the *pilawa*), next to his scattered jacket, socks and shoes. Was he now very drunk, or truly insane as I'd suspected; or was it the effect of drugs – or all three together?

I sensed a deeper cause, which filled me with awe. It worked through me, and him. A struggle was going on, involving much mightier powers than my soul and his.

My interest in him was beyond what psychology could suggest. I remembered reading an article after the hijacking of the Malaysian plane. The hostages expressed sympathy for their captors. Later on, three women even admitted having experienced strong attraction towards them.

Psychologists call it traumatic bonding; or Stockholm syndrome, I don't recall. Through identifying with the captor, they say, the ego tries to defend itself from the threat, becoming one with its cause. Stockholm isn't in Denmark, though.

And I didn't feel under threat anymore. I felt drawn towards this abusive man, spread half naked on the grass, his soul stripped of its affections, of its honour, of its breath.

By then, I knew *what* led me to him.

It was life. It was grace. As I stepped forward, he recoiled in horror, begging me this time, his eyes fixed on a distant object: "Away! Away! I hear the voice again! I must die! I must end it all! It's all ashes and blood! Ashes and blood!

"The voice speaks in me! The voice tells me to dread you, to sell them, to kill myself. The voice says: She's sent! The voice says: Don't let her touch you! The voice says: No redemption! Never!

"From the start, it was too late. Why did she not terminate me! I should never have left the womb! Why did she let me see my first sunrise? Why did I cease to be a baby boy! Why was life so full of tricks and traps!

"In this weather, in this windy storm, she should never have sent her child out! In this horror I was carried off... *Hinaus getragen*..."

Was he speaking Danish now? But he switched back to English: "And no father warned me, and no hand sheltered me..."

Later, much later on did I understand what he meant. For the present, he looked as in a trance, still lying on the ground. I was glad to see that the dagger now lay some distance away, by his jacket.

Still a bit frightened, I looked to the side to check that the bodyguard was at hand. Thankfully, Luke was watching us closely, concealed in the shade. He would reach me in no time, if anything went wrong.

I recollected myself for a second, and walked closer to the unfortunate Jonathan. So, *that* was the state of his mind? The poor man was carrying hell within him. He looked like a leper; and I was afraid of any closer contact with his destitute soul.

But a strength which wasn't mine empowered me. No redemption? Of course there *was* redemption. I should tell him!

An evil voice was speaking through him. I felt a different one inspire my weakness: "Jonathan! I have come to give you what you most want. I have come to give you what you crave. I have come to give you – mercy! I have come to reconcile you with your God and with your own soul."

He crawled a few steps aside as I affirmed: "Your *Hannibal*, as you once called Mansur, surely had many skills. But they shine brighter still as virtues and graces, in the Person of a greater Son, sent to you by a perfect Father. *Jesus* is the One Who saves our souls. Jesus, the Sun of Justice!"

He moved as though to creep further away; then remained immobile. I went on, coming one step closer to him, while a Spirit greater than mine prompted my memory, speaking through my lips: "And this is the declaration which I have heard from God, and declare unto you: That God is light, and in him there is no darkness."

He rose on his knees.

Coming nearer, I spoke louder: "God is love: and he that abides in love, abides in God, and God in him." I was by then standing a mere step away from him: "God is merciful: if your sins be as scarlet, they shall be made as white as snow: and if they be red as crimson, they shall be white as wool!"

At that moment, *he* was the one who moved closer to me. His eyes were shut, as if all the faculties of his mind were concentrated in his ears.

Seeing Luke, now a few yards away, about to run towards us, I gently waved at him to prevent it. He remained concealed while a green spot appeared on Jonathan's shoulder. It looked like a firefly, but I noticed the thin laser beam leading to Luke's handgun. Please, that he may *not* shoot!

Jonathan's arms very slowly rose from his knees towards my waist and embraced it, under my white burnous. A strong smell of vodka made me feel nauseous, for various reasons. My arms were extended in the air, horizontally, as I felt my utter disgust subdue, and my hatred fade away.

Could redemption reach *that* low?

Could it transit to him through *me*, of all channels?

His forehead now rested against my stomach. It hurt me to think that my cosy djellaba, the sign of my safety so recently regained, was spread under a brow filled with such criminal thoughts!

Meanwhile, the little green light – Luke's deadly firefly – moved up from

Jonathan's shoulder to his neck.

In a surprisingly pacified voice (or was his guardian angel speaking through him?) he asked, as if quoting: "How can a man be rejuvenated when he has grown old in sin? Can he enter a second time into his mother's womb, and be born anew?"

I wasn't sure what to answer. This sounded like baptism. I knew I'd discussed this with Sister at the convent, during our catechism classes.

Praying for inspiration, I spoke softly to Jonathan: "There's a Mother, who will have us back, after we go astray, if only we wish to be her children. She's pure and loving. She's truthful and fecund."

There was a silence, as he lifted his head, gazed at me intently and said: "If the face I see now can look at such *filth* as I am and not turn away... If the face I see now can be for me *her* Face, here and now...

"I will believe in such a Mother, and in her Son."

Chapter 89

How unbearable! He was setting conditions, again!
And again, was *I* the one to meet them? Why indeed would I *not* turn my face away from the monster at my feet? Why would I not crush him under my heel?

In my range of vision, his gun in his hand, Luke was looking intently at us – at *me*, I felt, as if begging for my permission to rid the earth of the repellent creature still holding me. Had Mansur told him how Jonathan had betrayed his family a year earlier?

I only needed to scream, perhaps even to nod... and death would follow, instantaneously. No court would question Luke's duty to save me from such an immediate threat, if I expressed the need... Of course, I didn't wish Jonathan *dead*! – but I wished myself *free* from his fate or future.

Just nod, I felt... as my former captor's arms tightened around me. *Just nod. His life isn't worth it, can't you see? He's an embarrassment to you and to society.*

Mansur! Kitty! Take me away! What had I done? I *had* to get free. Dear God, this was beyond me.

Yet, I had felt it might come to that, somehow; that Jonathan would seek absolution of his crime. In fact, I'd prayed for it in that horror car; and since. Traumatised as I was at the time, unable to think clearly, I still believe that, in an instant, I had offered my life for such an outcome.

But now that my prayer seemed to be granted, I felt torn apart. Contempt was fighting in my soul against self-denial; hatred against forgiveness. My hands wouldn't touch him. Nor would my eyes meet those of the moral leper who had the boldness of clinging to me now as his expected helper, after he'd treated me and my fiancé with utter cruelty!

I felt as a woman advised to get rid of an abnormal foetus. She – *I* – hadn't asked for *this*. In fact, it had been *forced* upon me. And Luke was only too willing to relieve me, painlessly. Down against my stomach, a living shape was awaiting my verdict, not knowing how literally his life was in my power.

Or rather – at my mercy...

Mercy?

Just nod. His finger on the trigger, another living shape, standing behind the bush, was also awaiting my decision, while images of dead bodies covered with blood, those of Nour and Azim, flashed back in my memory. *Just nod. It will be quick and clean. It will be hygienic. And it's* your *stomach, nobody else's, that this limpet is clinging to.*

Like a ladybug, but not innocuous, Luke's *firefly* slowly moved up from Jonathan's neck to the side of his head. I followed the green spot on the kneeling patient, but wouldn't meet his eyes.

Instead, I looked afar, beyond the two men, to the flowers, to the bushes against the fence.

Towards the gate: to go... to run... and to dump Jonathan at last, as he deserved!

But even as I formed the intention in my heart, my eyes discerned against the brick arch of the gate a shape I'd never noticed before. Had the shrubs been trimmed over there this morning? Why had I never looked up at it, the hundreds of times when I'd walked under that arch to reach the street?

It was a varnished relief of Our Lady. She was wearing a...

No! Dear God, why that! Why there!

Why me! Why him! Why now!

But it was too late. I'd seen the wide cloak that she was spreading over many kneeling figures, men and women.

Mary, Mother of the Church, Refuge of sinners – pray for me! Pray for him!

Pray for... us.

That train of thoughts had unfolded in an instant. I shook my head at Luke and slowly, I looked down, until my gaze met the top of Jonathan's head. I stopped and, breathing deeply, allowed my eyes to travel further down, and meet his.

To my surprise, I read in them no boast, no pride, no irony, no triumph; no madness; and no obvious effect of drug consumption either. I read extreme sorrow, abysmal contrition, and feeble – but actual – hope.

I also saw the greenish spot, now moving from his cheek to his temple, still unbeknownst to him.

My hands seized the edges of my burnous and, slowly, very slowly, brought either tail upon his shoulders; and tighter, even over his head, covering him entirely. I felt his warm breath exhale against my djellaba for over five seconds, in unexpected relief! His face pressed gently against my stomach, as if peering through the navel he'd nearly cut open thirty minutes earlier: would his soul now see the light?

My eyes could see another light, small and green, now more clearly noticeable over the even surface of my burnous. I put my hand under it. Like a genuine firefly, it nested inside my palm. I slowly led it away, assured that at the other end of the thin beam, Luke's finger would not pull the trigger.

At the same moment, under the shelter of my burnous, Jonathan started sobbing – as if his soul had reached safety and could eventually let go of the burden of self-hatred.

The green spark vanished.

My hands rested over his clothed silhouette and, before I was fully aware of it, started soothing him.

To the side, Luke was looking at me in utter dismay, still holding his gun, but not aiming at us anymore.

Was I, standing in that convent garden, in the middle of the night, embraced by my contrite captor and molester – was I for him... the face of the Church?

I looked at the white wool covering that human form: my mystical bump. We didn't remain in that posture for long, but enough for me to feel his tears. Finally, I delicately drew aside the tails of my burnous. His head appeared, slowly lifted up, and we looked at each other.

We said nothing. I didn't know what a mother felt when seeing her child for the first time. But perhaps, I thought, if God granted me the grace of conceiving, my first face to face with the new life formed in me would echo this moment.

I took from my neck the rosary beads and set it around his, explaining: "This is your umbilical cord to your new Mother. Never allow it to be cut until you enter eternity and thank Her face to face."

He stood up at last. I thought that he meant to say something. But what could be added? Please, please may he not say *thank you*. May he not say *sorry*. May he not say *goodbye*. We were beyond words, and they would make things uneasy.

However, in his old shy way, he asked: "Would you please... let me keep your burnous?"

I nearly laughed, nervously, at his ultimate gall. Had he not taken enough from me? But instantaneously, I realised that nothing was mine, of what he'd received. It was all God's merciful grace, and my joy was to have been called to channel it in that mysterious way. Besides, had not Our Lord urged us to let our cloak be taken away?

Nonetheless, I thought that this time I was entitled to some stipulations: "Jonathan, receive my cherished burnous as you wish, as my son and brother in the Lord – under two conditions. You must return it to me after your Baptism. And you must hand your weapon over to me forever: I think I've earned it! No more carving – only caring."

He bowed as I set my burnous around his shoulders. He was about to pick up the dagger, still lying on the grass. I stopped him just in time, putting my foot on the blade! I had remembered that such a gesture would mean instantaneous death – for him – as Luke would take no chances!

I said I would dispose of the weapon later, adding: "Have you got a pen? I will write the details of the one you must now visit, urgently."

Taking his jacket from the ground he gave me a ballpoint pen but, for want of paper he presented his hand. I wrote across his palm: *cath.chaplain@orly.fr*. Fr. Paul would be the best guide for Jonathan's full conversion and further instruction. Only then did I realise that both men had read inside my past, at Orly and in Cairo – but one to enlighten and to heal, the other to confuse and to wound.

As Jonathan made his way towards the gate (his jacket in hand, and my burnous on his shoulders), I came to the bodyguard, still hidden, and said: "Luke, everything's fine. Thank you so much for having watched over me. You're a guardian angel! Now, I would be *so* deeply obliged to you if you could take Mr. Amlødi's luggage from his car and drop him at once at the airport for his 6.09 a.m. flight. He shouldn't drive in his present state. Afterwards, rest all day, won't you?"

Pressing his hand (he'd finally put the gun away), I looked into his steel-blue eyes and, after a moment, he was generous enough to nod silently, agreeing to carry out this last part of his mission (surely not one he enjoyed much).

They left. I really liked Luke.

Chapter 90

Many mortals can inspect their coffin before use, I thought – *but very few* after.
I was gazing at the battered black Nissan, abandoned by the gate.
Something small glittered on the passenger's seat. I caught a tiny mother-of-pearl button and only then realised I'd lost one.
Can the skin remember?
For a second, I sensed his nails against me, trying to unfasten my shirt with one hand.
I felt the cool sensation of his blade... under my chin.
My fist tightened around the handle of the dagger. What a strange sensation to hold *that* end of the blade!
I was seized by an urge to stab the doors, the seats and the entire car with my weapon.
Through the window, the torn headliner caught my eye. He'd cut it open and revealed the original white colour.
I reached in and felt with my fingers the smooth surface of the metal, and the fabric edges spread apart. That slot wouldn't be stitched.
I was shaking, and walked back inside the building, breathing too fast.
I calmed down once I was kneeling before the tabernacle in thanksgiving. My sweet Jesus had carried me through an unexpected journey. I was His forever.
It was a rather feverish but happy lark – not a goose – that flew up to her cell.

Sitting on my bed, I remembered to email Fr. Paul, who had surely prayed for me.
I thought it fitting to paraphrase St. Paul's short note to his friend Philemon: *Dear Father in Christ, through your continued assistance, your daughter stands alive, and exhausted. She just made you a* grandfather, *though!*
I'm sending you my son Jonathan – older than I in age – whom I have begotten in my bonds. God has raised him to the life of grace through my unworthiness. Please, receive him as my own heart and make him strong in true love.
I had lost a burnous but not my life, and I'd gained a soul for my Beloved.
Beloved? Another beloved wanted to see me after the 8 a.m. Mass (and after my confession). I had less than three hours to rest.
Caressing the pearls and gems around my neck, I pulled the fly screen back in place, tightly against the window frame. For some reason, mosquitoes were no longer welcome in my cell.
My teeth started chattering a bit: I really needed sleep, and a very large

breakfast in the morning, with fresh goat's cheese, real crusty bread and, why not, a sip of Sancerre Sauvignon Blanc to drown this mild fever!

I lay down on my little bed, shivering but safe and at peace...

Or so I thought.

My blood flowed through my body – but it carried a virus. *Septicaemia* is what doctors call it – but who would call *them*, when everyone assumed that I was finally out of danger?

The last thing I remembered in my delirium was an ambulance siren wailing.

It sounded much louder than a mosquito.

I wondered why the ambulance would park just under my window, when I so desperately needed *quiet*. It made me feel sorry for the poor soul in trouble.

I must have sympathised quite a lot indeed, not realising that *I* was the one carried down on a stretcher!

Don't jerk me like this, I thought, *I will dance no more, I promise!*

PART THREE

Chapter 91

I love picnics.
What a good idea to have one here. Nothing like lying on the sand, with the sound of water around me, and... yes, the relaxing sensation of sunscreen being spread over me.
That must be Talitha.
Or Mansur.
Actually, I've never smelled such a fragrance. It's incredibly rich and deep. I let them do it, although I don't know why cream should be spread on my eyelids.
And on my ears, nostrils and lips.
Darling Talitha surely, trying to protect me thoroughly against the sun.
Now, that's better: hands and feet.

I wonder what we'll have for lunch. Grilled fish is my bet.
Let me check. Wahoo! What a lovely boat! Or is it a gondola? With eight oarsmen on either side, all clad in white.
Surely, we will eat on that island, over there. That's why I could not smell the food yet. But... this must be our *island! Are we then back at Ain Sukhna?*
Probably not, since we never went there with Azim and Nour. Here they are, though.
So, it must be Luxor, where the five of us shared lunch.
They look so tall and majestic, sitting on either side of the entrance to the temple, with their wide red tunics fluttering in the breeze.
How much I love them! My dear, my beloved brother and sister! I'm so glad they could join us for the occasion.
They stand up and, walking to the shore, wave at me out here in the boat. I must go to them.
But... I feel so heavy; so weary.
I just can't move my arms, or sit upright. Sorry, my beloved ones... I must lie longer over here. I must rest.
But what a joy: they're coming to me! They kiss me. They cuddle me like a baby.
What is it? Are we not ready yet?
Not yet? Really?
What a disappointment. That island over there, in the middle of the Nile, looks so peaceful! It shines like paradise.

It isn't lotus flowers...
It isn't bougainvilleas.

This is annoying: why can't I remember the name of the flowers I love most!

White. Tall. Trumpet-shaped. Long delineated petals – six.
But careful, their own coloured pollen stains them easily!
Sparse foliage. Sticky translucent sap. Inebriating fragrance...
I know: white lilies!
Why so many?
It can't be my First Holy Communion – I made it long ago.
It can't be my wedding either, since I've already brought forth a son to my... No! My son! My son! Where is the little soul? Where is my burnoued *baby boy?*

Please tell me, anyone!
I'm so tired.
It can't be my funeral – I seem to recall escaping from a tomb...
But it smells so nice. I feel a little breeze coming from the window. Are those seagulls, or larks, now singing so happily? I wish I knew.

Perhaps, I should rise now.
I must ask Mansur.
Mansur?
Mansur.
Mansur!
My love! Is it you? Are you here, next to me?
Where am I?
Thank God, it is *you!*
Those are your hands, holding mine.
Your face it is, so close to mine!
Your familiar perfume. Your tears, rolling down my cheeks.
Your lips, covering my brow.
Your voice, your sweet voice...

Chapter 92

Without Mother Joan-Maria, things would have gone badly.

I might not have died, or not overnight, but my condition was serious enough.

Having observed how exhausted I was that night, she suspected I needed attention. On not seeing me at Mass, she came to knock at my door and found me unconscious, lying in bed with burning brow and mild delirium.

She immediately called the ambulance, and Mansur.

I was diagnosed with blood poisoning, still in its early stages. Only later did I make the connection with Jonathan's blade cutting my navel.

At least it wasn't a mosquito, since for the first time in weeks I'd shut my window to them. But the doctor said that I could have been infected by a mosquito bite several days earlier.

The trauma undergone in the car park had made me more vulnerable.

After waking up, I managed to tell Mother Joan-Maria most of what had happened with Jonathan. Not to Mansur yet, as I didn't want him to become even more distressed. She said that I'd been through genuine mental torture.

She affirmed that, even though my body had been left mostly unscathed – if one discounts my cut navel and blood poisoning! – my mind and my soul had definitely been harmed.

Because of my "good heart and compassion" (I'm merely quoting her words), calculated deceit had wounded me more: "He poisoned your soul before poisoning your blood."

I'd never seen her weep, until that day, as she hugged me on my hospital bed with her wrinkled and motherly hands.

It took a day in the intensive care unit for my condition to stabilise.

The doctor was concerned and Abu Ephrem gave me Extreme Unction. Being unresponsive, I couldn't receive Holy Communion or make my Confession, as I had intended to. He was unable to assess whether I could hear and understand, and thus he absolved me conditionally before imparting to me the Papal Blessing for the dying, with the Plenary Indulgence.

So, if I'd died, I would have gone *straight* to heaven!

I'm not saying that I regret having survived... I'm grateful. But... Heaven...

Mansur and Talitha had stayed by me. My little daughter-to-be! I couldn't do *that* to her: I couldn't bereave her of a Mummy for the *third* time in her short life!

Abu Ephrem joined them. It might have been the very same room where I'd first seen them after the attack, a year earlier. It felt strange to be there again, all the four of us, but this time, with *me* lying and Mansur sitting: as if playing musical *beds*!

They kindly withdrew while – finally – I confessed to Abu Ephrem.

I didn't feel loaded with serious sins, thank God, but I desired very deeply to open myself totally to the mercy of my Saviour and to be objectively certain that He had forgiven me my imprudence, and whatever level of consent I had been guilty of.

Abu Ephrem was always succinct when hearing confessions – at least in my experience.

I knew that his questions, if any, would be intended strictly to help me and him to assess the gravity of a sin, or its absence.

On that occasion, I recalled that I had run after Jonathan's car by the garden; that I had eagerly let him fill and refill my glass with vodka; that I had imprudently danced with him on the terrace and before him in the car park; that I hadn't spoken soon and strongly enough against his first indelicacies.

My responsibility was lessened by my trust in him as a friend of both Mansur and me. Had I suspected Jonathan of lying, I would never have let my love for Mansur grow cold, and would have eluded from the start any ambiguity.

But he had so cleverly set actual truths as gems among his lies, and had manoeuvred my emotions by such unnoticeable stages, that I had been caught.

Abu Ephrem said that he wished to talk to Mansur and me, in the perspective of our marriage. Talitha stayed in the other room with her governess.

As Mansur wheeled himself back into the room, I felt that I was worthy of his sight again. Abu Ephrem, standing between Mansur and me, laid his hands on our shoulders. He led us in prayer for a few minutes.

Then he said that although our marriage preparation had been short in time, God had allowed for its peculiar intensity. He added that we had both experienced some essential aspects of true love, namely, endurance and forgiveness.

He had visited Ali's family in their new flat and he thanked Mansur for forgiving his former driver. I saw his hand rest in a fatherly way upon Mansur as he insisted: "*Another* culprit was in the prison; he'd harmed you and your family much more cruelly, and you let him go free, inviting him to repent. God will reward you, if He hasn't already."

I felt deeply proud of my fiancé.

Then Abu Ephrem said that, by God's grace, *I* had led my aggressor to repentance and conversion, demonstrating a kind of courage no less than that of the heroines of old!

Chapter 93

Five days later, I was declared strong enough to be discharged.

For another twelve days, my blood levels would need monitoring and complete rest was to be observed.

We flew off the hospital roof, in the helicopter. I was thrilled, like a child! It's strange how a mere sensation makes us forget the gravity of certain situations. Or, am I really shallow?

It had been decided (not by me) that I would convalesce on the *Cedrus*. I was a bit ill at ease, since after my trauma, I felt more than ever the importance of setting clear boundaries. I had never stayed the night on board. We weren't married yet, only betrothed, and I wished to appear before my bridegroom as his choicest lily!

But staying at the convent, on the third floor, with no lift and no en-suite bathroom, wasn't convenient for the staff and family to look after me, nor for the sisters. They offered to take care of me in their infirmary, but that would have made visits difficult.

Flying to the *Cedrus* from the hospital normally took only a few minutes. But Cairo was now long gone behind us, and our flight was lasting much longer than I had anticipated. Mansur wouldn't tell me anything and only smiled, ordering me to rest against him. We were apparently heading north.

Then, at a distance, I saw the sea! The *real* sea: the Mediterranean. The *Cedrus* had been transported by road to El-Agamy, to the west of Alexandria (she never stayed in her Cairo mooring after the winter months), and awaited us, freed from her shackles and impatient to take us anywhere across the open waters!

But as we landed, an even greater joy – the biggest in my life, at least since my ordeal – awaited me. A wheelchair. Not Mansur's. And not an *empty* one either.

Kitty!

How on earth! Kitty! How on the sea! How anywhere... And not only Kitty, but her mother-in-law, and Baby Javier!

My first reaction, while still in the helicopter, was to hug Mansur with all my strength (not a lot left). He whispered in my ear that Pilar would watch over me, and that an announcement would be made "instructing all male wheelchair users onboard to keep away from my suite, unless invited."

Kitty stayed in the adjacent room, but she wished to have her bed brought next to mine, at least for the beginning. In the suite opposite, Pilar was glad to have the opportunity to keep Baby Javier with her at night. What a loving grandmother!

Kitty and I found ourselves like little girls again, as in our shared bedroom in the West Point Grey family house in Vancouver, twenty years earlier. We recalled bittersweet memories, and truly happy ones. We even tried to remember our very early years in Montreal, and attempted a basic conversation in French, our first spoken language in kindergarten.

Incapacitated as we both were somehow, we perceived that our sisterly bond was growing even stronger. I loved her so much! We held hands as we fell asleep – *Kitty and Clarry*.

I woke up late, having slept better than I can ever remember. Kitty was standing by my bed (such a happy sight). She smiled at me and drew the curtains.

What a dream: we were in the middle of the sea! No coastline, no city could be seen. We breakfasted together, inasmuch as feeding Baby Javier at the same time allowed.

Looking at my dear sister and nephew, I longed for the time when I would carry my own child and, in my turn, would pour in his soul all the love of my heart, straight from my breast to his mouth.

The words I'd heard at Holy Mass, soon after Easter came back to my memory: *As new born babes, desire the rational milk without guile*. My dear God was feeding me with grace, and I would not detach myself from His Heart.

During those first blessed days of rest, rocked by gentle waves, out on the deck or in our cabin, Kitty and I spoke at length as sisters and as women; also as wives and mothers (or future ones in my case).

I told her my shame at now feeling so uncomfortable in the presence of men. The fact was, I breathed more peacefully when there were none around, and I was aware of a certain tension in my heart and other muscles even when Mansur merely caressed my arm.

Kitty helped me come to terms with the trauma I had gone through. I found her a thoughtful and wise person to talk to. She could understand my feelings and, through her affection, the impact of the violence inflicted on my soul lessened, and began to heal.

She encouraged me to talk with Mansur sooner rather than later, so that I might be cleansed from the poison of suspicion which Jonathan had instilled in my heart.

I read again a card found on my arrival. It was from Nurse Sheehan. While I was in hospital, she'd left to get engaged to a Muslim engineer she'd met in Cairo (so, *that* explained her learning Arabic). She apologised for any worries she might have caused me, and wished Mansur and me the very best.

He said that her departure was decided *before* my septicaemia. I was touched by her gesture. Once again, I seemed to have misjudged a good person. I sent her an affectionate reply (*not* suggesting we kept in touch though).

Mansur and I met in Nour's boudoir. I didn't need or wish to tell him everything I'd suffered. He knew or had guessed a lot already. We started by saying a Hail Mary together, facing Nour's private altar.

He spoke first, to let me know that he was going to go away for a couple of weeks, for improved rehabilitation and for business in the Middle-East. It would also give me time to rest and prepare for the wedding.

He meant to inform me prior to our important talk, to assure me that his departure was by no means a consequence of anything I would say. To put me at ease, he added that I might ask him anything I liked, as he kept no secrets from me.

I didn't dare look in his eyes, when I first asked if there had been anything more than friendship between Jonathan and him, or with any other man.

He said that he'd liked him from the start, at Oxford. He made him laugh and was imaginative. He confessed that he'd felt flattered by his praise and dedication.

Never until the past week, though, had he suspected the dangerous, obsessive degree to which Jonathan idolised him. He apologised to me, saying that he should have envisaged that Jonathan might retaliate, once dismissed.

He concluded by saying that he'd *never* contemplated love but with the opposite sex.

He confirmed that he'd meant the scene at Tora Prison to express his forgiveness to Jonathan, and not only to Ali (he didn't know, though, that his driver would be tied and half undressed).

He also flatly denied that there had been anything else between Nour and Azim than a deep spiritual friendship: "In the attack, a lover would have shielded his mistress, not her daughter."

Why had I never thought of that! Mansur's remark sounded even more accurate if the alleged lover had known his "mistress" to be pregnant with the child they meant to keep. (I didn't mention *that*, as the pregnancy was Jonathan's fabrication, after all.)

Mansur looked me in the eyes: "I knew my wife. And I knew our friend. They were trustworthy.

"Enough of that venom."

Chapter 94

I sighed in my heart with relief.

Next, I enquired about what in fact mattered to me more, because it was more plausible: the alleged charade about Nurse Sheehan and the gems!

I felt a trembling sensation, as referring to those horrible things made them vivid again in my memory, like ghosts springing out of a vault. He looked literally astonished by that second question, and then, frankly, angry.

I feared I'd touched a wound that would have been better forgotten. But Kitty had said that *now* was the time to put it all in the open, if I didn't want those seeds of death to haunt me all along my married life, and perhaps grow into strong liana or ivy, which could suffocate us. There were precedents.

Mansur took his phone out of his pocket: would he call a taxi and send me away forever? But we were in the middle of the sea and, more relevantly, *I* wasn't the one with whom he was angry.

He explained as he tapped on his phone: "Clara, darling, I seem to understand only now some of what you've been through. I would never have imagined that Jonathan's passion could have turned to such wicked hatred.

"He managed to twist minor truths and connect them together in such a convincing way, that I should be at a loss to justify myself if that video weren't stored somewhere among many others on my own phone.

"Where is it again? There, taken at the Cairo Beach Club – *not* at Ain Sukhna! – the afternoon *after* our row (in this very room), *not* the following day. I was exhausted and needed some fresh air. I took Talitha with me – and our usual staff. They have an artificial lake there."

The Cairo Beach Club? That was where Mansur had sent Talitha with permission to dive, I then remembered, the day before Nour's funeral.

He added: "I'd just sat down on the sand when Nurse Sheehan saw a long scratch below my ankle, which I asked her to tend. The loss of sensation causes me to hurt my legs unnoticed. Talitha was yelling at me from the diving board, asking me to watch her jump.

"I requested Jonathan, standing behind me, to film her swan dive with my phone: being higher, he had a better angle. But he misleadingly showed you only the second part of the film, which he soon after sent to his own phone as I can see on my log. Now the full video, if you care to watch it, for our sake."

The dreaded film played again in Mansur's hand. Jonathan had carefully skipped the innocent beginning which exonerated my beloved.

Talitha diving.

Mansur loudly congratulating her on her good dive.

Nurse Sheehan in dress, apron and cap, kneeling at Mansur's feet, starting to spread the unguent.

Talitha getting out of the water and proudly running towards her Dad – while wearing a much too long and glittering... necklace!

Mansur warning her not to wear it while diving or running, "as it could catch: it's dangerous."

Nurse Sheehan spreading the unguent.

Talitha taking the jewel off her neck, and from behind the nurse, tying it around the woman's waist.

Nurse Sheehan protesting that, "it isn't the time to play tricks."

Talitha running away giggling.

Nurse Sheehan embarrassed: "Just when my hands are sticky with unguent!"

Then came the part I'd been shown.

Ruth turning her head to the side and asking loudly in Talitha's direction: "Litha, come and help me rub Daddy now, and please take your toy back!"

Talitha coming back, still laughing mischievously.

Mansur's voice, kind but firm, requesting Nurse Sheehan, if she doesn't mind, rather to call Talitha by her full name, and kindly to refer to him as "Your father" when speaking to her. *I then recalled that Jonathan had turned the sound down when showing me that later part of the film, obviously to prevent me from hearing Mansur's reassuring stance.*

Nurse Sheehan blushing (matching her hair!) and apologising (never too late).

Talitha starting to spread the unguent.

Nurse Sheehan standing up, taking off the necklace-belt and putting it back into Talitha's pink beach case.

That was all.

Much ado about nothing. Looking at it with Mansur, I couldn't understand why I'd been so upset by it. Then I asked him: "But *where* does that necklace come from?"

He smiled and tapped on his phone again, showing me the number and name displayed – Van Amstel Jewellers, in Amsterdam with a 31 prefix – before dialling it: "Jan Van Amstel? Greetings, Mansur Al-Khoury here... Yes, very well, thank you... No, not in London... I'm with friends on the sea. You must join us, later in the summer.

"May I briefly ask you to check how many stones I bought from you last time, and what they were – don't mention the price, please."

We waited in silence, then the voice answered in English with a mild accent: "Hello Mansur. Your record came up straightaway. Your agent – Jonathan, isn't it – purchased five rubies on your behalf just two months ago. As usual, we added five replicas for you to work on your design. I wish I could see your necklace. We should subcontract you as a designer!

"Your previous acquisition was a set of very fine pearls, ten months ago.

Fifteen months ago, you also bought a pair of diamonds with remarkable scintillation, one carat each, for earrings."

Mansur thanked him for his time, and "Jan Van Amstel from Amsterdam" was gone from our boudoir.

Chapter 95

I was so grateful for the conversation.

Mansur said that Jonathan had simply displayed before my eyes the picture with the five genuine and the five fake rubies on the same tray.

He added that he'd first designed a longer necklace with the fake gems. But the pearls didn't fit well on that length, and the final result was my triple strand.

He called on his interphone, and Talitha was brought in by her governess: "Darling, do you still have the gold-painted jewel belt I gave you the other time?"

Talitha looked down, slightly embarrassed, and replied: "I hid it, Daddy. I promise that I won't swim wearing it anymore."

Mansur sat her on his lap and asked in a low voice: "Do you remember why Daddy was putting those nice plastic jewels together?"

She looked at him in dismay, then at me.

Mansur encouraged her: "Come, you can talk in front of Clara. She's already wearing the necklace, as you can see."

Talitha answered: "You said that you were preparing a surprise for my new Mummy, and I asked if I could have the plastic necklace, when you wouldn't need it anymore, because I wanted to look like my new Mummy; and you said yes, and that you would make it longer, so that I could also wear it as a belt if I liked."

He kissed his lovely daughter and whispered in her ear something I didn't grasp. She looked pensive for a while and kept silent. Then she ran out of the room and came back a few minutes later... with the belt.

For the first time, I was seeing it for real. So, *that* was the object that had nearly caused my fall, or at least, that had made me suffer!

I wouldn't touch it, as if it had been a talisman or a cursed item.

Mansur laid it on a cardboard tray and said: "Litha, do we now nearly have a Mummy?"

She ran to me, throwing her arms around my waist and said: "Yes, we do."

Mansur went on: "And since she's now wearing the *real* necklace, couldn't we do away with the fake one, and give you something beautiful, not in plastic, to wear instead and make her proud?"

She answered: "When Clara becomes my Mummy, I won't need anything!"

Then she left the room with a smile.

Mansur produced a lighter and, holding the dreaded counterfeit with a paper knife over a sheet of paper, started burning it. I nearly stopped him, finding it too dramatic.

But the plastic had already started melting. He kept the flame a long time under each fake ruby, until it bubbled out of its fake gold case. Tears of melted plastic fell slowly on the paper, like grease, among splashes of gold paint. It smelled horrible, and I went to open the windows of the boudoir, to give us fresh air and get rid of the heavy dark smoke.

Mansur asked me to wheel him to the window, as he was holding what remained of the enchanted jewel. It hung on either side of the paper knife, like a roasted snake.

I was strangely fascinated by it, feeling as if, with the help of my valiant future husband, we had just overcome some legendary monster!

He threw it through the window with the paper. It wasn't eco-friendly, but I exhaled a sigh from the depths of my soul, when I saw the 'beast' recoil on the top of a wave, and soon drown deep in the dark blue sea!

Let all the sharks feast on its flesh!

I jumped, as an ear-splitting sound blasted the silence. But Mansur held my arm, making signs that it was all right.

A steward quickly entered the room and, on seeing us, switched off a button in a control panel by the door.

Mansur told him: "Frank, I'm sorry to have caused you to run: I must have set off the smoke alarm when burning some plastic. Please tell everyone everything's fine now, and thank you for your speedy intervention."

Frank left with a professional "Yes, sir!" and I found myself alone, in the arms of the man I loved!

So, was everything all right now?

Reading my eyes, he asked: "Miss Cumberhart, the *Cedrus III* is currently bound for France. I've arranged for her mooring over there, whence you will be flown to a certain event to take place in less than three weeks, at a certain airport.

"Do you *wish* to pursue that course, or would you rather divert it, or stop the engine for a while? I'm eager to forward your instructions to the crew, whatever they are."

My lips conveyed – without uttering any words – my *instructions* to my beloved. To be safe however, I also verbalized them: "Across any sea, against any tides, I'm bound to your heart, forever please God."

I asked him: "God has forgiven me my imprudence and my doubts. Do *you* forgive me as well?"

He answered: "I forgive you with all my heart, and I give thanks for your preservation and recovery. And, do *you* forgive my blindness, as I should have expected retaliation, and left you exposed instead?"

I said: "I would not receive you as my *head* in matrimony (so does the Catechism teach) unless I trusted in your sight."

Chapter 96

The helicopter whirled my love away for three weeks.

I was left deserted amidst the blue sea – with merely twenty-five staff; plus Kitty, Pilar and Javier!

I remembered a last wound that wanted healing.

A young soul had suffered intensely in her very short life, probably more than I in four times her years. Her candour had brought about my betrothal to her father, and I owed her my impending happiness as the wife of such a generous man.

I didn't doubt the facts, despite the lies injected in my heart by a treacherous artist. But I needed our love to grow unabated. I met her in her room. It was my first visit to her little sanctuary. It reminded me of mine in Montreal when I was her age, as I told her.

I kept to myself my admiration for the simplicity of the decor. Mansur liked things to be plain for him and his family. It could have been the room of a little girl in any residential suburb in Vancouver or Houston, rather than on a 103-meter-long yacht.

You might have forgotten that she was the heir to the 849th world fortune. And, thank God, she didn't know it either.

She showed me her favourite doll, which we put to bed together. Then I asked: "Does she know her prayers?"

Talitha stopped for a while. I could see that she hadn't yet thought of applying that aspect of her life to her relationship with the doll. She was slightly sorry about it, but immediately set to the task, explaining: "No, she was never taught any. Can you help me teach her, please?"

The doll cooperated nicely and, getting out of bed, fell on her knees. I explained that it was safer to pray *outside* one's bed, for fear of falling asleep. I added that we should find a little picture of Our Lady, to stick above her tiny bed in the lovely doll house.

The idea delighted Talitha. It appeared to her that the installation for her beloved toy was scandalously incomplete without that essential element. And how could she have let her go to bed and spend so many nights without a holy picture to pray to!

I found one on a prayer-card inserted in an old hand missal, and I let her cut it out and set it against a nice blue surround. She then stuck it above the plastic bed, and we proceeded with catechising the doll! The three of us recited the Our Father and the Hail Mary.

The doll having fallen asleep – as one should after having prayed well – Talitha and I decided to go and swim.

There must have been two-thousand metres of water under our feet! I could see that she was apprehensive of the deep despite her armbands.

To be *very* honest, she wasn't the only one. I stupidly started fearing that the fatal plastic belt drowned by Mansur a few hours earlier might... reappear! What if it were *alive*? What if it suddenly wrapped around my leg and dragged me into the abyss?

There was little risk, admittedly, and we were in the Mediterranean, not in Loch Ness! I suggested to Talitha that we should swim all around the boat, and we began to do so, side by side.

After a while, I asked her if she wanted to lie against me, holding my shoulders as I swam on my back, and she readily accepted. I remembered her father's confidence, when carried on his nanny's back at a similar age, by the sea.

It was a moment of beautiful intimacy with my little daughter-to-be. I recalled that she was only six, and I, just turned twenty-five. So, I was nineteen when she'd seen the light of day: still in my teenage years...

What were nineteen years in the history of the world, and of humanity? The splendour of the sky and sea around us couldn't detract me from the contemplation of the treasure I carried with me: a human being, a vulnerable and candid little girl, soon entrusted to me by Divine Providence and by her father, as her new mother.

"I like your necklace very much," she told me.

I thanked her, saying that "Daddy" had designed it beautifully. I felt entitled to utter that name, which Mansur had rightly asked Nurse Sheehan *not* to use.

I thought I could venture further. "You know Litha, that necklace is one of the *two* most precious things I have. And the other is? Can you guess?"

After various unsuccessful attempts, I helped her: "My other treasure is a *letter*; the loveliest one I've ever received. Sent by a little girl whom I love more dearly every day."

She remembered gladly: "Ah, then it must be *my* letter! Did you like the colouring?"

I told her I did and she added: "I wrote it all by myself. I told Jonathan *not* to look, as it was a *secret*. But Daddy found the draft and after, he turned a bit red."

My heart was beating fast, as perhaps she could feel. But she was too young to interpret my emotions, when I finally asked: "Darling Litha... are you sure that you won't regret it when *I* become your Mummy?"

"Wouldn't you have preferred *another* Mummy, like... I don't know... Nurse Sheehan?"

I had the impression that I had just jumped from the deck and that, half way to the water, my course was suspended on the lips of that innocent creature.

She thought for a brief moment – I like the fact that she thinks before talking! – and said: "Nurse Sheehan was kind to Daddy. But she wasn't Azim's friend; and she wasn't with Daddy when he woke up in hospital.

"And Daddy can't live without *you* – he told me. And *I* can't live without you either!"

I felt as if my flight had ended; as if I'd eventually reached the surface, and my fingernails, my hands and arms, my head and my whole body and soul were entering a dimension of unconditional, uncalculated and unfaltering love.

I let myself be carried very deep into that love, as if I'd dived from the heights of adulthood, leaving behind the fears and shames inherent to sinful maturity, and was cleansed by the divine innocence of an unadulterated heart.

She thought *I* was carrying her upon my breast around the boat, but I was the one whose soul had just been secured in true peace, by *her* love. I was received anew – after the excruciating doubt – as her beloved *mother-to-be*.

I stopped swimming, and I hugged her tenderly. She did the same, her arms behind my back.

I said: "You'll be my beloved little daughter. Let's take our breath and I'll give you a kiss which will be just for you, not even for the sun to see."

We immersed ourselves in the water and I kissed her forehead in motherly anticipation, awaiting the day I would do so in the open air in Paris!

Chapter 97

The cruise across the Mediterranean and along the Atlantic coast of Spain and France was a timely transition between my life as a young single professional and my imminent wedding.

All I had to do was convalesce, chat with my beloved sister, relax in general – and pray! I was very grateful to Mansur for his thoughtfulness in withdrawing. I was sure that he was doing it entirely for *my* sake, as a costly personal sacrifice.

We went to Mass each Sunday on our visits ashore, and on other days whenever possible.

We first called in to Crete where we visited the ruins of the famous Labyrinth of Knossos.

I loved to picture the beautiful princess Ariadne, saving young Theseus from the bloodthirsty Minotaur. She gave him a ball of thread to unwind, that he might find his way back out of the maze.

I shivered in retrospect, recalling how *I* had attempted to help a certain Theseus out of his moral maze, only to find him turned into a Minotaur!

I soon felt as though I was leading a group of tourists (Kitty, Pilar, Talitha and occasional staff), telling them about the local history.

Malta was amazing, although they say that Napoleon stole most of the works of sacred art.

In Tunis, we prayed by St Louis' Cathedral in the old Carthage (*Hannibal's motherland*, as Jed made sure to text me, proudly). The church was built where St. Louis, the King of France, had died.

The local ruler Hussein Pasha Bey, although a Muslim, dedicated that plot of land in perpetuity for that purpose, impressed as he was by the virtues of the saintly king (an unsuccessful crusader in Egypt).

Casablanca was too far south for us to visit: a pity, as I'd have loved to see where my favourite film was shot!

But we saw Algiers, Gibraltar, Lisbon, Ribeira (with a short pilgrimage inland to Compostela); Brest, Mont-Saint-Michel (how was this shining sculpture of the archangel slaying the dragon carried so high up without a helicopter?); and lovely Honfleur where we moored eventually, as the River Seine was deemed too low by then for the *Cedrus* to navigate safely to Paris.

I looked back at my life and tried to put everything in order.

That included my money.

Kitty being a professional accountant, I asked her to tidy up my finances. I sent instructions to the Al-Khoury Charitable Trust to remove from my monthly salary the various days when I hadn't been at work over the recent weeks –

except when I'd been in hospital.

I also made a donation to the sisters for their hospitality of several months, which they'd meant to be free of charge.

Kitty was a bit annoyed with me – one of the rare occasions! – as it seemed to her an unsustainable paradox: "You are about to marry a billionaire, and you waste time on those trifles of yours?"

I explained that Mansur's money wasn't mine, and that I was proud of every cent I'd earned through my work, but didn't wish to take advantage of my forthcoming change of status to be indelicate in any way with my employer and benefactors.

Following their suggestion (aimed at relieving me from any unnecessary fatigue), I'd agreed to leave all the practical preparation for the wedding to Mansur and his parents – apart from the flowers. I *would* have my lilies!

Thanks to our webcams, Mansur and I spoke daily. How I missed him!

Fr. Paul and Kitty were involved as well, and I trusted their judgment entirely. Incidentally, she confirmed that he'd been in hospital recently for his lungs.

I emailed him: *Every time I saw Mansur's father light a cigar in Cairo, which was quite often, I was reminded to pray for you, that you may smoke less – as you asked me once.* He didn't answer.

The delicate question of the wedding dress had been solved.

Before we left Egypt, Mansur had told me of his desire to have a new one made. But Dior managed to make the coffee stain disappear entirely, and I insisted on wearing the original as a secret witness to our spiritual recovery.

The day before the wedding, we drove half an hour south, to Lisieux, where I spent the day in recollection at the shrine of the Little Flower, Saint Thérèse.

I also visited her family home, and prayed to her parents, Saints Louis and Zélie Martin, asking them to guide Mansur and me as spouses and parents.

I knew that they hadn't been spared trials: Zélie had died rather young, after a long illness; while Louis had suffered from dementia. But through their difficulties, they'd developed a deep conjugal and parental affection, grounded on their ardent love for Christ.

Looking at a picture with little Saint Thérèse and her parents, I begged God that the same grace might be granted to my family: that Mansur, Talitha and I might become saints.

Chapter 98

The wedding went as well as could have been hoped for.

A private suite and two lounges on the Chapel level had been booked for us, allowing me to prepare and dress without attracting attention. I would not have liked to be seen walking through the terminal in my wedding dress!

I went to confession with Fr. Paul just before the ceremony, as he'd told me that the sacrament bears added fruit in proportion to the purity of the souls at the time of the exchange of vows. I felt as if my soul had been clothed with grace, just as my body had been adorned with satin and lace.

I was very touched that, to please me, Daddy had come without Abigail, my stepmother (Mum wouldn't have attended otherwise). When I had called him to break the news six weeks earlier, he'd sounded truly pleased for me. Many things were forgotten, or better, forgiven, as he walked me down the aisle. I could feel his arm shake a bit under mine, and knew that he was truly proud of me, and happy.

Raising my joy to a climax, Mummy had travelled from Seoul. I didn't have time, at that moment, to dwell on what that meant for me and them and Kitty, but my heart registered their presence side by side, and it melted in thanksgiving. I resolved to pray ardently for their reunion, if God would grant it to them and us.

As we walked in, I first doubted whether it was the same rather gloomy and bare room where, thirteen months earlier, I'd been reborn to my faith.

It was now covered with marble of various colours – following an Italian pattern, I learnt later on. A few small statues punctuated the space.

In order to fit in more people, I suppose, the altar had been pushed back against the wall, under the tabernacle, and wasn't of aluminium anymore, but of marble, sumptuously dressed.

There were stained glass windows (electrically lit from behind, I found out later) with St. Vincent de Paul and St. Clare of Assisi, our two patron saints, and with our dearly beloved friends St. Anthony and St. Katarina!

I felt as if the place was populated with loving and powerful intercessors, as it was! But the most beautiful improvements were two Italian statues of the Sacred Heart of Jesus and of the Blessed Virgin Mary.

By what miracle that ordinary and dull underground room had been turned into a magnificent and shining chapel, I could only guess. I was told later on that the workers had taken night shifts to finish on time. Two men had made it possible – and both were awaiting me in the small sanctuary.

One was facing me, in his priestly vestments. His face was grave and radiated his fatherly affection.

I nearly cried when I realised *who* the other one was, his back still turned to me. Of course, I knew full well whom I was expecting to find on that red velvet seat to the right, by the Communion rail. But the man whose back I saw wasn't *sitting*.

I simply could not reconcile the place where he was and his posture. Until he turned his head towards me...

Mansur, standing! Mansur standing without any help! Mansur upright *in the air* before my eyes, not carried by the waves like at Ain Sukhna!

As he later confirmed, he'd spent most of the past three weeks at Dr. Schtreuli's clinic in Switzerland for intensive rehabilitation. And there he stood, tall and tanned; and he was my fiancé! What a delightful shock!

Dad supported my arm as I genuflected in front of the tabernacle, before kneeling side by side with my beloved. Only then did I recognise the rather mature altar server assisting Fr. Paul. *Nepomucen* looked deeply moved, and with good reason, having been the first one to see me out of the plane, and soon after in that chapel, thirteen months earlier.

My immaculate lilies had been set near the altar according to my wishes, and their fragrance would soon mix with that of sacred incense.

Fr. Paul preached on the sanctity of marriage as an icon of God's love for each soul, and as a gift to society.

At his invitation, Mansur and I then spoke the sacred words which made us husband and wife: "I, Mansur Al-Khoury take thee Clara Cumberhart, to my wedded wife; to have, and to hold; from this day forward; for better, for worse; for richer, for poorer; in sickness and in health; until death do us part; and thereto I plight thee my troth."

I answered: "I, Clara Cumberhart take thee Mansur Al-Khoury, to my wedded husband; to have, and to hold; from this day forward; for better, for worse; for richer, for poorer; in sickness and in health; until death do us part; and thereto I plight thee my troth."

Kitty was standing next to me as my Maid of Honour, and Jed on the other side as Mansur's Best Man. There was no clapping – just a loud heartbeat in my chest. When Mansur put the blessed ring onto my finger, I felt that we belonged to each other at last.

I followed Holy Mass with more recollection than usual. Some lovely booklets had been printed, with English and French translations alongside the Latin prayers. I realised that it was the first time I was attending Holy Mass offered by Fr. Paul. It was also the first time it was taking place in the refurbished chapel.

Kneeling so close behind him, I could admire his ancient-looking vestments (including the embroidered strip hanging from his forearm, like Abu Ephrem wore when saying Mass in Cairo).

Once Mansur and I had received Holy Communion, I saw more clearly than ever how the true Presence of our God and Saviour in us made us one.

Jesus in us was the Source of our unity.

All our attempts, all our efforts to deepen our relationship through mutual understanding, patience and forgiveness could only bear fruit as expressions of Our Lord's loving presence in us.

I gave thanks to the Saviour, Who had so generously and unexpectedly made me a daughter to Fr. Paul, Abu Ephrem and even Mother Joan-Maria; a sister to Azim and Nour; and a bride to Mansur.

He had also granted me motherhood, through the gift of my darling Litha; of my forty-eight rescued girls at Osly; and through another childbirth whose pangs were still too fresh for me to name their fruit, but whom I entrusted to God's mercy.

Chapter 99

We left the chapel and made our way out through a VIP exit.

To tell the truth, to me the party was by far the less important part of the event.

It took place in a beautiful private mansion south of Paris. I remember the magnificent garden and stream.

The owner told us a story about a squirrel (one of my favourite animals) climbing too close to the sun. Indeed, *squirrels* were depicted everywhere, carved on cornices, painted on wood panels and even embroidered on tapestries.

We had no more than forty guests, and the occasion was a rather quiet one. My delight was when Mansur, Talitha and I stood for pictures on the top of the steps leading to the grounds. We were holding the hands of our daughter.

Our daughter.

Two hours earlier, I was a single woman, and henceforth, I was a wife and a mother. We had become a *family*!

My heart was flowing with gratitude. I was flying! Mansur sat down, as his spine wasn't yet fully healed (and perhaps never would). But that didn't affect my joy, as it was a magnificent gift already to have been welcomed by him standing at the altar.

Thinking of the altar, I'd noticed something changed in Fr. Paul after Mass, when signing the registers. I couldn't exactly tell in what way, but he seemed different. He was now walking towards us across the lawn.

Our eyes growing moist as we looked at each other in silence for a short while, equally moved, as we both appreciated the distance travelled since our providential encounter thirteen months earlier.

As he was signing my brow with his thumb – another reminiscence – I realised what it was. The heavy smell of tobacco was totally gone! Perhaps replaced by a hint of Cologne (surely not *Givenchy*).

I teased him: "No pipe for you today, Father, even here outdoors? If you've lost it, Mansur could find you a hookah."

The three of us smiled and Fr. Paul changed the subject.

But the next morning, when opening our wedding presents, I found his pipe wrapped with a note: *Dear Clara, daughter, Doctor said again: Quit smoking or die. Said it many times. But I'm no hero. For what it is worth, I offered it up, as a wedding present.*

Will pray for your soul, whenever my hands find my pouch empty and my pipe missing: many times a day. Fr. Paul the Cleaner

P.S. I still have incense!

I was glad to meet with Mansur's extended family and friends.

Only then did I learn that Jeda, his mother, was a niece of the late Emperor of Iran. He'd died in Cairo, and Jeda liked to go and pray for his soul at the Al-Rifa'i Mosque where he lay buried, near the Cairo Citadel.

Jed confided to me later – half-joking, half-serious – that the Al-Khourys were "much more illustrious than the Pahlavis, since they could (almost) trace their genealogy back to King Hiram, who had given precious cedar wood to King Solomon to build the temple of Jerusalem."

So, my prince charming *was* some kind of prince after all. My own little prince.

However, had he been like me the son of immigrants to Canada (what part of England again did Dad come from: was it Yorkshire or Wiltshire?); but, I realised, Mansur's parents *were* immigrants to Canada, like mine!

Right: with or without his fortune – he would have been my prince and my love all the same!

The music was playing. I was careful not to drink too much Champagne (vodka I would not even look at, thank you – *Potocki* or not).

I had a little shock when meeting Vardah Wattles, Nour's first cousin. I'd been told in advance of their resemblance. Not so much the mouth or nose of Vardah, as her eyes and her voice, reminded me of Nour's.

I glanced at Mansur from the corner of my eyes, wondering how he would cope with the emotional impact. They simply embraced each other, warmly and briefly, before she hugged *me*!

She whispered in my ear: "You look *strong*, I'm glad."

I felt as if Nour herself was empowering me as her successor, and in my emotion I shed a few tears, (thanking Fr. Paul in my heart for his good cosmetic advice from the year before). I liked that woman, and didn't feel threatened by her, which was saying a lot (although I would not have minded if she'd been less skinny and stylish).

She begged us to come and see Stuart and her soon, near London. Before moving to another group, she looked as if she meant to add something, but smiled and went away.

Raúl had become a great chum to Mansur, and Talitha. That was very good as, after much hesitation, we had decided to leave her with Kitty (whom she loved) and Raúl for the first part of our honeymoon. Our darling had agreed, rather happily.

I'd noticed before that children like Raúl.

He was carrying Baby Javier, and allowed Talitha – sitting down – to hold him in her arms. My dear daughter was ecstatic! She couldn't take her eyes off the little boy, and seemed to feel as if she'd carried him all her life.

And to think that she would have been killed, that afternoon in Cairo, if it hadn't been for Azim...

But, I realised with a tremor, would Baby Javier himself not have been...

Once at Paris airport, thirteen months earlier, hadn't *someone* set her mind on preventing this baby nephew ever seeing the light of day?

Hadn't *someone* declared him to be in the wrong place at the wrong time – nothing personal – and resolved to use persuasive affection on her sister, intending the same lethal consequence on Javier as the Scimitars did with their guns on Talitha?

Wasn't that fatal decision made on the same day and at the same time as the Scimitars were loading their pistol? *What* made that "someone" different from those jihadists, then? Her clean hands? Her straw hat?

Azim had interfered and saved Talitha. *Who* had intervened for Javier to live? Who had died – or who might still die?

I couldn't face it.

Litha was holding Javier, while his tiny fingers caressed her cheek. Two *survivors*... Two small innocent survivors of the hypocrisy, selfishness and hatred of adults.

My throat felt suddenly dry and my legs trembled. The thought of falling down on my knees and begging for their forgiveness flashed through my soul.

My babies!

Oh! That I may atone, somehow, someday...

No, Clara, I said to myself – not *now* – you couldn't cope with that *now*! This is neither the place nor the time for such thoughts.

I should quickly divert my mind.

I stepped nearer and, leaning behind them, embraced both children, praying that God who had forgiven me would soon grant us the joy of my Litha holding her *own* baby brother or sister.

Chapter 100

Jed gave a beautiful Best Man's speech.

He managed to say a lot in a few words, with many gentle allusions to what we had all been through, and thanking God for the good achieved on that blessed day.

I really must remember to check if he *isn't* a Catholic; he didn't come to receive Holy Communion, unlike Jeda, but he seemed to know some of the prayers rather well.

Perhaps, I may still mention here his gracious compliment. Referring to my necklace, he said: "As we all know, natural pearls form when a tiny piece of rock or metal, or dust, enters the oyster and settles inside the shell.

"It causes irritation that the oyster overcomes through secreting layers of nacre to cover the irritant, eventually producing marvellous gleaming gems.

"Dear close relatives and friends, a year ago, the microcosm of my family suffered a devastating intrusion, of lasting consequences. It wasn't a piece of rock, but several pieces of lead. The best of us...

"The best of us... left this world. I now see..."

Dear Jed was visibly moved, in contrast with the strength he normally emanates.

After a slightly awkward silence, he went on: "I now see the affection and support demonstrated by our close family and friends, as so many *layers* of nacre, gradually set around our pain, with a soothing effect upon the hearts of Jeda, of Mansur, Talitha and on mine. I thank all present, and those united with us through affection from a distance.

"On this wedding day, I see and I sense an *added* protective layer on the convalescing heart of my family. This latest stage gleams before us today, and I give thanks for the radiance of such a gem, sitting in our midst, in her ivory dress.

"My son has found a *pearl* of great price, but he doesn't need to sell all our assets" – chuckles across the table – "because she *isn't* for sale.

"Mansur, you've paid the only price worthy of such a new daughter, your merciful and manly heart. May she further its healing, making you and us gleam and shine always brighter under God's sun."

He embraced me with emotion, like the very first time in Mansur's hospital room. He whispered into my ear: "Daughter, love my son with all your heart. Stand by him forever: you deserve each other."

I knew then that all the insinuations I'd heard in a certain car park were utter lies. That man, whatever his faith, was truthful and loving; and he set forgiveness as a condition to any healing. Jeda was no less affectionate.

I could see that they'd truly adopted me.

Later, we unwrapped their wedding present – a bronze replica of *The Cathedral,* a sculpture by a French artist I'd liked in Vancouver. Who could have told them about it: Kitty, Mansur, or Dad? I read that the Hornby Street Art Gallery had it on loan from a collection in Paris. (They wouldn't sell the original, I was told later, even to dear Jed! Hence the *replica*, which suited me well.)

The sculpture simply consists of two right hands, one of a man, the other of a woman, standing vertically, about to clasp. They seem to be dancing, as if in mutual love. It was originally called *The Ark of the Covenant*. I found it a deeply moving symbol of God's love for marriage and family.

Thinking of it, for my parents also, it was a very special day. What Kitty's wedding had rekindled in them, nearly one year earlier, grew stronger at mine. Their daughters' achievements subdued their mutual resentment.

Mum and Dad were brought closer to each other by these new steps in our own lives. They were a bit ill at ease with Mansur, whom they'd never met. But I was sure that their hearts would soon melt under the charm of my prince.

Dr. Yazir seemed perfectly in her element. Although we had kept in touch by email and occasionally by phone, it was our first meeting since San Antonio. We fell into each other's arms, my perfume mixing with her Chanel N°5.

She knew what an ordeal I'd gone through, having assisted me in the plane after I'd heard the news of the attack. I recalled her motherly dedication to me, an unknown tourist girl mercifully upgraded to Business Class.

She was now looking at my pearls. How mysteriously God works indeed... To think that those gems had shone around *her* neck just thirteen months earlier! What if I *hadn't* been late at the gate; what if the attack hadn't occurred; what if...

Her fingers were weighing up my necklace, as she complimented me: "My little contribution has been powerfully improved by your merit, and by the love of your husband. You wear them like a princess, Clara. I'm deeply pleased to be here.

"Now isn't the best time for you to answer this but, when convenient, could you suggest a couple of dates for my visit to your schools? My Department is definitively interested in the Al-Khoury Charitable Trust. Our respective aims look very compatible, and a possible partnership must now be explored."

Again I was impressed by her. She was a powerful and straightforward female leader. Although I chose to ignore a slight embarrassment, as I suddenly realised that I didn't share some of her views on *reproductive health* anymore. We would see.

I was also grateful to my few trusted friends from Canada who had travelled for the occasion, especially Emma and Sally. I knew that they were trying hard not to refer to the elephant in the room, as it would appear to them, namely, my stratospheric rise to fabulous wealth and influence.

I put them at ease: "Girls, please make sure to keep both my feet upon the ground. As soon as you detect that I sound less like the old Clara you knew, text me that you need my assistance to unblock your sink or paint your kitchen, and I will come and help."

They laughed, knowing in advance my limited practical skills. I challenged them, though: "Trust me: over the past three weeks on a boat, I've become an expert in changing my nephew's nappies. Kitty awarded a diploma to me!"

I also apologised for having frustrated their plans for a bridal shower, due to my convalescence; but we agreed that it was only postponed until after my honeymoon: never too late!

I had once said that I would never dance again. But that was in another life.

Most of us danced under the plane trees until dark: I with Dad, and with Jed; Mansur with Mum (an unexpected sight); I with Litha! – even Mansur with Kitty! I couldn't take my eyes off those two people I cherished most. Their wheelchairs folded away for a time, both were standing at present, dancing in a brotherly way.

They'd set foot on the dance floor a bit clumsily, due to their condition, but the sight of them captured us all, like a miracle. What a grace-filled *motion* it was, for once.

I caught Kitty's glance at Raúl and I as our pair was coming nearer to theirs, and my smile mirrored my sister's.

Chapter 101

The guests had left. Our close relatives stayed in the mansion.
Still wearing our wedding garments, Mansur and I walked to Talitha's bedroom.
For the first time, she called me "Mummy."
It was a moment of tranquil delight.
For the first time when talking to her, Mansur referred to me as "Mummy" as well.

What a mysterious thing a *relationship* was. How it developed, or degenerated; how it fulfilled or reviled us, according to the spirit that inspired it. I knew what I was talking about.
But better keep to *happy* relationships. I'd been a mere tourist coached by their late friend. I'd become an employee of her father. Then I became his fiancée. Now I was his wife, and her mother.
We lay by each other's side on Talitha's little bed, saying nothing.
We imbibed the glory of being simply that: a family.
Father; mother; daughter... I'd never felt more intimately close to anyone else, than now, with this man and this child: my husband and our daughter.
We let our modest network of relationships take root deep inside our hearts, along the channels that, months in advance, we'd prepared for them. We let ourselves be husband to wife; wife to husband; parents to child; and daughter to Mom and Dad.
And further out: son-in-law and daughter-in-law; grand-daughter; brother-in-law; niece and cousin; uncle... We let our humble cell, our nuclear family, connect with the wider organism of mankind across generations.
And what of "Uncle" Anthony the Hermit, and "Auntie" Katarina the Martyr, and all the saints and angels? May our souls beat in unison with this even broader family of God's children, the Church.

The three of us got on our knees, in front of Nour's image of Our Lady taken from the *Cedrus* (Mansur thought of everything). Having examined our conscience for the sins of the day, we recited an Our Father, a Hail Mary and a Glory Be.
I saw that Talitha awaited something. Was it a kiss? Was it a hug? Had I missed anything in this tender protocol, putting her to bed as her new Mum for the very first time?
She looked up at Mansur, who nodded at her with a light smile, and took from his wallet an old prayer-card that he handed me, while the two of them began, "Glory be to Thee, sweetest, most gentle, most benign, sovereign,

transcendent, effulgent, and ever-peaceful Trinity, for the roseate wounds of Jesus Christ, my only Love!" They said five times that rather old fashioned but short prayer. I caught up with them soon enough.

Talitha didn't glance at the card once. She knew it all by heart, like Mansur. Did she understand every word?

On the card, under the prayer, I saw the name of St. Gertrude, and the picture of an old crimson banner bearing the pierced Hands, Feet and Sacred Heart of Our Lord with a chalice in the middle. I made a sign of the cross upon my new daughter's forehead, now lying in her bed.

She threw her arms around my neck, saying that she had the most beautiful Mummy in the world, and the nicest Daddy also! I couldn't object, at least to the second claim.

Mansur and I stayed at the other end of the park, in a separate pavilion, enclosed with its own grounds, and a swimming pool. No one was to be admitted but he and I (nurses, carers and bodyguards would kindly keep out). What a luxury!

As we slowly walked towards our quarters, he explained: "Nour had a great devotion to the Five Sacred Wounds. I started reciting that prayer along with her and Litha, years before converting. As you guessed, it was part of their evening routine. You don't mind, do you?"

Five?

We stopped under the majestic beeches and plane trees, shading us from the moon, while another light started glimmering in my heart.

Five wounds?

But I didn't dare to ask, in case I was wrong. Instinctively though, the fingers of my right hand came to rest upon my throat, upon five...

He smiled almost shyly, as if found out: "Yes, I designed your necklace as a reminder of the Five Wounds. Each ruby stands for one. I wished my new wife to be adorned as richly and gloriously as possible and, rather than multiply the gems, I selected those according to colour and number, as an echo of redemptive suffering.

"Seeing you wear it helped me a lot. Do you really not mind, now that you know?"

Sweet Jesus – this was my best wedding present! So, my beloved wasn't indulging in a rich man's hobby when designing my set of gems. He wasn't subtly trying to bind me either, when insisting on my wearing it.

He was asking God for assistance, through me. He was presenting me to God as the successor of his lost wife, I assumed, and as a claim to God's mercy.

I took his hand and set it over my right hand upon my throat, saying: "Darling, I will wear your necklace even more proudly, now that I know its full meaning."

We hugged gently, and slowly started dancing, close against each other, among the tall beeches, living pillars, a natural temple to our delight. Then we walked on towards the gate of our domain.

We walked. He *walked*. I still wasn't used to it.

His arm across my back, his hand upon my hip, this man walked like a prince and could pray like a saint – and he was my *husband*. I walked alongside my spouse and let him show the way.

What You have joined together, O beloved Saviour, and purified, and inebriated and sealed with your Precious Blood, let no man put asunder (and no woman either).

Chapter 102

Rome was our first call.

We received the blessing bestowed upon several newlywed couples by the Holy Father.

I was struck by that grace. Not so much in terms of emotions, since I didn't *feel* anything particular as I stood in my wedding dress with Mansur in St. Peter's Square. But more on reflection, when considering that the man who had extended upon us God's protection was the direct Successor of the first Pope, St. Peter.

An unbroken line of hundreds of pontiffs, many of them martyred, linked our modest couple with the very One Who had chosen and empowered Peter to teach, sanctify and govern His Church in His Name. I recalled the moving expression of another Katarina, calling the Sovereign Pontiff "the sweet Christ on earth."

We entrusted our newly founded family to the protection of the Holy Apostles, and of the many saints whose innumerable relics and charitable deeds make Rome a furnace of grace.

We had supper with a Cardinal, Patron of charitable Works for Middle-Eastern Catholics. He seemed to know my beloved well, and was appreciative of his convictions and support. Every day, I was discovering new traits of Mansur's discreet generosity.

The Nuncio to Sudan was present. I thanked him for having relayed to London Nepomucen's call thirteen months earlier, saving innocent lives. He gave thanks to God for the rescue, adding with a slight smile that, if ever the Nunciature had been involved, it would have occurred during the interim, before his assignment to Khartoum.

We also tried every possible type of pasta. I didn't know that so many palatable variations were possible on that rather plain theme. But the best thing with pasta is that, after, you get a gelato! Or two, if you smile at your prince nicely enough, until he lets you try his, and in fact is grateful to you for slurping it all for him.

After Rome, we visited Florence and Turin, staying with friends. At a shrine, the priest told us about the local saint, famous Don Bosco, "who had prophetic dreams, and led so many young people to God." I wished he'd lived in Vancouver when *I* was in my teens. The relic of Our Lord's shroud is also kept in Turin, but it wasn't on display, sadly.

We then flew to Lourdes, in the French Pyrenees. What a treat! I'd always wanted to see the place where Our Lady had announced to the world that she was the Immaculate Conception.

For years, I'd thought that her title meant the Blessed Virgin Mary had been conceived in her mother's womb *not* as the result of the marital act, and that we were supposed to admire her for *that*, as if the normal way was sinful.

I felt so ashamed of my ignorance – and relieved – when learning that "Immaculate Conception" in reality meant that her soul had been preserved from any stain of sin from the very first moment of her existence.

She was conceived by her parents in the normal way, like you and me.

So, what the Church invites the whole world to celebrate is the purity of a human soul in whom God was *always* pleased.

I lit many candles at the Grotto, for all my family and friends, and very much in thanksgiving for the unexpected improvement of Mansur's health (we had been warned not to call it "healing" too soon).

We were both a bit apprehensive of the baths, but decided to try anyway. The volunteers treated us with a lot of respect and everything went prayerfully and peacefully.

After, I went to confession to a French priest who spoke with a very high-pitched voice and a strong accent from Provence, and nearly made me laugh – which perhaps wasn't very proper – but gave me great encouragement.

Before leaving, we visited "the Cell," as the flat of St Bernadette's family is called. It was the town prison, and was found to be so insalubrious, even for inmates, that it was vacated.

The Soubirous family, having become destitute, could only find refuge there. It confirmed to me that wealth was no prerequisite to raise a saintly family, and a blessed daughter. I wished Litha had been with us.

We fetched her in Paris as had been planned, on our way to England. I was so glad to have our little treasure with us again! We hugged each other as if it had been ten months rather than ten days.

Mansur thought that I would like to visit the motherland of the British Empire, as I only knew Heathrow Airport! Although my grandfather was Irish, Dad was English by birth; from Yorkshire, if I remember (I would text him for confirmation).

I think that Mansur also wanted to show me the places where he'd spent most of his youth, at a boarding school in the North, and at Oxford.

I kept my professional lenses on while visiting tourist sites, wondering how I could lead a group there, if ever I decided to work again. But I knew that was unlikely – unless it was humanitarian work, as I'd started doing for the schools in the Middle-East.

While in London, an incident occurred at the Royal Albert Hall, during the Proms. The day had been rather hectic and hot; Talitha was in bed at our house; and I simply relished sitting back in the concert hall, whatever the music. I liked the melody playing, although it sounded a bit sad; and must have fallen asleep, as often happens to me when it's warm, peaceful and dark.

As in a dream, I realised after some time that the music had become very familiar to me. But not at all in a *happy* way.

I knew each cadence and interval; I knew when any violin was to stop and play again – and the cellos...

I felt as if the sheet music had been carved into my heart with a blade not very long ago. Every minute, it seemed, I was sweating more abundantly and felt more nauseous.

I didn't need to check the programme.

I knew very, very well the composer's name and the title of the work. *Why* had I not bothered to read it before sitting down! I tried to pull myself together: *Clara, you* must *overcome this. Be a big girl now!*

But it was stronger than me and, trembling, I grabbed Mansur's hand.

He turned to me and realised that I was unwell. He asked me if I needed to go out and, seeing the sweat on my face, and feeling my burning hands, knew the answer right away.

He supported me out to the corridor and we sat together, while Mansur's carer was dispatched to bring me water.

Chapter 103

I was feeling much better already.

We walked out of the Albert Hall and on to *The White Hart*, a lovely little restaurant on the edge of Hyde Park, sitting just the two of us in a private room (one bodyguard only stood by, while his colleague and the carer had been given a table in the main area).

The eyes of my beloved and his gentle smile brought my balance back.

I wanted strength and shamelessly ordered a roast leg of lamb, Indian style, marinated with mixed spices, and French fries! Mansur chose an excellent red wine (*Château Musar*, from Lebanon) and helped us both to it.

It puzzled me that he wasn't asking what the matter had been with me, while a very discreet smile kept appearing on his lips.

Did I blush faintly when the thought occurred to me that he might think me, well... No, surely, *that* was too soon. Categorically too soon.

I decided to spare him any disappointment after a premature joy, and plainly explained that the andante of *Death and the Maiden* evoked very unpleasant memories of my last evening with Jonathan.

He didn't smile at all then. But *I* did, taking his hand across the table, and I assured him that poor Schubert couldn't have foreseen the bad use made of his music played in loop. He filled our glasses again and we drank to the health of Schubert.

In fact, we spent one of our happiest evenings so far.

We even spoke French, and I tried Arabic.

Mansur was altogether very caring and very funny. I hadn't seen him like that before – so funny I mean – since considerate, he always is (no fit of anger had occurred again).

We knew that we were drinking a tiny drop more than needed, but we were in love, and so happy to have found each other.

Let the violins play then: with such a prince to protect me, I feared nothing and no one.

Back at the house, we met with Talitha's governess who said that our darling was fast asleep and tired after her long day of sightseeing. I went to the bedroom of my little daughter and looked at her while she slept. What a delight!

Mansur joined me and, in a very low voice, we said our usual evening prayer over and for our little treasure, and for the two of us.

Lying in bed later that night, with my cherished blue and white djellaba on, I looked at the moonlit shape of my dear husband, now sleeping against me.

I didn't know what to expect when he'd mentioned his *family house* in Chelsea. Actually, I liked the place very much, with the gigantic plane trees in the not so small garden. I knew that we could not really spend our lives on the *Cedrus* and, when the time came to settle down in a proper house, this one would suit me very well.

The Thames was down the road and Battersea Park across the river, to go jogging. Vardah Wattles had told me that there were two excellent hospitals nearby (and Sloane Street for fashion!)

I'd also noticed the Oratory Church, and the museums, and I'd heard good things about the Oratory School (although Fr. Paul had recommended homeschooling, which was becoming more and more popular). Talking of an oratory, I wished to convert our smaller drawing-room here into a private chapel. I would ask Mansur.

In the morning, we woke up to find Talitha lying between us.

It was the first time she did so. Birds were chirping through the open window, and tiny grains of dust were dancing in the sunbeams reaching our bed through the curtains. It felt so peaceful to be in our own house, with my husband and darling daughter.

She'd brought along her favourite comic, *Tintin and the Picaros*, and Mansur read to her part of the story.

Looking at them, I gave thanks in my heart for such a grace, and begged for God's assistance to help me live up to His bounty for another new day. I remembered that it was the feast of Our Lady of Mount Carmel, which increased my joy.

The *Tintin* reading had ended and Talitha, in a playful mood, started tickling me and Mansur. Her attempt prompted retaliation, and we ended up in a fierce tickling battle, punctuated by much laughter and culminating in a pillow fight!

We took our breakfast in bed, with several hot croissants per person. How we managed not to spill any coffee or orange juice on the sheets, I don't know.

A little cloud appeared on my sunny firmament though, when from the bathroom, Mansur's voice *innocently* asked: "Darling, you remember that I promised to ignore any business matter during our honeymoon?"

I said that I recalled his pledge very well indeed, and was *truly glad* that he was keeping it so faithfully. He then asked if I liked football.

I didn't see the connection, as I thought that sport was leisure, not business.

He explained: "Al-Khoury Sports Corporation is about to increase significantly its participation in the Chelsea Football Club. The team has been revamped and will play tonight unofficially against Arsenal. It's a bit like the Proms for football. My father texted me that it would be very good if I attended... ideally with *you*.

"But we won't go unless you like the idea. Fulham is five minutes from here; we would be out of it by 10 p.m. Kundomo will play – Arsenal's new striker! *We* couldn't afford him, but I know many men who would dream of getting his shirt."

That *was* a cloud! I knew nothing about football (let alone about Mr. Kundomo and his shirt!), having only learned from Azim that eleven players per team were needed.

Hockey, that was something I could watch (or even play). But *football*? And right in the middle of our honeymoon.

I *was* upset.

Then I remembered that marriage was very much about pleasing one's spouse, in anything good or indifferent. Could I say that ninety minutes over there would be culpably spent? Not really.

So, I tried to make my voice sound as interested as possible without lying when I answered: "Darling, I didn't know that you loved football, or that your family had invested in it. But if you think it's important, I will come along with pleasure."

With *pleasure*, truly? Sunrays still flowed upon our bed. What was that glint on my left hand?

Ah, yes... I kissed my wedding ring.

Chapter 104

I emailed Dr. Yasir about something important I had to do. Then, Mansur, Talitha, and I went out for lunch, and shopping.

I bought her a lovely little summer dress of woven cotton with exquisite floral, striped and *broderie* tiered design. She loved the shirred top and the pretty frill straps. Mansur said that it suited her very well.

I then announced that I would meet them later at the house, as it was good for father and daughter to spend a little time on their own. As I was leaving, Mansur embraced me, asking: "Sweetheart, I really hope that you aren't upset about the football event this evening?"

I kissed him and said: "If I remember, we leave London tomorrow, by boat! Once you are locked up in there with me and Talitha, we won't let you escape. But you may bring a football on board and teach us how to play."

He saw that I wasn't really annoyed and waved at me as I walked away. Sometimes, taking a little distance makes us appreciate our happiness better, doesn't it? I loved them enormously.

Meanwhile, Nasreen had emailed back and, twenty minutes later, I met with her friend in Kensington. Kindly, she'd agreed to see me immediately, despite her busy schedule. She kept me less than a quarter of an hour.

I felt dizzy on leaving the building and wished to sit down for a while. Was that a steeple, in the distance? Yes, there was a church further down, across the street.

I didn't know its name, but it might be Catholic. On entering, I discovered that it happened to be *Our Lady of Mount Carmel* Church: *today*'s feast according to my e-calendar. What a wonderful hint of divine Providence!

I fell on my knees by the Lady's altar.

There we were. How to begin?

My life had taken me through momentous stages over the past thirteen months. But *this* latest one was perhaps the most moving, if possible.

I simply couldn't integrate the news.

It was too sublime; too awesome; too sacred. What could I say, but thank God and Our Lady, and my guardian angel, and my patron saint, and the whole celestial court for such an unexpected and quick fulfilment of my deepest aspiration?

And thank Mansur, my spouse... I was in tears again, in front of the statue of Mary carrying her divine Child.

O Mother, please, teach me! Please guide my every step and word and thought. You know how inexperienced I am. You know how selfish and impatient! How can I respond to such a mission, to such trust?

I must spell it out: I'm inhabited.
I'm lived in.
I'm indwelt.
For the first time, I was going to speak to him, or her, I didn't know.
I couldn't say "it": *Child. My child. Our child.*
How astonishing those two words. My relationship with Talitha deepened every day. I was fulfilled in it. But I'd somehow caught up with her life, from the time she was five, or six years old. Another woman had given her life.
Today, I was catching up with the life of a younger child, now aged a fortnight! And I was with him or her from the start.

My treasured little one...
When you're old, long past fifty, after I'm gone, I pray that you may rest assured of one thing: right on hearing of your presence in me, my heart leapt with joy and my soul embraced yours in my womb. I felt humbled and glorified as never before.
You are. You are, nested in the most sheltered part of my body. You live. Our God has done such a favour to me as to make me the mother of yet another of His cherished children: you – promised by Him to everlasting joy in the contemplation of His splendour. I love you with all my heart, dear child!
I thank God and you with all my strength, for the indescribable wonder of your occurring, and for the promise of your blessed future. I confess my surprise, as I experience a rise of glee *that I'd never have thought possible, so high above the clouds I'd already been raised, by the mercy of our God and the love of your dear father.*
Child. My child. Our child – although your father doesn't yet know that, for fifteen days already, you've been with the both of us. I recall those blessed two weeks since we gave ourselves to one another. So, in Rome, you were with us? In Lourdes, you were with us. In London, you are with us...
And we're with you, now and forever.

Today, kneeling before our heavenly Mother, I pray that when your father and I will leave this earth, we may be with you still in spirit, and that from the bosom of the Blessed Trinity, we may help prepare for you a place of rest and fulfilment.
I pray that your mansion in God's eternal love may be as close to the Sacred Heart of Jesus as His Providence disposes. I pray that as your mother, I may help you reach that place as safely and fruitfully as possible, by the grace of God.
Dear child, it's as if my heart has mysteriously moved from my chest to my womb. I feel as if henceforth you *were my heart.*
I can't find a reason why my blood would flow through my body, anymore, other than for your growth.
Why would my mouth open and my throat swallow food any further, but for your nourishment?

Why would I lie and rest, tonight and any future nights, but for restoring my strength as the dedicated bearer of your precious life?

Why would I laugh, if not to provide you with a foretaste of the joy found ultimately in God?

Why would I hum a lullaby, if not for you to perceive, however faintly as yet, the tunes of tenderness and of expectation of which you are the cause?

Why would I pray, if it were not to besiege the heavenly mercy with a mother's humble petitions for the fruit of her womb, and to give thanks for such a joy!

I have conceived. I carry life. I'm a mother.

In your coming, beloved child, God has exalted me greatly.

What dignity may a creature ever aspire to, after she's been made what I am to you, and what you are to me? An immortal soul, united to a beautiful body, chosen and designed by God from all eternity, to be bathed in His grace and rejoice in His sight, forever and ever.

Kneeling by her altar in this London church, I see the little brown patches of cloth handed by Our Mother to the saintly friar. How ardently I pray, dear child, that this the most important grace of all may be granted you: to die in the love of God, so as to be born into eternal happiness.

And for you to die well, I know that you must live well.

My child, my joy isn't exempt from fear, when I think that after nine months you will leave the haven of my body, and move by yourself, perhaps getting hurt.

But my fear is greater for your soul, much greater, as I realise that after seven years or so, having reached the age of reason or discretion, you will start answering for yourself before God, for each of your thoughts, words and deeds.

Ah, that I may keep over your soul during your entire earthly life the protection that I now give your body!

That you may never offend God and, from the time of your Baptism, that you may keep in yourself His sanctifying grace, as the life of your life and the soul of your soul!

Chapter 105

Ding!

I hadn't noticed the time fly by, when a bell rang in the sanctuary, the sacristy door opened and Holy Mass started.

Holy Mass! Attending it would be my first practical decision as a mother. It was only 6 p.m. but, to spare Mansur any concern, I texted him where I was and the expected time of my return.

I refrained from sharing the stupendous news.

First, because its nature called for breaking it face to face. Second, because I thought it fairer to inform him only *after* his football evening was over. There was no need to cancel our coming to the event, as it seemed important to him and his father. And I would not have the treasure in me be used as a pretext to save me from an entertainment I didn't look forward to.

I followed the Mass with ease and deep recollection.

After Holy Communion, I was suddenly struck by the thought of the close contact between my God and my child in me. I knew that the Real Presence lasts no more than fifteen minutes after swallowing the Sacred Host, until our body digests It. So, it appeared to me, my Beloved Saviour was in me then, with His Body, Precious Blood, Soul and Divinity, as physically close as can be to my little Baby.

What distance is there, literally, between my stomach and my womb?

Are they not part of the same organism, sheltered under the same skin? Yes, my God was visiting His little one *in* me. I was transported with joy at the idea of their silent meeting in me, and I spent my thanksgiving in begging Jesus to give my child all the graces needed to make him or her just the saint He had planned.

If a *temple* is a place designed to facilitate encounter between man and God, I knew myself to be, kneeling at my pew, a temple within a greater temple.

Holy Mass had ended when the priest carried out of the sacristy a glazed casket containing, he explained, the arm of St. Simon Stock, which was only displayed on today's feast, once a year.

We were invited to venerate it, touching the glass with our hand or kissing it. I'd never done that and, at first, thought it a bit morbid. That was the sort of thing non-Catholics objected to, I remembered.

I looked at the faithful waiting their turn. I saw them gently kneel by the casket, and kiss it with no fuss, one after the other. A Filipino woman was holding her little boy up, so that his lips could reach the casket.

Then I recalled Azim's body in the morgue, and his blood on my dress and skin. What was the difference?

Perhaps, St. Simon Stock had a sister or a niece, who would have venerated his remains as spontaneously as I'd done for my dead friends. It struck me that we, members of Christ, truly are one family across space and time.

I was about to walk to the casket after all, when the priest said: "And now, would all those who have prayed the novena come forward to be enrolled in the Brown Scapular."

Too late for me: I'd missed the kiss!

But what were the "novena," and the "scapular," I wondered?

I mustn't have been the only ignorant person present, since the priest pointed at the statue of Our Lady behind him, explaining: "Here the Mother of God is handing the Brown Scapular to St. Simon Stock, the English Carmelite friar. According to ancient tradition, this apparition took place on July the sixteenth, 1251, here in England, in Kent.

"Our Lady promised that her children who die wearing it will be saved if they entrust themselves totally to Her protection. We should all have recourse to her maternal intercession, and pray daily."

That, I was *already* doing! The priest then showed us a scapular: "As you see from the one I hold in my hand, the scapular consists of two small pieces of brown cloth with one segment hanging on the wearer's chest, and the other hanging on the back. These pieces are joined by two straps or strings which hang over each shoulder — hence the word *scapular* (*shoulder blade* in Latin)."

I observed that if, as Mansur had said, men would do anything to get the *shirt* of a mere football player, thinking that it would bring them happiness and success in this life, it made even more sense to be clothed by the heavenly Mother to die well, under Her protection, and rejoice eternally.

Not having prepared for it, I stayed in my pew, watching members of the faithful receive the scapular.

I suddenly felt a deep yearning to be enrolled when possible, and resolved to ask what the conditions were.

Now a mother to my own child, I better understood my relationship to the Blessed Virgin. According to God's design, I was clothing with flesh the soul of my baby; she would clothe mine with grace – as well as his or hers.

Before leaving, I walked to the casket and knelt to kiss it.

Standing up again, I was inspired to lightly press my stomach against the glass, begging the holy friar to channel to my tiny baby, through his dead arm, the graces he'd received from our Immaculate Mother.

I did so with a slight feeling of embarrassment, half pretending that I was only looking at the contents, as if I were *stealing* grace and feared a sensor would set the alarm off! But everything remained still, thank God.

Azim was right: a God incarnate made all the difference in the world, and His Hands were not tied up in Heaven, but reaching us in our concrete circumstances through His Church, His sacraments, His saints and their glorious remains.

Yes, in its own way, that arm in the gilded casket extended over my child a protection more lasting than the one of the gynaecologist I'd just met.

Chapter 106

The world was totally renewed. Nothing would ever be like before.

For instance, I realised that I now had a *second* guardian angel to protect me: my baby's.

Back into the street however, I noticed that pedestrians didn't gaze at me in awe, and that cars and buses drove by as if unaware of the marvel that had occurred to me.

I knew why. There were all waiting for the happy dad to be told the great news, as was his right, before anyone else could express their joy.

Walking home did me good and, on arriving, my newfound motherhood had ceased to be something unknown to tackle.

Rather, it clothed me more naturally than my skin. It was no effort to behave as normal in Mansur's company. In fact, I wasn't hiding from him information to which he was entitled – I was keeping it lovingly wrapped until his mind, soul and body would be fully available to welcome it.

We arrived at the stadium in good time for the game.

Champagne was served in the VIP lounge.

Despite the fact that the season was long over, the stadium was full. How daunting for the players to see so many faces all around, and to know that twice as many eyes watch every gesture of their feet, not to mention the thousands of spectators online or in front of their televisions.

But many more angels and saints watch our every thought and action as we make our way through life. They cheer us through their example, and support us through their intercession.

The big talk in the lounge was the "purchase" by Arsenal of Lass Kundomo, a Namibian player, for only... thirty-four million pounds! I *must* have misunderstood the amount.

He was allegedly a fierce striker, and the Chelsea team (Mansur's team in fact) were eager to play against him on that informal occasion, in preparation for the real business at the next season. "Lass is a demanding customer," Mansur mentioned, "according to Vardah Wattles who's designing his new penthouse in Kingston."

Had she *told him that?*

When?

Never mind...

I saw the men walk out of a tunnel onto the field: blue against red. Of course, I wished "our" men would win. They were holding a big *Chelsea* banner bearing a blue... Yes, it looked like a panther, not a *leaping* one, though, as it stood with a sort of hockey stick in its claws. The *Arsenal* emblem, fittingly, was a golden gun against a red background.

Strangely, I started taking the game more seriously than I had anticipated. Despite my very poor knowledge of the rules, I could still appreciate the strength and even the beauty of the moves, and the powerful collaboration among the players on either side.

Soon the first half was over, with not a single goal scored. I thought that those who had paid thirty-four million pounds for Kundomo must have been feeling a bit nervous. For the price, would they at least get one of his shirts?

The second half was no more eventful, despite a few narrow escapes.

To be honest, I was starting to wonder what the strategy was, when Mansur led me by the hand to watch the last fifteen minutes on the field. We stood by the front seats among photographers, right behind the nets. Mansur said that "we" had just been awarded a corner kick.

I saw the blues and the reds position themselves near the goal.

I could read the names on their shirts.

A blue player sent the ball towards his team, and the ferocious Kundomo, like a red devil, jumped to intercept it – don't you dare!

But in vain: another blue had come to the rescue with his head and the ball travelled in our direction towards the right bottom corner of the goal.

It flew in and, but for the nets, would have ended straight into my lap!

All around, everyone was shouting for joy, or whistling!

Why? Just because a leather ball had nested inside a net? Just because on that occasion, nothing had stopped it from reaching its expected end? I smiled, thinking of another nesting, which deserved the deepest thanksgivings...

The emotion and the noise were enormous. *We* – that is, Chelsea – had won the game 1-0! We walked back into the VIP lounge, where everyone was singing the praises of Tekko Fideles, from Dakar, the Senegalese player who had scored our last-minute goal.

Those in the know had had little hope of victory against such an impressive defence as the Arsenal warriors, galvanised by Kundomo.

The autographed football and Tekko's blue shirt (he'd just put on a *dry* one instead, hum...) were presented to Mansur. He thoughtfully offered the ball to me (not the unwashed shirt!). Everyone clapped (it was apparently a great honour).

On our way home, Mansur thanked me for having let him attend, and for having accompanied me.

I smiled, holding the ball on my lap. He asked me if I wanted to go out, but I suggested we spent the remainder of the evening together, just the two of us. I wasn't sure of the best moment to break the news of my pregnancy to my beloved husband.

I gazed at the man who knew well that he was my spouse. He knew that he and I were parents to Talitha, our darling. But he was still unaware of being a father *biologically*, to *someone* inside me.

That new relationship between him and our child was as real as invisible, and yet unknown to him. What was it made of? Genes and material inheritance; authority and responsibility?

Love...

Chapter 107

"Darling?"

Once lying in bed, in my cherished djellaba, I simply said that I had *something* to tell him. He looked a bit alarmed and came to lie next to me, resting on his elbow so that he was looking at my face.

I improvised: "We truly are the winners tonight, darling. Against very fierce opposition, it seems as if we have scored for real."

Looking even more puzzled, he answered: "Well, I didn't know that you were such a football enthusiast!"

I went on, smiling lightly: "Could you bring me that ball, with a pen?"

As he presented both to me, I whispered: "It wants *your* name." And I wrote in capital letters, above the surname of Tekko Fideles: MANSUR.

The ball became less steady in his hands.

We didn't move for a while, apart from my lips, as my smile broadened. His eyes looked at the ball and at me, alternatively.

Until he asked: "Clara, please, is there something you mean to say? Something vital to me, and you?"

I took his hand off the ball and laid it against my stomach.

His eyes became shiny and moist, as he said: "Is that possible? When?"

I told him about my pregnancy test, performed by Nasreen's doctor friend that afternoon and concluded: "Darling, our *baby* is just a fortnight old and should be born at Easter.

"Congratulations. And thank you."

He wrote on the ball, under Fideles' surname: CLARA.

I noticed that he didn't ask if it was a *boy*. He perhaps knew that it was too early. Or simply, he was like me overwhelmed with the joy of parenthood.

We looked at each other with a hint of... awe.

I wasn't sure what caused that feeling. In retrospect, I think it was *glory*. I know 'glory' sounds a bit too solemn. But it's how it felt.

Let me see... This is how I'd put it: our shared responsibility in a new human life, we felt, increased our *dignity*.

Mansur said that he didn't need Tekko Fideles' shirt now. Instead, he would have the Club produce two bespoke "official" Chelsea shirts with the words *THANK* and *YOU*, for he and I to wear when jogging, side by side.

Then he looked at me gravely: "Wait a minute, perhaps you *shouldn't* jog from now on – too risky for the baby."

"And not *swim* either.

"Perhaps not even *walk*...

"In fact, I'll keep you *in my arms* for nine months, to rest, while you carry our baby."

We hugged each other tenderly.

Later on that evening, as I was falling asleep, memories of the game floated in my imagination.

Mansur might have wondered why I smiled with my eyes shut.

The players' blue shirts displayed utterly *surreal* surnames. Behind Tekko Fideles, the *Chelsea* players were called *Strong, Fecund, Sacrifice, Fearless, Parent...*

At the other end of the field – which for some reason proved to be at the bottom of the sea! – Lass Kundomo was leading his *Arsenal* strikers against us, whose red shirts bore surnames even less plausible: *Pistol, Pill, Scimitar, Diaphragm, Dagger...*

I'm pretty sure I was *asleep* by then.

Movements looked very slow underwater, but grace-filled, like classical dancing.

Azim appeared, dressed in blue. A skilled goalkeeper, he blocked several shots from the red fighters. Right behind him, Talitha applauded.

Our team counter-attacked, gliding towards the opposite goal, which looked like a gleaming seashell, ajar and of vast proportions. The red goalkeeper smiled like a piranha.

He missed, and the seashell received the gift – of *life*.

So I recalled, on waking up before dawn, and tried not to laugh, for fear Mansur might suspect that pregnancy made me mentally unstable.

Girls, I've turned into a football fan: there's simply no more thrilling game on earth! That's what I texted Emma and Sally.

Would they be impressed?

Chapter 108

As planned, we travelled from West London to Oxford by boat on the River Thames.

The three of us (or four, rather) shared a lovely narrowboat, pompously named *Lady Caversham*. It comprised one double berth and two single ones in separate cabins, a tiny kitchen, a compact bathroom and a lounge-dining room (no prayer room). The entire boat would have fitted within the dining room of the *Cedrus*!

Mansur couldn't help laughing at our spectacular downsizing: "In our circumstances, *extra* space should have been needed instead."

In fact, shrinking to that floating caravan suited us all very well.

Talitha was running from one end to the next, pushing every button, opening every door and asking every minute if we could swim (alas, no more than in the Nile, I had to tell her).

Mansur commented that his Phoenician descent made him comfortable on boats, which was why, even in Cairo, he preferred to stay on the *Cedrus*. He asked if I didn't mind a "boat family." I said that since Our Lord was often seen preaching and even sleeping on ships, so I was happy to become a *Catholic Phoenician*.

A much larger escort boat was following us closely, with the inevitable and dedicated bodyguards, carer, governess and (new) personal assistant.

I'd won a great victory, persuading Mansur to entrust his precious telephone to me for the duration of the cruise. There really couldn't be *any* more business calls (unless his personal assistant deemed it an emergency)! Out of fairness, I also switched off *my* phone.

My beloved would be totally mine (that is, ours), for the following three days. Far from the romantic feel of the Rhine Valley for instance (I'd taken a group there once), the Thames still proved amiably picturesque. As we glided along flowery banks, looked at by meditative cows, we enjoyed the bucolic quiet, the utter tranquillity and peace of such a modest cruise.

After venerating the hand of St. James the Apostle himself, kept in a village by the river, we had lunch on the way at the Wattles', who lived on a small island by a lock, amidst the Thames, near Henley.

It was our first proper encounter with the trendy couple, if one discounts our wedding. As Nour's first cousin, Vardah was part of the family. As to Stuart, about to play *James Bond* for the third time, he was the sort of casual Hollywood celebrity.

I was glad to see them again, Vardah in particular. I wished to ask her advice for the interior design of our London house.

More importantly, she was someone with whom I felt I could discuss personal matters – although we had decided to keep our big news secret for a couple of months, even from Talitha.

It was very hot, and after lunch, while our husbands smoked in the shade, Vardah showed me her garden, surrounded by the river. She said that I should visit again in the spring, when it would all be in bloom. I kept to myself that I would not be fit for travelling by then.

But, how ridiculous of me to feel slightly *jealous* of the fashionable blue leather garden-belt she'd put on!

It definitely enhanced her thin silhouette, a bit like a cartridge belt worn by a video game heroine. Her husband had bought it for her from *Le Prince Jardinier* at the Chelsea Flower Show, she told me, as she buckled the belt around my hips instead: "I love it! Look, it adjusts to your waist and enables you to always keep your trowel, secateurs, phone and seeds at hand while on your knees in a flower bed.

"I even wear it indoors sometimes. And, as a tip, there's nothing like a few gardening tools scattered across one's interior to make it feel lived in."

She said the belt suited me well (now *I* was the heroine!) and that I should wear one in our London garden. Rather than in London, I could picture myself back at Osly, elegantly equipped with the same garden-belt – apart from the colour, as I would choose purple rather than blue, to match my bougainvilleas.

Vardah would email me the link to the shop – or better, to Mansur, as a gift suggestion. My eagerness was short-lived, as I soon recalled that of late, to please me, my then-fiancé had *burned* another belt and might not think a new one would delight me so soon.

You spoiled woman! – I told myself – *be consistent: belt or no belt?* With a shade of regret, like an overindulged child trying to make a small effort, I handed the belt back to Vardah.

Her mention of *waist adjustment* made me wonder if she'd found me out – or did I look plump to her? But no, surely, even a woman couldn't have guessed yet what tiny treasure I carried. I was *still* skinny!

We sat by the grassy bank, dipping our bare feet in the delightfully cool water. As I liked her (and it seemed reciprocated), I was tempted to break the great news to her there and then, under the willow tree. She would be very happy for me, and dear Nour would smile at me through the face of her cousin.

I looked at her from the corner of my eyes as she was gently drawing away from my shoulder a long willow-bough covered with thin silvery leaves and, at its end, a couple of late catkins.

Pointing at a creamy-white swan gracefully paddling towards us with her cygnets (the latter not graceful, but so cute!), she observed: "She comes for bread, but I brought none." For a moment, the lovely bird seemed to me as the floating reflection of my friend.

She added: "Those tiny ones appeared last Tuesday. Lucky parents, who need to wait only six weeks for their babies to hatch. Did you ever hear that swans remain together for life and will even mourn their lost mate?"

Yes, Vardah sounded like Nour, from what I remembered. Her eyes looked like Nour's, especially on that picture in Talitha's bedroom. So, would I tell her? *Could* I? It cost me a little to admit that in my heart, I knew that it was *too early* to speak; and Mansur *didn't wish* our secret to be shared *yet*.

We remained sitting in silence for a while, side by side, enjoying the quiet and inhaling the warm smells from the river.

Vardah took me by surprise when she confided: "I would like to share a secret with you, Clara. I'm nearly eight weeks pregnant."

Chapter 109

I was taken aback, and congratulated her (hoping *I* would look as thin in six weeks' time).

But she went on: "No, listen... We *can't* have children."

Her statement made me smile since, obviously, they *could*...

She explained: "I mean, we *mustn't,* not just yet. Stuart's career (and mine) simply won't allow it. I booked an appointment last month to "do the right thing," as Stuart is still expecting. But soon after, I came across that video on the *Daily Mail* website, with a fourteen-week-old foetus *singing* when classical music was played near the womb!

"I thought at first that it was the usual anti-choice propaganda. But I found that the obstetrics centre in Madrid who released the film provides the full range of normal reproductive services, regardless of gender or marital status.

"Watching that short video, I thought of Nour, my singer cousin. Had *she* sung in the womb, before singing on stage? And now, she's dead.

"I didn't turn up to the appointment. It's been three weeks now and I just can't make up my mind. Nour couldn't have children. I know she would have kept any child."

Vardah didn't ask me for advice, as if not daring to. I held her hand in silence for a while. Talitha was coming in our direction, followed by Mansur and Stuart.

I whispered: "I can't wait to hear your baby sing!"

Eventually she responded, with some anxiety: "But what would *you* do?"

Her question made me realise how much I'd changed.

The choice, I felt, had been made *earlier*, when deciding to get married. If new life followed, love would support it. But how to share this with Vardah without making her think I was lecturing her?

Remembering the arm of St. Simon Stock under whose protection I'd so recently placed my two-week-old baby in the Kensington church, I ventured: "I would do like Nour. And if I were you, I would enter St. Peter's Church in Marlow, twenty minutes downstream, and would ask to see the hand of St. James, Christ's Apostle. It came from Spain, like your video."

Vardah looked at me, puzzled, as if I was making fun of her.

I explained: "On some invisible instrument, I believe, the hand that touched God can play for your child and his parents music that your hearts will recognise – happy music."

I helped her stand up and with a kiss urged: "Oh yes, ten thousand times, yes – let's keep all our children!"

As Mansur was helping me step aboard our little boat, I thought that I needed no garden-belt after all. The arms of my prince adjusted around me more tightly than any gardening equipment, and his love shone into me as if I were a living greenhouse.

As to being a *heroine*, I saw no greater role than that of welcoming and giving life. Soon I would show Vardah my cygnet, expecting no bread but sisterly joy.

From her smile as our boat started upstream, I felt that she might well be speaking to her soul just the same words.

Our first night suffered a slight disruption.

We had all been asleep for a while, when I heard the voice of Talitha, clearly frightened.

I ran to her cabin where I found her lying on the floor. My beloved daughter had fallen from her narrow berth and, not being used to the new environment, was unable to find the light and get back into bed.

I took her in my arms with soothing words. She was in tears, gradually awakening from what seemed to have been an awful nightmare. It sounded rather incoherent, as dreams often are.

She'd fallen down the very steep steps of the pyramid when *Tintin* had jumped to rescue her, but masked *picaros* had prevented him and, instead, had taken him and his dog *Snowy* prisoner; and *Captain Haddock* was lying on the steps and said she was covered with whisky.

And *Professor Calculus* said that whisky was wrong and he brought water instead. And she tried to explain that it wasn't her whisky, but that of *Tintin* and *Snowy*, and she didn't dare to tell the *Captain* that he was also covered with whisky...

I hugged her even more tenderly, realising that another fall, down some other steps, still haunted her memory. My darling child would definitely need all my attention to ensure that the trauma of the attack thirteen months earlier healed as thoroughly as possible.

I sometimes had bad dreams as well, so I knew how it felt.

To start with, Litha would sleep with us the following nights, if Mansur agreed

The most memorable aspect of our cruise was to feel so cut off from the world. We were in a modern country, but pleasantly withdrawn from it, seeing few cars and shops, and not receiving any emails at all.

The second evening, the *Lady Caversham* moored alongside a beautifully curved bank.

We had a very joyful dinner, cooked by Mansur and Talitha. My role was to taste each course, blindfolded, and to name the ingredients.

I nearly believed Mansur when he said that he'd caught the salmon in the river during my siesta. But wildlife in Berkshire comes in smaller sizes than in Vancouver – no wild salmon, but no bears either (just as well!).

Then we played cards, said some prayers, and went to bed.

Talitha was lying in-between us. She was wearing a cute djellaba which I'd ordered at her request (a small-scale replica of mine, in actual fact), as she wanted "to look just like Mummy." Through the small portholes, moonlight was flowing upon us like heavenly milk.

A few birds could still be heard, mingled with the sweet sound of water rippling against the hull, and of the wind in the branches. Mansur's fingers gently played on my stomach, while Litha rested upon my chest, already fast asleep.

My heart gave thanks for the simple joy of spending time together, as a family. I included, of course, our little baby, still invisible, so small under his father's protective hand.

My eyes could see the stars. I knew of a wider hand extended upon us. Compared with our minute child, we were like giants, in size and in might; but under the hand of God, even we adults were more needy than the tiny embryo nested inside me.

And yet, God loved us all similarly, and treated us with equal respect, compassion and tenderness. I offered Him anew my life and all my family. When would we die? When would we see God? He knew.

But whether our cruise lasted three days or a hundred years, God was with us and carried us along with His grace, like our humble boat on the water:

For in Him we live, and move, and are.

For we are also His offspring.

Chapter 110

We had just disembarked at Oxford, when the world caught us back in its claws!

Switching on his mobile for the first time in three days (an unprecedented sacrifice!), Mansur first looked puzzled by the message displayed, and soon smiled, asking: "Darling, why did you not tell me that you were such an amazing dancer? You've generated a real buzz on the Internet."

My heart jumped, as I immediately feared that the CCTV footage of my fatal ballet before Jonathan, in the underground car park, might have been emailed to my husband...

I didn't want that horrible memory to be revived, and least of all in Mansur's company – and during our honeymoon! Please, sweet Jesus, spare me this dreadful interference! Later, anything later...

He went on: "My people emailed me several times yesterday, asking for instructions. Your performance passed half a million views on YouTube."

I was in agony, wanting to look at his screen to check what it was all about, but dreading to have the shameful truth thrown into my face. Music was now playing on his phone: not by Schubert, for sure.

Mansur obviously hadn't noticed my emotion and only meant to tease me further, tenderly, as he quoted the news: "Need quick cash? *Very* big and *very* quick? Learn from *Clara Cumberhart*, the orphan girl who raised two billion in twenty seconds!

"Her 'Sphinx Dance' for Egyptian billionaire Mansur Al-Khoury made the most eligible widower of the year fall into her arms. The video of her performance by the Pyramids has become a web phenomenon, with a dedicated blog and over ninety-three-thousand likes on Facebook in two days.

"Following the successful dance, the couple were married in secret in Paris last week. Cumberhart may give up modelling but not dancing, she says.

"Meanwhile, dozens of girls are queuing at the Cairo Pyramids to perform the now famous *Sphinx Dance*, the latest fad which makes you rich overnight."

Mansur stopped and, taking his eyes off the screen, saw that I wasn't amused. "Darling! What's the matter? It's nothing at all, I assure you.

"I've a team in charge of hunting down indiscreet videos and pictures of my family and business. One email, and this bubble is squashed. I'm sorry, I thought you would find it funny. When did you dance at Giza anyway? Not in *my* time."

He took me in his arms as I furtively tried to dry my eyes, pretty red and wet by then. How can one be altogether humiliated and relieved? So, it wasn't the video I dreaded.

But this one wasn't much more edifying...

I'd completely forgotten about that occasion. Yes, I'd meant to attract

Azim. That was true. But obviously not *Mansur*, whom I'd only met once and who wasn't even present in Giza on that day. There had been that guide, I remembered, who had come by the Sphinx and had filmed me dancing.

But who could have posted the video online, and added that music? (Pretty good rhythm, actually.)

And why? Nobody knew me! Dear God, are all our silly actions recorded somewhere, ready to appear and be displayed before the entire world? Is that what judgment will be like, at the end of history? Oh Jesus, please, help me think, speak and act always in a way that will make You and those I love proud of me...

After a long hug in silence, I finally answered Mansur: "Darling, I was with Azim that day. But as you know, nothing ever happened between us. Not that I would have turned away. I don't know."

"He was such a noble soul. He *is*. Like *you* are."

"But all the rest is rubbish! You weren't there, and you aren't even Egyptian. And I'm not an orphan (Dad will be furious if he reads this nonsense)! And I never spoke to any journalist, and I'm not a model – I only had pictures taken by a photographer who loved me. And I love you regardless of your wealth, not *for* it. And I'll never *ever* dance again (except for God). And for you. Please, can you take it all down?"

He smiled again, holding me tight: "Clara, darling, please don't get upset! I never doubted you for one second! I don't believe half of what I read in the media. This silly incident proves again how much caution is needed. But it could have been much worse. You don't know what paparazzi are like."

He typed a reply on his screen: *Kindly smash it now* – and, taking my finger, pressed with it the *Send* icon, saying: "It will cost a little money. For my reward, may I keep the video – just for me?"

I answered with a kiss, and we walked out, over Folly Bridge.

I wished our sins and shames could be erased with a finger or two.

Actually – they *can*.

Mansur was pleased to show me Oxford.

Although, I felt that he was finding it difficult sometimes to skip any reference to Jonathan, who had shared so much with him in that city. I told him I was feeling more at peace now, and that he shouldn't worry too much about the impact on me.

He'd been deeply hurt as well. Perhaps more than I, actually. He'd managed to forgive him the first time, after hearing his involvement in the attack on his family. Forgiving him again, for his attempt to seduce me, his betrothed, proved more difficult.

In the afternoon, we were sitting on our own inside the shady cloisters of New College, which looked rather *ancient* to me. Talitha was asleep on my lap. A beautiful oak tree stood majestically by the gothic arches. The air was very hot and all was quiet, apart from the rustle of the leafy branches in the breeze.

Speaking low, Mansur asked me if I'd received any news from Jonathan.

I answered that Fr. Paul had met him twice, and was reasonably hopeful. But it would be a long way to full conversion. For the first time, Mansur and I prayed together for our former friend and forgiven enemy.

Afterwards, we looked at Talitha, our little treasure still asleep on my lap, and neither of us felt like moving.

I was surprised when my beloved added, pressing my hand into his: "You know, the day after I'd treated you so badly, during the fitting of your wedding dress, Jonathan confessed to me what he'd done. I was devastated.

"I wonder though if the shock of discovering how my best friend had betrayed me wasn't just what I needed to realise my selfishness and my pride.

"If I could have so dreadfully misjudged Jonathan's sentiments towards me, what about yours? I'd treated you as my enemy, while the one I called my friend was plotting against me. By contrast, that crisis revealed to me how precious your affection was to me – and by consequence, also your principles."

I was touched that he wished to share this with me.

The air was hot and moist, but the wall against which we sat was refreshingly cool.

Mansur paid *no attention* to the red squirrel (I thought they were extinct in England) jumping down the lowest branch of the oak tree and standing amusingly on the grass before us, in obvious expectation of a gift.

Poor little thing! He must feel so hot wearing that fur coat...

I would have thrown a nut or some fruit, but I had none and, besides, my dear husband was still busy revisiting that terrible day: "Forgiving Ali sounded less unbearable to me, compared with what I now felt against Jonathan. That's when your idea of visiting Tora Prison appeared to me in a new light.

"I felt utterly incapable of even looking at Jonathan again, but having him witness my encounter with Ali might be the best parting in our circumstances. Thank God, you were there with me, or I would never have kept calm."

Litha woke up.

The squirrel hopped away as we walked out.

I would have loved Mansur to *notice* the animal and say how cute it was. But he was focused on less happy thoughts and I offered up the joy of chatting about the squirrel.

Can there be heroism – or can love show – in such tiny sacrifices?

If I ever designed a dating website, I would insert a conspicuous "Loves squirrels" box to tick!

Abu Ephrem's praise of us before leaving Cairo sounded in my memory: yes, the two of us had shared a lot in a short time, through decisive acts of forgiveness.

As we were walking to our van, Mansur pointed at a gate: "*Corpus Christi*: that was his college. May he soon discover the Presence behind the name."

I'm often surprised to find the faith of my husband deeper than I remember. A greater Love speaks through him – even though he's squirrel-blind.

Chapter 111

Fifteen minutes later, we were taking off at Oxford Airport on board the family jet bound for York.

And Mansur was flying it! Or rather, he was allowed to *co-pilot* for limited amounts of time (not yet to fly without assistance again).

He boasted as men do: "This *Falcon* can reach a speed of six hundred miles per hour while using less fuel than other jets in its category, with reduced carbon footprints!"

I congratulated him on the performance, adding that I was even *more* impressed by the little prayer corner at the rear of the cabin.

The Häagen-Dazs pints found in the freezer, I heroically tried to ignore: *Rich, aromatic cappuccino ice cream with pieces of velvety rich truffle!* – until I realised that *milk* was an essential ice-cream ingredient!

But *who* fed essentially on milk? Babies.

And *who* was carrying a baby? Clarry!

I couldn't deprive my child of what was so necessary to his or her growth, could I? Besides, I would share the pint with Talitha, and even with Mansur (if that was allowed in the cockpit).

Mansur wasn't the only one whose phone had stored up messages while switched off during our cruise. I read again Dad's response to my query. Since I'd left Vancouver, we'd begun emailing each other more often.

I realised for the first time that, perhaps, he missed his two grown-up daughters: *Dear Clarry, of course not Wiltshire: that's where* Stonehenge *is. As I explained to you more than once, but you seem to have forgotten, Ripon is where* Mum *(my own mother) is buried. It's a town in Yorkshire – nearly a village I believe, by modern city standards.*

I have no memories of her, obviously. You recall, I hope, that she died in childbirth. It sounds like the Middle Ages! Actually, Yorkshire was very much lagging behind, and not every house had a telephone, or the midwife would have arrived sooner.

Rather than return to Ireland, Dad migrated to Canada before I was one. Kitty and you were about six and five when we left Montreal, moving further west to Vancouver. I never had a chance to go back to England, or to Ripon for that matter.

You may be able to locate Mum's grave on the cemetery register. There can't be many Madeleine Cumberharts who died on twenty-fourth September 1962 – also my date of birth, by definition. Send me a picture, will you, if you find it.

Greetings to Mansur, and a kiss to Talitha. Talk to you soon, Dad.

Dear Daddy...

Why did he have to make it sound so incidental, as if pretending that such a tragedy had had no impact on his personality and on his life?

Was he trying to protect himself? I felt a surge of tenderness for him, for all his failures.

And "Madeleine"? I knew well that he'd lost his English mother while still in infancy. But it was true that I didn't recall the circumstances; if Dad had ever shared them with me as he now assured. (I would check with Kitty.)

Madeleine, then?

My little grandmother, cut short on a sunny September day, like a vine branch, having just brought into the world that tiny, living fruit, my father... I knew that it was better for me and my family not to start thinking too much about that story.

I owed my husband and daughter cheerfulness; brooding upon the sad end of my grandmother wasn't going to help.

Through the porthole, I could see the English countryside, a tapestry of fields and villages (was it already Ripon, over there?). Talitha was asleep, her head resting on my lap (her little stomach filled with ice-cream). I gave thanks to God for her life, and for the protection He had extended over us all, so far.

Our flight to York had lasted a mere thirty minutes and we landed at a small airport near the former imperial capital. "Many more gliders than planes on the tarmac," Mansur pointed out, wishing he might soon be allowed to fly one.

Once we were standing outside the *Minster*, our guide explained that the first Christian Emperor, Constantine, had been called to power while staying in York.

He added wittily: "For those living in the Big Apple, *York* is the city founded in seventy-one A.D., a mere 1,553 years before New York City!"

I was thrilled to be there. Was I not half a Yorkshire girl? *Look at me...* Well, perhaps my Asian blood made me less credible as a native. Think what you want: I simply felt at home.

I enjoyed visiting the school of my dear husband. It was situated in a picturesque valley, next to a large Benedictine monastery. He introduced me to a few monks who remembered him. They were very gracious and congratulated us.

I hadn't realised, then, how much we owe to those who take care of us during our formative years. When I look back at my *own* upbringing, and after the decades I spent trying to educate children, I reckon that dedication alone doesn't suffice for us to become great educators, unless sound principles direct us.

We stayed the night at the Guest House, Mansur taking a trip down memory lane.

I walked with him.

That evening, though, our first small conjugal incident occurred. I was brushing my teeth in the bathroom when, from the bedroom, I heard: "Clara, thank you for not having interrupted me earlier, today, at New College."

Busy as I was over the basin, I muttered that I didn't know what he meant.

He replied: "As I was telling you about Jonathan, I noticed that you were more interested in the meaningless *animal* jumping before you. If you had found my confidences less important than a tumbling squirrel, I would have been quite upset. Yes, I would have been upset, and I'm glad you avoided that mistake."

I unconsciously stopped brushing my teeth, not daring to look in the mirror in case I met his gaze. Had I really just heard *that*?

Having washed my mouth, I went to sit by the window, not answering.

He soon came to me and a kiss reconciled us. The power of toothpaste!

But, had my fresh breath really made that little cloud vanish?

As I lay awake beside my husband, later that night, I felt slightly troubled, trying to ignore the very subtle impression of *threat* conveyed by his words.

Were storms looming ahead?

Was it what Jonathan and Jeda had warned me about?

Chapter 112

The next day, in York, the discovery of St. Margaret Clitherow impressed me deeply.

I'd never heard of the "Pearl of York," and it was a revelation.

Can I say that I *fell in love* with her? Yes, I did. An encounter which stimulates the best of what we are, and spurs us to develop and fulfil it, is a gift of love.

This is what I have gleaned about her, from various websites – thank God for the Internet (sometimes).

My "Pearl" (the meaning of the name "Margaret," I learned) had received everything and given it all up for the love of Jesus.

She was merry, pretty and strong-minded; she had wit and wealth; she was successfully involved in the family business; she enjoyed the affection of a loving husband and of delightful children.

Married at fifteen as was customary, she converted to Catholicism at eighteen (which was illegal).

She won the loyal affection of those around her, including her family, clients and servants who trusted her as if they'd been her own children. At least two hours daily were spent in mental prayer, with Mass whenever possible (attending it was considered treason).

But her devotions didn't interfere with her duties as wife, mother and assistant in her husband's business.

Twelve years after converting to the faith, aged barely thirty, she died a martyr for having harboured Catholic priests, who offered Mass in her attic and ministered underground to the persecuted Catholic population.

She's typically depicted in sculptures and paintings carrying a chalice and a missal, to show that she died for the Holy Sacrifice of the Mass, the priesthood and the Church of Christ.

Summoned before the York assizes for questioning, she replied softly: "I know of no offense whereof I should confess myself guilty. Having made no offense, I need no trial."

By refusing to be tried for having peacefully assisted Catholic souls, she also meant to spare her children questioning and, possibly, torture.

But as she knew, the barbaric punishment for those refusing trial was "*peine forte et dure*," as the judge stipulated:

"You must return from whence you came, and there, in the lowest part of the prison, be stripped naked, laid down, your back on the ground, and as much weight laid upon you as you are able to bear, and so to continue for three days without meat or drink, and on the third day to be pressed to death, your hands and feet tied to posts, and a sharp stone under your back."

The date was set for 25 March, 1586, the Annunciation, and that year Good Friday – thus "commemorating at the same time the beginning and the fulfilment of our Redemption by Jesus, through Mary."

She spent most of her last night praying.

Saint Margaret had a handkerchief tied across her face before being laid over a sharp rock roughly the size of a man's fist, the rock touching in the small of her back.

Her hands she joined towards her face. Then the Sheriff said, "Nay, you must have your hands bound." So the two sergeants parted them.

The door of her own house was placed on top of her and then slowly loaded with heavy rocks and stones. The combination would cause the small sharp rock to break her back, thus causing her immense pain before death.

My heroic friend would only wait fifteen minutes under the incredible eight-hundred pound weight before her martyrdom was complete.

She was pregnant with her fourth child.

In his agony on hearing of his wife's sentence, her Protestant husband who, "fared like a man out of his wits," betrayed his real sentiments by exclaiming that she was "the best Catholic in all England."

Her children were questioned about their religion and, when they professed the Catholic faith, were severely flogged.

Anne, a girl of twelve, was even imprisoned. Finally she became a nun abroad, at Saint Ursula's in Leuven.

A son, Henry, had already been sent to the Continent, to Douai, where he became a priest; as also did his brother William.

Before her execution, the judge had challenged Margaret: "Mistress Clitherow, you must remember and confess that you die for treason," which brought the response: "No, no, Master Sheriff, I die for the love of my Lord Jesu."

Her last words were: "Jesu! Jesu! Jesu! Have mercy on me!"

Chapter 113

I knelt for a long time at the Bar Convent chapel nearby.

There, the right hand of the martyred mother was displayed in a blessing posture.

My recent encounter with the arm of St. Simon Stock had increased my love for relics (after Azim's blood had turned my own dress into one).

Margaret's hand was thin and beautiful. Those long fingers had held brooms, meat, flowers, candles and rosary beads... That palm had clasped a husband's shoulder, offered bread to hunted priests, and caressed children's young heads... That wrist had been cruelly tied to a post while weight was piled upon the expectant martyr...

I recalled another limb.

That of St. James the Apostle, seen by the River Thames only two days earlier. Another martyr; another lover of Christ. That left hand of his had offered fish to the Son of God; it had opened in awe at the raising of the dead twelve-year-old daughter of Jairus; it had joined with the right hand in adoration on Mount Tabor; it was spread against the ground in slumber at Gethsemane; and opened towards heaven at the Ascension...

And there *I* was, a Canadian-Asian girl (or wife and mother, rather), kneeling in England under the hands of a Galilean fisherman and of the wife of a York butcher. In my heart, both hands met as a gracious arch, a bridge of love embodying the mysterious circulation of God's grace over oceans and across centuries.

Jed and Jeda's wedding present flashed back in my memory – with another arch. Not that long ago, in Egypt, my soul had walked under the joined hands of Azim and Nour. And now, Mansur and I extended yet another arch over Litha and her tiny sibling.

I was deeply grateful to be part of that living architecture, adding to it the modest "flying buttresses" of my marriage and motherhood.

The three of us walked out of the convent, holding hands.

Mansur announced it was time for lunch.

I said I wasn't very hungry, but he seemed to know exactly where he was going. In a narrow street by the river, we came across a timber framed house with an ornate wrought-iron sign to which I didn't pay much attention at first. But reading the name The Grey Squirrel Inn revived in my memory the incident on the previous evening.

I looked at Mansur who smiled and said: "I apologize; I found no *Red* Squirrel place to eat..."

It was his way of saying sorry. I accepted, and would remember the lunch, long after the menu had faded from my mind. Jeda surely knew her son...

Afterwards, we strolled along the River Ouse nearby, then across the bridge to the basement of the toll booth, where, down in a damp dungeon, Margaret had died.

Mansur and Talitha left me at The Shambles, the shrine located where her house used to stand, near York Minster. In my memory, a certain underground car park, also beside a river, collided with the cell by this other river 'in the lowest part of the prison', where my new friend had suffered. But *she* was a saint, whereas *I*'d been a fool.

I prayed to my new sister Margaret, asking her protection on me as a woman, as a wife, and as a mother.

I prayed to her for every woman persecuted for the love of Our Lord and His Church and the Sacraments; for every woman abused physically and spiritually; for every woman threatened or attacked in her family, and in her offspring born or unborn.

Her example stirred a very deep aspiration in my soul. I wasn't able to tell *what* it was, but I knew that within me, something precious and strong had been touched, or implanted.

If I had needed proof that saints interact with us, my unexpected encounter with the lovely Pearl of York would have amply convinced me.

She was five years older than I when she died. Would *I* live that long? How could I best glorify my Beloved Saviour in that amount of time? How?

I knew. By applying all the energies of my body and soul to serving my God, my husband and children, in the ordinariness of my daily duties. How much deeper than romanticism had she gently led me! Margaret was deeply grounded and balanced. She was altruistic and committed to life.

But above all, and through it all, she loved in truth, led by a light she'd found as a young adult, a light of which she never took her eyes off. And by so doing, she mirrored and radiated the same light of grace across oceans and centuries, all the way down to us.

Beloved Margaret! Take us by the hand! To Jesus.

"Clara?"

Mansur called to me from the threshold of the little shrine, looking surprised to find me still on my knees. He'd taken Litha for a walk along the medieval streets. She was licking the last traces of an appetising chocolate (and pistachio?) ice-cream from her fingers. It had been topped, she informed me, with Chantilly!

Strangely, getting one didn't appeal to me at that moment (though a slice of Stilton would have been tempting). But it was time to do what I'd prayed for: to live for *them*. I walked out hand-in-hand with my dear husband and daughter – and *did* get an ice-cream for my reward.

We stayed at a nearby moated manor, the ancestral home of an old school friend of Mansur's.

A banner, very similar to the one on Nour's prayer card, hung in their Great Hall. They explained that the *Rising of the North* had started in their very courtyard. Only then did I learn of the context in which the devotion to the Five Wounds of Christ had taken historical shape.

Upon a wall, engravings displayed the Catholic pilgrims marching under the Banner of the Five Wounds of Christ. Alas, Henry VIII killed their leaders, including the valiant Robert Aske.

The faith and courage of those men and women had earned us, I realised, the freedom to travel and worship as Catholics in modern England. Emancipation would take another three hundred years, but they'd sown the seeds.

Eager to escape the scorching heat, we jumped with delight into the swimming pool (that is, Litha and I dived, while Mansur slowly went down the ladder).

That evening, the three of us recited our evening prayers with more attention than usual.

Later on, Mansur and I were lying upon our ornate canopy bed.

It was still hot, despite the thick walls; and unlike in Cairo, there was no air conditioning (not even a fan as in my convent cell).

I liked the fact that Mansur respected my silence – for some time...

He eventually asked: "Darling, are you *all right*? You seem rather pensive today."

He was right; although I wondered if the cause was my pregnancy, or my encounter with Margaret, or both. I'd assumed that he hadn't paid much attention to the shrine, even less to the echo of Margaret's story in my heart.

He surprised me: "My cherished little *pearl* Clara... Father was right in his Best Man's speech. *You* are the Pearl that was sent to our family. You've coated our suffering with your smile, and turned our pain into joy.

"John was a lucky man, but I would not change my wife for his!"

I asked: "Which *John*? I thought your Head of Legal was still single."

He answered: "John Clitherow, your wealthy butcher. And you're *my* Margaret. You're my beloved *Pearl*. I spent enough time at school near York to remember her story, even though I was a Muslim. How was God so generous as to make you appear in my life: once in Luxor when I needed nothing; and later, by my hospital bed, after I'd lost everything?"

I was moved: "Darling... so, you like Margaret as well?"

He nodded: "I suppose I do. And perhaps, five hundred years from now, somewhere in Egypt, a couple will ask each other the same question. But the name she will speak will be *yours*; and the medal he will admire on her neck will bear your lovely features.

"I only ask you not to go to God before me. Not without me. I couldn't take it. I couldn't wake up in hospital again, and again see my heart flown away. Not after such a successful transplant. Your priests are good surgeons."

I answered: "Mansur, how can you know me so well? By God's leave, we'll go together to Him."

Since his father's speech, I'd become a mother. Hence, it occurred to me that I was less the *pearl* now, as the *mantle* carrying it, sheltered under the shell of my husband's broad shoulders.

What a beautiful *oyster* the three of us made!

Long may we keep hidden in the depths.

Chapter 114

On the way back to the airport, I saw a sign for *Ripon*.
I had meant to ask Mansur to take me there, but my encounter with Margaret had made me forget. Would we have time before take-off?
Apparently, I hadn't yet acquired the reflexes proper to my new status. One of the advantages of a *private* jet, as it turns out, is that it waits for *you*.

Ripon isn't a village at all. It's of a good size and the cathedral is magnificent.
Finding the graveyard was easy enough; but not the tomb. We walked along many rows, deciphered dozens of names and dates, drawing a certain joy from it (at least I did) as if saluting each of those souls, with respect and love.
There wasn't anyone around to guide us and the plan by the gate didn't include graves older than fifty years. Daddy might have known in which row Madeleine Cumberhart lay, but it was much too early in Vancouver to ring him. After all, if he'd known more, he would probably have told me.
Mansur found an online register and, after browsing through it unsuccessfully, concluded that my grandmother must have been buried in another cemetery.
We were walking out, disappointed, when the thought occurred to me that we might try to identify her by entering her maiden name, Meddleton (I remembered that clue from my teens, as I'd boasted of the similarity with the surname of Prince William's then-bride and allowed Sally to wonder if, perhaps, I wasn't related to the future Queen of England).
Thankfully, Mansur located it online and I followed Litha, nearly running, to a line of ancient yew trees where...

So, that was it?
A rather plain stone monument, with several names on it. It was a family tomb. I read in a sort of awe: *In loving memory of Madeleine Meddleton, 1936-1962, our darling daughter gone too soon.*
Further below, other names were followed by the inscriptions *Father of the above and much missed husband* and below *Mother of the above, dutiful wife and beloved Nan.*
I was surprised: no *Cumberharts*? Why was our *own* surname not displayed anywhere?
Had grief been so acute that her family didn't feel capable of referring their daughter's inscription to her *husband*? But did that justify it?
Or was anger part of the explanation? But why be angry at a disconsolate widower, my grandfather? Or...

With some level of embarrassment, I started wondering if I hadn't, quite unwittingly, dug up a family secret that would have been better left untouched. Granddad had died two years earlier in Vancouver. Had he lived, would I have asked him?

Meanwhile, I explained to Litha, with very simple words so as not to shock her, how my own father had been born as his mother was dying. She looked admiring rather than concerned, commenting: "So, she gave her life to her little baby."

Mansur had caught up with us (sorry darling, how selfish of me not to have walked at your pace). His hand rested on my shoulder as he stood next to me. We remained silent for a while and I hoped that no one would notice the detail that had just struck me on my grandmother's inscription.

Instead, I tried to imagine the world when she was born in 1936, before World War II. Long before the Internet, when gigantic cruisers, rather than long-haul aircrafts, would take you across the Atlantic. What did Ripon look like in 1936? At least the cathedral would have stood just the same.

What had Madeleine's mother, my great-grandmother, wished for her baby when she held her in her arms for the first time after giving birth?

That she would be very happy? Of course.

That she would marry a handsome Yorkshireman and live in a cosy cottage?

That she would be a saint?

One thing was certain: she would not have hoped for her daughter to die so young, with not even the name of a husband to give her baby boy... Dad. Baby Niall.

And I... What if Madeleine's mother hadn't met her husband? Or if Madeleine had lived and Granddad had remained in Ripon all his life? None of us would be there, standing by that grave. I wouldn't *exist*. I wouldn't have met Azim. He might not actually have died and Nour might still live, with Mansur and Talitha...

How accidental it all seemed.

If only *one* encounter had failed, so many lives would have been different, or wouldn't have come into existence in the first place. But on the other hand, it made what we had and who we were even more precious, as a wonderful gift of life, a smile of God's providence. We should be grateful, and make the best of it.

Talitha interrupted my meditation, asking with a very down-to-earth sense of the occasion: "Mummy, is it now that we pray for your Jeda?"

I took her in my arms and the three of us recited a decade of the rosary for the repose of the souls of all those buried at our feet. Then I took the picture to email Dad, as he'd requested.

Mansur and Talitha were walking back to the gate, hand in hand. I was glad that *apparently* neither of them had noticed, from the inscription on the tomb, the coincidence that I'd tried to forget. Or, was Mansur just ignoring it for my sake?

Glancing one last time at Madeleine Meddleton's name, I sent my unknown grandmother all my love and asked for her protection on my family and me. In many years, would a mother read my name incised in gold on a marble tomb and tell her husband and children: *Let us pray for the repose of the soul of Great-grandmother Clara*?

In the car to the airport, Talitha was counting on her fingers, frowning in deep concentration. Until she triumphantly exclaimed: "Mummy, neither you nor Daddy paid attention, but *I* did. I read it on the tomb."

His arm around her, Mansur asked: "What is it you've seen, little monkey: tell us?"

There! So my secret had probably *not* escaped the candid curiosity of my darling. Anticipating an awkward moment, I braced my soul, preparing my lips to display a calm smile.

With the charming naiveté of her age, Talitha announced: "Why! Mummy is only *one* year younger than Jeda Madeleine when she died with Granddad still in her tummy."

Mansur patted her, answering: "We have a future accountant here – I will tell Aunty Kitty that you're nearly as good as her with figures!"

Meanwhile, his other arm embraced my back and shoulders powerfully, as pouring within me all the strength from his soul. He whispered into my ear: "Remember Clara Pearl: we go nowhere without each other. *No-where*. Don't even *think* of it!"

His warmth dispelled my anxiety.
No! Our happiness wasn't doomed!
Yes, our baby would be fine, and so would I.
Sweet Jesus, thank you for such a good husband, who knows me so well.
Am I afraid to die then?
Yes, and no. I carry life; and Life carries me – and us.

Chapter 115

The honeymoon had come to an end.
For the foreseeable future, the *Cedrus* was to remain our home, presently moored in Beirut.
There were worse living conditions!
But I started discussing with Mansur the best place to settle. He agreed that, with children in particular, we needed a stable address. I felt like a swan anxious to find a warm and safe corner for her *cygnet* to hatch. London was my preferred option; but Paris wasn't ruled out, since we both spoke acceptable French.
Meanwhile, I wished to invest time in our charitable schools before my pregnancy started hindering my mobility too much. That led me to spend many days on sites in Lebanon, Eritrea, and Sudan.

I also had to answer the many letters congratulating us on our wedding. From my former boss and colleagues in Vancouver; from University teachers who'd heard about it and written to Dad's address; etc.
One card touched me particularly. It was signed *Mrs. Kamilah Fawad and Family*.
At first I couldn't figure out who she was, and assumed the sender was one of Mansur's relations. A picture of a groom and bride kneeling on either side of a large red cross was enclosed. It was drawn in colour by a child's hand. Mansur and I felt rather strange after he remembered – and explained – that she was the wife of his former driver Ali (still in prison).
We sent her a nice card in return, thanking her and her children for their picture. It wasn't our easiest thank you letter.

Another letter surprised me. It was from Dad.
It displayed unusual affection and, as well as expressing his best wishes to Mansur and me, it referred for the first time to the picture I'd emailed him, taken at his mother's tomb in Ripon. He seemed to have known the tragic circumstances of her death. I was glad to see how, unexpectedly, some links were activated or perhaps repaired among us and across the generations.
In particular, I felt it was time for me to make peace with Mum. Had I forgiven her for deserting us, even though it hadn't been *her* choice?
She'd sent me a long and thoughtful letter after the wedding. The most important aspect of it for me was to see that she was happy, and still loved me.
Why did I ever doubt it?
A line struck me: "As your mother, I was so glad to see you supported by a strong and loving husband and in-laws, and your Talitha is a jewel. I found you

more confident than usual. You know Clarry, you were always a bit apprehensive. In fact you and I are closer in temperament, whereas Kitty is more like your Father."

Sitting outside in an armchair upon the deck of the *Cedrus*, her letter in my hand, I reflected: did I think myself *apprehensive*? Was I? Was she?

The slight problem with mums is that they know pretty well *where* we come from and how we grew up, so that when they tell us who we are, like it or not, they're less likely to be mistaken.

I looked towards the east and travelled in my memory across the Asian continent to visit in Seoul my... mother.

We only flew there once, as a family, before our parents separated.

We went to *Lotte World* and I remember proudly holding hands with *Lorry*, the Park's mascot! There must be a picture of us somewhere in a file in Vancouver. Crucial question: was Lorry a *squirrel* or a *racoon* (the shape of her tail escapes my memory)?

Never mind, I loved her red polka dress with white dots, over a petticoat. I was so taken aback by the entertainments that I got lost! Poor Mummy freaked out, apparently. But Kitty – or Daddy? – found me.

Many years later, I tried to imagine Mum's life, single in Seoul... She had close family there, in Sillim-dong, but no daughters and no husband. Dad had been the one to blame, and truly, Mum was the victim.

I admitted it and yet, emotionally, I still struggled to forgive her disappearance. I knew that she'd been given no choice, legally, and that the verdict could only have been overturned by hiring a better lawyer, which she couldn't afford.

But the want of her had burned in my adolescent heart so painfully that only through becoming a mother in my turn was I able to truly heal my relationship with her.

I sent her a note:

Thank you, Mum. Bless you. You're the first person I'm telling this to, apart from Mansur. Although it's very early, please come to Beirut for Easter when I will... give birth!

Baby will have Jeda, but you must be Grandma *(of course your trip is taken care of.)*

Your loving daughter, Clarry, who misses you.

Chapter 116

While Mansur was away on business in Dubai, Emma and Sally organised my promised "post-bridal shower" in Beirut.

It started with a relaxing massage at *Le Royal Hôtel* in Dbayeh, allegedly the best spa in town. (I managed to ignore a certain girl with ginger hair, seen from a distance, who could well have been... hum, nobody.)
We were then dressed up as Oriental women, and Lebanese pastry tasting followed; my favourite were *jazarieh* (pumpkin jam) and *mafroukeh* (semolina, clotted cream, syrup and nuts).
After a siesta and a swim, they insisted we should spend the evening at the White Club (*"the ultimate chic playground for upscale party-goers"* according to their guide) in remembrance of our frantic nightclubbing in Vancouver as teenagers!
A table had been booked under my name, they announced, with a bottle of Dom Perignon awaiting us.
But I managed to make them change their minds, arguing that it might seem awkward if anyone identified me there without my husband.
We found instead a traditional Lebanese restaurant and they loved it (although I skipped the deserts, having eaten my fill of them in the afternoon).
The "shower" ended the following day with a cultural trip to Byblos (the first writings on paper in human history were exported from there, as Jed had proudly taught me).
On the way, the origin of the word *Bible*, linked with our destination, prompted a discussion about the faith. Emma and Sally's remembrance of school catechism was hazy. I was glad to find my old friends rather curious to know more about Our Lord, the Holy Eucharist and Our Lady; and not only to *please* me, I reckoned.

But I missed my husband!
He was awaiting me in London, after some weeks on the *Cedrus* as his base.
The day I arrived, Mansur came to sit in front of me and said that I shouldn't have gone to a nightclub in Beirut.
How did he know? He looked upset, and I started to fear another little clash.
"Darling," I answered, "I agree with you. I told Emma and Sally that it would not be fitting for me to be seen there without you."
He enquired suspiciously whether I'd gone to the White Club at all. The owner, a business relation, had apologised to him for not having welcomed us in

person after we had booked. I told him that I'd asked Emma and Sally to change the plan.

He kissed me on the forehead with a condescending "That's my girl!" adding that with the name I now bore, I had to be more careful.

This time, I couldn't let it pass! I asked him coldly if he feared for my safety or for his honour. The blank look that followed was eloquent enough.

As he left the room, I tried to cast away the memory of the terrible scene during the fitting of my wedding dress.

Being scolded like a schoolgirl for something I hadn't done was good for my humility! But deeper inside, I feared I was identifying a possible trait of Mansur's character against which I'd been warned.

Was my beloved really the controlling type?

In that case, was I supposed to endure it, or should I resist, for his own good and that of our relationship? And what if it became worse?

I would ask Emma for advice. Meanwhile, that evening, I showed myself sulky on purpose.

At breakfast, Mansur begun: "Darling, I'm sorry for what I said yesterday." Then he announced: "I won't be outdone by Emma and Sally! Let's go on a 'post-honeymoon' cruise, to Ain Sukhna! That is, if you would like it." He knew that it was a very special place for both of us.

We flew back to the *Cedrus* two days later.

This time, we swam to our paradise island not from the shore (to the west) but from the deep sea (to the east), where we were anchored. Mansur and I escorted Talitha, who proudly covered the distance with her armbands. No fluorescent lifejacket hung from the trees, and no mosquitoes visited us either.

We lay on the warm rocks again, saying little.

Mansur and I could appreciate the stages we had gone through since our first and only visit to that blessed islet.

We had taken risks; I had been imprudent; we had been united through shared forgiveness towards our aggressors; until the sacrament made us husband and wife.

I'd adopted his darling daughter. And now, I carried our child. We had so much to give thanks to God for!

While Talitha slept in the shade, Mansur and I gazed at each other, fully conscious of harvesting a joy that our patience had sown before our marriage, and in preparation for it.

On the way back, the three of us hugged underwater, like happy triplets before birth!

After two days, Mansur was back to work, travelling a lot. I wonder if, on some occasions, he couldn't have managed more of his business from the *Cedrus*. But I suspected that flying his jet again (albeit as co-pilot only) was such a boost to his morale, after over a year stranded, that he needed it.

Horse riding was still forbidden him, but he'd bought Litha a gentle Arab pony and was initiating her into his former passion. I witnessed the first lesson he gave to our daughter, at Hyde Park.

It was bareback riding. Mansur insisted that no good rider learned in a saddle: "You see, Litha, it's like when I took you in my glider, before the... ahem, two years ago. Good jet pilots will fly *gliders* first, to learn to feel the wind freely, like swimming through the sky."

"Well done, Litha!" I proudly cheered her on.

Whether or not our darling understood her father's comparison, she did her best to overcome her apprehension.

So did *I*...

Chapter 117

Of all our school sites, Osly, by the Nile in Sudan, was the one I liked best, for obvious reasons.

My dear Azim had died for those girls to be free (and possibly to enjoy further education). I'd carried (unbeknown) over the Mediterranean the message that set into motion the process of their rescue.

Thus, on my first visit after the honeymoon, I told the girls and the population the full story. Some of them had seen a few items of news on television, but the connection between the attack in Cairo and the attempted abduction in Osly hadn't yet been made public, and perhaps never would.

However, our remote oasis clearly showed on somebody's map as I discovered, when, that afternoon, a vaguely familiar face appeared in the school window.

I wouldn't have recognised Agent N'Guyen.

The *C.I.A.* in Osly!

It seemed such a long time since our encounter at San Antonio Airport. A young Arab woman accompanying her, probably her guide, remained silent.

Agent N'Guyen updated me (confidentially) on the Sobek network, asking if I'd heard anything myself about them in Osly or anywhere else.

I hadn't.

The C.I.A. was collaborating with the Mukhabarat (the Egyptian Intelligence Agency) to counter Sobek: the sex trade was one of the various sources of income for Scimitars of Islam. Some members had been arrested and tried.

She played on her tablet a series of short videos to see if I could identify any of the prisoners, but in vain. There was even a *woman* among them! How could she!

Agent N'Guyen confirmed that the Scimitars had left North Sudan. But she recommended prudence, as in this isolated area, wealthy people like Mansur and I – and Talitha – might attract kidnappers.

I showed them around. To my surprise, they liked my bougainvilleas! Why did I think that female agents – who had probably killed people – wouldn't like flowers?

As they left, Agent N'Guyen informed me that Osly remained under satellite surveillance. From on high – I wondered – can they count the petals?

Mansur was away, but I immediately told him everything over the phone. He said that he knew already, through his father, who kept in touch with Intelligence people. Mansur asked me if I preferred to leave Osly until more guards were sent (he'd thought it better not to alarm me). But I wouldn't abandon my girls!

From the start our aim wasn't to set up a parallel school, but simply to upgrade theirs, providing resources that were totally beyond the reach of the village community.

Their response had been very encouraging.

We were planning to provide education in practical skills such as cleaning, cooking, sowing and basic nursing; but also genuine academic formation, with grants for university studies for the more intellectually able girls. That latter offer sounded like the moon to them, but some were eager to try.

I was as thrilled as they were!

Dr. Yasir visited twice. As she'd mentioned again at our wedding, she hoped to affiliate the Al-Khoury Charitable Trust to her UN Department. I was treading very softly, not so much because Jonathan had given her the idea, as because I'd come to realise that her views differed from mine.

She hadn't changed, though. *I* had. Her presence and knowledge helped me deepen my understanding of reproductive health and education. We had long chats on the veranda, surrounded by my luxuriant bougainvilleas (which she much admired).

On one occasion, our conversation moved to psychological health. It brought back to my mind a website about mental disorders, to which Emma had referred me. (She'd left her boyfriend, thinking him bipolar. It was cruel of her, but what could I do?)

After some hesitation, I ventured: "And what about narcissistic personality disorder? Is it as common as the Internet seems to assume?"

Nasreen paused for a moment as if weighing up various considerations. Then she answered: "Of course I'm not a psychopathologist. But in my opinion, there are fewer people with *NPD* – narcissistic personality disorder – than one might think. Perplexing reactions don't necessarily amount to a syndrome. For instance, someone may have a very strong will, without lacking in respect or even compassion."

My throat tightened. She must have guessed *whom* I was concerned about, but she tactfully spoke in general terms.

She went on: "In fact, giving someone a label like NPD can be a form of violence. Because his or her attitude sometimes hurts us, we lock up the 'offender' inside a pathological definition – and thus a pattern of behaviour – which doesn't truly define him or her. By so doing, we make it impossible for him – or her – to improve in our eyes.

"We also dispense ourselves from examining our *own* failings. In fact, unless there are explicit threats, such casual diagnoses freeze the relationship at either end. Avoiding them preserves the momentum of life and leaves space and hope for improvement."

I felt enlightened by her explanation, and perhaps unfair to Mansur in retrospect. I asked Nasreen: "So, do you think it better to stand exposed, for the sake of love?"

She smiled affectionately: "You, the Christian one, are asking me? Is that not just what you believe Christ did? Mind you, I'm not condoning abuse either. You know that I oppose coercion, equally harmful under the guise of tribal or religious customs."

Her principles, I noticed, didn't suffice to protect voiceless babies obviously *coerced* during abortions. But her explanations helped me regain confidence in my relationship with Mansur. For that, I was truly grateful to Nasreen.

My doctor friend also assisted me as my acting obstetrician. Our mini hospital was completed and she supervised its launching, being satisfied that we had the best equipment. Actually, I was the first patient on whom the ultrasound was used. When first visiting in mid-September, she said that my baby was doing well. I was so glad to be told about him or her, although I asked her not to specify the sex of my child.

One month later though, on her second visit, a very big surprise occurred. Nasreen was looking at the screen and enquired: "Clara, you said you didn't mind either a boy or a girl, didn't you?" I confirmed and she smiled, adding: "What if it were *both*?"

I could not believe my ears, as my eyes followed her finger on the screen. She said that there were definitely *two* foetuses, not one, and most probably of opposite sexes. I was captivated by the sight of those two little shapes, actually moving, as my hand felt their gentle kicks against my stomach. It was almost as if I could *hear* them too.

Nasreen successively closed up on either baby with the 3D ultrasound. I couldn't take my eyes off their lovely figures. Was it possible that, within me, *two* such little creatures were actually alive, and growing? We could see their faces, their limbs, and even their tiny fingertips and yes, she confirmed that it was a boy and a girl, adding that twins were to be expected after *in vitro* fertilisation.

She looked surprised when I said that the conception had occurred naturally.

Partly to change the subject, I told her that I would email Kitty the short video of the ultrasound: a life manifesto, after the dreadful CCTV footage watched at San Antonio Airport the previous year, also sent from Africa to Texas!

To keep things on a happy note, I mentioned to Nasreen the great maternity wear that I'd found. We agreed that there was absolutely no reason why an expectant mother shouldn't look fashionable.

I'd bought online some lovely dresses (quite cheap, as well!) combining comfort and beauty. Nasreen complimented me on the one I was wearing that day: a dark blue polka dot maternity dress made of soft stretch jersey that would adjust to my growing bump.

When the temperature dropped in the evening, here in the desert, I only needed to slip on a cropped cardigan (in white stretch knit). I also had a pair of rather classy wide leg trousers with a turn up and adjustable waist.

Nasreen had good taste and I was glad to have her approval.

Chapter 118

Mansur arrived that afternoon to spend a few days with us. His pilot flew the helicopter from Port Sudan, by the Red Sea, where the *Cedrus* was moored.

I was standing in the wind by the helipad, behind the school. On the nearby playground, dozens of girls were looking in awe at the noisy bird slowly coming down towards us in a cloud of dust. Litha was with them, and got permission to join me, soon holding my hand.

The rotor wash pressed my dress against my bump, making it seem all the bigger, I felt. As Mansur stepped out of the aircraft (after his bodyguard), my broad smile soon alerted him to some happy secret. He was ecstatic when I broke the news to him, unnoticed by our darling.

We decided to tell Talitha without delay. I was slightly apprehensive of her reaction, in case she would feel... outnumbered. She'd taken the news of one forthcoming baby well, but *two* of them might unsettle her. She might even wonder whether more would not appear later on during the pregnancy! An invasion of babies!

That evening, the three of us were lying on our bed. I asked her if she would like to have more than one little brother or sister to play with.

She seemed rather pleased with the prospect, and said: "Yes, there's enough space in my room to play with many more."

Relieved, I produced the scan of her siblings printed out by Nasreen, introducing her to them. Talitha was fascinated. She actually spread the picture upon my stomach, as if peering at the living twins through a window. Mansur whispered into my ear that he would have a portrait of our family painted in that telling posture.

Meanwhile, Talitha kept gazing at the paper, looking rather serious, until she pressed her little lips against each printed silhouette, welcoming her brother and sister with a first kiss. She then asked: "Mummy, will I have to wait for them to make my First Holy Communion?" And: "What are their names, Daddy?"

Those were important questions.

The first one was quickly answered, and darling Litha was secretly relieved not to have to wait any longer than planned to receive Jesus, for which Abu Ephrem and I had just started preparing her.

Mansur and I dealt with the second question that evening. Our little boy would be called Francis, after the poor and joyful saint of Assisi (who had gained favour with Sultan al-Kamil of Egypt, and encouraged him in his lenient treatment of Christians). Our baby girl, we would name Margaret, after the Pearl of York, the new star shining bright in my mystical firmament.

Our children would have other patron saints to give them inspiration and to intercede for them. Why be mean, as it secured for them an effective spiritual genealogy – free of charge! Thus, Francis was to bear also the names of Anthony, Yusuf, Athanasius and Mary. In addition, Margaret would be called Lucy, Madeleine, Katarina and Mary.

Lying on my back that night, my hands spread over my stomach, I whispered their names for the first time, feeling a deep and peaceful emotion. They were asleep, and so was Mansur.

I murmured, almost shyly: "My dear son Francis Anthony Yusuf Athanasius Mary, I love you with all my heart and soul. May God protect you always and may Our Lady keep you safe.

"My beloved daughter Margaret Lucy Madeleine Katarina Mary, I give you all that I am and I pray God and Our Lady to guide you safely to them in paradise."

I listened to the sounds of the desert. It was mid-October, and still hot during the day, but not in the evening. The wind had subsided. Some wild animal – fox or bird, I didn't know – howled in the distance, by the Nile. Through the window, the constellations shone brighter than ever; not like in Cairo or London, where pollution and artificial lights screen the sky. At my side, Mansur lay deep in his dreams.

My first meeting with our twins delighted me.

It was my first moment alone since the scan earlier in the morning, and I wished to consider this great surprise.

After hearing that I was pregnant, three months earlier, I had gone through what every mother experiences. I had started interacting with my tiny inhabitant.

What a mysterious thing a relationship is!

How exactly to describe that invisible bond that connects us with other people?

I had such a link with my parents, of course. But it had been damaged (not destroyed) when they separated, leaving me in a state of emotional helplessness. Other bonds, and strong ones indeed, attached me to my beloved Kitty; and to Azim, and Nour. And to my other heavenly friends: Anthony, Katarina, Simon Stock and Margaret, to name just a few.

Many more ties, of a lesser strength, intertwined, weaving my life with those of many other people, either acquaintances, or former teachers, or collaborators. There were other more challenging relationships, such as with my stepmother Abigail, with Nurse Sheehan and with Jonathan.

My link to Talitha – my beloved treasure – was a most cherished one. Blessedly, on becoming Mansur's wife, I knew that I'd been made one with him, through the union of our souls.

That was expressed in the most striking way through the presence of the child I was carrying. Daily I'd talked to my baby, and prayed with and for him or her. I'd taken him or her to our God, at every Holy Communion, when the

Sacred Host would come and dwell in me, so dizzily close to my child.

But since that morning, I had become aware of an added relationship: *in* me this time, rather than *with* me. That was the great novelty.

On the screen, I'd seen them move against each other within the tight space available. One was sucking his thumb; another folding her legs. They had a life of their own, and they interacted not only with me, but also with each other.

It was a *triangular* relationship, not merely reciprocal.

Did I feel excluded?

Not at all.

Rather, I was happy to see Francis and Margaret enriched through that added dimension of kinship. Trying to explain to myself what I felt, I found that I was even more fulfilled as a mother, now that I knew them to be siblings.

Spouses can become bored or even selfish, unless in time their one-to-one relationship expands to include a *third* person through parenting (or through some charitable endeavour, if sadly they can't conceive).

For the same reason, my mother-to-child relationship was broadened by the presence of a third person, our second child.

Beware of deserts: they make you think!

I gazed at the thin moon through the window. The night was beautiful, pregnant with light.

Chapter 119

Large four-wheel drives weren't uncommon around Osly (we have two).

But I had yet to see one with diplomatic plates, as occurred later that morning. I was watering my bougainvilleas when a car drove in and parked near the school.

It couldn't be Nasreen, as she was already staying with us, and had travelled from Khartoum in a rented car, out of discretion, rather than in an official UN vehicle. Was it Agent N'Guyen again?

Our guards were already standing by the car door, checking the visitors' identities and inspecting their boot. Two men eventually stepped out, young and old. The older one walked towards me with a large smile.

What a surprise! I couldn't believe it! Nepomucen! Here?

I'd insisted on his attending the reception after the wedding in Paris, but he'd declined, saying that he was glad to have served the Mass, and would remain in the chapel "in thanksgiving."

By what miracle was he now materialising here in Sudan four months later, in the middle of nowhere? (Osly not really being the sort of place where you travel for tourism.)

Then I remembered that he *was* Sudanese, having only come to France as a refugee.

He held out his hand, but I felt that, although we had seen each other only three times, and so briefly on each occasion, we had shared so much supernaturally that a formal greeting would simply not do. Letting my hose fall down among the shrubs, I opened my arms and we embraced each other.

Life is so mysterious: who could have predicted that I would one day hug a cleaner-cum-secret agent from Orly Airport, here by the Nile at Osly Ford; sixteen months after he'd deciphered my boarding card on my exit from the Cairo flight; had prayed for me in the underground chapel in Paris; and four months after he'd served my wedding Mass in the same location!

He introduced the younger man to me: "Clara, this is my son Lewis."

I was taken by surprise, having assumed that he was Nepomucen's *driver*.

Actually, he *was* a driver, as I then recalled. A light thrill went through my spine as I shook hands with the chauffeur of the Papal Nunciature. Now I could put a *face* on the name.

The voice of Agent Bloomen sounded afresh into my ears, as heard at San Antonio Airport, when he'd identified the two missing links in the chain of transmission of the vital information which had saved the lives of forty-eight Muslim girls, here at Osly: "Nepomucen and Lewis Kanisah."

Slightly troubled by the depth of Lewis' gaze, I managed to smile in a natural way: "I'm delighted to meet you at last, Lewis. I don't know why, I'd always imagined you older, as Nepomucen's *brother*." He'd something military about him, but also very tender.

Lewis shook my hand vigorously.

He looked a bit like... Azim. Rather handsome as well! Or was it just because he and Azim were about the same age? Was this unforeseen visit a gift from my late beloved brother, from beyond the grave? Hopefully, he – *they* – would stay the night and we could evoke those crucial hours, at length.

I would make sure he was comfortable – would the smaller guestroom near the chapel do for him? And why was I so distant with him? I should have embraced this young man, as I had hugged his father.

Like a dark meteorite across a clear desert night, a glittering and unsolicited shadow crossed my imagination, instantaneously vanishing: Lewis and I, alone upon a bench, under a fig tree. Lewis' arm reaching my waist. And I...

No! Please!

The vision was gone.

Later that day, when examining my conscience before going to bed, I observed with dismay that during that instant Mansur, our children, Kitty and the schools had literally flattened like familiar shapes on the wallpaper of my life; while any remembrance of Our Lord, Our Lady and the saints had utterly evaporated!

What had happened to me? Could a temptation be so sudden and overpowering?

Objectively, however, Lewis was looking at me with deep interest.

Or was it admiration?

I was still standing in front of my guests. That trick of my imagination couldn't have taken longer than a few seconds to unfold. Realising how unsafe such wondering was, I was prompted to utter mentally: *Jesus, help me!*

At that moment, another man's arm, which had touched my body and soul and nearly my offspring through a gilded casket in a London church, gleamed in my memory. Immobile as it was, it seemed to wave at me. *St. Simon Stock, come to my aid! Shelter me under Our Lady's cloak!*

Turning to Nepomucen, I inquired as artlessly as I could: "So, you're back from exile? Were you recalled? Is this what explains your joyful apparition in our little desert? What an amazing surprise! But come and sit down under the veranda, while I ask for coffee."

As we rested in the shade, Nepomucen explained that he'd come to bury his wife. She'd died of cancer several months earlier, and the Nunciature had granted him diplomatic status temporarily (hence the car), so that he might finally bring her mortal remains back to Sudan. Her body now lay in their native village, less than two hours from Osly.

Fr. Paul had emailed them that I was on site and they'd decided on an impromptu visit. It pleased me much, I insisted, despite the sad circumstances. Fr. Paul had told me of the death of Nepomucen's wife at the time, but I was glad to be able to offer my condolences face-to-face to both father and... son.

Our conversation gradually moved to less grave topics, as I described our work at the school. I showed them around and both expressed admiration at the quality of the buildings and grounds.

We stood in silence in front of the very simple monument commemorating Azim's sacrifice.

The epitaph read: *To the memory of Anthony Azim Nebankh, Egyptian guide, who died age twenty-three, that many might live. 'Greater love than this no man hath, that a man lay down his life for his friends' (John 15:13). Requiescat in pace.*

We also prayed in the chapel. They remained kneeling for quite a while, actually. It reminded me of another chapel where that old man and I had prayed, one after the other. I left them after ten minutes and came back to fetch them just as recreation time began.

The girls were running out of their classrooms towards the playground. The three of us kept silent, equally moved by the wonderful sight. In various capacities, we had been instrumental in such a pleasant outcome, whereas, had any one of us acted differently sixteen months earlier, most of these girls would now be dead or – nearly as bad – sold as sex slaves by the Sobek network.

Instead of the joyful sounds of games and children's laughter, one would only hear mourning parents. Where my bougainvilleas now grew, one would have seen but bloodstains.

Blood *had* been shed, here and in Cairo, but not that of my girls, thank God.

We walked together down by the Nile, at the end of the village and stood in the little cemetery, around the tomb of the school bus driver shot by the Scimitars in the attack. His daughter was one of our pupils. I liked her particularly.

Unexpectedly, Lewis announced that he would go and rest under the veranda, before driving back... So, they wouldn't stay the night? Part of me was disappointed, but it wasn't my better part.

My fingers, I realised, were clutching under my shawl another piece of cloth: my Brown Scapular (I'd been enrolled a few months earlier). I gave thanks to Our Heavenly Mother for having kept me under her mantle.

Letting my hand go, I managed *not* to look at Lewis as he started walking back up the dusty street, while I remained alone by the great river, with Nepomucen.

Chapter 120

The old man wanted to talk, I could sense.

But I would leave it to him, if and when he chose.

After a few minutes walking along the bank, he confided: "I feel awkward without my wife. Her tumours were thought to have healed a year ago. But in late May she was taken to hospital in an emergency. New tumours had appeared and metastasized.

"She knew the end had come. She told me that she would offer up her sufferings for our country. I think your intentions were included, because of what you'd done for our girls, down here. She died peacefully a week later."

That was all.

That woman whom I'd never met had thought of me in her last days. In heaven only would we know how this all fitted together.

For the present time, I saw that I'd become accustomed to this exchange of prayers, of sufferings, of merits and intercession within "the network," God's extended family – His beloved Church. I also knew that many more such connections were occurring daily, most of them unknown to us, at every Mass, and at any smaller sacrifice offered in union with Jesus.

I thanked my friend for his message and said that I was grateful to his wife and to him.

A raft was crossing the Nile, loaded with goats, two cows and even a camel; plus some farmers and a motorbike. As it floated across the ford thanks to a cable, a few young men were actually pushing at the rear, with water up to their neck, holding the railing. From April onwards, the Nile would swell and a heavier, safer barge would be used for crossing.

Nepomucen spoke further: "It reminds me of the River Jordan, in the Old Testament account. After having left Egypt, the Hebrew people had been wandering in the desert for forty years and at last, were encamped by the river, about to enter the Promised Land."

I remembered this episode, first heard at children's catechism.

He went on: "But first, they sent two spies to reconnoitre the country. They were sheltered by the prostitute Rahab and her family in Jericho, thus escaping the local police. Only Rahab's family was spared, when the Hebrew army invaded the country and took the city.

"Would you agree, Clara, that our time on earth as members of Christ is about spying for the Lord's army? We are the Hebrew spies by the River Jordan (I don't mean the *Mossad*). We are sent as a vanguard, to inspect the territory and share the good news of the forthcoming liberation with as many souls of good will as possible so that, when the days of wrath come, they may be spared, and us with them."

I smiled and said: "I knew you were a *spy*, Nepomucen. But a *good* one. A spy for God's network, the Church. I didn't give out your name, even when that C.I.A. man, Agent Bloomen, was trying to identify you as the missing link. And to think that I didn't know who my contact was, let alone that I carried a message for him!"

He smiled back and added: "That's the safest way to smuggle information. But you learned fast. In no time, you were down at Headquarters to receive the main message."

I wasn't sure what he meant, but he explained: "Seeing you in the chapel so soon after you had showed me your boarding card didn't surprise me. Where else could you have been called to better connect with the Word Himself; with the Lord Jesus? He's *the* Message of the Father to the world.

"In His 'network' as you say, my friend, you soon became a trusted agent, equipped with the weapons of prayer, humility, purity and faith. I was with Fr. Paul during the prayer sessions over Jonathan (he wouldn't mind my mentioning this to you). We couldn't have started assisting him if you hadn't first 'exfiltrated' him from enemy territory. From the realm of darkness."

I was a bit embarrassed: "Nepomucen, I had no notion of it. I only meant to help a friend, when I started slipping onto treacherous ground. Later on that evening, he appeared as my enemy; and then God touched him. I wouldn't call my imprudence (for want of a stronger word) an act of virtue."

The old man took my hand and answered: "God knows how weak we all are, and what responsibility we bear for our falls. But His mercy and almightiness can give even our shortcomings a fruitful outcome, if we truly repent and beg for His help."

I had repented. And I had begged for God's help.

We stood downhill from the school.

I'd taken off my sandals, and the two of us started walking in the shallow water along the bank.

I asked, partly to tease him: "So, are we two spies here on the west bank? But I can't see Christ's army on the opposite side, awaiting our report to crossover and liberate the land..."

Shielding his eyes with his hand, he looked attentively towards the east, over the half-kilometre-wide river.

After a moment, he whispered, as if in a dream: "I *see* them.

"I *see* the holy angels, the archangels, the cherubim. I *see* the martyrs, the confessors and the virgins. I *see* the innocents; I *see* the penitents. I *see* all those who have died in God's peace and are now ravished in the contemplation of His Face."

I wasn't smiling any more, but felt captivated, as he described further: "Above all, I *see* Our Blessed Lady, the perfect worshipper of the Blessed Trinity, and the true Mother of God made Man, Jesus Christ. She 'cometh forth as the morning rising, fair as the moon, bright as the sun, terrible as an army set in array'! I see them. And they see me. They see *us*.

"Only to our eyes of flesh do they seem to stand at some distance from our needs. In reality, they are *among* us. They shield us. They guide us. They inform us. With them, we are Christ's gentle spies. We spy... On behalf of love, against hatred. Against revenge, on behalf of mercy. We prepare the ways of the Lord in every heart, for His glorious return."

I was fascinated by his prophetic posture, as he stood in the sun, like Moses facing the Red Sea, translating his vision for my sake, average believer that I was.

On the opposite bank, passengers had disembarked the little raft.

They'd reached the other side, and were now walking uphill under the palm trees. It struck me as an image of our journey on earth, from birth to death, or rather from first to second birth (apart from the camel, goats and cows, which I was sure we wouldn't take along with us after death – no more than yachts, helicopters, Chanel jackets or Häagen-Dazs truffles).

I felt very clearly that, if the twins I *carried* were at an early stage of preparation for entering the "real life" after birth, to a greater extent Nepomucen and I standing on our side of the Nile were *carried* or ferried by the Ark of Salvation, the Church.

Her motherly protection prepared us for the "real life" of eternity after death.

Think of it: is there a single instant spent in the womb that doesn't aim at our fulfilment after birth?

No.

Just the same then: does everything we do or omit until death shape our eternity?

Yes.

For example, the tiny battle I'd just fought against my imagination about Lewis was part of the shaping of my soul.

Not one of our thoughts was in vain; none of our assents without consequence.

Chapter 121

Nepomucen was still looking silently towards the East.

Was he thinking about his late wife – perhaps talking to her?

The sun was now very high up and the air was pretty hot. I would soon need to go and hide under the shade, just like across the river the group had wisely sat down under the trees. I couldn't see distinctly. Some seemed to begin eating, while children were kicking a ball. Surely, some of their sisters attended our school.

The raft was coming back towards our side of the river, pushed by two young men immersed in the water. They were laughing. Were they coming to fetch us?

Actually, I'd have loved to go for a swim, right then! Touching my stomach, I thought:

Lucky babies, enjoying a nine-month swim!

As I *had*; only, I didn't remember.

I'd seen Baby Javier just a few hours after he'd been born. But what was *birth*?

Abu Ephrem once mentioned that the day when a saint or a martyr died is commemorated not as his *end*, but as the day of his *birth* – to eternal life.

I wondered: had Archangel Raphael, the holy hermit Anthony and the bright virgin Katarina tenderly smiled at Azim and Nour, on that last afternoon, when they were *born*?

Azim...

It was really getting too hot.

I strapped my sandals on again and, as we climbed up the bank back to the school, I asked Nepomucen: "Did you see Azim and Nour, and your wife, on the other side?"

He confirmed that they were there.

I burned to hear more from him about Azim in particular, remembering that he knew him personally. But I didn't want to be indiscrete. I thought I would ask indirectly: "Nepomucen, do you think Fr. Paul knew about Azim, when he met me in the chapel after you'd left?"

Nepomucen smiled: "No, he'd never heard of Azim before. But as a priest, he's used to taking genuine interest in anyone's sorrows and joys, and to look at them in the light of God."

I said: "But then, was it not very risky of Azim to make the entire rescue depend on my keeping the encoded boarding card? I could have lost it – actually I *did*, for a time. Surely it would have been far safer for him to have texted to you directly from the Cairo Airport lounge what he wrote on my card?"

Nepomucen remained silent for a moment, before answering: "If I remember, you only misplaced the card *after* I'd made use of it. Azim didn't text me the intel from the phone booth, because he feared interception if unencrypted, and rightly so.

"If the C.I.A. could read it, as your Agent admitted in Texas, why not others? Such caution might have been unnecessary, who knows? But Azim knew that his enemies had accomplices within governmental agencies. He wanted to be sure that the Scimitars wouldn't find out what he knew, so that they would be caught red-handed – and Sobek uprooted."

And so it had happened... How it all made sense to me now!

As if guessing that I wished to hear more about my dead friend, Nepomucen went on: "Azim was a beautiful soul. This is how we met... He was still a Muslim, fresh from training with some Western unit – British SAS, if I recall. Unofficial cooperation was taking place between Egypt and Sudan, to try and secure stability.

"I was a Baptist, recently converted from animism. We shared information, political and military. But soon it also involved religion. Our souls gradually converged toward the Church. It's a long story. He always liked the desert."

Nepomucen became silent for a while, as if revisiting his memories.

We had stopped halfway up. The majestic Nile was shining under the sun. Despite it being October, the breeze was very hot. However, it wasn't why light perspiration appeared on my brow, when my friend added: "Azim loved you. Not that he told me. But I know it."

It was so good to hear those words. I let them sink deep inside me; I let myself soak in their power: 'Azim loved me.'

After a silence, I answered: "Thank you, Nepomucen. But, I've always wondered: if he loved me, as I know he did, why not openly entrust me with his rescue plan for the girls? Why did he involve me without letting me know?"

Nepomucen looked into my eyes and, after a while, replied: "It's true. Azim clearly meant to have you involved, even though unknowingly. Why? Perhaps that was his message to you. A message you could only read in *retrospect*, in the light of a Love grown stronger in your heart after his sacrifice. Ask yourself: would you have passed on his intel to me, had you known it would probably result in his death?"

I slowly looked away, towards the wide river... He was right.
Why hadn't it struck me sooner?
Of course... Had I known...
Had I known that my boarding card was his death sentence...
Had I held in one hand my exotic flirt and in the other forty-eight unknown girls, I would have chosen... romance, against sacrifice.

I said, almost for myself, confessing and giving thanks: "Now I understand what he felt towards me. He wished me to reach deeper in true love and knew that I was too weak to consent, then. He led me blindfolded to our greater Love, and the blindfold was a screen of petals, and he walked ahead and still holds my hand."

I was on my knees, facing the water, peacefully crying. A shadow met mine. It was Nepomucen, standing between me and the sun.

We remained silent for a little while, until he stated: "There's no use imagining what would have happened if Azim had lived. He made his choice. Rather, he chose to answer an invitation to Love eternal (as carved on his stone at the school) and this with our help.

"But he isn't gone. He's here.

"They're here.

"You are here, *Lord*, Who promised: 'I am with you all days, even to the consummation of the world.'"

We walked side by side, up the sandy bank and back to the school. The girls were playing before lunch break. As they often did, on seeing us, they ran towards me to touch my hands, caress my bump, and hug me. My "petals" were pressing against me, full of life, and my eyes gave thanks for such a happy sight. I could speak to them in local Arabic now – just the odd word, but still a great joy.

The sun looked huge above the desert.

I remained standing in the shade, my gaze attracted to the opposite bank, long after the diplomatic vehicle had disappeared amidst a cloud of dust, towards the south. It had fulfilled its embassy.

A message had been sent from on high, and lowly received, and gratefully. And I stood stronger, and more confident, thus watched over by an army set in array.

My weakness was backed up by the legions of Love, as invisible as invincible. And the man I loved, alive and strong, was standing next to me. Mansur and I walked back into the house, hand in hand.

Chapter 122

I lay awake on our bed that evening, in a meditative and peaceful mood.
How many more galaxies are yet to be discovered, I wondered?
Who knew?
In fact, many things exist unbeknown to me, or to any other man or woman.
Closer to us: how many types of Camembert are there? I should know, having visited Normandy just over three months earlier.
Closer still: how many teeth are there in my mouth? I don't even know that... and yet, I can't doubt their existence – wait until they meet a Camembert!
An easy one, finally: how many babies are in my...
My reflections were interrupted by Mansur, who turned to his other side in his sleep, now leaning against me. I raised myself up on my elbow to look at his familiar and beloved face. A hint of a smile passed on his features, like the caress of a summer breeze over a flowery field.

I kissed his brow.
What dream was crossing his mind? Was he thinking of me? Or of our three children? Not of his *helicopter*, I hoped!
Suddenly he frowned. It was just the same expression as earlier that day, I recalled, when he had informed me that "Luke wouldn't give me swimming lessons any longer." Only suspicion could have motivated Mansur's decision. It hurt me. Didn't he know that we had stopped swimming together as soon as I had become engaged?
Before my eyes, the *only* man I loved... was asleep. He was unaware of my presence, but conscious enough for his imagination and his memory to show on his face.
During his coma, fifteen months earlier, he didn't perceive or express anything.
What a mystery we human beings are! What specifically does make us *human*?
It can't be consciousness, since that can be lost or interrupted without our becoming something else.
We can forget that we exist, and other people can ignore it as well: does it suspend our humanity? Are we then turned into rabbits, or into smartphones?
Obviously not!
Neither does our size, or wealth, or power modify essentially who we are. My rich husband and my swelling bump didn't make me *more* Clara than four months earlier, when both my bank account and my waist were thinner!
So, there must be something deeper and more permanent that makes us

members of the human race.

It can't be what we or others think or say about us, because that varies as well, and can be contradictory.

It must be our *nature*, full stop.

It's what from the start we share with all human beings, and not with cats or flowers. Nasreen could surprise me with the *number* of children I carried, but not with their *nature*: neither kittens, nor white lilies – no matter how much I loved them – would come out of my womb...

And that was just as well, since I'd ordered a sample of the cutest ever baby clothes from *Bonpoint* (the ultimate Parisian chic for children) and I would surely not have a kitten wear them, or a squirrel!

Well, I was turned into a true philosopher that night! I should ask Kitty if she was thinking that deeply when she expected Javier! Or, is it a normal symptom for twins?

What then with triplets: I would surely write a *treatise*!

Did anyone mention *Camembert* recently? I suddenly felt hungry.

Hunger... Food. Ah, *that* was known territory!

Fridge!

Tomato juice, with ice, and the spicy powder on the top.

But Mansur was lying against me and I was afraid I would wake him up. What if Margaret needed to stretch her legs (as she likes doing) while Francis was resting?

Looking at our adult shapes under the sheet, I realised how *little* separated us from our children. We lay like bigger twins under the cotton cloth, just like our babies under my djellaba.

They didn't *know* about us – or very vaguely, through the protection and nutrition we (sorry, *I*!) granted them. Surely, beyond the vast veil of the sky, other Persons (I don't mean aliens) are looking at us adults, and smile at our busy lives and mighty concerns, when all we need to do is let ourselves be nurtured and shaped, in preparation for real life after death.

I looked again at the thin moon crescent and figured that it was a shining slot *incised* in the dark blue sky, the cosmic membrane separating us from the "other side" where full light blazes.

Are we not all in gestation, adults included, in a vast sub-lunar lounge, preparing for transit through that bright slot, into the sun? When will our mystical c-section occur?

Questions to ask Nasreen urgently: do foetuses *dream*?

In general: do they plan, interpret and react? Perhaps, for tiny Margaret, a slight kick from Francis would be tantamount to a slap in the face for me? How does she cope with such aggression, poor sweetheart?

Time for tomato juice – sorry darling, I simply *must* visit that fridge! I mean *we* must, Francis, Margaret and I – while you rest and keep happily dreaming...

I came back to bed and fell asleep, only to have an unpleasant awakening two hours later, wet with sweat.

Calm down, Clara! Everything's fine!

But, what a dream... I'm having nightmares just like Talitha now.

Mine don't involve *Tintin* and *Peter Rabbit* – though I wish they would!

What time is it?

Barely past 3 a.m.

Did I drink too much tomato juice? Or perhaps that spicy powder isn't recommended when expecting? I must tell Mansur (and Nasreen) about my horrendous dream. Not just now though. He's asleep.

So, a *referendum* was taking place, no less! The question put to the population was quite simply the existence of... *me*! It was organised in my womb and I was watching it live with Nasreen on the pregnancy scan screen.

Francis voted against; Talitha in favour; and Margaret hesitated. Francis persuaded her that there was no scientific evidence.

When Talitha pointed at his umbilical cord, he answered that it was a purely functional device pumping resources from the soil. Plans were afoot, he added, to go cordless soon and not to be tied down any longer.

Margaret was intimidated and didn't protest when Francis declared that the referendum had concluded against my existence.

Talitha was in tears, saying that she couldn't believe there was *no one* outside the womb.

As she would not keep it a strictly private opinion, but meant to convince Margaret, and perhaps Francis – he decided to expel her from my womb! But instead, a suction device appeared and Francis was vacuumed out.

That's when I woke up, perspiring. I put my hands on my stomach, palpating it... My babies! Of course I'm here.

How could I not exist, since I love you so much?

I will tell Mansur and Arous at breakfast.

What a dream! They will laugh, for sure. It's perhaps the best reaction.

I hope that they won't have a vote, as they drink their coffee, against the existence of the sun, and kick me out in the dark if I persist in calling it light.

Chapter 123

Months had gone by and my last significant trip was to England, to see Vardah's baby, born on the twenty-second of February.

I had a shock when arriving at our house in Chelsea, on my way from Heathrow. The smaller drawing room had been turned into an oratory *in my absence*. A note on the door welcomed me on behalf of Mansur. A poignant painting of St. Margaret Clitherow hung above the little altar.
He'd wished it to be a surprise.
Was I selfish? Although the final result was magnificent, it upset me.
When I'd mentioned that project to him during our honeymoon, I'd enthused about choosing the colours, the furniture and the paintings. Vardah had agreed to give me some advice. Why had he so flatly ignored my wishes?
I felt excluded from an undertaking which was very dear to my heart, and it grieved me that my husband hadn't understood it.
I had intended to involve Mansur as well, if he had time. I would have enjoyed sharing our ideas. In due course, I would ask Vardah if she'd been consulted at all.

Meanwhile, what a lovely little girl she had!
One could not tell yet what colour her hair would be: fair like Stuart's or brown like Vardah's. They decided to call her Jacqueline, which didn't strike me as very trendy – I mean, considering the style of Stuart and Vardah – unless they have Kennedy connections.
But never mind! I was so grateful to God for the safe birth of that child, whose future in the womb wasn't so secure when I'd last met her mother.
I wondered what had made Vardah change her mind. I'd prayed for it of course, but some concrete circumstance must have occurred and led her out of doubt, to do the *true* "right thing."
Even more surprising was Stuart's *passion* for his daughter. It seemed quasi-animal, as if the slightest perceived threat to his chick's well-being turned the sociable actor into a gorilla or a bear.
Stressing her qualified position as Jacqueline's mother, Vardah regularly had to urge him to let the child rest as he would have kept her in his arms all day long.
Worst of all (for *James Bond*'s fans, not for his family), he'd cancelled at the last minute his attendance at the Oscars ceremony! His agent was still in the hall, nearly in tears, when Vardah let me in.
The poor man pestered Stuart in vain: "For the last time, will you *reconsider*? We could *still* arrive in time at Los Angeles. We can be at Heathrow

in forty minutes, rush through the VIP gate and catch the last flight. No doubt you will receive the award, if you deign to show up! Please Stuart, I *beg* you..."

I was slightly embarrassed to witness the scene, not least because I hadn't seen his last film.

But Stuart dismissed it all with a kiss – to his baby; adding: "Dan, you *do* realise that it will be the middle of the night for us here, and feeding time for Jacquie (I'll be awake as well, as *Best Supporting Actor*). However, if Vardah permits, we will sit in front of my webcam and show you all in Hollywood *why* I couldn't come.

"I can picture it on the wide screen at the Dolby Theatre, with all the celebs! Believe me, they will *adore* it, and my producer will bless you for the scoop!"

Well, *that* was a change of heart, for sure.

Stuart's trust in me touched me all the more, when he put his little treasure in *my* arms, adding: "May I introduce Miss Jacqueline Wattles, Vardah's most satisfied customer? She was so pleased with my wife's bespoke *interior design* that she stayed in for nine full months!

"She only came out to pay her bill – in yawns and smiles. There! Just look at her! She's doing it again; look everyone!"

To which Vardah replied tit for tat: "Clara, may I introduce the definitive *James Bond Girl* instead? For the *first* time in the series, a woman managed to wrap *007* around her little finger. She's convinced him that from now on *she* is his mission! Well done Jacqueline!"

I rejoiced, seeing how Stuart and Vardah teased each other only to express their inebriating happiness as first-time parents. I also thought of other little "customers" of mine and hoped they were just as pleased with *my* "interior." They hadn't stepped out to complain so far; that was a good sign.

No word was spoken about having Jacqueline *baptised*, but Stuart came from a Christian background and I hoped that he and Vardah might gradually realise what a blessing their baby would receive if they entrusted her to God, body and soul.

On my smartphone, I cunningly showed Vardah the lovely baptism gown that I'd bought in advance from *Bonpoint* for Margaret (and the same for Francis). It came with a gorgeous matching lace trim bonnet, fastening underneath with a delicate satin ribbon.

She loved it! – and promised to attend the ceremony in April, if her baby was strong enough to travel. Meanwhile, Jacqueline was as happy as can be on her parents' island amidst the River Thames.

Leaving her daughter to rest (in Stuart's arms!), Vardah and I walked back to the willow, smiling. As expected in February, it was rather chilly and damp by the river, and no swan came to greet us.

But my friend put her arm around my shoulders, saying: "Clara, if I may ask, are things going *well* with Mansur? I meant to speak with you at the wedding, but it seemed out of place then; and here last summer, I was too worried about my decision regarding the pregnancy, so that I forgot."

I felt awkward, guessing what was on her mind.

"Nour never complained," she went on. "But she offered up a lot. Mansur, as you surely have experienced, can be domineering. If ever you need to speak to someone who knows the situation well, I'll be pleased to help. I've done it before."

I replied: "I thank you for your concerns. Mansur treats me with affection and respect. I'm glad of it because what he went through would have made better men than him bitter."

After a brief silence, I added: "Come to think of it, though, did *you* help at all in designing our new private oratory in Chelsea?"

She remembered well offering her services, but didn't know that the job had now been done.

Seeing the upset on my face, she quickly shifted to another confidence: "There's something else. It's about Jacqueline. I wasn't sure how to tell you, last July. I was afraid of what you might say about keeping the baby.

"Your suggestion to go and see a mummy's hand was the last thing I expected! You know, we actually *went* to Marlow, half-jokingly. Stuart said he loved relics and that kind of medieval stuff. He made up a whole scenario for a modern action movie.

"But when we came back home, he said that, while looking at the glazed casket, he'd felt as if the fragile piece of flesh inside was a baby in a little coffin, or in an incubator.

"We didn't change our minds, but our hearts. I'd like to say thank you, simply, for having listened to me last time. And what a joy, now, to see that you expect twins! Soon, they will play with Jacqueline."

I was looking forward to it.

I would also stand up to my husband, for his good, if he tried again to control me.

Chapter 124

It was a month since my trip to England.
I'd gradually shifted my attention from friends and schools to... my stomach. There was no use denying the evidence: it *was* big.
Very.
I'd stopped visiting our school sites. If Nasreen's count was correct, in less than four weeks – at Easter – I would hold in my arms little Francis and Margaret! I would have them baptised at once.
Fr. Paul had told me once that, while expecting him, his mother had cut the bottom of her wedding veil to sew a pall (a small square piece of material covering the chalice during Holy Mass, as he explained). She didn't know the sex of her baby yet, but hoped he would become a priest. He laid the pall over the chalice at his first Mass.
I thought that I would do the same for Francis, whatever his calling; and a mantilla for Margaret.

I was also preparing Talitha for her First Holy Communion.
It was planned to take place at Abu Ephrem's parish in June, but Litha was so motivated that her Eucharistic faith was more articulate than that of many adults. In fact, she'd asked several times since the beginning of Lent if she could not receive Jesus even *before* Easter.
I discussed the issue with Mansur and Abu Ephrem, who said that, since our wandering family wasn't really part of a parish community yet, Talitha might receive the sacrament on her own sooner, if circumstances allowed.
Meanwhile, the *Cedrus* was a very comfortable and safe place to spend the remainder of my pregnancy.
It allowed me to stay close to my busy husband, as the ship was his main office. She was also quick enough to avoid rough seas, which I wouldn't have liked *at all*, especially in my condition. After a few business cruises to Beirut, Dubai and Kuwait, the *Cedrus* was back in Cairo, in its usual mooring until the summer.

This was when news reached me of unrest in North Sudan, east of the Nile. After a full year of quiet, new acts of violence had occurred in villages, about an hour east of Osly.
Thank God, "my" girls were doing well at the school, and some of the older ones were actively preparing for distance examination, with a very tenuous hope of admission into an English university.
Was it one of those strange pregnancy cravings? I'd been rather good as far as food was concerned, but I fell for *flowers*.

I started missing Osly more and more and, when the gardener texted me that fourteen of my bougainvilleas had died, probably due to desert nights having been colder than usual over the winter that year, I felt an urge to go and remedy the situation (with or without a garden-belt).

I knew my flowers! And our good people down there were manifestly unskilled to take care of more delicate plants...

As a diversion perhaps, the gardener added that a young woman had come to look at Azim's monument and had left a large envelope with his name and mine on it.

A woman? With mail for Azim and I?

I couldn't take the risk of having the letter forwarded to me across the desert, could I? On the contrary, was it not an added motive for me to fly there and find out?

Mansur opposed my plan as *selfishly imprudent*.

I hadn't felt contradicted by him for a while and I wondered if in this latest instance he wasn't simply right and I wrong (after all, it *might* happen).

But I also remembered my resolution to resist his domineering tendency.

For the first time, I put my foot down...

Raising my voice deliberately, I said that he had *no* experience of what a pregnant woman needs; that I was feeling *seasick* onboard, even at the Cairo marina; and that if any more of my bougainvilleas died I would hold *him* responsible.

In truth, I was a bit unfair, but he was taken by surprise, having never seen me like that. He backed down, and it seemed as if I had won that battle.

In retrospect, I wish I *hadn't* – but who could have known?

On my consulting her, Nasreen sent us both a conciliatory email.

She stated that as a friend of our family she would not take sides, but that as far as travel regulations were concerned, airlines allowed women pregnant with twins to fly up to the end of the thirty-second week. I was still under the limit and would be fine, especially if we took the helicopter from Khartoum, (*driving* for hours along those rough roads in my condition being out of the question).

As a rearguard action, Mansur made it a condition that Abu Ephrem would come from Cairo with us and would give Talitha her First Holy Communion in the new chapel at Osly on *Laetare* Sunday. I liked his way of saving face, and I happily complied.

Litha was ecstatic! Our dear priest admitted to me that he was glad to take some rest, in anticipation of the busy Holy Week ahead. His young curate had energy to spare and could take care of things for a couple of days.

At Osly, the local priest had permission from the Bishop to come and offer Mass once a week (he lived forty minutes south), but Abu Ephrem would also assist local Catholics on his rare visits. On this occasion, he readily agreed to take Holy Communion to the mother of our trainee doctor, Arous, who was gravely ill, down in the village.

I couldn't wait to arrive at Osly.

Mansur had put the chapel under the patronage of St. Anthony, and the cherished icon that had saved his life was hanging against the wall above the altar. I was very glad to see that the place had become increasingly dear to my beloved. Memories of Nour and Azim visiting there two years earlier were attached to it, both for him and for me.

We felt that, out of the dozen schools run by the Al-Khoury Charitable Trust in various Middle-Eastern countries, St. Anthony's at "Osly-upon-the-Nile" was the one most special to our family.

Nasreen was in Khartoum that week.

She hoped to bring to bear the weight of the UN to obtain the pardon of a Christian woman sentenced to death by a Muslim tribunal for "apostasy". Adding to the horror, the accused was pregnant, and shackled by the ankles in her cell. I had heard of her case before and prayed ardently that she would live.

Nasreen would travel to Osly by helicopter with us, as she too felt the need for a break. She also liked our little oasis, nested in between the Nile and the desert (and she might not have totally given up on affiliating us to the UN). She confirmed the rumours of unrest to the east, but said that our region was absolutely fine.

Out of precaution however, several weeks earlier, Mansur had organised for armed men to reside at the school. Anyway, we would only stay for two days, as I meant to get back and stay still until birth in Cairo. I was expected the following month at the As-Salam International Hospital.

My ankles were swollen, even more than during the earlier months. Nasreen insisted that it was caused by my body holding on to more fluid than usual – nothing alarming for a pregnant woman. She would examine me at Osly.

But worse, my *face* now was looking puffy. How depressing! A quote from Scripture came back to my mind: *All the glory of the king's daughter is within.*

Still, to cheer me up, I'd decided to put on my favourite maternity dress, the dark blue one with the ivory polka dots.

Jeda once confided to me that, while aged seventeen in Teheran, she'd done "maternity catwalk" (she was hiding a cushion against her stomach!) for her aunt, Empress Farah of Iran, who was expecting her last child, Leila. I would not mind modelling in that context.

I don't know why, but when we flew off the deck of the *Cedrus* that tenth of March afternoon, on our way to Cairo Airport, I felt a bit sad. I'd spent so many important moments aboard that beautiful boat... Pregnancy made me emotional – I mean, more than usual – and slightly apprehensive, as Mum would say.

It took Mansur's jet less than two hours to reach Khartoum Airport, where we all boarded a large helicopter. Soon, I was thrilled to find myself high in the air with my husband and my three children (born and unborn), and our friends

Abu Ephrem and Nasreen.

Before long, the sun set on our left, far across the desert. For a moment, the horizon of sand and rock turned to red, and then to milky blue, under a fairly bright moon. There were many more lights in the sky than on the ground.

Talitha was asleep, her head on my lap.

Mansur was sitting next to me, on the other side, behind the pilot and the bodyguards. His condition made it still too risky for him to fly a helicopter across the desert.

I let my head lean against his shoulder.

Finding ourselves enclosed in that flying bubble of Plexiglas and resin, surrounded by the night, fostered a particular sensation of peace and security. There was less space inside than in my former cell at the Convent, and more of us sitting in it, like in a flying abdomen!

The dim light from the instrument panel projected shadows on our faces, like candles. We sat comfortably together, without talking, but Mansur's hand came to lay upon my bump with fatherly tenderness, speaking deeper than words.

I liked to feel him communicate with our children, through me. Presently, his hand moved to Talitha's little head, tight against my stomach. Truly, very thin was the veil between her, outside, and our twins within; or between us all in there and those on the other side of heaven.

Then I dozed off, I suppose.

Chapter 125

We must have been near our destination, when the helicopter started shaking and the moon disappeared. And the stars. In fact, soon we could see practically nothing at all. Mansur became concerned.

His pilot assured us that, having checked the weather forecast, no storm was signalled on our itinerary, although the windy season had just begun. Abu Ephrem was praying his rosary, and Nasreen had given up reading her tablet.

Our flight became bumpier and bumpier.

I prayed that we might not be caught in a sandstorm.

Mansur strapped Talitha in properly, right at the back, and I covered her with a blanket.

Worried as I was for my children, I tried to distract my mind...

My beautiful Egyptian hat with its protective veil might be put to good use at last – to shield Talitha.

But Mansur's bodyguard rang from the school. As far as I could understand from the pilot's answers, an unexpected sand cloud was indeed sweeping eastward and left little visibility.

Mansur was speaking loudly into the microphone: "Luke, there at Osly, are you already out of the *habūb*? ...Yes, the *sand cloud*... Okay, but it's still safer for us to land at the school rather than at random in the desert... Yes... Certainly... Although the area where the unrest occurred is much further east.

"Turn all the lights on to help us locate the landing zone, and have your men ready to find us quickly in case the sand cloud hasn't totally dispersed when we arrive... Say again?... Yes, then the risk to the rotor is limited. It's just been serviced anyway. Follow us on your screen and geolocate us when we land. I can't say more now."

Mansur tried to reassure me: "Darling, this will be over shortly. I went through worse two years ago, further north, in Egypt. We're nearly there."

But the conversation had left me acutely anxious, especially for our twins! The shaking and the noise only seemed to increase. One could see absolutely *nothing* outside the cockpit.

I remained silent, holding Mansur's shoulder very tight, until a formidable blast sounded in my ears and the moon, or the sun, or several of them, flashed into my eyes.

My head banged against the window and all became quiet and dark...

I can't say for how long I remained unconscious.

I woke up as our bodyguards were trying to extract me from the helicopter.

We had crashed into the Nile, in shallow water by the west bank, and sand was flying everywhere through the cockpit.

I glimpsed Mansur slumped beside me on the seat, showing no sign of life.

A wet sensation first made me think that water from the Nile had got into the helicopter, but I soon feared that my *own* waters had broken...

What of our babies!

Such a panic took possession of me that I even forgot to ask how Talitha was, tucked away under her blanket at the rear, while our guards were carrying me out of the aircraft.

Abu Ephrem had vanished, apparently; but Nasreen appeared.

The sand flying in our faces prevented me from seeing distinctly, and hearing her was difficult. I tried to tell her that I was losing the babies. Shouting to cover the sound of the wind, she urged me to calm down: "Clara, please stop yelling! We will soon be safe inside the building and then you will receive all the care you need."

With great difficulty, our group carried me to the shore, led by Luke, Mansur's head bodyguard.

As we began walking uphill towards the school, gunshots were heard from opposite directions. With sand still flying into my face, I could barely see further than my feet.

Our guards pressed me down onto the ground and crouched around me, weapons in hand. We waited several minutes without saying a word, while the wind finally abated.

Some silhouettes materialised in the distance, as if out of the floating dust, gliding down the bank towards us. Their masks reminded me of a Halloween show I'd taken part in with Emma and Sally, while at school: it was called "Danse Macabre."

Those silhouettes definitely looked hostile in their black overalls, and they carried guns. They dramatically outnumbered us.

I asked Luke to order our men *not* to resist, or we would all die.

One of them was lagging behind and hadn't heard Luke's order. He opened fire and was immediately shot. (If we needed confirmation of just how critical our situation was...)

As his body slumped lifeless to the ground, the others reluctantly threw down their weapons.

Torchlight was shone into our faces as a voice shouted in Arabic. Another one added in English: "It's *her* all right. But her *husband* is missing, the apostate. Find him at once, we have little time."

Please, let them not find Mansur – and let him be alive*!*

Where were our other armed men from the school?

Where was everybody?

Soon after, a jeep arrived by the bank. More masked men dragged out of it – oh no!

Abu Ephrem... bleeding.

Flashing a torch into the face of our dear priest, the leader said: "It's not Al-Khoury – keep looking, he can't be far."

As the jeep drove off, he shouted: "Keep their guards by the bank for now. But take those three to the river! Hurry up!"

My hands were quickly tied behind my back, and Nasreen, Abu Ephrem and I were dragged down to the Nile and made to kneel in the shallow water, perhaps five inches deep.

The moon had become visible again and its milky light coated the smashed cockpit of the half sunken aircraft, a few dozen yards away. Our broken shell...

One after the other, we were ordered to shout "Allahu Akbar." I would readily confess that "God is most great" in any language, Arabic or Chinese, but the implication then was that the Holy Trinity did not exist. For a Christian, it was apostasy.

Nasreen complied, assuring them that she was a Muslim. The leader seemed to have been aware of it.

As they spoke to one another, Abu Ephrem whispered to me: "Child: remember that God is love; that Jesus is God; and that the Host is Jesus. And now, I absolve you from all your sins, in the name of the Father, and of the Son, and of the Holy Ghost. And pray for me as I will for you. All shall be well!"

I said the quickest act of contrition in my life: "Jesus, mercy!"

The leader turned to Abu Ephrem: "You coward! You were running away when we caught you!"

He answered: "Running away? I was preparing to assist m..."

But the man interrupted him: "A sorcerer like you can't assist anyone. You mustn't! Never, ever! Is that your *magic*, hanging from your neck?"

The blade of his long dagger flashed in the moonlight against Abu Ephrem's already bloodied torso. Without awaiting a response, he cut off the pouch that the priest was carrying around his neck and opened it. He sounded delighted as he exclaimed: "Just as I guessed: magic bread! You see, I know all your tricks. That surprises you, doesn't it?

"Now, we don't have much time. Say *Allahu Akbar*, or die!"

Chapter 126

It happened very quickly, and simply.

The priest's voice was fatherly, when he said: "My friend, you are terribly mistaken." The other raged: "Stop your preaching, you pig! and say: *Allahu Akbar* – now!"

I heard in response: "Jesus, true God and true Man, Saviour of all mankind, have mercy on me a sinner, and on these your children!"

A vicious stroke followed, from the masked guard near the priest, but no sound. Our friend slowly fell on his back into the water, which grew darker all around him.

They forced me to go on kneeling there next to him, bathing in his blood.

Meanwhile, the masked men shouted from the helicopter. They'd found Mansur still unconscious. He *was* alive, then!

The leader shouted back: "Wake him up, if you can!" Then, turning towards me: "Here we are, Clara Al-Khoury, the wife of the fainted billionaire! We know all about you! And we won't trust your words, whatever you may confess. From you, it will take deeds."

Speaking to a couple of silhouettes standing to one side with a handheld spotlight, he snapped: "Start filming!"

One masked person took a device out of his backpack and directed it towards us.

Looking towards the camera, the leader warned: "Infidels of the West, this is our live channel. What you will see tonight is a lesson and a warning. Leave your sinful ways! Renounce prostitution and idolatry. Submit to the truth, join us and you will be saved from the wrath to come!"

He kicked the body of Abu Ephrem, then spread the burse out on his chest, placing the open pyx on it. Then he barked at me: "You, *spit* on the Christian magic bread, and you will live."

On the bloodied robe of my martyred friend, like upon an altar, my eyes caught the shape of the small white disc within the gilded receptacle. It shone like a tiny moon under the real one, so high above us. But, which one was more *real*?

I knew now why unconsciously I'd wished to come back here. I didn't mean to die. But I wanted to love, and to be loved further. To love to the end, as I had been loved. God had given me so much over the past two years. He'd showered upon me graces of every kind.

Images appeared in my memory.

My friendship with Azim; my conversion in the underground chapel; the funeral; the first schools; Talitha and Mansur; my ordeal in the car park and the conversion of my aggressor; my coma and fortunate recovery; my wedding and honeymoon; Margaret of York, the beloved martyr; then, my pregnancy...

I'd had a wonderful life. I wished it could continue, but...

"Think of your *children*!"
Who had spoken?
That was Nasreen's voice.
She was trying to help; but she caused the opposite.
My *children*!
All of a sudden, the horror of my position overwhelmed me! If I didn't desecrate the Host, my dear babies would surely die – with me.

Could I not prevent it? Would God not forgive me? Who would see, if I did as the fanatic demanded?

Who?

Well, I knew that I was being filmed, and probably broadcasted live through satellite. Those people needed the media. That was how modern terror worked. And, now, I was part of the action. And no stuntman offered to take my place...

Someone, please wake me from this nightmare!

But the terrorist was still pressing me. I couldn't escape choosing.

Even if no one was watching on earth, millions of saints and angels were, on high... And Our Blessed Lady. And the Most Holy Trinity. So many men had died – one just a minute ago – for *that* truth and its ultimate consequences.

I was tested to the extreme limit of my faith. My eyes were burning, so intently fixed were they upon the small white disc on Abu Ephrem's chest.

Was *this* truly my God? Would I die to assert it?

A voice yelled in my mind: *Bread! Bread! Bread! Don't die for a crumb! Let your children live!* My children? God knows that I would give anything for their life, starting with mine, a thousand times!

But if I gave in and now betrayed my Saviour, how long would it be until the same voice shouted even louder, against my babies: *Tissue! Tissue! Mere fetal tissue! Don't die for a lump! Just save your own life!*

And if after my God, I forsook my children, soon that voice would claim further, this time against me: *Dust! Nonsense! Farce! Don't prolong the sham! Get out of this life!* Actually I'd heard it before suggest just the same thing, and I'd listened, as the scar across my wrist still showed.

And at the end, upon my trampled God, my slaughtered children and my bled body, that voice would laugh out loud at my soul... in hell.

No.
God forbid.
I would speak to them, for the last time on earth, until we met above. A mother somewhere, perhaps Margaret Clitherow, was praying for me. She

inspired in my heart those words, a mother's prayer once read in the Bible: *Beloved children, heart of my heart! I know not how you were formed in my womb: for I neither gave you breath, nor soul, nor life, neither did I frame any of your limbs.*

I don't know how you grew in my womb, nor did I grant the breath of life to you or arrange what makes you who you are. But the Creator of the world, who shaped the beginning of man and devised the origin of all things, He will restore to you again in His mercy, both breath and life, as now we despise ourselves for the sake of His love!

I looked at the moon on high, so beautiful... and leaned slowly towards the pyx.

"Spit on it now, and you will live!"

My tongue touched the Sacred Host, I swallowed It and My God was in me, and closer to my dear children than ever! Abu Ephrem meant to bring the sacrament to a dying mother. His intention wouldn't be frustrated.

O sweet Jesus, Thy will be done.

Chapter 127

The leader was enraged.

His face darkened in wrath and he looked straight into the camera. "What shame possesses this whore! She doesn't even care about her child! Watch and learn, then, O infidels, the fate of all who choose superstition over truth!"

Then, turning to the man holding me, he drew his long blade and said deliberately: "Give her to me!"

His rough hands were dragging my head back, baring my throat. *O Lord, into your hands I commit my spirit...* I waited for the stroke, seeing men and stars from a dizzying angle.

And from that strange angle, I saw the man who had killed Abu Ephrem raise his pistol and shoot ...his leader.

As I dropped limply towards the water, a fusillade of gunshots sounded all around... then my head plunged under the surface and everything faded to black.

Hands were dragging at me, pulling me up out of the water... my head broke the surface... I was being rushed towards our tiny hospital and down into the basement theatre; I stumbled, almost being dragged. The sound of rattling wheels rang in my ears, but I could see no gurney...

Nasreen was whispering into my ear: "I'm certain that the one filming is actually Agent N'Guyen. The C.I.A. must have sent her to infiltrate, and she will soon intervene. But we must buy time, Clara! Whatever happens, whatever I say or do, trust me!"

Agent N'Guyen? Was that not too good to be true? Although we were already inside the building, I couldn't take my eyes off the shrinking shape of the dear priest in the water, the moonlit pyx on his chest – empty. His heart beat in me. Why could I see him still?

I could hear a voice, speaking urgently... *get her in, get her in here, quickly...* it sounded like Nasreen, but her mouth wasn't moving.

Five of our captors entered the theatre, pushing Nasreen in, and locking the heavy door behind them – captors? – was the leader not just killed? Am I still a prisoner? My *babies*... I began to struggle as hard as I could.

"Tie her down!" – a woman's voice! She repeated the command in Arabic. She sounded familiar, frighteningly so. Her skinny overall revealed a thin and athletic body. She seemed to be in charge. Agent N'Guyen? With her mask on, I couldn't tell.

Tie her down... tie her down... we have no choice... the order continued, ringing in my ears, though the woman had stopped speaking...

As they were tying my limbs against the operating table, Nasreen pleaded on my behalf: "She may die of infection if her children aren't delivered now. I think her waters have broken. Let me help her!"

The woman leader snarled at us: "*Help* her? We will make an example of her! She will be tried."

Where had I heard that voice? They were tearing off my dark blue polka dot dress and spreading over me a wide orange burnous, like a shroud. I'd seen their victims clothed in that colour before. It was part of their ritual, which looked rather impressive when watched on a screen.

...*Cut it, just cut it*... said the voices in my ears.

Turning to the camera, the woman proclaimed: "Let the trial begin. I will accuse; Dr. Yasir – that's your name, isn't it – will defend; and our audience will judge.

"Clara Cumberhart, you are charged with the felony of wilful seduction of two good Muslim men, leading them away from their fathers' faith through the vilest means. Defence, what do you say? Look at the camera!"

Nasreen was at a loss: "This is totally out of place. You've no jurisdiction. And it's all nonsense! Who are you to say she's seduced anyone?"

The leader tore off her mask, and a splendid red mane spread over her shoulders: "Because I saw it! I was there when she danced by the Sphinx at Giza."

I couldn't believe it. If a nightmare is a bad dream, *what* do you call the most horrendous of all possible nightmares? Ruth Sheehan! And she looked sublime: as death. How on earth had she turned into a jihadi bride! Just nine months earlier, she was my husband's nurse!

Nasreen objected: "Under Sharia Law, a woman's testimony is worth half that of a man. You must produce two witnesses of your claim for it to be valid evidence. But your accomplices killed Azim; and I can't see Mansur supporting your allegation."

Ruth simply laughed: "Time's running out. The case is clear and I demand that the accused should be flogged a hundred times and stoned to death as the law foresees in cases of fornication, her marriage being null and void under the current legislation; and that her accomplice – the one she calls her husband – should be crucified as an apostate."

Nasreen was flabbergasted. After a little silence she said, looking straight into the camera: "I'm a Muslim myself, and I cannot accept that punishments of such gravity should be inflicted so summarily. If you're a Muslim and are watching this now, or later, know that millions of my fellow believers support my views."

...*Hurry up! Haven't you found the... Aren't they ready yet...* whispered the voices. Who was speaking?

Ruth challenged her: "Tell us your views then, Doctor, if you dare!"

Nasreen closed her eyes for a while, as if praying, and then affirmed, looking at the camera: "My Muslim brethren, Allah, the Almighty, Who created the minds and the throats even of unbelievers can't wish us to cut their throats after we have failed to persuade their minds – even less so *before* we have peacefully tried to explain our reasons.

"The Most High would never lower Himself to becoming mere *flesh*, as the Christians believe! He is the divine Spirit. Well then, *spiritual* arguments are those in keeping with His nature, not *muscular* ones."

Ruth interrupted: "Very well, for the sake of the women of the West who are watching us now, we wish this judgment to be exemplarily fair.

"Hence, your appeal is granted, as follows. If the accused converted, submitted, and got married, she would be considered a Muslim mother and would be allowed to give birth.

"Since she refuses, let the fruit of her fornication be *erased*, that she may not answer for her crime at the cost of her life. She will be free to go her own way, as will her accomplice.

"Dr. Yasir, we empower you to proceed with the operation here and now and, as a last token of our clemency, we will assist you according to our good medical training."

Chapter 128

What? I could not be hearing correctly!

Nasreen and Ruth were arguing, Nasreen declaring that I would never consent to such termination of the life I bore, even to save my own life.

Ruth just looked at her scornfully, laying her hand on my stomach: "How unprofessional, Doctor! You know full well that whatever she hides under my fingers doesn't meet the legal criteria in force across this territory to qualify as *offspring*. By law, there is nothing in there but *fetal matter*. No doubt you are familiar with the consequences."

Nasreen was deadly pale when she finally admitted: "As an obstetrician I have no objection to the procedure – but as a Muslim, I emphatically oppose the validity of this sentence.

"In this very country, the Islamic court permitted eight-month-pregnant Meriam Ibrahim to give birth, before she was supposed to be hanged for apostasy. Therefore, unless you confirm that my religion has nothing to do with this, I will *not* cooperate."

Ruth conceded: "Didn't you take the Hippocratic Oath? Even though you claim to keep your faith out of this, at least do your duty as a physician! It's her, or her foetus. Only you can save the life of this woman, and of her accomplice."

...save her life... we must proceed quickly... Who was whispering?

Hesitantly, Nasreen stepped nearer, and leaned towards me. She would take care of me. I could smell her strong Chanel N°5 perfume, just like the first time on the plane, when I'd woken up after my collapse.

Collapse? Was I dreaming? Was I to awake soon? I felt it was high time.

Without meeting my eyes, she whispered: "Clara, I'm terribly sorry, but I will have to proceed, for your own good. I commit to surgically safe assistance. There will be other occasions to give birth, I promise you. This isn't China! Your reproductive powers won't be affected. This is only postponing things for you."

Was it so? She was betraying me! Help! Help anyone! Was my brief suspicion at San Antonio Airport confirmed after all? Was Nasreen a murderess infiltrated among doctors, rather than the opposite? Had she fooled me from the start?

My hands being tied, I could not grab her sleeve, but I begged her with all the strength in my heart: "Nasreen, how can you say that you value me, when you intend to act so crucially against my will and against innocent lives?

"You wrote and said that those operations 'should never be coerced.' I'm surely not sick and I want my children; and I *forbid* you to terminate their lives!"

She looked deeply embarrassed, as she replied: "Clara, please don't quote my former positions, stated in different contexts. What choice do I have? The law defines your children as fetal tissues.

"Besides, one should not call this *coercion* if, above the individual, a medical authority, or, further above it, the State, deemed the procedure beneficial to the public interest. Then in conscience, every subordinate level should collaborate, and personal reluctance, while understandable, should be overcome. Regrettably, we are in just that situation."

She nodded to Ruth, and both put on surgical gloves and masks. Nasreen was now barely identifiable among the captors standing around me. Their masks were black and hers green, just a paler shade. I tried to yell and started to struggle again, but no sound would come out of my throat.

...Quickly... give her some of the...

I felt the sting of a syringe and, all of a sudden, became very relaxed.

Why did the thought of Margaret, my Pearl of York, then flash into my memory? Our ordeals were similar. Instead of the door of her house though, that camera was remotely pressing against my skin with no discretion or mercy. That *was* heavy!

The sentence and its execution, Ruth had announced, were to be broadcasted live across the globe, as a warning and a lesson. May my fellow-women learn, then! No less importantly, may they pray for me, and for the children...

Ruth produced a dagger and laid it against my throat. My eyes almost crossed as I took in the decoration on the hilt – a snake-head hilt I'd seen before in Jonathan's hand...

With a flick, Ruth – *snap* – cut through my necklace. The pearls rolled along my limbs in every direction as if for shelter, camouflaged among the printed dots of my polka dress (or what remained of it), under the burnous.

...Yes... give it to me... better out of the way... Who said that?

But the five rubies, Ruth swiftly scooped up! Shortly, she would pluck two more gems, also a gift from my husband, but infinitely more valuable, out of my stomach.

Thank God, I realised, she'd left intact my Brown Scapular. That thought spread over my soul as a wave of soothing warmth. Whatever happened, I remained under the protection of the best of mothers.

She wasn't pledged to save us from earthly death, but from an eternal one. She would hold my mind and my will in Her faithful hands, as She had assisted Her own Son in His Passion.

Jesu! Jesu! Jesu! Have mercy on me!

All that followed can't have lasted longer than a few seconds, and yet my thoughts seemed to grow in accuracy and sharpness as the horror loomed closer. My anguish forbade speech, or at least I couldn't hear myself.

But in my conscience, possessed by womanly indignation, my protest blasted out...

Chapter 129

Woe to me and to you!

The holiest place in me, you are desecrating! Its walls had been tenderly lined with membranes more precious than the finest cedar wood but, leaving it void of the cherished presence, you bring in instead the abomination of desolation!

Your surgical gloves are but sullied boots, splashing into the clear water of my womb! Your scalpels are poisoned fangs, raking a woman's glory.

The most secure nook in the world, where innocents are nurtured in peace, you turn into a haunted den, a labyrinth where a beastly Minotaur dispatches young princes and fair princesses!

Children! My children! Go and hide at the rear! Move away from the access! Make your tiny shape smaller if you can, under the folds of my mantle, and lay still until danger is past!

They will show no mercy! Modern Cleopatras, they will hunt my pearls down and drop them as sweeteners to dissolve in the vinegar of their lies – as if ultimately, the snake would not bite them! May they gulp me alive then, miserable oyster, as already they've discarded your father like one more empty shell!

What profit can they make? Your skin is too tender and tragically too small. They will sell off your cells as rich in energy! They will burn you for heat in the hospital stoves!

Ruth was now spreading sanitizer over my lower abdomen. Why? Why was she putting it there…?

I went on: *The accuser's finger is upon their stomachs: can they not read its mark? Under their scrubs and gowns, is it not a navel? How did it come to gape across our adult skin?*

Were we not once allowed to nest and grow and reach the blessed light of day? Were we not spared? Were we not protected? Were we not loved? Were we not deemed human?

We strike our breast about the tragedies of war and about deadly ideologies and wail 'Never again!' – while we circle our wombs with razor barbed wire and deny those inside human citizenship!

We mourn the odious loss of abused innocence – for those of our children whom we allowed to live! We talk of preventing further molestation – ignoring the carnage perpetrated daily where cameras won't film and where justice is shunned!

We set up peace meetings, campaign for cease-fires, singing 'Peace be with us!' – while all around the globe, and every night and day, weapons of mass destruction butcher silent unborn – the dreaded invaders of our selfish comfort!

We spend gold on our pets in our supermarkets; we walk them to the park for a well deserved stroll – by the abortion mill...

I pleaded inwardly: *O women of the west, of the north and the south, of the east and the moon and the sun if you wish: we were all made by God and none of us was born outside His embrace!*

Let not our soul suffer the ultimate assault. Life made us. How could we be less alive when accepting to carry life in our turn? Human life. Let us not call 'matter' the baby we shelter – or else, just call 'immaterial' whatever you cherish!

Gloved claws entered into me, like thieves into Fort Knox or terrorists in a nuclear reactor. My riches, my power, my life as a mother was being torn from me, turning me into a living sarcophagus. They might as well display me at the museum in Cairo, until I returned to dust...

Many women aren't granted the joy of becoming mothers; some renounce it for an even greater love. But whenever nature and circumstances – even unplanned or adverse – make us the living containers of the most innocent and most vulnerable creatures in this hostile world, please, let none of us call 'dust' and 'waste' the tiny human to whom we are everything!

At what stage of our life before birth were we malignant tumours – that we should treat as such the life growing in us? Rather, from conception, let us acknowledge, cherish and protect our greatest treasure: this little boy, that little girl – or both, as in my case! Let us bring life into the light.

Chapter 130

There was nothing more I could do, but pray.
Words came back to my memory: *Hope in none other, have I had ever, but in Thou Saviour...* I closed my eyes, abandoning myself to God's holy will.
May my sacrifice be of some merit, please God, for the protection of so many innocents, and for the conversion of so many perpetrators.
Francis! Margaret! My babies! I'd offered up all: the life of my life...
...Carefully... that's it... just a little more...
I was floating, as described in near-death experiences. Only later did I put words to my sensations. My heart felt... lucidly disencumbered.

The sequence turned into a holy dream after the nightmare, for the room being underground, no bright sky could have shown, even less so a... tall white deer!
"What a beautiful animal... It stands unharnessed: it can't be Christmas then. I know these gentle friends smiling on either side. Katarina; Anthony. Nour; Azim! Where have you been all this time?"
A stirring fragrance reached my nostrils, as of lilies distilled with incense. Surely, antlers don't normally blossom. But those on my deer were now covered with petals, which started falling all around as snowflakes, draping me and my flattened stomach with graceful folds, and soothing freshness.

God had shown mercy to me. The most displeasing sound to the ears of strangers, and the most exquisite music for a first-time mother – called me back to life. An infant, crying. Crying loud. An infant alive.
Not crying anymore, but... No! Unthinkable! That baby had just been laid against my breast, and... sucked it. Another cry. Another infant. Another breast. Another little mouth drinking me alive!
And my arms untied eventually. My arms gently arranged around my children, and a warm blanket over the three of us.
Where was I? What had happened? Was this a dream? Definitely, the nightmare had stopped. If it was dream, I wouldn't wake up, ever! I was a mother, and my babies lay against me. We were skin to skin, and we were alive!
My head ached. But I didn't mind. My stomach ached. But who cared? I had to try and open my eyes. At least one... The light was dim. Just as well.
A man's face smiled at me, from a chair next to my bed. His arm was bandaged; his cheeks bruised; his eyes tearful... In fact, I liked his face very much. I would have liked to know him better, soon.
I felt as if I'd been through this all before. No lilies around but – yes: bougainvilleas!

"And now, let me see... I know *who* you are. Are you not... my husband?"

My husband? Next to me? And smiling? Then, there couldn't be any danger anymore?

Mansur! Mansur! Mansur!

His free arm came around me. Around us! While another small arm embraced me – Litha! So you escaped! You were hidden at the back of the helicopter.

I felt as if I'd crawled across the desert alone...

Daddy now nodded at another man. This was impossible! I had seen him down in the river. I had seen him fall. Under the blanket covering his shoulders, I now could see his djellaba still red with blood. Was he... Could he be Abu Ephrem? Yes, I knew this long beard. He smiled, also with moist eyes...

What was the matter with them all? He explained that, with my permission, it would be good to baptise the children immediately, as Mansur suggested. Of course I agreed. Isn't Baptism the most important gift to a newborn babe? Even more than milk?

Is God not impatient – so to speak – to embrace them as His adopted children? I wouldn't have kept my Saviour waiting for one second: "Let Holy Mother Church nurture the souls of my babes with the water of grace, one after the other, while happy mother Clara feeds their bodies with milk: *As newborn babes, desire the rational milk without guile...*"

I soon heard a music that sounded even more wonderful, if possible, than the one which had woken me up a few minutes earlier: "Francis Anthony Yusuf Athanasius Mary, I baptise you in the name of the Father, and of the Son, and of the Holy Ghost.

"Margaret Lucy Madeleine Katarina Mary, I baptise you in the name of the Father, and of the Son, and of the Holy Ghost."

What a joy! They were God's!

Now I could die...

The sun was rising.

Chapter 131

Everything was still. Through the open window I could see sand spread everywhere over the patio and grounds.

Some grains even fell from my hair.

It was merely a squall, they said, not a full sandstorm.

I'd slept for several hours and could now hear a few birds chirping. They started early down here. In three weeks it would be Easter. Today was *Laetare* Sunday.

Mansur still looked very shaken by our ordeal.

He told me in outline what happened.

We'd met with a sand cloud on our approach to Osly. It wasn't dense enough to damage the rotor, but it suppressed visibility and destabilised the aircraft when it began to descend.

The pilot missed our landing zone and touched down into the shallow water by the ford nearby. It was a blessing in disguise, as the water absorbed most of the impact and prevented fire.

But what if we'd fallen into deep water, rather than by the bank? I later realised that it was about the same area where, a few months earlier, Nepomucen and I had stood, when he was describing the invisible presence of God's army around us.

The Scimitars had attacked Osly as we were approaching.

Obviously, somebody local, a member of staff or a villager, had leaked to the enemy the news of our impromptu flight to the school.

The C.I.A. had intercepted a message in which the leaders of the Sobek network and of the Scimitars planned to meet at Osly that evening to celebrate our capture!

Code-named *Operation Omen*, their attack was intended to shock international public opinion. They meant to broadcast the abduction, trial and execution of the two of us well-known philanthropists, convicting us of "culpably spreading Christian influence" across Muslim countries.

The American and Egyptian Intelligence Agencies thought it a unique opportunity to catch *both* leaders, never before known to have been in the same place at the same time. Their eagerness explained why they dared to use our family as *bait*! – telling us *nothing* of the forthcoming threat...

In preparation, a full one hundred commandoes had been secretly deployed. They allowed us to be captured, waiting for the two leaders to arrive. But neither of the real bosses, whether of the Scimitars or of Sobek, was to be found anywhere.

Dr. Yasir described what had followed our crash landing. Our armed men managed to locate us down by the Nile and rescue us quickly. More sand than water had got into the cockpit, coating us passengers with crusty mud.

I seemed to be knocked out, just like Mansur, my right temple heavily swollen and ecchymosed. They couldn't assess on site how badly hurt we were, so Abu Ephrem, superficially wounded, walked straight to the chapel to bring back the Blessed Sacrament and give me the Rite of the Dying (again).

Mansur was knocked out but, thankfully, he "only" had a broken arm and a superficial wound to his head, while his spine hadn't suffered.

Strapped in at the rear, Talitha was left with bruises caused by her seatbelt, but nothing more. The Scimitars were so pleased to have found Mansur (still unconscious) in the helicopter that they didn't properly check the back seat. There, Talitha's small form was hidden under the blanket. She'd pulled it right over her head, first against the sand flying everywhere, and later in her terror of the armed men.

And Abu Ephrem? While we were kneeling in the river, Agent Bloomen was the one who had "killed" him. Pretending to strike a lethal blow, he'd only cut him superficially, breathing in his ear the moment before the stroke: "Play dead, *right now*..."

According to their message intercepted by the C.I.A., the Scimitars and Sobek bosses planned to make a show of our death.

Why hadn't they turned up for our imminent execution?

This had all been in vain...

The C.I.A.'s plan having failed, exposing our lives any longer had become useless. Throwing off the mask, Agent Bloomen shot my executioner *in extremis*, immediately backed up by the hidden commandoes (including frogmen immersed behind the reeds).

Saving us was the very *least* they could do, after having so cynically used us as *bait*! Granted, our helicopter crash wasn't *their* fault. But to think that they coldly let us fall into such a trap instead of warning us...

We all nearly died – as one of our guards did for real, trying to protect us. May he rest in peace.

As soon as we'd been set free, I was hurried from the Nile into our hospital theatre, where Nasreen examined me. She was chiefly concerned for the twins, especially after ascertaining that my waters *had* broken.

She couldn't see much on the ultrasound and feared an infection, a risk increased by my immersion in the Nile. I was feverish and spoke incoherently. Since I was due merely three weeks later, early delivery wouldn't put the babies at risk. She performed an emergency c-section.

I was tied up so that, in my delirium, I wouldn't impede the operation. No one had filmed anything at the theatre. And – a capital point – strictly *no* redhaired nurse had assisted Nasreen, just Arous our local trainee.

Truly? I could have sworn I had *seen*... Ruth Sheehan!

Poor Nasreen must have found me very ungrateful when I jumped and shrieked at her on her first entering the room after my awakening. It took a little while to convince me that she meant to help, rather than harm me. She was bringing me back my precious necklace, removed by Arous prior to the operation.

I felt that her smile was unconvincing, as if she knew better than I what a narrow escape we'd had, and was trying not to upset me retrospectively. Mansur was sitting right by my bedside, showing no sign of alarm, but looking equally downcast.

Despite my joy at holding Francis and Margaret against me, I was exhausted. Besides, I vaguely remembered some of Nasreen's nightmarish replies to "Ruth" (to Arous, in reality) and found some of them perplexingly consistent with what I knew of her ethical convictions.

There would be a time to discuss this in depth.

Meanwhile, Arous was doing her best to nurse the wounded, but she needed extra help, since the military doctor had left with the commandoes. Mansur had hired a doctor and a nurse from Khartoum to spend the next couple of days at Osly while I recuperated. They were on their way.

After a quick inspection and an encouraging but weary smile, Nasreen left us alone with our babies. I expected Mansur to ask if I wanted my necklace on again, as he'd done in the past on various occasions.

But he didn't seem to notice it.

When I reminded him that we hadn't decided on the godparents yet, he gave a pained smile and said: "Just as well, or they could have got shot like two years ago, at Azim's baptism. This time at least, my *wife* survived."

He laid his hand on my shoulder, while against my chest, tenderly held in my arms, our two most precious gems were as secure as ever.

Chapter 132

Alone for the first time, I took a look at my stomach.

Mansur had left me to rest, after Arous had carried the twins to sleep in their cradles in the next room.

My skin told another story, or a complementary part of the same narrative. Unfastening my watch, I laid my wrist against my abdomen.

Scar against scar.

The one across my limb betrayed my teenage loneliness. The wider one on my abdomen exalted motherhood. The former meant death escaped; the latter showed life shared.

I mentally followed the path from one to the other, made of painful stitches: the scars from the flogging on Azim's chest, shoulders and side, and the impacts of bullets all over; those on Nour's body; and on Mansur's torso...

I was in awe.

God had allowed the wickedness of assassins and the helplessness of victims to mark our skins in such a tragic way.

Was it devilish scribbling or sacred writing?

Hellish tattooing or providential calligraphy?

One thing was certain, the story it told was no rosy one, but no dark one either. All along, I sensed, light had been at work, and no shadows would ever shroud its rising.

Arous entered to ask if I wished to attend Holy Mass.

Mass? Was it Sunday? Ah, yes: three weeks to Easter. I had forgotten.

I was exhausted and had assumed that our dear priest wouldn't be able to offer Mass so soon. Even though his two wounds were superficial, he'd been badly shaken and would need weeks to recuperate, if not months.

But he wouldn't be deterred: "I may not be able to genuflect or even bow, but this day, of all days, the sacrifice of Christ on Calvary *must* be offered anew, in reparation and intercession. Later, my child, you'll understand."

He added that it was better for Talitha not to postpone her First Holy Communion, which had been planned for that day. Mansur agreed. The sacrament would bring her grace and joy to help her overcome the shock of the accident, and would also help our family recover after the ordeal.

Abu Ephrem had suggested offering Holy Mass in my room, so as to keep me and the babies warm and comfortable, but I felt well enough to be wheeled on my bed to the chapel at the end of the corridor.

For safety reasons, Mansur explained, no pupils attended – no one from the village, either (only our local staff). I regretted it for Talitha. But her young friends sent a cake they'd baked for the occasion, the previous day.

Abu Ephrem wore rose and the altar was dressed in the same colour.

What a joy to see my little Talitha – from now on, the oldest of my three – kneel in her white dress at the rail, and receive our Blessed Lord for the very first time! And what an added blessing that her two siblings were with her, witnessing their very first Holy Mass ever, on their first day under God's sun.

The readings were so uplifting: *Rejoice with Jerusalem, and be glad with her, all you that love her: rejoice for joy with her, all you that mourn for her. That you may suck, and be filled with the breasts of her consolations.*

Abu Ephrem sounded as if in mourning, though – as did everyone else but Talitha and I. What a strange contrast it was!

For the first time ever, I saw him *sit down* to preach.

With a shaking voice, he told us that the Holy Gospel that Sunday – the multiplication of the loaves – prefigured the Holy Eucharist: "Our Lord Jesus," he remarked, "teaches His apostles and us that, to come near us and feed us with His love, He will make Himself present even within the small dimensions of a crumb."

He stopped, breathing heavily. I feared he wouldn't be able to complete the Mass.

After a silence, he resumed: "The Lord commands: 'Gather up the fragments that remain, lest they be lost.' That is His loving warning. We will render an account of our treatment of His hidden presence, whether sacramental in the Host, or spiritual in the most vulnerable of His children.

"The more we believe in the first, the less we can ignore the second."

Abu Ephrem had just concluded his sermon when, changing his mind, he added with a very grave face: "My children, Christ's presence in the Holy Eucharist is our strongest hope in the midst of adversity."

Despite the heavy atmosphere, despite my own pain and my trauma, joy reigned in my heart.

I gathered my twins against me, feeling like a momentary reflection of the New Jerusalem, the mystical Bride of Jesus: His Church. I gave thanks for being a tiny but not quite barren branch of the Vine, Christ's mysterious and all-encompassing love network. For the first time I received my Lord lying down, due to my condition.

I was forever His.

The icon of St. Anthony hung above the altar. The impact of bullets still showed. They would soon be two years old. After Holy Mass, I was wheeled back into my room. My dear husband was holding me. I fell asleep, and didn't dream.

Mansur had informed our close relatives and friends of the happy births.

A few days later, a parcel reached me from France. I don't know why it had been sent to the Khartoum Nunciature, via the diplomatic bag. Lewis Kanisah, the Nuncio's chauffeur, had delivered it.

I tried not to laugh (bad for the scar across my stomach!) on reading the first line in Fr. Paul's note: *Dear Daughter in Christ, congratulations on the happy birth of your triplets.* Thank you, dear Father: but I only had *twins*, actually. Men are all the same... Since they don't have a womb with which to carry life, they can be grossly inattentive to our womanly achievements. I'm sure that they don't mean to be careless, though.

However, I was proven wrong again in my judgement of character when reading further down:

Dear Clara, Francisco agreed that it was just as well for me to write rather than him. He allowed me to share the following.

Was baptised on Laetare *Sunday, the day when your twins were born. Due to his circumstances, I preferred to proceed before Passiontide to secure quiet for his sake. After his initial visits nine months ago, seemed to lose interest, or courage. I had to burn a lot of incense.*

As you known, his past was like an infected wound, deep in his soul. He disappeared for two months, apparently for choreographic work in San Francisco. When he came back, I saw that he was ready to commit. Knew quite a lot about the faith.

Is particularly devoted to the Immaculate Heart of Mary. He's left Paris now, to be some kind of a caretaker in Portugal, at Fatima. He chose Francisco as his baptismal name, after the little Fatima seer. We keep in contact. The enclosed, he said, belongs to you.

Affectionately, Fr. Paul the Cleaner.

There was a postscript in different handwriting:

With the gratitude of a spiritual son who was lost, and who was found again, through the self-denial and mercy of a motherly soul.

Francisco – Unworthy child of the Church.

I unfolded what proved to be... a *burnous*. It wasn't orange, but creamy white. I had to try it on... Yes, it really suited me. I'd forgotten. It was wide enough to cover me and my babies, and my Litha; and even my beloved husband. All was well. And... I would soon order new bougainvillea plants to be delivered!

As soon as I could walk, I would spread Azim's fifty dried petals: they belonged here (sand grains, I bet, reaching everywhere, would be found even inside the envelope).

Chapter 133

An envelope...
All of a sudden, I recalled the text message sent to me by the gardener, a mere few days earlier (although it felt like years).
Was it not about some woman leaving by Azim's monument a letter, with his name and mine on it? Not knowing what to expect, I preferred not to involve Mansur and I asked Arous to bring it to me.
She laid it by my bed as I was asleep.
I caught sight of it on awakening and remembered my curiosity. What could it contain? It was a thick packet made of brown paper. Only the names *Azim & Clara* showed, in rather elegant handwriting – probably a woman's.

It made me rather suspicious.
Was it a complaint against my dear friend? Worse, was it a revelation casting an unpleasant shade on him? Jumping out of nowhere like a Jack-in-the-box, the most dreadful thought crossed my mind... What if...
What if certain insinuations in a certain car park were not totally invented? Was it not precisely here, at Osly, that Azim and Nour had become lovers – well, according to Jonathan. But he'd denied it afterwards! How absurd of me. I tried to check my apprehension: *Clara dear, why is your imagination still so quick to expect the worst?*
Although, admittedly, I wished I'd suspected the worst on *previous* occasions, like during my last evening with Jonathan. Thus, my fear wasn't necessarily unfounded. What if my pure and heroic Azim hadn't been the model and inspiration I still cherished in my heart?
My fingers weighed the envelope, which I couldn't persuade myself to open. It could wait, could it not? As I laid it aside (rather cowardly), I found other words written at the back: *Jamila Nebankh, c/o Abu Ephrem, Risen Christ Church, al-Warraq, Greater Cairo, Egypt.* A great warmth washed over me as I realised...

Jamila. His sister!
He'd wanted me to meet her.
And she'd come all the way to this desert in Sudan, taking great risks, to pay homage to her fallen brother among the children he'd saved. I opened the envelope and drew out of it a leather-bound volume.
Intricate embossed designs adorned its front cover. Inside, I saw many pages covered with handwriting I immediately recognised, despite the language being – Arabic! From right to left, I presumed, apart from the numbers on the top of every page. Were those perhaps dates?

It was a diary! Azim's diary.

The last entry, nearly two years ago, shifted to English: *June 1st. Clara dearest, if you're reading these words, you know by now how much closer I'm to you than we ever dreamed of. I asked Jamila to bring this journal to you if anything happened to me. I've prayed that you may find God and be fulfilled in His love, now and forever. By the time you read this, I hope to have been called deep into His Sacred Heart. My little Asian star, meet me soon in that Sun.*

Looking at the picture of Azim and his sister, inserted in the last page, I whispered: "Beautiful Jamila, held tight by your brother. Thank you, unknown sister, for having shared him with me. I love your brown eyes, even though they seem a bit sad. Have I not met you before at Osly?

"In fact, you look strikingly like the young Arab woman who accompanied Agent N'Guyen on her first visit here! Could you be the same person? I will look for you when I get back; if you wish. In a way, you are here."

Certainly, *Azim* was here. All of us connected through the mystical vine, God's all-encompassing network of love, were present to each other in Him. We breathed the One Who is. We inhaled His Spirit. He inspired our lives. We were made His members.

As I shut the diary, I became aware of a change in me.
Something was detaching itself from my soul, as if peeling off.
What was it?
Fear.
Fear?
How strange to name it and yet not to be frightened. It was happening very peacefully; almost unnoticeably. I realised that I'd lived for years with some level of fear; perhaps all my life, in various ways. But only now, as fear was unexpectedly falling away from my soul, was I able to acknowledge it.

What could I compare it to? Fear was to my soul like the gold wrapping around St. Anthony's icon. Once the treasured picture reached its destination, here at Osly, the paper could go.

Lying on my bed with my scarred stomach, I felt a bit like a replica of the sacred icon with its bullet holes, hanging in our chapel.

I must have fallen asleep since, through the window, the sun was now setting.

Judging from how still the bougainvilleas stood, the wind had settled. On the patio, a desert bird was playfully hopping in the deep layer of sand yet to be swept away. It flew off – a lark? – as Mansur walked into the room with Nasreen, each carrying a (hungry) baby!

Talitha was the only one joyful.

Her resilience was miraculous, after such a trauma as the crash and the attack. Definitely, maintaining her Holy Communion had been the right decision. In comparison, all the adults looked distressed.

Our little daughter dropped the blinds, as she likes doing.

Nasreen checked that I was well and discreetly departed, leaving the five of us as one family. What a blessing to be there, together, even though bruised, fractured, traumatized, torn open and stitched up.

Stranded in Sudan then – for want of a new helicopter – but not planning a journey soon anyway. Unlike Nasreen, I recalled, and Abu Ephrem... On our way from Khartoum, she'd envisaged travelling back with him. Now she would wait until Friday, when the doctor and the nurse would arrive.

Note: suggest that he should take up her offer, even if it means flying back to Cairo one day later than he'd planned. Who knows, the good doctor might have important questions to ask a man of God on the way.

Little did I suspect that Cairo was no more. There'd be no going back.

Chapter 134

Cairo?

Alas, what was left of Cairo – and of Egypt!

I might have been the only one in the world unaware of what was happening.

Nasreen was adamant that my phone and tablet would be restored to me only when I was stronger; while television, radio and newspapers were also kept away from me. Later I understood why they'd waited five days before breaking the news to me.

In my condition, and after my ordeal, it was essential that not only my body but also my mind should rest.

On seeing their faces so gloomy when we had all survived (apart from our poor guard), I asked them several times what the matter was. They must have made huge efforts to spare me the truth. Thankfully, Talitha was also kept in ignorance, and was sent to spend as much time with me as possible, to cheer me up.

The following Friday, Mansur disclosed the truth.

The night of the attack, after our aggressors had been defeated, all were safe and my twins safely born.

Before dawn, Agent N'Guyen rushed in, asking to speak with Mansur and Nasreen at once. She asked if they'd heard the news. Far from it, so exhausted were they: they'd simply tried to sleep a couple of hours, when not checking on me.

Agent N'Guyen announced: "They've blown up the Aswan Dam!

"It happened last night. The attack here was a mere *diversion* to distract the Intelligence. Their message was faked. *Operation Omen* was a setup from the start. To make it more credible, they even sacrificed their own men, not telling them that possibly our commandoes were awaiting them.

"The leaders of the Scimitars and of Sobek *never* meant to meet here. I'm sorry that Agent Bloomen had to wait until the last moment to intervene. We were still hoping to catch their leaders, which could have saved thousands of lives. But they tricked *us* instead.

"I came to tell you to keep away from Cairo. In fact, stay out of Egypt. What's happening is likely to escalate dramatically in the next few days, and violence will surely erupt."

Abu Ephrem arrived, having just heard the news. Stunned, the priest said: "The Aswan Dam! How could they? My children, the apocalypse has started."

They all looked at each other in utter dismay.

Agent N'Guyen went on: "The tidal wave has already destroyed a third of the Nile Valley and should reach Cairo shortly. It won't be high by then, but it's loaded with debris and mud. Evacuation began last night in the capital, but erratically since everyone was asleep.

"When the population realised what was coming, the panic was such that many died, crushed, trampled upon or drowned when falling off the cramped bridges. Already, several million have died from Aswan downstream.

"Scimitars of Islam have posted a video, or *S.I.*, as they now call themselves. It shows a man they say is a Coptic monk. Under torture he confesses to having been part of the Dam Plot, with many Christian accomplices.

"The Scimitars *lie*. The man's body was identified three weeks ago, long before yesterday's attack. He was one of *our* agents.

"The Coptic Patriarch denied their accusation, stating that vast number of Copts have already died as victims, together with the Muslims. However, in the last few hours, already eleven churches were set aflame in Egypt; some more in various African countries, some in Asia, two in France and one in Britain.

"Egypt declared martial law."

Nasreen fell to her knees, hiding her face in her hands. Sobbing, she repeated: "Not in our name... Not in our name!"

Abu Ephrem knelt beside her and laid his hand on her shoulder compassionately, whispering: "No, my dear friend, not in your name.

"And not in His."

Chapter 135

There was no time to lose.

Abu Ephrem was very anxious to get back to whatever remained of his flock in Cairo, while Nasreen made her way to Geneva for a UN crisis meeting. She left as soon as my new doctor arrived from Khartoum. The latter stayed only for a day, showing our trainee Arous how to take care of me, as he had to go and help in Egypt.

It took me a while to assimilate the magnitude of the catastrophe. Our lives would never be the same again. But at least, we hadn't *lost* them, unlike millions along the Nile valley.

That Friday after the flood, after having shown me some news on his tablet, Mansur prevented me from watching any more, arguing that I'd seen enough of the carnage. He was adamant that my main task was to rest, and to feed the babies. He even refused to tell me what had happened to the *Cedrus*.

In fact, my dear husband seemed obsessed with the tragedy, at the expense of our relationship. He was constantly on the phone with his father, or sending emails, and would barely come to my room and see our children.

I was dreading the moment when he would announce that he had to go, leaving me behind at Osly.

Eight days had elapsed since our ordeal and the flood, and Mansur was showing himself itchy and distant, almost hostile. I prayed to St Joseph (the nineteenth of March was his feast) for assistance for my husband.

I felt that I needed to address the situation and insisted on talking it through. I was still in my pyjamas that Monday morning, feeding Margaret, when Arous asked if she could check how my scar was doing. I let her do so.

Mansur entered the room (forgetting to knock), his face frowning. Seeing our little one in my arms seemed to upset him even more. He asked if he should come back later. I invited him to stay but, feeling that there might be trouble, I let Arous take away the child, now crying.

Our conversation went horribly. Mansur's attitude reminded me of that terrible scene on the *Cedrus*, during my wedding dress fitting. Pointing at my belly, he first asked if my scar was healing correctly.

At first, I thought it considerate of him and, with a welcoming smile, I answered that Arous was pleased with me. He replied bitterly that *he* wasn't, since my scar was a mark of *shame*.

I said I didn't understand.

Raising his voice, he replied that if I hadn't selfishly insisted on flying to Osly to see my stupid bougainvilleas, the helicopter crash wouldn't have happened, we could have left Cairo before the flood and I would have carried my pregnancy to term and given birth normally in London or Zurich.

Over there, we would have been safe, whereas now we were stuck in this desert until I and my premature children were fit enough to travel!

Meanwhile, he complained, our friends were being martyred in Cairo and we couldn't help them. His voice was very loud by then, and he sounded dangerously frustrated.

I became afraid.

Reaching for the little vase with flowers on my bed table, he threw it into the wall, shouting that he'd yielded to my caprices one time too many, and that from now on, I would learn *submission*.

Too shocked to find any words in reply, I kept looking at the petals scattered across the tiles, among the fragments of shattered glass. He walked to the window, apparently gazing at the sand dunes. But I could see his hands clenching together behind his back, as if to prevent himself from raising them against me.

It got worse.

Still not looking at me, he added that it would be irresponsible to beget any more children in this world gone mad, and that he would see to it that we had no more.

I managed to answer that, as his wife, I had a say in that matter.

He replied that if I was *his* wife, I'd better stop always comparing him with *Azim*.

Azim?

This came totally out of the blue! I started shaking, now that the discussion was getting out of control.

But Mansur went on, saying that he'd been shot at like Azim; he bore a scar on his stomach like Azim – not a selfish scar like mine; he'd been baptised like Azim. Was it *his* fault, he shouted, if *he* had survived? Why should Azim always stand between us?

I was completely taken by surprise, realising for the first time that he must have been feeling that way all along.

Surely Azim wasn't always on *my* mind, and I deeply loved Mansur, without comparing him to my dead friend. Was it not rather that Mansur was feeling ashamed of his own bad temper, and tried to throw the responsibility onto someone else?

It became clear to me that he felt torn between his family duties keeping him with me and the children at Osly, and his sympathy for the numerous victims of the flood, whom he yearned to assist.

As a consequence, like the psychological equivalent to the blown up Aswan Dam, Mansur's self control seemed greatly damaged, letting violence erupt.

The realisation that we hadn't yet overcome that flaw I knew too well in his character saddened me, even though I knew such things couldn't improve overnight – if ever.

As he walked out, dropping my phone and tablet on my bed, he informed me that a revolution was likely to occur in Egypt, and that I should be less selfish, and sympathise more with the many families already destroyed by the current conflict.

In tears, I replied that it didn't have to be *our* fate.

His hand on the door handle, he added after a silence: "By the way, it appears that we've lost the *Cedrus* for good. When hit by the flood, she got caught in the mud, and in Cairo, the new Coalition Government has other priorities than relocating the homeless who have sought refuge on board our ship, the property of a wealthy 'apostate' – your husband. We tried everything to get her back. Give up any hope of ever sleeping in our cabin again."

I knew how much that loss would have affected him (as it grieved *me* as well). The *Cedrus* was much more than a sublime yacht. It was our family home; a part of our identity.

Mansur left later that day, I was told.

Before departing, I remembered to spread Azim's fifty petals in our private garden, outside our bedroom. They were completely dry, like scraps of coloured silk paper. I scattered them at the foot of my bougainvilleas, asking my dear friend to intercede for my husband – and for our family.

London didn't feel much safer than Osly, when we finally reached it, the children and I. Out of Africa, and stranded in Europe. It felt of déjà vu... Mansur had organised everything and we were under constant protection. But his absence left me emotionally vulnerable.

I had access to the news and started to realise the global repercussions of the Aswan catastrophe.

From Beirut, Mansur texted me that he would be gone for a while, as required by his business (the Al-Khoury Middle Eastern operations needed all his attention).

A *video* was attached to his message, in which he offered me a thorough and far-reaching apology. He said that he was unworthy of me and of our children.

Through my affection over the past two years, he said, he'd felt as if his domineering tendency was gradually being subdued, but the impact on him of the recent events had reawakened the "monster" and made his efforts seem fruitless.

He begged me to allow him to redeem himself in a definitive way, in my eyes and in his, adding that the children and I would receive all the support we needed in his absence.

But what could we ever want, I replied to him, more than his presence; more than his arms; more than his smile?

Weeks went by and, as was to be feared, *S.I.* seized power in Egypt. Mansur never told me when he'd started living in Cairo, risking his life daily for a Church in dire straits under the Scimitars' rule.

But I soon suspected that he was there.

Chapter 136

Four months later, the shooting at Harrods, in the heart of London, was a turning point.

Fifty-two had died in the luxurious department store (where *I* had popped in just the previous day). Until that eighteenth of July, everyone had tried to ignore the growing tension. Previous terrorist attacks in Bradford, Gatwick Airport, Glasgow, Manchester and Brighton had been described as isolated events.

But the Harrods shooting had been claimed by S.I. as part of a global strategy, and Downing Street couldn't deny any longer that the violence which had escalated since the eleventh of March – Flood Day – indicated a well coordinated scheme.

Safety couldn't be taken for granted anymore in large cities. The beginning of the school holidays was a good pretext to take families away to the country. Elderly people compared it with the evacuation before the Blitz, in 1940, when they were children.

Vardah insisted on our moving to her mansion near Henley, amidst the Thames, west of London. I accepted. Stuart had had the whole island fenced and was taking shooting lessons (quite appropriate for *James Bond*). He had me try. But after a few shots, I felt awkward with a gun in my hands and was glad to hold my babies again instead – *my* favourite weapons. Meanwhile, Vardah had turned half the grounds into vegetable gardens, with the ambition of becoming self-sufficient within a year!

The children and I felt so relieved. We could all focus on leading a simple life amidst nature.

Despite the suffering which Mansur's desertion caused me, I was able to relax and to find consolation in motherhood. I became more aware of my responsibility to shape the souls and minds of my children, making them good and holy people, with God's grace.

Begetting children was only the first part of my mission – of *our* mission – as parents, also the simpler. The second part was no less important. It was the education of our little ones according to natural law and to the enlightening commandments of God.

Alas, even such commendable aims were now undermined in the official curriculums. I seriously considered starting to homeschool after the summer, as it was still legal then. As a run up, I began teaching catechism to Talitha and to three young children from the area. On occasions, I would also teach them bits of history and English.

Soon enough, Francis, Margaret and Jacqueline would join us for colouring sessions.

Vardah earnestly tried to help me understand *why* Mansur had left me. She wondered if I hadn't made a mistake when opposing his intention to have no further children. I reminded her that according to Catholic teaching based on the very nature of the marital act, contraception was *always* a grave sin.

She was puzzled: "Surely, Clara, there must be *some* exceptions, even for you. You convinced me last year about *abortion*. Thank you truly for your advice back then. But contraception isn't the same. You invoke theology, but millions of innocents have died in Egypt and the country is in complete chaos.

"For the foreseeable future, should not any responsible adult spare children the pain of being born into such a mess. Your husband is there trying to help. Don't you think he would come back and be reconciled if you texted him that you now mean to support him as his wife – in *whatever* way he needs?"

I could only tell Vardah that contraception was *always* harmful. "God help us: I would never do anything which would make my husband – or I – offend God and lose His grace." I explained to her that if a couple thought they shouldn't have another child too soon, then they should either abstain, or unite in times of infertility (if gravely adverse circumstances justified that second option, which I didn't think was our case).

Looking at me doubtfully, she commented: "Well, consider yourself lucky if Mansur doesn't undergo *surgery*. Stuart mentioned it to me once, as an option. That was *before* Jacqueline, though. I wouldn't like it. But Stuart and I *do* use contraception. And see, we live together here and are perfectly happy."

Unwittingly, her implication was that I would still have my husband by me if I were *reasonable*. How could I tell her that if marital intimacy selfishly excluded life, it left the spouses far apart, their souls lying light-years from each other? Mansur and I, with the Thames and the Nile between us, and even oceans and deserts, could be closely united if our wills acknowledged fecundity as the supreme good of marriage, even if we chose to abstain for a while; even if we never had any more children.

We had our tea and spoke of gardening, to change the subject. Birds were chirping and small butterflies danced around us: *they* didn't carry our moral burdens. But also, they couldn't *love*.

In October, Mansur rang me for the first time.

It had been seven months since we had spoken, at Osly. Hearing his voice caused me such joy, and great pain.

He apologised: "Clara, please understand that I *had* to go and help them. They are my people."

"But we are your *flesh*."

"These fanatics butcher everyone. They desecrated tombs, not only those of Nour and Azim, but even Muslim ones, like my great-uncle's, the Shah, whom they say was a *bad* Muslim."

"But your absence kills *us* too! It's in me like a sword! You are our head, our protection. You're my life and the hope of our children. Your calling is to *us*, before any victim in Cairo."

"You don't understand, Clara. I do it for you, and for the children. I want you to be proud of me. I want them to remember me as a man generously spent. I want to do what Azim did. Without this tragedy, I might never have dared."

"Please, Mansur – Azim has nothing to do with our marriage!"

"Yes, he has. Don't think I didn't see what lay on your bed the day of the Flood. You had just given birth in daunting circumstances; Aswan Dam had broken (although you didn't know it yet), but your consolation was Azim's *journal*. Yes, *his* journal."

"This is unfair, Mansur. His sister Jamila had just brought it to Osly, two years after his death."

He paused for a little while.

I feared he might hang up on me, but he resumed the conversation: "First time you've mentioned this to me, darling. But I ask no explanation. I trust you, and always have. While you slept, that dreadful day, I opened the leather-bound diary. It was no secret, or you wouldn't have left it in sight. I merely browsed through it. You don't read Arabic, but you were right in your appreciation of Azim. I understand why he's been your constant inspiration."

"He hasn't! Not more than you, anyway. *You* are the man I married, Mansur."

"Yes, once *he* had died. Don't think me jealous, Clara. I simply realised that the Scimitars' madness could have at least this advantage, that I could prove myself as generous as Azim. Since against them my power can't prevail, I'm learning patience and humility, while doing quite a lot of good."

"Mansur, I love you as you are! I will *always* love you! Please, you told me that you'd *never* leave me. You repeated it: 'We go nowhere without each other. No-where' – you said! I love you so deeply, so strongly! Come back to me, with all that you are, even with your anger! We'll seek counselling. We'll get help and will overcome this together. We need you so badly! My love, my love, my love!"

He hadn't interrupted me.

He answered, very calmly: "I *am* with you, Clara. I've never felt closer to you. I think of you and the children night and day! But they've taken Abu Ephrem now. We can't let them get away with it, can we? I have a plan. Give me just another few of months...

"Clara darling... are you still there?"

"Yes, I am... Mansur, Talitha's having nightmares again. She spoke your name in her sleep. Will you speak to her now?"

"I'd... I'd rather not. It would break me. Please, darling... You're the soul of my soul... If anything happens to me, tell the children, our beloved children, that their daddy loved them greatly. Let's face it, it really might be... better that way..."

I couldn't hold back a huge sob. He heard it.

"No, no, don't cry, Clara. I don't mean it. I *will* see you again, soon. Give me just a few months and I'll be back. Forgive me."

Vardah found me in tears and, as usual, did her best to soothe me. Thank God for her.

Meanwhile (talking of friends), Nepomucen was back in Sudan.

His government meant to prevent instability from spreading from Egypt across its northern border. To that end, Khartoum needed support from Western democracies and, among various tokens of goodwill, Christian exiles such as Nepomucen were allowed to return.

After a month spent in his native village, where his wife lay buried, he asked me if he could move to Osly, two hours north, "to keep an eye on the school and property." We had staff in charge there of course, but I was delighted that such a personal friend would live among them. He loved our chapel and started acting as sacristan.

Chapter 137

Mansur hadn't called me again, "for fear of being identified and of putting the Cairo Christian network at greater risk."

Danger was genuine, I admitted, but I also suspected that he used it as a pretext to avoid direct communication with me and the children, which he couldn't face, for some mysterious reason. He sent regular text messages, though – never twice from the same phone.

His absence was unjustifiable, considering his primary duty to us, his family. By then, I couldn't deny the fact that something must have gone wrong in his head. It was deeply worrying for our family, and also humiliating, as far as other people suspected it.

Kitty was supportive, assuring me that modern life made *burnouts* increasingly frequent for high-achievers such as Mansur. In his case, the Scimitars' attack at Osly, coinciding with the Flood, could have been the catalyst precipitating the crisis, couldn't it?

However, she later on agreed with Nasreen that there was more to it than burnout. Rather, a deep-seated controlling tendency would need to be tackled. Nasreen said that it was often a reaction to cover up one's vulnerabilities. Did Mansur ever mention that he wasn't up to some task, unable to meet the standards set for him by someone else?

I hadn't noticed. What was certain was that he needed psychological assistance. But how to get it to him?

We were still on Vardah's little haven island, amidst the Thames. It felt a bit like on board the *Cedrus*, in the good old days. I had dealt with our prolonged marital crisis the best I could, and tried to minimise the impact on Talitha (Francis and Margaret were still much too young to suffer from it).

I longed for Mansur's weekly text message.

His parents had tried everything to get him out of Cairo. After several months, Jed had sent Luke, the head bodyguard, with a rescue team, to bring Mansur back by persuasion, but to no avail.

Reluctantly, Jeda agreed with Nasreen that her dear son needed psychological assessment and medical support.

But Mansur was in blunt denial. He texted me once that "our situation wasn't different from that of so many families separated by the necessities of war."

I texted back that he hadn't enlisted and wasn't a soldier. I also asked him if Abu Ephrem supported his exposing his life. For the first time, I dared to mention that he needed to consult a psychologist. I gave him the contact details of one in Beirut, recommended by Jeda.

He didn't reply – possibly because he had switched phones again.

A thin layer of snow covered the island, that nineteenth of December. As I watched the children make a snowman, I tallied up that my beloved would from now on have spent more time estranged from me than with me, since our wedding. In fact, we had been together even *less* than nine months as husband and wife: eight months and nineteen days... Over the phone, Sally thought herself *helpful* when she enquired about marriage *annulments* in the Catholic Church... I nearly hung up on her.

Winter came to an end. On nineteenth March, the first anniversary of Mansur's departure from Osly, I begged St. Joseph to give me strength to bear the suffering; to bring my spouse back to me and their daddy to our children.

Months went by...

The Aswan tragedy should have diverted my attention from our marital difficulties. The Nile flood was sending ripples all over the world. The English countryside was still safe. But from Egypt, violence was spreading abroad, and everyone was becoming anxious; not only around us, but also more broadly across the Western world.

Without too much struggle, I had lived half way through my *second* summer without a husband... Mansur had been gone fifteen months when I heard his voice over the phone again.

He'd left Egypt! – ringing me from Osly, where he had come to rest.

"Darling, I have news. I spoke with Nepomucen – he loves it here at Osly and sends his regards. He says that with the new army bases between the border and Osly, this place has actually become safer than England. There are Russian, British, French and American troops stationed, with patrols in every village. Not even a *goat* could walk by the ford without having to show its ID. I know that you love Osly..."

"So many memories..."

"Clarry, I've been thinking... Would you *like* to come here with the children?"

I kept silent.

I wasn't sure what to say.

Of course, it was a pleasant idea, generally speaking, since I couldn't impose for too long on the hospitality of Stuart and Vardah. But it came so much out of the blue, as if he had just left home for work that morning and suggested a picnic at the local park...

As if *nothing* had happened... Fifteen months of solitude, of dejection, of agony... Fifteen months raising our newborns, Francis and Margaret, without a husband, as if they had no father... And Talitha crying, unwilling even to ride her pony... And family and friends wondering... And the occasional echoes of soul-shattering gossip such as: "See how one ends up, with too much religion... A husband needs fun, not holy water... She led him to it with her *faith* commitments. No wonder... She's got kids and money now; it won't be long until she finds a better match..."

Mansur went on, apologetically: "You know, darling, I went for counselling... Although I was upset when I read your suggestion, several months ago, I went to see your psychologist in Beirut. I'm not sure it helped much. I don't know.

"His theory is that from childhood, I've been unconsciously undermined by my father's dynastic expectations. Apparently, being 'heir to an empire' was too heavy for me. I couldn't handle it well and I didn't want to admit it, for fear of disappointing Jed.

"It caused tensions in me, which manifested themselves in my controlling attitude. I told the psychologist that I thought I was handling things rather well, on the contrary, since I hadn't crashed the family business, but successively increased it.

"His point is that the pressure was – or is – unconscious, and was bound to reach a critical stage sooner or later. Anyway, he says I'm not *mad*. That's reassuring! We met five times and he can fix me, he assures. By the way, he says that it might be good to meet *you* as well."

I was so taken aback that, after a further silence I could only say: "I love you Mansur. I've always loved you, and always will."

Sounding more confident now, he announced what he must have had in mind from the beginning of the conversation: "Clara... I've been thinking... Nepomucen made an interesting suggestion the other day. He said that supporting my own family would be my most powerful contribution to ease the horror in Cairo. He said: 'Family is about life, about hope, about the future. A man with a family is a true asset to society.' He added that outside Cairo, I could still do a tremendous amount of good among the refugees from Egypt, who are parked in camps two hours north from Osly."

My heart started beating frantically: would our separation end soon? Would we soon meet again and resume life as a family? I asked plainly: "Mansur, *what* exactly do you suggest?"

He confessed: "Listen, darling! I'm sure you need a change of setting. And I want to see you and the children, if you haven't totally given up on me... Have you? That's why I called. Come to Osly next Thursday, the twenty-second. Everything is arranged for your journey."

As I didn't answer, he went on: "Did Arous tell you that they'd started planting, between the school and the Nile? I thought the soil was definitely too poor, but with daily watering, a few vegetables have sprouted already. It was *your* idea – wise and generous, as always. 'In the current economic context,' I remember you said, 'better try to become self-sustaining'.

"As it happens, I'm going to accompany a small convoy from Port Sudan. It's humanitarian supply for the refugees, by the border. But I've added to it all sorts of agricultural equipment. As for you, would you *please* bring the children! All three of them! I mean... if you think it's not too much for them.

"And we'll pray together, as I know you like."

"Mansur!"

He was gone.

Chapter 138

Coming to Osly in July, what an idea!
The place hadn't changed much and was dreadfully hot, especially arriving from England. But the rainy season could start anytime. Oh yes, let it pour – I was *melting*.
Thankfully, our air-conditioning still worked perfectly: a prerequisite for bringing the children along. The (limited) risk to them was worth taking, if one considered how unexpected this opportunity was of being together again as a family, after over a year of trial. They should meet their father...

Coming back prompted bittersweet memories. So much had happened there, connecting the lives of the forty-eight Muslim girls, of Azim, of Nepomucen and later, of Abu Ephrem, Nasreen, Mansur and I. Lastly, our beloved babies had been born there, fifteen months earlier. Outside my room, in our private garden, my bougainvilleas had survived the heat, thanks to our irrigation system.
That afternoon, the temperature was unbearable. It felt so dry and dusty, with a hot wind blowing and some clouds growing fast. I stood under the shade, on the top of the little hill where the school was located, looking across the Nile, towards the east. The river was still wide but very low, after a long dry season.
Happy shouts were heard downhill, as villagers started pushing the usual raft into the water. Children stood on it, waving towards the opposite bank where several trucks had stopped, loaded with boxes and pallets.
Mansur's convoy!

There were also soldiers, unsurprisingly. After enquiring as to the depth of the water by the ford, I assumed, the first army vehicle started across. It had water over its wheels and I wondered if they wouldn't all get stuck in the middle of the wide – if shallow – river.
Meanwhile, the sky had turned to dark as the clouds grew bigger over our heads. I prayed that they wouldn't be *sand* clouds... The memories of our ordeal on this very site flashed back. *The helicopter crashing, the attack...*
Yells interrupted my reminiscences.
I walked halfway downhill. *Mansur* was on the first truck. This had to be *him*, although it looked as if he had... grown a beard. He had spotted me from afar and was frantically waving at me. I waved back, deeply moved. To think... that this silhouette across the water was my *husband*. The human being I loved most after Our Lord – and Our Lady!
At that moment, I felt a wet drop on my arm. Could it be? Could the rain begin at last, after so many months? It was already falling on the opposite bank.

But no one was looking for shelter! After so much dust and sweat, every drop was a long-awaited blessing from heaven.

I didn't move either, when the first cloud broke over the west bank where I stood. Within a few seconds, I was delightfully drenched. Too bad for my smart cotton dress (it wasn't by *Kayamashi* anyway). But by the river, the rain made the crossing less smooth for the first truck – and for those following. In fact, one couldn't see clearly anymore. I walked to the water to welcome my husband, whenever he would reach my side of the river.

His truck had a hundred yards left to drive, when it jerked and several boxes on the top fell into the water. Soldiers dived to catch them, as did the villagers around me. All were laughing, with water up to their shoulders.

The rain was becoming heavier. Mansur had dived like the others. I could see his strong strokes directing him towards a plastic barrel floating down the current. His *legs* were moving as well, vigorously. I remembered how, at Ain Sukna, I had devised a way of helping him reach the shore, before his body had healed.

And why would I not help him *again*? I couldn't get any wetter than currently, under that blissful downpour. I took off my sandals, ran into the water and started swimming towards the barrel, as if someone's life were at stake. I could hear Mansur laugh: "Save the cabbage seeds!"

He'd seen me come towards him. We were getting closer – he, the barrel and I. But *I* was the first to reach it and held it tightly. I was nearly out of my depth, on tiptoes like a ballerina, barely touching the muddy bottom of the river – when I shrieked, feeling myself *caught* from below.

Startled, the villagers nearer to me, in the water, looked in my direction. They soon started clapping and singing, when realising that Mansur had taken hold of me and was now lifting me up in his arms – while I still held the barrel against my chest, laughing and crying.

The pouring rain prevented me from seeing much at a distance, but it sounded as if the soldiers joined in, blurred silhouettes spread all across the ford, and it felt as if the whole river was celebrating our reunion. From the arms of my husband, I smiled at the young men near us: they looked like children. Were they even eighteen years old? Among the villagers were many of my schoolgirls. Such lovely youth!

They had no suspicion of what Mansur and I had been through (was it *over*, by the way?) but what a joy to see them happy, unknowingly encouraging us through their simple demonstration of affection.

Mansur wouldn't let me loose. He hugged me like an anaconda (surely the first one to be seen in the Nile), then carried me all the way to the shore, pushing the floating barrel before him with his knees. The rain was still pouring, as dense – and refreshing – as before, while the last truck was reaching the west bank. Mansur gave orders for the cargo to be stored safely, and we danced, rather than walked, uphill to the school.

As we entered Talitha's room (with muddy toes and our clothes still drenched), she didn't run into Mansur's open arms. He seemed surprised. Instead, she considered him from a distance. I told her that it *was* Daddy for real, even though his *beard* made him look different. But none of us were mistaken. It would take time for our darling Litha to get used to the idea of her father disappearing, and popping up again.

She wasn't even thinking in terms of debt and forgiveness, surely. She'd simply suffered, a lot, from his absence and from my tears. After a silence, he fell on his knees before her and said: "Talitha, my little daughter: I'm so sorry that I made you sad. You see, I wasn't well. But I love you so much. Please, will you forgive your daddy?"

She walked very slowly towards him, her face expressing a gravity beyond her age. After looking in his eyes, she said: "Why do you smell so strongly of mud, and also of petrol, Daddy?" She drew a tiny cross on his forehead, as she had seen me do to him and the children often – and fell in tears against his chest.

I left them together and went to put dry clothes on.

Chapter 139

Mansur insisted on helping Francis and Margaret with eating their sliced bananas.
   He was moderately bad at guiding the spoon, and I let him try, with the help of their nanny. Then he cooked with his own hands, using some of the very first vegetables grown in our field.
   Would he wish to learn to change nappies?

   He *looked* different, obviously making some efforts.
   But *inside*, was he altered, I wondered?
   The five of us stayed on the sofa for some time after, chatting. Mansur had changed clothes and washed.
   Fearing it was all too good to be true, I eyed him as he cuddled our little ones.
   What future did he envisage for us as a family?
   Had my husband changed his mind since, in this very house fifteen months earlier, he'd declared never to want children again in this world gone mad? Having absented himself for over a year, he'd forced strict abstinence upon us as a couple, *de facto*. But what would he expect now, if anything?
   He knew that contraception was out of the question... I realised that, since our wedding night, circumstances had never again allowed us to conceive. Estrangement had followed pregnancy – ...and now? It was two years and twenty-two days since we had exchanged vows.

   Eventually, the twins were laid in their little beds and Litha in hers, prayers done.
   Before supper, Mansur and I had put on dry clothes in our respective bedrooms, the ones we occupied on our last stay in Osly, fifteen months earlier. Now the evening was over and I didn't know what to say or expect. The initiative, if any, should be his.
   Whatever he did or chose, I felt that his presence gave me peace, deep inside. For that, at least, I was grateful.
   He gazed at me as we stood in the corridor, by my door. We didn't dare to move, so fragile that instant was, and so crucial. Perhaps, *he* didn't know what to do either. After a while, I said I would be in the chapel praying my rosary. He replied that he would go and look at the children as they slept. He had been deprived of their sight for so long.
   We wished each other goodnight, as if nothing had ever come between us.
   Twenty minutes later, I wasn't surprised to see him enter and kneel next to me, in the dark. The gilded frame and halo on St. Anthony's icon, above the

altar, reflected the glittering light of the sanctuary lamp. It was too dark to see the bullet impacts.

After a little while, I felt my hand being reverently seized and his lips kissing it, remaining on it for a *long* time. Then he walked to the sanctuary steps and crouched there, immobile. I had finished my rosary and, since Mansur hadn't moved, I left the chapel in silence.

It was one of life's very simple joys to find on my bed, neatly folded and perfumed with lavender, my cherished djellaba. I had forgotten to take it with me on leaving Osly, after the tragedy, so shocked had I been then by all that had occurred…

Here at Osly, our housekeeper had washed and ironed it for me, whereas its very existence had escaped my memory. Now feeling nearly cold with the air conditioning, I took a warm shower before going to bed, putting on with delight my embroidered nightdress.

I couldn't sleep, though, and, opening wide the French window, I stepped onto the terrace. A puff of warm wind and light mist entered the room, loaded with the scent of wet soil and plants. It smelt wonderfully fresh. The rain had ceased, but it had resuscitated the perfumes of herbs and flowers in our enclosed garden, lushly released after months of dryness.

The soil felt spongy under my bare feet. I knelt by the bougainvilleas, along my bedroom wall. The grass was thick under my favourite shrubs, watered daily. Alas, the strength of the downpour had made most of the petals fall to the ground. I smelled their thick and scentful layer.

Drops of rain still fell occasionally, also dripping from the shrubs. But most clouds were gone and I could see the first stars reappearing and soon, a magnificent moon. Night birds could be heard further away, among the trees and downhill, by the Nile.

Someone walked out of my bedroom, into our garden.

I didn't turn my head.

I knew whose shadow stretched across the grass, meeting mine.

I knew whose hands robed me with fresh bougainvillea petals, lighter and softer than any seamstress would ever assemble.

I knew whose face eclipsed the moon, over mine.

I knew whose soul mingled with mine, spousally.

The one who'd received me for his wife, long ago – the same I had received for my husband, blissfully.

I knew by Whose mercy.

Chapter 140

Looking back, I am still grateful for that happiest month in my life – ever since.

I remember choosing as spiritual reading during those weeks the *Song of Solomon*, as it fitted so well our sentiments: conjugal love truly was an icon of God's love for each soul.

My beloved to me, and I to him who feedeth among the lilies...

Could it ever have got better? I harvested bliss as it came, knowing it might not last.

We lived by the Nile as a family. We planted a (small) field. We swam and laughed a lot. Mansur gave Litha more riding lessons.

After three weeks he nearly cried, when I smiled, announcing I was pregnant again. He requested *triplets*, this time, as if *I* could decide. "From so kind a mother," he said, "I would wish many more. Please, let there be at least one girl among them and we'll name her *Hope*." Arous said that it truly was an "Osly child."

Mansur wanted to know how many more children we could have: "Tell us Arous: *you* are the doctor here." With candid exactness, Arous started: "Well, a woman the age of Mrs. Al-Khoury would still have about three hundred thousand eggs, and..." Mansur interrupted her, saying: "Imagine, three hundred thousand Clarries! That's heaven on earth!"

I laughed, as his vision of paradise sounded rather nightmarish to *me*.

I even got my camel trek. My *Lawrence of Arabia* took me for three days in the desert, just the two of us. This time, Luke let him slip off unguarded. After all, Mansur had survived a year in Cairo under the Scimitars' rule – and he carried a gun.

Across the dunes I held him fast, sitting close behind him. The starry nights felt cool. He called my scar 'glorious' and said that more children should be our best retaliation to the Flood.

It had rained the whole morning. Sitting under the shade, we opened our hearts to one another. There was so much we had wished to share over the past year and a half, and hadn't been able to.

I described for him my life in London and further, on Vardah's island, near Henley; the children; the prayers; the tears.

Mansur told me that Abu Ephrem was free again, although hiding. In Cairo, the previous month, he had confirmed the opinion of the psychologist from Beirut: "He thinks I coped poorly with being 'heir to an empire.' Of course, his perspective is that of a priest: *Every inheritance can collapse,* Abu

Ephrem said, *every possession can fail us. But as God's adopted son, through baptism, you are* heir *to the Kingdom of Heaven.* That *empire*, he stressed, *no one could ever ruin or even merely harm.* Abu Ephrem quoted the Bible – St. Paul, I recall: *And if sons, heirs also; heirs indeed of God, and joint heirs with Christ: yet so, if we suffer with him, that we may be also glorified with him."*

The second night, I found Mansur's mat empty before dawn. He was kneeling outside, a hundred yards away, facing east. The Nile glittered further down. A basic cross stood nearby, made of two sticks of wood. Not a sound... I had never experienced such silence.

I wouldn't disturb him, but could join him in prayer, from the tent. We had so much to give thanks for.

After three rosaries, though, I came to kneel by him. We didn't speak. Our hands weren't even touching. Never had I felt so close to my spouse. I surrendered anew, in my heart, everything to the Lord.

Back at Osly, in our garden he spoke, that afternoon: "Darling, Abu Ephrem has been released, as you know. With his involvement, I have a plan in place that could make the Church strong for years, right under the nose of the Scimitars. It would secure access to the sacraments, giving spiritual strength to persecuted souls. But I won't go back unless *you* freely grant me leave. If you say no, I will happily stay. In fact, I'd rather *not* go. But I'm the only one who has all the contacts, with Rome and locally. If you granted me *two* months, not a single day more... I solemnly promise I would be back within two months from now."

He knelt before me (as he hadn't been able to do when proposing to me, I recalled, in another garden). I knew that this further trip was no escapism. He had come back to me, to us for real. I knew that he wouldn't expose his life unless it could make a lasting difference for the Church – for the Bride of Christ.

I thought of all the persecuted souls, further down the very same river where we, happily, enjoyed peace. I thought of the children, fevered. I thought of the mothers, losing hope. I thought of the fathers, powerless.

But what would be the difference with his *previous* absence, my heart objected? He would leave us again and again expose his life, wouldn't he?

Yes, but this time it would be a *shared* decision. It would be a gift *we* would make as a couple. It wouldn't be *stolen* from me, his wife. This time it would be by my leave – if I consented...

And yet, did I have the *right*? Even if *I* made such a sacrifice as his wife, did our children not require the presence and protection of their father (even more so the tiny one I now carried), before any children in Cairo? Sweet Jesus, what would *You* want me to choose?

I looked at the man at my feet, the husband Christ had given me. Could I deter him from such a plan he had? Since he could make a real difference, down the Nile, in the hell of Cairo... Since he could ease the pain and revive the courage of so many souls... So many families, our sisters... So many crucified families...

And had he not spent a whole year down there, and come back unscathed? And Abu Ephrem was part of the plan, I recalled. Abu Ephrem, who had nearly died a martyr here at Osly, in this river. Abu Ephrem who had given me the Last Rites twice – and here I was, alive.

With a shaking hand, I blessed my beloved, tearfully.

"No, no, don't cry, Clarry. Please God, I *will* be back. It will be my *last* time. Your faith is my light, Clara. Hatred may flood the world, but you're my beloved ark."

He went.

In my anguish, my prayer for him and our children became even more ardent. I was sure that God would bring us together again. I knew my beloved had realised that *home* was the first place where his virtues should shine, and that a hero was no use to me if I lost my *spouse*, and our children their *daddy*.

I dried my tears, begging God that the war might not have the last word; that the little treasure I carried might soon meet with his or her father.

And begging, and begging.

As the weeks passed, with a few text messages from intermediaries assuring things were going well, all according to plan.

Sometimes a little voice would whisper to me that the "monster" within my husband – the controlling side of him – would never truly be tamed, that I would live to regret his return. I drove the voice away, locked it out, fought it with almost as much force as I put into my prayers.

God would bring him home to me; to us. All would be well.

It would.

Chapter 141

Two large four-wheel-drives parked before the school, that morning.
Lewis Kanisah was a familiar face at Osly, but Jeda had never visited us there.
Seeing her, I guessed.

When I heard Mansur was *dead*, something broke in my soul. It felt like a very thin spring overstretched, within the complex mechanism of a clock. The agony it caused...
I felt the pain in my body as well. For several days, I truly believed that I had lost our baby. Arous wasn't sure and told me simply to wait.
The child was fine, thankfully, but my soul wouldn't work properly again without external intervention.

Getting Mansur's body out of Egypt had been extremely difficult. Jed never told me how he'd achieved it in just three days. Luke and Lewis had been involved, I heard. A lot of money had been spent, and perhaps recourse to force had been necessary.
Mansur was to be buried at Osly. This place truly had become our *home*.

There would be no classes that eleventh October. All our girls – seventy of them by now – were lined up outside the school, wearing their best uniforms. Our staff were present as well, and the villagers.
Shading his eyes as he looked towards the horizon, Nepomucen whispered to me: "I hear them come."
The sound was first very faint, nearly covered by the sobs. But it soon increased and became extremely loud. We were facing the Nile, towards the east. Above the opposite bank, far away, three small spots were slowly growing.
The voice of my beloved, behold he cometh leaping upon the mountains, skipping over the hills...
The one in the middle was smaller, but it carried a load, hanging from a cable. It shone powerfully, like a jewel at the end of a silver chain.
Verses from the *Song of Solomon* kept flashing back in my memory.
A bundle of myrrh is my beloved to me, he shall abide between my breasts.

In ten seconds, the three helicopters flew over the wide Nile and hovered over the esplanade outside the school. Despite the morning rain, clouds of dust spread all around, as if it were a *habūb*, a sandstorm. At closer look, the silvery load now looked like a giant cello case.
They landed, the rotors stopped and the dust settled.

Followed by the Papal Nuncio, Jed stepped out of the middle chopper and walked towards the oblong casket, set on trestles by Luke and Lewis. Anastasis troops jumped out of the two army aircrafts and lined up on either side, led by officers.

Jeda and Nasreen stood close to me. Further back, Raúl was holding hands with Mum and Dad (Kitty was expecting her second child and couldn't travel, just like Vardah).

I laid my hand on Talitha's shoulder while Arous held Francis and Margaret. On reflection, despite their very young age, I had found that I owed them that last meeting with their father.

Nobody had moved.

Jed opened the isotherm container inside which the fibreglass coffin lay. The inner lid was finally removed, and the father looked at his son, the young heir to his lost expectations, now sleeping in his shining sarcophagus. I forgot my own pain, imagining his. Had his *empire* collapsed? Had ancient *Phoenicia* failed?

Dear, dear Jed... I never saw such suffering on a man's face. His eyes crossed mine and didn't even have the energy to look away. It was as if he was asking *me* for strength. I knew he felt responsible for the death of his son – my life.

Litha and I walked towards Mansur. I had almost no sensation, as if I were numb. His face looked serene, but I couldn't come any closer. After a little while, Litha took my hand and gently laid it on her father's. I remained in that posture for a while, and found the strength to kiss him one last time.

I adjure you, O ye daughters of Jerusalem, by the roes and the harts of the fields, that you stir not up, nor make the beloved to awake, till he please.

The coffin was carried into the chapel for the Requiem Mass. Soldiers spread upon it the Anastasis flag, which I had never seen before in real life.

The Nuncio praised Mansur, who had given up his life for the Church in Cairo. He said that, while any such sacrifice was unique and worthy of our gratitude, Mansur "had done more than any man so far to implant the life of grace anew in the midst of the most dreadful persecution."

Concern for the Church's safety forbade him to be more explicit, but the future would no doubt let all know the importance of Mansur's sacrifice.

On that occasion, I was struck by the words spoken by the Celebrant at Communion. Hundreds of time I had heard them said in Latin while the Sacred Host was laid upon my tongue: *May the Body of our Lord Jesus Christ preserve your soul unto life everlasting. Amen.* But only then did I realise that the purpose of this rite, of this sacrament, was to lead me to life eternal where, as I hoped, my beloved awaited me.

Later on, I recalled that Jed had received Holy Communion that day for the first time since I'd known him. Jeda was holding his hand. It made me hope that *Phoenicia* was saved.

The tomb chosen was simple and allowed for *my* coffin to lie along his, in God's time.
May it come soon.
Very Soon.
Now.

Chapter 142

Abu Ephrem couldn't be reached for consolation, although I knew he was praying for us.

From Paris, Fr. Paul helped me for as long as he could.

He said that I had spent years convinced of Azim's presence at my side, even though I couldn't *see* him anymore. I was better prepared than others, he suggested, to continue my relationship with Mansur in God, despite the tragedy of his death.

I gave birth that following April, on the twenty-fifth. There were no terrorists, no red-haired midwife and no c-section! If a boy, I would have named him Mark, after the first Bishop of Alexandria whose feast fell on that day. I called our lovely daughter *Hope*, as her father had wished.

Time flew. I felt busy and lonely.

What led me to Portugal three years after Mansur's death, ignoring Fr. Paul's cautions?

Was it anger?

A young widow with a two-year-old daughter, with five-year-old twins and another daughter in her early teens, with war raging all around me, I had honourable motives. I merely sought affection from a friend, a spiritual son once called *Jonathan*.

But I meant more than that. Part of me wished to *deface* the memory of my love for Mansur, who had abandoned us, so I felt at the time. (No wonder Margaret never forgave her father.)

I remembered that I had given my husband leave to go on that fatal mission. But how could I be sure that he wouldn't have deserted us a second time against my wishes? Had his last trip not been, like the first one, merely a sign of his controlling bent? Shouldn't he have simply ruled it out, regardless of Abu Ephrem's backing? Why had he mentioned it to me at all? Especially since he knew by then that I carried our fourth child, so tiny, so vulnerable...

He had me cornered.

Deep inside, I resented God's providence that had let our generosity as a couple meet with such an outcome. At the time, I had allowed the eventuality of Mansur's death, for the love of God and the needs of His Church in Cairo. But I couldn't accept that God should have welcomed my surrender so literally and quickly, taking my beloved from us.

I couldn't forgive *myself* either for having let Mansur leave... for having been generous towards strangers (the Cairo Christians) beyond my strength and to the detriment of my children's needs.

That afternoon in Fatima, Jonathan and I (or "Francisco" rather, according to his baptismal name) were standing on the terrace, while the children rested indoors. We were discussing the troubled times the world was in. He felt sorry for me as a young widow.

Half humorously, I suggested we should get married. My late husband's former personal assistant (and failed Best Man) gently dismissed the idea, though he must have guessed I *wasn't* joking.

It made me feel humiliated and helpless.

The thought of luring him occurred to me. I had nothing to lose, and after all, lay oblates like Jonathan *are* allowed to marry.

Would I try? Hadn't *he*, years earlier, in a certain car park?

Before I could make up my mind, my three younger ones walked in, dressed up as the three Fatima shepherds, while Talitha played Our Lady. They looked so cute... It was meant to be 'a surprise for Mummy'.

But I'll never forget the look on Litha's face. I felt as if, somehow, she'd *seen* inside my heart and stood in shock, an embodiment of innocence confronted with untruthfulness.

Mansur hadn't married me with the intention of erasing or offending the memory of Nour. He'd been at peace with his late wife. But I think that Talitha guessed, rightly, that I was intent against Mansur's memory, or against the memory of our marriage.

Even if Jonathan gave in, I saw that I couldn't marry him for... for *revenge* against Mansur, or worse, against divine Providence. It wouldn't have been true love. And... even though at times Mansur had been controlling, and for all my resentment since he'd felt called to help in Cairo, my late husband still claimed my deepest affection.

And how could I challenge *Francisco*'s calling, if the Mother of God wanted him as oblate (a celibate one) at her shrine?

The next day, we flew back to Casablanca.

When Fr. Paul got killed during the Paris bombing, I felt even more abandoned.

In vain I sought consolation in the writings of saints who had undergone special tribulations. I read of St. Teresa of Avila complaining to the Lord of her treatment, and hearing Him answer, "Teresa, whom the Lord loves, He chastises. This is how I treat all my friends." She replied wittily, "No wonder You have so few!"

But the saints had kept hoping, believing and loving. *I* on the contrary was feeling increasingly *dry*. I busied myself with the education of my children. I gradually got involved in programmes of assistance for children who were victims of the war and of persecution. But while I cared for those little ones, I felt like a fraud, having lost touch with the Holy One I knew counted most – the Child *Jesus*.

I wept my soul dry.

The war was raging worldwide, but my *inner* battle was against resentment.

I tried my best not to be cross with God.

Over the years, I clothed and fed thousands of children, and yet *I* was the one longing to be pampered and kissed. I yearned for the milk of consolation – and He fed me with gloom.

Rare were the times when a *sunbeam* would pierce through my interior clouds.

I begged God not to treat me as His "friend," as I couldn't bear desolation any further.

When did I last call Him *Father*?

EPILOGUE

Our Anastasis troops are still being ferried across the Nile this morning. It must have gone on all night. Can it really be twenty-five years since I last saw Cairo?

We boarded our own hovercraft and are now crossing over to the East Bank, our security drones flying ahead of us, like well tamed falcons.

On either side of us, vessels loaded with soldiers and vehicles move towards the opposite shore. They see our Government flag and salute us – most of them Chinese, it seems. Russians crossed first, yesterday. They move west; we move east.

It really feels as if I'm going back in time.

I haven't slept much.

Where will the First Mass take place? There can't be any churches left, after S.I. burnt down those the Flood had spared. Even that one where Azim and Nour lay buried, so I heard.

And it's still too soon for new churches to have been built. If not in a bunker, I suspect that we will have to squeeze under some military tent.

Or could it be at my old Convent? Actually, I prefer not to think about what may have happened to the sisters, let alone to the building.

I'm grateful to Fatimah for accompanying me. Especially as she's the only Muslim among the Anastasis Cabinet members. A Muslim with firm Catholic principles on essential issues such as the protection of life (quite a journey, compared with her previous convictions).

She's been such a support. I wouldn't have accepted an administrative position in Kiev if it hadn't been for her insistence. Why she decided to be called by her second name instead of *Nasreen*, I don't know. I realise now that in all these years, we haven't talked religion.

Our hovercraft is slowing down, slaloming through a putrid archipelago.

After the Flood, the Nile remained spread broadly, wherever the banks had burst, as occurred in Cairo. Most of the water doesn't flow. This wider area is a loosely connected network of dead backwaters and vast pools clogged with mud, debris and silt. It looks like the bayous in Louisiana, only with smaller trees.

In the political chaos that followed, then the war, things were left nearly as we find them twenty-five years later.

Half emerging from the unstable ground, all sorts of carcasses show. Not only recent ones such as cows or even crocodiles, but also rusting riverboats, a telephone booth, several buses and train coaches, many cars and vans, all entangled in bushes and young trees.

The East Bank, ahead of us, is where most of the surviving population live. But we can't hear or see much.

Our guards and staff alight first. Nasreen and I follow them on a clay jetty and start walking along a paved alley, in between high fences crowned with barbed wire.

Nearby, a few towers still show, seemingly abandoned. Actually, I recognise this tall red one: it used to stand very close to the marina.

Everything looks derelict. We reach a gate leading to what resembles a makeshift bunker. I was right, we will have Mass underground.

For some reason, I feel a bit apprehensive and take a last look at the outside world. My drone still hovers around and won't follow me inside. I must face this defenceless.

A young seminarian wearing a cassock and a middle-aged sister (fully veiled) greet our group as we walk in (she looks vaguely familiar). Indoors, when stepping up the narrow stairway, a strange sensation occurs, as if I'd been there before. But only when we reach the deck, at the top of the edifice, do I understand. We *are* where the Cairo Marina used to be, or very near it. Over there, this *was* the Business District. And under my feet...

Under my feet *is*...

Can it be?

Our clerical guide is visibly impressed that Dr. Fatimah Yasir, the Health Minister of the Anastasis, is coming in person with her retinue to attend the First Mass. Does he know she is a Muslim? He explains that the Bishop chose to remain where he'd been tortured and later imprisoned for years. He still sleeps in his former cell. Only, the main room of the prison has now been turned into a chapel.

"Of course," the young man remarks, "it wasn't built as a gaol. Before the Flood, it was a big yacht with very rich people living on it.

"When the wave hit Cairo, this boat was one of the few which did not capsize, because its hull was designed for the deep sea, unlike the riverboats around. It simply got stuck in the mud and gradually buried in it, while trees grew all around.

"The story goes that in the old days, twice a year, the owner would have the motorway closed down overnight to get his boat carried to the Mediterranean before summer, and back in winter. Imagine!

"The Bishop baptised the owner's son, in fact. He told us that they'd left Cairo on a helicopter the very day before the Flood. S.I. used the fact against Christians, as if it proved they knew the Aswan Dam was to be blown up..."

We now stand inside a sort of vestibule. Its sole decoration is a framed picture of the Holy Father in Yamoussoukro with, in the background, the papal basilica of Our Lady of Peace.

The sister is looking at me. Surely we never met before, or not in Kiev.

The seminarian explains further: "Our Bishop doesn't like it when we call him *the father of the Cairo Church*. He says, 'the Church existed, suffered and sanctified all around here long before our time, and She will continue long after us, if we become saints. But as to the past twenty-five years,' he insists, 'I could have done very little without Fr. Yusuf's own father'. He says: 'If you call me *the father of this Church*, then remember that Mr. Mansur Al-Khoury is the *grandfather* of the Cairo Church.'"

The young cleric smiles at us candidly before concluding: "And today, the *grandson* will say his First Mass here: our own Fr. Yusuf, on his family boat.

What a treat!"

Nasreen and I keep silent. I didn't expect all this. I am moved.

We've got slightly lost in the recent *genealogy* of the Cairo Church. The seminarian looks at Nasreen, and announces with a head bow: "Madam Minister, Sister Jamila will now show you to the chapel where the other officials are already sitting. Fr Yusuf expects his mother to arrive shortly and asked me to inform him as soon as she does.

"You may have met her before at government functions: she's the famous *Million-Baby Mother*, as he likes to remind us, because she saved so many children during the war. Hopefully, she'll allow us all seminarians to remain on her boat. Where would we go?"

Nasreen smiles at me as our young guide disappears, still unaware of my identity.

Unlike the sister... Our eyes need a few seconds only: *it is you – it is I – he sent you – we mourned him – we loved him – he's with us... Azim...*

Beautiful Jamila. She is in her mid-forties. The veil suits her lovely face, which doesn't look sad anymore. While she leads our little group along the narrow corridors (smelling of bleach), I reflect...

Mother?

Is it *I*?

For two years, I haven't seen my son. The war prevented it. I even had to miss his ordination last week, but he said he would wait for my arrival to offer his First Mass. Also, I resented Yusuf's decision to be trained for the underground priesthood. I thought it an unnecessary risk, when he could have completed his formation in Yamoussoukro.

Isn't Talitha safe over there, as well as useful, working for the Holy See? I told him that he should not expose his life. Was it not enough that his father had died, and that Margaret was gone with an S.I. captain?

I felt betrayed when Abu Ephrem accepted Yusuf in his clandestine seminary.

But we've arrived at the chapel.

Now my son is on his knees. He won't stand up.

This is annoying. I must bless him as his mother, he demands, before he blesses me as a newly ordained priest, if I wish. He knows that God is far from me. But now, everybody's watching. He has me cornered.

So much like his father! I suppose I have no choice.

I lay my hand upon his head, and request lasting peace and joy to be granted him. His brow rests against my stomach. I think I hear him sigh. And then, at the worst moment, the memory of another young man in a Cairo garden, kneeling before me and begging me to intercede with God on his behalf, superimposes...

My *son*! My beloved Francis Anthony Yusuf Athanasius Mary!

I hug him with all my strength, standing in silence. He rises with tears in his eyes.

But I'm not ready to ask for his blessing in return and, as a diversion, I take out of my handbag my ordination present, which will count also for his twenty-fifth birthday, falling today.

I don't have the strength to explain, especially with people around us. I put in his hand the chalice pall I sewed from my own wedding veil, in another life, while expecting him. Perhaps, he will understand.

He wants to share some great news if I wish to hear it, but I ask him to wait. *After* Mass. After...

The chapel used to be our dining room. I remember my first meal here with Mr and Mrs Al-Khoury – Jed and Jeda – the day he asked me to take up Azim's vacant position as Coordinator of the charitable Schools.

The room was cedar-panelled then.

It smelt wonderfully.

Now, I see only the underlying metal sheets, whose rust is barely concealed by new paint and damask hangings.

Hope is already here. To think she never knew that boat... I'm so glad that she's stayed on after Yusuf's ordination last week. We hug. She looks magnificent, my little baby (now twenty-three, I admit). She's the *businessman* of the family, gifted like her father. I'll tell her to sort out any paperwork for the seminary to remain here as long as they want – obviously. Still, what a strange sensation when I heard this boat referred to as *mine*... Mine.

Ours.

I stay at the back during Mass, with my veil on. Bishop Ephrem, I suspect, is the one who puts his hand on my shoulder before it begins. But I keep my face buried in my hands, as I don't wish to see him or anyone until it's all over.

All sit down for his homily. He quotes the Gospel for the Mass of today, which I read on our basic service sheet: *Woman, hath no one condemned thee? No one, Lord. Neither do I condemn thee; go, and sin no more.*

What I was told is true: the poor man *was* beaten up, even tortured.

He walks hesitantly; one of his eyes remains nearly closed; his nose is broken and – how horrible – some fingers are definitely missing from his right hand, laid on the edge of the lectern.

"Beloved brethren, we just heard twice the words No One, spoken by the Lord Jesus and by the accused woman. 'Nemo – No One'. What, or who, do we mean by No One?" the Bishop asks. His gaze seems to caress the audience as a wing, resting in a fatherly way upon each face.

He goes on: "Hatred negates the other person.

"To hate is to call our brother or sister 'Nobody,' or 'No One' – the opposite of a name.

"If we call our fellow human being 'No One,' then according to the Lord's sentence, '*No One* condemns us.' That is, God will avenge the brother or the sister we denied.

"But if we recognise our brethren as human persons, loving them as ourselves, then *no one* will condemn us, least of all God.

"Christ's sacrifice reveals to us sinners the divine Persons, Who love each other and love each of us as persons. This in turn teaches us to love our neighbour as the person God calls him or her to be.

"Christ died as No One, that we may forget No One, and, as brethren, may love the One Who is."

Before the Consecration, the service sheet mentions that a relic of the Cairo martyr Azim Anthony Nebankh, beatified last month, is sealed inside the altar. So, *he*'s there, under the corporal, upon which my son lays the wafer again; and genuflects again before taking off from the chalice the pall I gave him. And his father must be there as well, proudly – Mansur... – it is *his* boat after all, even more than mine.

That makes many persons present in that action; visible and invisible ones, especially if *God* is there, rather than bread.

As he slowly walks me back to the hovercraft, Abu... – I mean, Bishop Ephrem – apologises: "Clara my child... You don't mind if I call you my child, do you? I'm sorry that you knew nothing of where we live. It must be a shock to you. Many times I meant to tell you all that happened here. I couldn't.

"Mansur didn't mention it either, I assume. This was our decision to avoid the *slightest* risk of compromising our work in Cairo. Since the Liberation, I left it to Yusuf to give you any details, if he thought it would not hurt you more."

I keep silent, not being sure if I wish to hear it, after all these years.

Behind us, Yusuf chats with Fatimah. They haven't seen much of each other since she extracted him from my belly... exactly twenty-five years ago. It took place by this very river, over a thousand miles south, in Sudan.

That place was called... Osly.

Bishop Ephrem puts his hand on my arm, partly for me to support him, I guess, partly to express affection: "When Tora Prison was taken, your former driver, Ali Fawad, rose to prominence among the many inmates. They knew that he'd cooperated with S.I. to kill your husband, a wealthy Westernised Muslim... An 'apostate', as they would depict him.

"Under S.I. rule, Ali was considered a hero.

"Like many other private buildings and properties, the *Cedrus* had been turned into a prison. Steel-built and stranded as it was in the middle of this filthy laguna, it was suitable for confinement. Ali was put in charge of it.

"He couldn't prevent many of the horrors which took place here, as in many other gaols. As you know, the first crocodiles appeared in Cairo soon after the Flood, feeding on the thousands of corpses. In the beginning, they were few and small. But in the following years, they proliferated.

"Prisoners sentenced to death were taken by boat and dropped on the muddy mound over there, tied up, for the beasts to feed on. They hunt mostly by night. We would hear the screams in the dark, followed by a brutal silence."

The Bishop points at a patch of dried mud, some hundred yards away. It's covered with crosses.

He goes on: "But in secret, Ali assisted us. I never told this to anyone, but I want you to know. When I got arrested for hiding alcohol (communion wine, of course), S.I. never found out that I was a Christian, let alone a priest. They would have killed me at once!

"But Ali knew well who I was. I'd brought food to his family (later drowned in the Flood) and visited him many times in prison. He managed to get me transferred to the *Cedrus*.

"After some weeks (spent recuperating after they'd questioned me), Ali let me walk around and assist the prisoners in their needs, both in body and soul.

"The Patriarch and the Bishops had been massacred. Through his connections in Rome, and without telling *me* anything beforehand, Mansur caused my appointment as Vicar Apostolic for Cairo. He and Ali took great risks for my episcopal consecration, which occurred twenty-three years ago, at the hands of a courageous missionary bishop.

"Here at the prison, the guards were told that he was an engineer called in to fix our *power supply*. It was true."

After a brief smile, he looks grave again.

"The news spread like fire across our people. Everyone realised that we now had a future. That we would *not* back down. That Rome our Mother hadn't forgotten us. We were scattered and doomed no longer. All the sacraments would be available, and leadership would be exercised. Through the gift of episcopacy, God was granting us a fresh spring of grace, here, right into the heart of hell – if hell had a *heart*.

"This is how the Church rose again in Cairo after the Flood – still underground, but alive.

"The Scimitars tried everything to find out *who* that new bishop was, and were he hid. They never succeeded. *I* was only *Abdul*, the prison cook. Eventually, they said it was a lie, a myth.

"Mansur was shot while helping the visiting bishop avoid a checkpoint on his way out, the day after my consecration. I was immediately called for. Your husband died in my arms an hour later. Bishop Murzello escaped unhurt and reported to Rome that his mission was fulfilled."

Yes, I heard this last month. Truly, the secret was well kept... To think that I, Mansur's widow, should have been left in the dark for twenty-three years...

I look at the brass ring around one of the remaining fingers of Bishop Ephrem. I know the Church's teaching. This cheap jewel, with its tiny amethyst, is the sign of his commitment to his flock – of his spousal bond with the local Church. I admire how faithful he's been to his *spouse*...

But *mine*, he took away from us, as he later did my son.

And now, they want *me*?

Then I realise that my own husband made that very bond possible, between Bishop Ephrem and his flock, when he obtained a new Bishop for the persecuted

Church in Cairo. I have long ago sold Mansur's sumptuous necklace; but I feel as if, on Bishop Ephrem's finger, my husband has offered me a gem no less valuable.

I don't kiss it though, as Catholics would: I'm not ready.

The Bishop resumes: "When I was released, we decided that there was no safer place for me to lead the underground Church from, than the *Cedrus*. Ali appointed me prison cook and, under that cover, I continued my ministry undetected until the Liberation.

"Sadly, I was absent when the Anastasis took the *Cedrus* and Ali got shot by mistake, due to his S.I. uniform. He was attracted to Catholicism, but hadn't formally asked for Baptism, yet. May God Who rewards each person according to their conduct have mercy on his soul. And may the Lord forgive me if my words and deeds in any way delayed his conversion."

Yes, I think, looking at the sun reflected on the ripples against our hovercraft, some people need longer time than others to trust in a hidden God, or to come back to Him. Some are wounded; some are tired; some are lazy; some are selfish.

What am *I*?

Angry? Still?

Was it anger that led me to Portugal, twenty years ago?

Like Talitha on that day in Fatima, today Bishop Ephrem seems to read my soul: "Mansur admitted to me that your relationship had suffered from his decision to come to Cairo the first time. How could it not! In case you aren't sure, and for all my gratitude to him, he stayed against my advice. We celibates can take more risks than those with families.

"Talking of families, be prepared for a great surprise. Fr. Yusuf and I meant to tell you before Mass. It was confirmed last night that Margaret has been found in Libya. She's in a refugee camp in Benghazi (that's my hometown, by the way).

"She is single, but not alone, as *Baby Vincent* was born two months ago. Fr. Yusuf will baptise his nephew shortly. He wonders if there is any chance you could attend."

Is this possible? A baby? The words seem not to make sense to me. I will need time to realise what they imply. New life? A daughter back, and a grandson – to me?

Vincent... That's the English equivalent of *Mansur*'s name... In Arabic: "*the one who is victorious*."

Victory...

As I keep silent, Bishop Ephrem goes on: "Clara, your husband genuinely meant to come back to you and the children as soon as possible. But leaving Cairo was almost more dangerous than hiding in it. You may not believe it, but even texting you was unsafe, as S.I. could trace our communications. We would only use handwritten notes.

"As soon as I'd been made a bishop, Mansur's only desire was to be reunited with you, his family. Everything was arranged for his departure.

"Fr. Yusuf never knew his father, but he was deeply relieved to hear that I gave Mansur the Last Rites, as I think he told you. How sorry your husband was for leaving you all behind! He urged me to bear witness of it to you. Dying far away from his wife and children was a suffering to him worse than many tortures.

"But his soul was at peace. He looked fulfilled when, uttering your name, he died with a smile."

Now, *I* am the one resting upon the bishop's shoulder.

I can't sit down in the mud though. I must be strong.

"Here's something he left for you. I used it for prayer all those years, while I was cooking for our hundred inmates – only, I'd hidden it behind the oven, for safety. Mansur made it with splinters saved from the panelling in the main room – whatever hadn't been burnt for heat in winter."

I unwrap a little cross carved in scentful cedar wood, whose arms bear the words "Clara" and "Arca."

Mansur called me... *his ark.*

My husband...

The sun is already fairly high in the sky. The breeze rises, and on it, a lark.

As our hovercraft slowly moves away from the grassy wharf, I wave at the Bishop, imperceptibly.

Behind him, like a sail unfurling over the *Cedrus*, a large Anastasis flag is now floating in the wind. I see the five red stars set all around the Face. I see the closed eyelids. And then I realise what puzzled me yesterday at Giza, when I walked into the residence.

Pointing at the flag, I ask Fatimah: "Did you ever notice – His nose is broken?"

With a smile, she answers: "Clara Al-Khoury, if you had read *A Surgeon at Calvary*, a purposely short book given you *last* Easter by one Doctor Yasir, you would remember that it occurred when the Christ fell on His Face, carrying the Cross. You've three weeks left to read the book though, before *next* Easter."

I try not to move. I feel something reconnecting within me, so deep, so fragile, so precious...

Fatimah holds my hand. Over the whir of the hovercraft fan, she exclaims: "What a radiant smile! Suddenly, you look half younger!"

I stare at the flag, flapping in the wind.

If this be a shroud, it now shows empty. No one lies in it – "nemo Domine"...

Has a mighty beast leaped across the Nile? No Egyptian Sphinx, but One aptly named "Lion of Judah?"

Has "Father-of-Dread," or "Father-of-Lies," a pagan idol, been at last

eclipsed by "Father-of-Lights" – "Father-of-Mercies," Whose Face is the Son?
Yusuf has joined Bishop Ephrem, both now getting smaller on the East Bank, by the former prison, our boat.

They slowly raise their hands.
They bless.
We kneel.

THE END

Made in the USA
Middletown, DE
08 June 2024

55488866R00243